A Sound and a Shadow

ISBN: 978-1-60920-092-3
Printed in the United States of America
© 2013 Susan Flach
© 2020 (second edition) Susan Flach
All Rights Reserved

Library of Congress Cataloging-in-Publication Data

API
Ajoyin Publishing, Inc.
P.O. 342
Three Rivers, MI 49093

Please direct your inquiries to
admin@ajoyin.com

A Sound and a Shadow
(second edition)

SUSAN K. FLACH

Acknowledgements

I want to continue thanking God for all the blessings in my life, writing being one of them.

~~~Also, I want to thank all of the people who have shared in the excitement of this series. My husband, Steve, who always has a positive word for me. My parents, whose support is unwavering. My family and friends who have embraced these books with whole hearted enthusiasm. The girls on the North Pavilion who have encouraged me more than they'll ever know, not only by eagerly reading the series, but by throwing parties and book signings, writing reviews, and helping to spread the word. I'm pretty sure it is partially your fault that I keep writing. A special thanks to my mom, Nancy Root, and my daughter, Haley Flach, who have not only read my manuscripts and held nothing back, but are continually lifting me up during every step of the process. Also, Maggie Comben, Chris McDonough, and Corrie McArthur for reading the rough draft and offering their opinions. And to the many encouraging people who have told me that they couldn't put A Song and Seashell down...and that they can't wait for the sequel. Here it is.

~~~Thank you~~~

Prologue

(Summer 2008)

The day is unusually warm, oppressive and thick with humidity. The sun filters through the haze, adding to already high temperatures. Turquoise waves shimmer somewhere in the background as they lap onto a sandy shoreline. A welcomed breeze finds its way to the unscathed landscape, swaying the trees, sluggishly reaching for the ground—rustling through the untamed foliage. A hawk circles high above looking for prey. Small, furry creatures scuttle here and there trying to avoid the threat. Mostly, it is the type of day best spent attempting to conserve energy. A wise individual would find a cool spot and lodge there, unmoving, until the heat is finally swallowed up by the darkness of the night.

But for a young girl of thirteen bent on a quest, this isn't an option. It's the same undertaking she's been called to for as long as she can remember, and the feverish weather will do little to deter her today. Absentmindedly she takes a hand and runs it across her cheekbones in effort to wipe away the sweat that has pooled there. Her brown, shagged hair feels sticky, and her pink, heat-swollen lips are cracked and dry. For just a moment she envisions cool, crisp water and how lovely it would feel right now flowing over her skin—how refreshing it would taste on her tongue. Briefly she considers going back. Then shaking the notion away, she continues on, focusing her gray eyes on the junglelike landscape surrounding her. Using her hands as a scythe, she presses on through the maze of brutish plants that are trying to block her way. After what seems like hours of her petite frame fighting with nature, she reaches a clearing in the terrain. Peering around one last, giant leaf that stands between her and an uncluttered parcel of land, she sucks in a breath.

Suddenly it's worth every ounce of agonizing effort spent.

Standing in front of her, only yards away, is a boy of fourteen hard at work. Air held tightly in her lungs, she watches the boy's blond, unruly hair as it sticks to the back of his neck. From her angle, the girl can barely detect the perfectly chiseled features on his face that she has memorized by heart. The boy bends to pick up a piece of lumber, maneuvering it into just the right spot before securing it into place. Youthful, newly-formed muscles flex with each movement. Unwittingly, an ache spreads through the girl's body, and without thinking she loses her balance, stumbling into a large plant beside her.

Instantly, the boy's young frame whips around to confront the noise, and green eyes lock onto gray. Almost immediately his startled expression is replaced with irritation. A large sigh escapes his lips.

"What are you *doing* here?"

The girl's pixielike features are frozen in place, eyes wide. She has a hard time recovering her breath. "I…ah…I just wanted to…" Explanation abandoned, her words disintegrate into thin air. Wandering across the meadow, she begins eying the partially constructed configuration that lies at the boy's feet. "Hey, what are you making here anyway?" She uses an index finger to trace a crack in one of the pieces of his wood, ignoring the intimidating expression that is confronting her.

The boy's jaw tightens as he runs a hand through his tousled, blond hair. Once again he sighs as if it is inconveniencing him to give her an answer. "It's a raft. I'm making a raft."

The girl overlooks the obvious irritation in his voice and continues to explore his work. "Really…why?"

The boy shrugs his spry, adolescent shoulders. "I don't know… just because I can…and I want to."

"Oh."

Apparently satisfied with the explanation, the girl asks no further questions, settling herself instead on a patch of grass to sit and watch. The boy shakes his head before turning his back to the girl, resuming his previous work. The gray eyes that stare longingly at his lithe form while he cuts and positions each log into place go undetected by his line of vision. And yet he can feel them boring into him, penetrating his skin with each movement he makes.

Time passes and soon the rhythm of the job takes over, erasing the spectator from the boy's mind. So when a small voice interrupts his train of thought, it momentarily startles him.

"You know…you are really starting to get tan. Does that worry you?"

The boy stops what he is doing and slowly turns to face his forgotten companion. "Well here's a thought for you…if you stay out here too long, you are going to have too much sun too. You'd better get going."

Disappointment flickers across the girl's features before she glances up at the sky and then back down at the skin on her arms. Finally she stands to her feet. Lips pressed together, she nods one time and turns to leave. The temperature surrounding her is suffocating, but it's not the thick air that causes her to almost choke. Silently she begins to make the passage back through the dense vegetation the way she came, all the while fighting the burning sensation that is building in the back of her throat.

Much to her discouragement, her mission has been thwarted once again.

Chapter One
(Summer 2016)

Adrenaline rushes through my veins. My heart begins pounding as reverberations from a tune that has become as intimate to me as breathing itself reaches my ears. *Could it be?* Hope surges through every part of me. Impulsively, I abandon my spot on the sand and head toward the sound. Running down the beach, I dodge scattered rocks and pieces of driftwood, doing my best not to trip. Finally reaching a bend in the shoreline, I pause, trying to determine if I'm heading in the right direction. Straining my ears, I listen for the music. Is it getting louder, or is it fading away? A gust of wind whips across my face, and for a moment or two the tune completely disappears. *No!* Did I just imagine the whole thing after all? I calm the panic that is circulating in my chest. With purposeful focus, I clear my mind of the extra clutter around me—the whistle of the ocean breeze, the constant roar of the sea waves, the deafening beat of my heart.

And finally—it's there—once again.

Joy swells to the forefront of my emotions. I keep walking, increasing my tempo to a jog. This time I know I'm heading in the right direction and that just ahead, around the next corner, I will find the author of the song.

But then—what is this?

I stop. My breathing is loud but I ignore it, listening. There is something about the ballad that has changed. The chords of the guitar are being strummed in a slightly different key, distorting the original melody. My skin prickles. Something is not quite right. My footsteps slow to a cautious pace as I continue forward, rounding the final curve in the coastline.

Holding my breath, I stop short and stare.

Then instinctively, I take a step back.

The sea green eyes that I'd expected are not the ones that greet me. Instead, the person in front of me that is raising his gaze slowly to mine—*is someone new.* Amber eyes framed by hair the color of midnight pierce my own. Bewildered, I study his face. There is something about his perfectly chiseled cheekbones that seems so familiar. A knowing smile closely resembling a smirk crosses over his striking features. It's as if he is enjoying a secret—like he'd been biding his time, playing, waiting for me to arrive—as he knew I would. Unhurriedly, he puts down the guitar, his eyes never leaving my face.

"Well, hello there." His voice sounds deep and dangerous, and without warning, I jump.

He laughs. "Are *you* okay?"

I am breathless from running and from the uneasiness that is now playing havoc with my mind. Wrapping shaky arms around my mid-section, I try to soothe away my unkempt appearance and my nerves at the same time. My heart is slamming against my chest wall. *I'll just go.* I'll tell him that I'll just be going.

"I…ah…I heard the song…and I thought—" I am having trouble communicating my thoughts. I have no doubts, I need no introductions. I know exactly who this person is sitting so casually on the log in front of me.

Effortlessly, the stranger—yet somehow not stranger—rises to a standing position and holds out a hand. "Hi, my name is Keuran. What is yours?"

I suck in a breath. Suddenly I am anxious. The sound of Mr. Horton's voice resonates in my ears—the story of Keuran and how Tristan thought he was the yacht murderer. My eyes dart around looking for a way to escape.

Keuran chuckles lightly while his amber eyes search my own. "Why do you look so nervous? You look like a deer caught in the headlights." *An unlikely phrase coming from a sea creature.* What does he know about deer? But I realize he must be right; I am frozen in place and I can't seem to find my voice.

"So," he tries again. "Do you have a name? Or are you from the wild…raised by wolves, can't speak and all that." *You mean raised in the wild like you…only in your case it was raised by sharks?* I clear my throat.

"My name is…Bethany."

"Well, hi…Bethany. I hope I didn't scare you. You look so… frightened. I take it you didn't expect to come upon me while you were on your jog. Is that what you were doing—jogging?"

"Um…not really, I was just visiting the shore….out for a walk. And no…I guess I wasn't expecting anyone…" My voice trails off into the quiet. How much should I be saying to this guy before I tell him that I'll just be on my way? I begin slowly backing up, trying to ease into my escape gracefully.

"Well, I definitely have to say…you made *my* day. The shoreline is nice, but I wasn't expecting such beautiful scenery today."

In spite of the apprehension that has a grip on me, I can't help myself—I roll my eyes. *So, infamous Keuran has lines.* Very unlike Tristan.

Tristan. As I think his name, disappointment floods through me. The initial threat of finding Keuran is beginning to wear off a bit. Although I am still uneasy in his presence, I am not feeling any imminent danger. Now it finally hits me just how high my hopes were for those few precious moments in time. Just how close I'd thought I was to actually finding what I now realize my body still craves like an addictive drug. Tristan. Only it wasn't him at all, and now the letdown is ruthless. I shake my head. It's still there. All I'd worked to suppress for the past four years is still there lurking below the surface, just waiting for a trigger.

7

Will it never end? Will these feelings never go away so I can just get on with my life? Isn't that what I was here to do today— lay these feelings to rest and finally move on? Instead, the opposite has happened, and the old emotions and memories are getting all stirred up. Not meaning to, I sigh out loud. *This just sucks!*

All the while these thoughts are occupying my mind, Keuran is talking, and it occurs to me that I'm not hearing a word that is coming from his lips. Stopping midsentence, a flash of irritation crosses over his features. Pressing his lips together tightly, he narrows his eyes in frustration over my apparent impassivity. But then just as quickly, his expression softens, and he becomes well composed again. It occurs to me then how rude I've been, not paying attention to his conversation, so I attempt a smile and make eye contact.

"I'm sorry, what were you saying? I've traveled a long way today, and I think I'm a little worn out from the ride."

He studies my face, trying to read into my statement. It hits me then how similar his facial structure is to Tristan's. Alike, and yet different at the same time. His fine-boned features along with his dark hair and intense, amber eyes could best be described as striking. In comparison, there is one main word that frequently comes to mind when I conjure up Tristan in my memory: beautiful. But still, in spite of the variances, the obvious relation is there.

"Traveled...so I take it you are not from around here?"

"No...Philadelphia."

He seems pleased that he once again has me engaged in conversation. "So...first time here then?" His eyes never leave mine while he waits for an answer. It's as if he's challenging me, daring me to offer the right reply. I decide to go with the truth.

"No, not the first time. I've been here before. A few years ago my family vacationed in Watch Hill."

His lips fight back a smile, and it's almost as if he's privy to a private joke. "Well, I hope you'll stay for a bit...after you drove all that way. You must have really liked this place if you were willing to make the drive back." He waits for my response.

"Well, I wasn't really planning to stay for too long—"

"Long enough to sit and take a load off, I hope." He points to a piece of driftwood. My gaze drifts to the log. *I really shouldn't.* But now I'm curious. There is so much I'd like to know about him, about Tristan, about the last four years. Maybe he will have some answers. I glance back up at his face as he runs a hand through his dark, spikey hair waiting for my answer. I contemplate his invitation. Actually, in many ways he *is* different than Tristan. Even his hair is so unlike Tristan's perpetually windblown, tousled, blond locks. But *really*—does he seem all *that* bad?

I hesitate. "Maybe for just a *little* while."

I walk over to the piece of timber he's suggested and sit down. In the back of my mind I realize that I need to tread carefully where Keuran is concerned, if he's as dangerous as Tristan would say. But there *is* something I really need to know.

"That song…that you were just playing, it sounded so familiar. Where did you learn it?"

Keuran glances at his guitar that is now resting against a rock. He shrugs his shoulders. "That song? I'm actually not sure. I must have heard it somewhere. It just happened to be the tune I was playing right then…Why? Have *you* heard it before?"

It's only my very own personal anthem. "It kind of sounded like a song I used to know...but I may have been wrong. It's not important." I force myself to sound nonchalant. Once again the glint in Keuran's eyes and the slight twitch of his mouth tell me that there is more information that he isn't sharing. In sudden frustration I blurt. "So you are Keuran…from the sea…right?"

Keuran goes very still. In the few minutes that I've gotten to know him, I can tell that he is not a guy that is easily surprised. But in that one question, I'd just revealed so much about myself. He appears stunned.

"I ...*am.*" He draws the words out slowly, all the while watching my face.

"Tristan's cousin?" I spit out. I am on a roll, and I can't seem to stop myself.

Silently Keuran runs a finger across his lips before clasping both of his hands together like he's getting ready to pray. His eyes flash. "You know Tris then?"

Tris? I nod my head.

He speaks cautiously, like he's trying to decide how much to reveal. "Well, we do share the same name. I'm Keuran Alexander."

At once, I begin to feel nervous. What will he do now? Now that he knows I am privy to such confidential information. Will he assume that I've heard about his villainous reputation? Eyeing the shoreline, I begin to think of the best possible getaway route—if need be. But then he smiles at me, and I feel more at ease.

"This day just keeps getting better. There aren't many that know about us here on land. You are one of the very few. This is truly a delight...Bethany. To be honest, it's nice being around someone I don't have to pretend with." He seems sincere enough, and it makes me feel better.

"So how often do you come on land?" I really want to ask—how often does Tristan come on land and how he has been lately, but I remember Mr. Horton's exhortation about the years of deep-seated jealously that exists between the cousins.

"Not much really. Just once in a while to see how things are going with you people." He stops momentarily to smile. "Probably more often if I had a friend that I felt comfortable around—if I didn't have to work so hard to hide who I really was."

"That's understandable." I watch the ocean waves as they keep a steady rhythm pushing onto the shoreline. Inhaling deeply, I taste the salty air that surrounds me. I've missed the sea so much, and all that goes with it. With much effort, I try to suppress the desire to ask all kinds of questions about Tristan. It's difficult though, because I really, *really* want to. I glance over at Keuran's strong profile. This is nice. I can't be with Tristan right now. Maybe I will never be with him again. But sitting here now, talking with someone who is so close to him, this is okay too. It is definitely the next best thing—but maybe it's all I'll ever have.

"So serious." Keuran's voice breaks through my reverie. "Do you like the water? You must or you wouldn't have wanted to come back. That's all there is around here, water and more water." Rising to a standing position, he pads through the sand and holds out a hand in my direction. I hesitate before resting my fingers over his palm, letting him pull me to my feet.

He leads me to the water's edge. "You're not afraid of getting a little wet, are you?"

I shake my head. What does he have in mind? Eyeing my shorts which are resting midthigh followed by the stirred-up water in front of me, I look back up at Keuran's face. He chuckles, reading into my uncertainty. "You won't get all *that* wet. See that big rock over there? We can wade out to it pretty easily. Once you are on it you will be completely surrounded by water and waves. It feels somewhat like an oasis. I'm going to bet you'll like it."

Tentatively, I take a step into the ocean. It has been so long since I've stuck my toes in this massive body of water and allowed the warm, salty liquid to wash over my feet and legs. I close my eyes and sigh, feeling the sun warming my lids. Suddenly I have an overpowering sensation of coming home.

Wading out to the rock, I try to finagle my way onto its slippery crest, but with little success. I am amid fighting back a measure of frustration, when somewhere close behind me I hear a "May I?" I pause only briefly before allowing Keuran's strong arms to give me a boost. We are both laughing by the time we get settled onto the boulder, massive as it is. Taking a second to catch my breath, I look down at my tan shorts and pale-colored pink tee shirt. I am completely soaked. How do these "sea boys" manage to do this to me? Keuran notices me regarding my wet gear and wrinkles his nose.

"Sorry. I didn't *think* you'd get that wet."

I narrow my eyes in jest. "Really!" It's then that I observe *his* waterlogged attire and just shake my head. He doesn't seem to mind his drenched clothing at all. *Of course!*

But he is right. The rock is a sanctuary in the middle of an unbridled sea. I could easily sit here for hours and watch the waves as they try to reach up and lick the bottom of my feet. Water is everywhere and I am stationed serenely in the midst of it, safe. I glance over at Keuran and get a momentary chill—well, *hopefully* safe.

Some time goes by and eventually we head back to land. Falling onto the sand, we will the sun to do its thing and dry our clothes. I find Keuran is unexpectedly easy to talk to, and the conversation between us is carried on quite effortlessly. He is busy telling me how to effectively evade drawing the attention of sharks should I ever encounter one, when he catches me eyeing his guitar.

"Do you play?"

I laugh. "No."

"Do you want me to teach you a few things?"

Again I laugh. "No."

"Yes, you do. I can tell. I'm going to." Not giving me a chance to protest, Keuran jumps up and grabs his instrument before settling back in at my side. "Here." He offers it to me.

"But I'm still wet."

"Trust me, it's not the first drop of water this thing has ever felt." I contemplate his cavalier statement. So different from Tristan, who seemed to completely revere his own guitar.

I am unsure, but I take it in my arms anyway, gingerly and with a degree of apprehension. Keuran crouches behind me. "Get your fingers used to the feel of the strings, and then I'll show you a chord or two."

I try to brush away the uneasiness of him sitting so close, brushing my back with chest, his arms circling around from behind showing me where to hold my hands. It's hard to concentrate. Somehow this seems like an intimate act, something I'd imagined sharing with Tristan. But here it is Keuran instead, and it feels all wrong somehow. I exhale slowly; I am clearly making too much of this. This is just one person teaching another to play a guitar. Taking a cleansing breath, I make every effort to pay attention to his words of instruction.

"Take your second finger and put it here. Now put your first finger here on the fifth string. And then your third finger on the first string, right here. Okay, now curl your fingers and play."

The musical tone rings out, interrupting the monotony of the ocean waves. "Nice. That's called a G chord."

I smile. I'd be jumping to conclusions to call myself a future rock star, but it's a good start for an amateur, and I am proud. After learning two more chords and then trying them all together, creating a little ditty, I hand the guitar back over to Keuran. He settles in, resting the instrument on his lap as if he's getting ready to play.

"Do you ever worry—" I start, then stop, and he looks up. I try again. "Do you ever worry about the effect your playing will have on a human?" He stares, bewildered, and all of a sudden I feel stupid. "Like…you know…it might put them in a trance or something?"

"No," Keuran shakes his head. "No, not really." *Oh.* "But… clearly you do." He pauses. "You feel worried about that…don't you?" Setting his guitar off to the side, he looks at me. "You're not a worrier, are you, Bethany?"

Involuntarily, I shiver. What is it about his questioning tone that has me feeling a little on edge? "I don't know…um…I don't think so." *Should I be? Worried?*

Everything is quiet for a minute, and I contemplate how to word my next question. Soon it will be time for me to get going, and I will never forgive myself if I don't ask the one thing that I am dying to know. Even if the question will bug Keuran to no end. I clear my throat.

"So, I'm curious…how is your cousin Tristan doing?"

I hold my breath waiting for an answer. A flash of anger darts through Keuran's amber eyes. And just as quickly disappears. He breaks into laughter. When he finally does speak, I begin quarreling with my imagination, wondering whether his voice sounds forced. Almost *too* nonchalant. "Tris?" He laughs again as if just the thought of him brings to mind some funny memory. "I think he is doing *just* fine. That boy likes to stay busy." He watches my face for a reaction, still smiling, as if I should get what he means by that statement.

Only I am confused. *Likes to stay busy?* What does that mean? *Busy how?* I want to ask him to clarify, but there is a small part of me that isn't so certain that I do. Surely the statement isn't holding a negative connotation, is it? Refusing to bring any ugliness to my recollection of Tristan, I decide to let it go. Keuran falls quiet and I feel stuck. Well, so much for the information I crave. It appears I wouldn't be getting any.

My mind wanders back to four summers ago, when I had spent so much time right here in this very town, together with Tristan. I remember his intense, green eyes, and the way his lips felt when they came in contact with mine. Such a new, wonderful sensation—I will never forget that. Or how his body felt when he held me so tightly to him. The way he made me laugh. How he took my breath away the first time he told me he loved me. I press my lips together, working hard to suppress the sigh that wants to escape. I'm regressing. It is time for me to go. Leave this place and never look back.

I begin rising to my feet. "Well…I think I'll get going. It was nice meeting you, Keuran. It's a long drive back, and I really want to make it before dark."

"Don't go."

What?

"If you go now, you are going to miss River Glow. No one in their right mind would miss River Glow." His bait is obvious.

I press my lips together. "Okay, tell me, what is River Glow?"

"A really cool festival in downtown Westerly on the Pawcatuck River, where they have floating bonfires."

"Really…that does sound cool."

"Better than cool. It's an awesome sight and one I've only watched from the water, but I bet it would be quite a spectacle from the land side of things, too. Plus there is live music, jugglers, belly dancers, and a lot of good food too."

"Well, belly dancers…why didn't you just say?" I laugh before shaking my head. "Really, the festival does sound like fun, but I think I should go."

"You have a job you need to go back to?"

"Well, no…not yet."

"Didn't you say earlier that you just graduated from college? Penn State? I'll bet that was four years of hard work. I might be wrong, but it seems to me you could use a couple of days to celebrate a job well done. Besides, I always wanted to attend River Glow on land, but I won't if I have to go alone."

I sigh, heaving my shoulders. "I know you are right…I probably should stay and have some fun. Thank you for the invitation, but I'm going to go."

Keuran shakes his head, resignation written on his features. He is done trying. "Okay…well, drive safe."

I nod my head. "Nice to meet you," I say with resolution in my voice before turning to walk away. Winding my way back along the shoreline, I keep one ear open, listening for footsteps behind me. Part of my wants to roll my eyes in response to my own behavior. What was I expecting anyway— that maleficent Keuran would be trailing me, sneaking up on my shadow, capturing and tying me up, holding me captive against my will, eventually feeding me to sharks? I shake my head, smiling. I definitely need to tame my overactive imagination.

I eye the ocean, just to my left. How can something so stirred up and wild be so pacifying at the same time? Frothy whitecaps spill onto the shore, reaching for my footprints. On quick glance I spy sailboats rocking against the horizon, weathering the frantic surf. The sand sticks to my toes as I scoot around an occasional protruding rock. The paste created from the mix of seedy, pale granules and salty liquid feels like a day at the spa on my bare feet. In a few short minutes I will be leaving this all behind. Again. Most likely not to return for a long, *long* time. *Geez,* I missed this. But it is making me miss Tristan too, bringing back all sorts of raw hurt that I am having a hard time getting a grip on. If I just keep walking, I can leave it all behind and get over it all—eventually.

But *geez, I missed this.*

The farther I get away from Keuran, the more I relax. He is not coming after me. I am free to go. Go home and what? Maybe he is right after all. I should stay. For a couple of days anyway. Just to enjoy that river-fire-thing he was talking about. I really *did* work hard at college, and I really *do* deserve a celebration.

I stop dead in my tracks. Gazing out at the ocean, I search for an answer. *What should I do?* But of course, the ocean would tell me to stay, relax, and enjoy. Folding my hands together, I press my thumbs against my lips in a rhythmic motion, thinking. *What should I do?*

Oh, to hell with it!

I turn back around.

When I reach Keuran he is still sitting on the piece of driftwood where I originally found him, guitar supported in his arms. He doesn't look at all surprised to see me. Once again his smile is more of a smirk.

"How long can you stay?"

"Two days."

He nods his head in acknowledgement. "All right then. Two days it is."

I bite my lip, warily eyeing my new companion for the next couple of days. The roar of the ocean waves is almost deafening as they sweep toward us, victorious, creating a backdrop for our conversation. All the while, in my mind I am shaking my head in defeat.

Would this place never cease to have a hold on me?

Chapter Two

I find a room to rent right in the town of Watch Hill, on Plimpton Road. I assure the business manager that I'll only be needing the room for two nights. And he assures me that I better be sure about that, 'cause the rooms go fast around here. And I reassure him that oh I'm very sure.

Just like he told me he would, Keuran arrives to pick me up for the festival on time—even early. As he pulls his ride, a red Lexus ES, up to the curb, I contemplate where he keeps it stowed while he's in the water, which, according to him, is most of the time. Dressed in shorts and a button-down shirt with sleeves rolled to the elbow, he looks sharp. My eyes take him in as he stands at my front doorframe waiting to enter my room; he is not an unattractive date. His build is similar to Tristan's, only maybe slightly smaller. My gaze travels to his face, and I notice that his dark hair is wet, causing me to wonder if it's due to a recent swim or if it's been gelled into place. Either way, it's not a bad look.

I'd spent the afternoon moseying around town visiting some of my old haunts: St. Clair Annex, Ocean House, Flying Horse Carousel. Each place I lay eyes on gives me a jab of memories bittersweet. No longer is the town of Watch Hill just a location on Google maps. Every structure I encounter has a story to tell from four summers ago. So many good remembrances—but that just makes the dull ache in my chest all the greater. I stop in at Jan's Boutique and find a few items of clothing to get me through the next couple of days—a graduation present to myself.

As I exit the building, stepping onto the boardwalk next to the exterior of the shop, my gaze is intrinsically pulled to the waves that are lapping onto Napatree Point. For an overwhelming moment I find myself staring longingly, waiting, hoping. Then, almost immediately, I chide myself, rubbing my eyes with my fists as if to wipe away the thought. And it works for the time being. As I head back to my rented room, I focus on my upcoming night with Keuran at River Glow. I'm just not sure what to think of him. He seems friendly enough—definitely persuasive—but there is something about him that has me feeling a little cautious too. I shrug off the notion, realizing that it originated from someone else's opinion. I am fully capable of drawing my own conclusions.

Now I am sliding into the gray, leather interior of Keuran's Lexus ES, heading out for a promised evening of fun. Traffic is congested and we have to park several blocks away from the hub of the festival. After wedging our car into a lot, we set off on foot finally reaching the Pawcatuck River. In an instant, I am sucked in by the energy of the event. People are everywhere, packed into the streets and the riverfront park. Food venders line the walkways, and carnival-like activities are scattered here and there, luring susceptible participants. Jazz music fills the evening air, keeping the gala lively. And when the daylight finally fades to dark, the much-anticipated floating bonfires are set loose on the river, lighting up the night. It truly is a spectacular sight. Keuran stands close by me as we watch each glowing bundle float by. For a split second during the midst of the drifting parade, I glance in his direction and catch him watching the expression on my face. *Oh no!* We both turn away awkwardly, and I breathe a sigh of relief. I am not ready for *that*. May never be ready for *that*—with him.

The rest of the evening progresses, and thankfully there are no more *moments*. I arrive back to my room safe and sound, thinking to myself—see, Keuran is *not* that bad. Before he leaves me at my door, he asks me for my number to text, and I am surprised.

"You text?"

"Yeah…" he draws the word out slowly. "Don't you?"

"Yes…but, I just thought—Never mind; it's not important." I give him my number.

He narrows his eyes at me questionably. "You know you act surprised when I tell you I do a lot of things, and I'm not sure why—"

I shove my hands in my pockets and shrug my shoulders at the same time. "I guess it's because of the water and all…no big deal. Text me." *And because Tristan made me think in certain ways about certain things, and now you are doing everything the opposite, and it catches me off guard, that's all.*

The next morning he texts me, and I am happy he does, because my microwave has gone on the fritz, and I have been trying to get ahold of the business manager to no avail. When Keuran arrives at my door, I am standing in the kitchenette dressed in yoga pants and a gray tee-shirt, cup of coffee in hand. His eyes rake me over quickly, and he smiles.

"Would you like a cup?"

He crinkles up his nose. "No, thanks."

I show him the microwave, and quickly he figures out it's a fuse. Less than a minute of tinkering and just like that it's fixed and ready for use once again. I am impressed.

"Where did you learn to do stuff like that? I'm sure you don't have to deal with fuses and electricity in the water very much."

"Actually, Tristan taught me that one." Goose bumps cover my skin. Hearing Keuran speak about Tristan is unexpected. I rub my arms trying to soothe away the reaction to just the sound of his name. "Yeah, good old Tris. Speaking of Tris, you know, he seems to be doing pretty good lately. For the last long while really. He finally seems…I don't know…happy."

"Happy?" I manage to mutter, though my voice sounds choked and funny.

"Yeah, we've been pretty close for as long as I can remember, and there were times over the years when he seemed unhappy or like he was struggling with something. At times I would find him off by himself, acting moody, wanting to be alone. But a few summers ago he seemed to snap out of it...get over whatever it was that was bugging him."

Keuran pauses for a moment to press a button in the fuse box before closing the door. "Now...he is finally carefree again, happy." He laughs. "Maybe a little too carefree, if you know what I mean."

Suddenly, I realize I've been holding my breath as I listen. Now I let it go. Simultaneously my heart sinks. *No.* I don't know what he means. What *does* he mean? He's moved on then—and is happy. Well, I'd only want the best for him, so I'm happy—glad he is finally happy. *Wait—no, I'm not.* Oh geez, truth is, I wish he had been miserable for the past four years just like me! I force myself not to think too deeply about the whole thing, because the tears that are lurking behind my eyes at the thought are only seconds away, and I don't want to start crying in front of Keuran.

But I have to wonder though—how long did *that* take? How long after I left, or rather after *he* left, did it take for him to move on and be happy—carefree even? Gathering up courage, I turn toward Keuran. "When...did you notice the change in him?"

"Let's see...when *was* it?" He taps a thumb on his lips, contemplating an answer. "Oh yeah...I do remember, it was right before that big hurricane hit. Hurricane Sandy."

Fight back the tears. Fight back the tears. He doesn't have to say another word. I know exactly when he means. I remember how Hurricane Sandy hit soon after our summer together was over, and how I worried about Tristan and how he was doing while his home was being turned into a complete upheaval. Well, apparently I didn't have to worry too much. Sounds like he was off having a great time. Must have just needed to get me out of his system. I turn away from Keuran and close my eyes briefly. *Glad I could help him out with that!*

Keuran hangs around for a bit longer. Finding the remote to the TV, he begins flipping through the channels with obvious enjoyment. A real novelty for him, I'm sure. I'm glad he is having a good time, but now I can't seem to shake this melancholy mood that has settled over me. Why am I even here in this town? This just hurts too bad. I should never have agreed to stay, even for two days.

In the midst of his remote control frenzy, Keuran glances over at me, pauses mid-flip, and presses the off button. Apparently I'm not very good at hiding things, or else he is a mind reader and can tell I'm about to bolt.

"You know, there is a really great beach party tonight at the Fredericks. It's going to be huge. I'm invited and I really don't want to go alone. You can't beat a good beach party to liven things up...will you go with me? Say you'll go. I know you want to go. You said two days. Just smile at me and say, yes, Keuran, I'd love to go."

I can't help myself, I laugh. "Yes...okay, yes, I'll go."

Once again Keuran shows up in the red Lexus ES, and I'm glad he likes to drive instead of traveling on foot, taking the shoreline route. Most of the places I'd gone with Tristan in the Watch Hill area, we'd walked beside the ocean. The water was so much a part of him, it was like he always wanted it in sight. I had loved that about him, and I grew to feel the same way. But it is hard for me to think about sharing that same familiarity with someone else.

Keuran is right: the Fredericks' party is huge. Once again it seems as though we have to park miles away. Finally after a long walk, we arrive at the monstrosity of a house where the festivity is being held. The exterior is brick-sided, impressively decorated in pillars and arches. The lawn is lush, trimmed with well-kept shrubbery and flowering bushes. The main driveway is gated and closely guarded by a watchman. *Holy cow!* I glance down at my less-than-formal attire. White shorts and peach blouse.

"Am I dressed okay for this?"

Keuran chuckles lightly. "You are going to be overdressed when it comes time to play volleyball. You look just fine. Great, really."

I glance around at the others arriving and realize he is right. I guess big, fancy house doesn't equate big, fancy clothes. Girls are dressed in anything from bikini tops and Daisy Dukes to casual sundresses. We merge with the oncoming crowd and make our way through the entrance. The lavish front lawn is filled with partygoers milling around, drink in hand. Food and beverage stations are strategically placed just feet away at any given time. In the side yard a dance floor is pulsating with music and lights. Toward the shore two volleyball nets have been erected, and both courts are already in use. Onlookers are gathered on the sidelines, watching and waiting for their turn. Briefly, I wonder if I'll have a hard time getting in on a game.

I've taken only a few sips from my fruity drink when Keuran pulls me toward the dance floor. Dubstep music is blaring from the surround-sound speakers, thudding loudly, vibrating my body as I begin moving to the rhythm. Keuran makes a great dance partner, keeping time easily, and soon we are both carried away into a world of frenzied tempos and flashing illuminations. For a few moments in time, there is only this dance floor and nothing else.

And it feels breathlessly good.

After two songs come and go, we are in the midst of dancing, flickers of light dodging across our skin, face, and hair, when for a few heart-stopping seconds a glow catches the iris of Keuran's eyes, and they become iridescent. In a momentary panic I think I'm going to scream, but then I realize no one would hear me above the musical pandemonium even if I did. As I try to make sense of what I'm seeing, my heart beats more loudly than the pounding cadence of the song. Then, as quickly as it came, the glimmer is gone, and it is just Keuran and his amber eyes once again. I shake my head, trying to focus my mind. It feels like I'm going crazy. I motion to Keuran to let him know I'm ready to be done for a while, and he follows me off the dance floor.

"Good idea. Let's go get some food." His voice comes across slightly winded after the vigorous workout. We head to a linen-covered food bar and begin to fill our plates. As I peruse the mouthwatering spread laid out in front of us, I begin placing a variety of fruits, cheeses, and bread on mine, deciding to skip over the seafood section for Keuran's benefit. But when we arrive at our table, I realize that there was no need to forgo. Resting on his dish amongst the other heaping pile of delicacies are crab legs and some shrimp.

I try to ignore the fact that it's there, but when he takes a piece of iced shrimp cocktail and dips it into a soufflé cup filled with sauce and then sucks it slowly into his mouth, all the while watching my face, I can't help but think that it is for my benefit. Goose bumps cover my flesh as I recall Tristan's words. *For us, it's practically cannibalism.*

I imagine the look on my face is less than pleased, and Keuran breaks out into dark laughter before finally turning his head away. I swallow down the rising bile in my throat, feeling a little creeped-out. Suddenly, I've lost my appetite. Deciding I've had enough Keuran time for a while, I push back my plate and tell him I'm going to play some volleyball. I'll catch up with him later.

As I head toward the courts, I remove my flimsy, peach blouse and throw it over my arm. My camisole beneath will be much more conducive to playing a competitive game. After several rounds I am finally all played out and a little too hot for a bonfire, but I head in that direction anyway. Situated close to the ocean, the sound of the waves welcomes me as a pacifying backdrop against the flames.

I am relaxing, making small talk with the others that are gathered around, when I begin to contemplate Keuran. Last night his behavior had been golden, and I was so sure the others had been wrong about him. But tonight, there've been moments when I was getting a weird vibe from him and it has me feeling a little less sure. And yet, on each occasion, it may have been just me making too much out of nothing. I mean like the shrimp—it's just food—that *I* eat all the time. So what? And the lights—*well, that was just creepy*—but who knows, maybe the strobe effect was making my eyes appear the same way.

I am lost in thought, imagining all sorts of scenarios where Keuran is concerned, when for a few minutes the techno music from across the lawn pauses. In comparison all seems quiet.

Except for the gentle, melodic sound of a strumming guitar from somewhere in the distance.

Unwittingly, my heart begins pounding, and I glance in all directions in search of Keuran. Did he bring his guitar to the party? Because I don't remember him carrying it. After a few scans across the lawn, I find Keuran talking and laughing with a group of girls, no guitar in sight. *Not him then!*

Still the music continues—softly thrumming, fading into the sounds of the evening tide.

My pulse is throbbing triple-time, and my mind instantly becomes scattered. I look all around, planning my escape from the crowd in order to go in search of the sound.

Leaving the glow of the fire behind, I make my way down to the beachfront. Pausing for a second, I strain to listen, making sure I'm heading in the right direction. With each step I take the chords become clearer. I round one bend in the shoreline and then another. The ocean is right beside me, only millimeters away, seemingly cheering me on. My brain becomes an emotional blur. I can tell I'm close now. The nearer the strumming sound, the louder my heart beats, like a drum that is accompanying the guitar. I edge around one more curve in the nautical landscape, and the instrument inside my chest stops playing.

One –two –three –four—beats.

And there sitting before me, ensconced in a sandy alcove, is a guy with blond, tousled hair, head bent, lost in his music. I blink. Is it an apparition? I gasp for breath. I can't breathe. *God, please help me—I can't breathe!*

The person hears me then, stops playing, and turns.

Shocked, green eyes stare back into mine. I am unprepared for my reaction. I begin trembling all over. A tidal wave of emotions surges through my veins. Time stops and we are frozen, watching each other. He is more beautiful than I remembered. All the pictures that I had conjured up of him in my mind over the years had not done him justice. I'd forgotten.

Finally his voice comes at me—just a whisper in the wind. "Bethany?"

He shakes his head as if to clear his sight, his tone becoming louder. "Holy geez, Bethany, is that you?"

"Tristan," I murmur, but I'm not sure if I actually say the word aloud.

Then standing up, setting his guitar off to the side, he gives me the opening I need. All thoughts of anywhere and anyone else in the universe become muted and distant as I run into his arms. He squeezes me tightly to him. His biceps feel so strong, enveloping me, pressing me to his chest. *Oh my...Tristan, it's really you! After four years, I can't believe it's you!* I burrow closer and closer. Our embrace is both smothering and desperate. We stay that way for a long time, as if either one of us is afraid to let go—as if this might just be a dream, and when we pull apart, it will all vanish right before our very eyes.

When we finally do separate, it is only for him to cradle me in his arms as he looks me up and down. "Geez, Bethany, you look so beautiful. If possible even more beautiful than before—" He pauses, seemingly at a loss for words. He shakes his head. "I ...have...missed...you! Have missed you *soooo* much!"

"Tristan—" I mouth his name. I am so overwhelmed. He frees a hand and runs a thumb across my cheekbone. To wipe away my tears? I didn't even realize I'd been crying. "I...I can't believe...I...it's really you." I don't recognize my own voice.

He groans. "Baby...it's been so long." His green eyes are resting on my mouth and immediately I begin to tremble. And then he's leaning toward me, as if in slow motion, until finally I feel his lips coming in contact with mine.

Instantly, I react.

I've waited four years for this, for him. And I am so ready. My fingers reach for his blond, disheveled hair. It's a little shorter than before, but still just long enough. I shudder as I feel his strong hands running through my own long strands, up and down my back, pulling me to him at the same time. My breath comes in short gasps as I reach for the solid muscles of his back. *Holy...wow!* I'd forgotten how good he feels. I am so hungry. It's like I haven't eaten in such a long time, and now I am starved. The kiss continues and we are devouring each other, telling each other how much we missed each other with the reaction of our bodies.

Eventually we pull apart, and Tristan rests his forehead on the top of my head. My face is looking into his chest, watching its heaving motion. I can feel the breathlessness that is racking my own body. We are still for many moments waiting for some sort of calm to settle over us. Then I feel his arms moving, his hands reaching for the front of my shirt. His fingers slip inside my blouse and I hold my breath. We've never gone this far, but it's been four years and we're both older, not kids anymore—surely it's time. I'm afraid to breathe, preparing myself for the sensation of his touch. I still love him—I never stopped. The light touch of his fingertips is like fire as it trails across my chest, just below my breastbone. Then his hand comes in contact with the shell that rests around my neck and he clasps it between his thumb and first finger, eventually resting it in the palm of his hand. *Oh, he was looking for the necklace.* I'd forgotten it was still there. It had become so much a part of me—I'd never taken it off. *Yes, it is still there where you put it. I never forgot about it, never forgot about you. I still love you.*

Finally I pull back and look up into his face. The look in his green eyes is so tender. It gives me all the encouragement I need to speak. If only I can find my voice. "Tristan—" I shake my head and then smile. What else can I do but smile, this is just so unbelievable! "I can't believe it's really you. I didn't know if I'd ever see you again." At that statement I want to cry once more, and I have to fight back the tears. I am an emotional mess.

"Awe...baby—" He pulls me in to his chest. "You are like a vision...I can't believe this is real!" He curves his arm around my shoulder and leads me to a soft blanket of sand. We sit side by side. "I've missed you. Have I told you how much I've missed you?"

I smile once again through the fading tears. "I think so... and I've missed you too. So much—" My last words are just a whisper, and he squeezes my shoulder. "How...how have you been?" I look up into his green eyes.

"Okay." *Okay? Please tell me you've been miserable every second we've been apart, that you can't breathe without me by your side!* He nudges me with his shoulder. "How have *you* been? Did you make it through school?"

I nod. "Yep...I made it. I just graduated recently."

He grins from ear to ear. "Awesome job! What did you major in?"

"Marine biology."

He laughs out loud. "You would! Yes, that's definitely you... good for you!" Pausing, he looks at me. "Well...don't you want to know...about me...and school?"

"Of course!" I'd forgotten how cute he could be when he gets that excited schoolboy look. His enthusiasm is contagious. "Did you end up going to college?"

"I did." Pressing his lips together, he tries to stifle an all-out grin.

"And—? What did *you* major in?"

"Ocean and coastal engineering."

I shake my head, so proud of him. "That is so perfect. I'm glad. You are really going to help your people!"

"I hope. That is the goal." He stops talking and watches my face with a certain look in his eyes that makes me blush. *Oh…my goodness…it's like I'm still seventeen!* He is still *so* hot! Even hotter than I remember! Is that even possible—or had I just forgotten?

"What will you do now?" His voice breaks through the moment, forcing my mind out of the spell that he so easily weaves over me.

"I'm not sure. Look for a job, eventually. It all just happened, so I need a minute to figure out what it is I want to be doing." *But none of that matters, because I just found you again and I'm here with you now.* "What…what about you?"

He doesn't hesitate. "I got a job working for NEC Systems Group. I'm consulting companies on how to best set up structures to protect the ocean environment."

"Is it…is it around here then?"

"Yes, I'm based right here in Rhode Island, but I travel around to consult the companies…only to coastal cities, of course."

"Perfect." I have to fight down the growing ache that is working its way into my chest. It sounds like he has it all planned out. His whole life is falling into place, and there has been no plan for me to fit into it anywhere. I'm not even an afterthought.

"Hey—" His fingers reach for my chin, and he gently turns my face towards him.

I pull back away. I won't look at him. The waves push to shore, filling in the gap of my withdrawal. Finally I pinch my lips together, eyes narrowing, interfering with their cadence. "Why did you leave that summer, Tristan?"

Silence. The sound of the water once again takes forefront. "You don't know?" He pauses. More waves. "I know you talked to Mr. Horton."

"I know…what Mr. Horton said." My voice is edged with bitterness and hurt. "But why didn't you tell me good-bye? You could have told me good-bye. Could have trusted me enough to confide in me…if you wanted to."

"Is that what you think…that I didn't want to?"

"What else am I led to believe? You didn't give me a chance to believe anything else—you just left." Rising to a standing position, I look back at him still sitting in the sand. He is staring hard at the water, the muscle in his jaw twitching. My heart aches. I want him so much it is making me crazy. But if he wants me too, there has to be some new ground rules laid out. Then another thought occurs to me. *What if he doesn't want me too?* I gasp for air, brushing away that last thought.

"It's complicated. But know this: I didn't want to hurt you. I hurt too."

I spin around to face him directly. "If you were hurting that bad…you could have come to find me in Philadelphia." He is shaking his head, but I ignore him, continuing on. "You know it has occurred to me, Tristan…I spent that whole summer chasing you…waiting for you…always waiting for you. But I'm over it. If you want me…come find *me*! For once!"

Finally my rampage is finished, and he looks up at me with a troubled expression.

And I am this close to retracting my statement and falling into his arms, kissing away the hurt from every inch of his beautiful face.

"Where are you staying?" His deep voice is subdued.

"You figure it out!" I say before turning around and retracing my steps back to the Fredericks' lavish front lawn. All the while my heart is left behind to lay face-down in the sand.

Chapter Three

Oh! My! Word! What have I done?

I have just arrived back to my rented room, and my back is pressed up against the door. Motionless, I stand replaying the words that I'd flung at Tristan less than two hours ago. After my encounter with him on the shore, it was so hard to focus on having fun at the party, followed up by the difficult task of trying to make sense of Keuran's chatter on the drive home. If I was able to pull that whole charade off without making Keuran suspicious that something was up, I really needed to think about an acting career.

And now that I am finally alone with my thoughts, the reality of what I've just done is assaulting my mind. *Am I just crazy?* How long have I waited to see Tristan again? How many minutes of the past four years had been spent thinking about him? How many times had I envisioned our reunion and how that when I'd finally be in his arms again, I would never let him go, not for a split second? The wooden structure of the door behind me is all that is holding me upright as I bury my face in my hands and groan. Tristan. *Oh— my—goodness!* I just saw Tristan!

And now he's gone!

And all because I basically told him off and offered him an ultimatum. On shaky feet, I walk away from the entrance of my room, stunned. I told him he needed to pursue *me* this time. That if he wanted me, he should chase after me. Only I didn't even tell him where I was staying. My double bed bounces lightly as I plop on top, kicking off my sandals. The physical ache that is spreading across my limbs is very real, and there in part because I know I just did the right thing. But it hurts so bad, because I am unsure of what the outcome will be.

Unhurriedly, I begin pulling off my clothes in preparation for bed. As I tug my shirt over my head, unexpectedly my senses become assaulted because etched into the fabric is the smell of *him!* Tristan—left over from the hug. I stop in midmotion, inhaling the soapy, salty fragrance, and close my eyes in agony. *I didn't do the right thing after all!* He could be here with me right now—on this very bed. *Oh crap!* Setting my shirt gently beside my pillow, I wander over to the sink to finish my nighttime routine. No, it *really* was the right thing to do. I can't keep living my life shadowing a boy who is always just beyond my reach. I had to lay out my terms—let him know where I'd set the bar. But will he come after me? Does he even still want me—or will this be it? He acted like he was truly happy to see me, but is it enough? Or will he realize he was really okay without me these last few years after all? Either way this had to happen; I know I did the right thing.

But I'm so scared!

The following morning, I approach the business manager in an attempt to extend my room rental. I have to give Tristan some time to come find me before I leave town for good. Furrowing his brow, the manager clicks his tongue several times before telling me that *he told me these rooms rent fast.* I just nod my head in polite acknowledgement, secretly hoping he'll be able to finagle something. I try to ignore the stern look on his countenance as he peruses the computer screen in front of him. Finally, he glances back up at my face while informing me through narrowed eyes that the only way it could happen is if I book it for a whole week. In return, I smile sweetly as I tell him that a week will be just fine.

Unsure of what to do with myself next, I decide to take a jaunt on the boardwalk through town, heading toward the marinas. It will be nice to see everyone at the boatworks again; not sure who *everyone* is now, four years later. Watching the boats sway back and forth from the gentle pressure of the waves as they push toward the docks, my attention is drawn away from the water by the ring of a high-pitched voice.

"Miss Bethany Kuiper...is that you?"

As the sound of my name reaches my ears, I begin searching the crowd for the owner of the exuberant greeting. It's not long before I find who I'm looking for on the other side of Bay Street, enthusiastically waving at me for all he is worth. I smile as the person belonging to the voice proceeds to recklessly dodge cars while running in my direction.

"Jonathan!"

We wrap our arms around each other in a gregarious hug.

"Just look at you! It's so good to see you! What are you doing here?" His words run all together.

I smile uninhibitedly. "In town for a visit."

He takes a step back from me. "Girl...a few years away and just look at you, all blessed with curves."

I can feel my jaw dropping.

"And no...I don't mean fat curves...I know how you girls worry. I mean swimsuit-model curves."

Now I'm pretty sure I'm blushing. "Thanks—I think?"

"As you can tell, I've really beefed up these last few years myself. Very soon I'll be winning bodybuilding competitions." He pulls an arm upward in an attempt to flex a muscle.

Shaking my head in laughter, I eye his small, boyish frame. It seems he hasn't changed a bit. But it is so good to see him. "You still live in town then?"

"Only for the summer. I'm at the University of Connecticut the rest of the time."

"Oh, good for you."

"Well, not that good. I'm on the six- or seven-year plan trying to complete a four-year degree."

I chuckle lightly. "Still, that's good. Stick with it."

He tells me he's working at a small surfing apparel shop in the area, and though he's only on break, he will definitely get ahold of me later. During our few minutes together, we walk down by the docks, and he briefly fills me in on the rest of our summer crew.

"You should really go visit Kate. She'd love to see you. She's still at the same place."

I tell him I will and on a sudden whim begin heading in the direction of her house. I'd catch up with the marina employees at a different time. As I wind my way up through the center of town, I contemplate what it will be like to see my old friend Kate again. How had things turned out with her and Nick? Will she be happy to see me? Neither of us had put much effort into keeping in contact over the years. Soon, her address comes into view. Pushing away the nerves that are hovering just below the surface of my skin, I knock on her front door.

Minutes go by and no one answers. Feeling slightly deflated, I try one more time before eventually turning to leave. My retreat is slow, lacking momentum. Reaching the last step on the deck that doubles as a front porch, I hear the sound of a doorknob twisting behind me, and I turn back around.

Peering through the now opened screen door, I find not one, but two pairs of large, brown eyes staring back at me.

"Hi, Kate," I say slowly. For a second or two she watches me with a guarded expression, before recognition sets in and she breaks into a tired grin. "How are you...and—" I nod toward the miniature version of Kate that is attached her hip.

She smiles more brightly then, the weariness in her countenance receding momentarily. "This is Hannah." Pride is evident in her features. Then as if suddenly remembering her manners, she shakes her head in surprise. "Bethany!...Bethany Kuiper...how are you? It's been so long."

"I know! Wow though!" I motion to the small creature on Kate's hip. "She is so pretty—she looks just like you." Large, chocolate eyes framed by wispy, brown curls and perfectly formed pink lips watch me warily as I take in her every detail. In speechless amazement I study the young child that Kate is holding in her arms, all delicate features and baby-soft skin. Finally, as if tired of being scrutinized, miniature Kate turns away and buries her face in her mom's shoulder.

Kate smiles. "Sorry…she's a little shy."

"Different than her mom, then," I say, and Kate laughs outright at that.

"Yeah…I guess that is different than me. But I don't know, I've changed some too. I might not be exactly like you remember."

I eye my once-carefree summertime companion, imagining the multitude of ways motherhood could change someone. "How old is she?"

"Fifteen months old."

She invites me in then, and we sit in her living room talking, while baby Hannah stands beside her mom, hanging onto her legs, burying her face into her knees—occasionally peeking around to get a look at the stranger that has invaded her house. I offer a friendly smile each time she does, and eventually her serious, brown eyes begin to crinkle at the edges. Kate tells me the story of how she made it through two semesters of school at Community College of Rhode Island before she found out she was pregnant and dropped out. She had broken the news of impending fatherhood to the boy involved and never heard from him again. Now she lives here with her mom and waitresses evenings at Misquamicut Beach restaurant. *Nick?* I silently wonder and contemplate how to broach the topic.

"What happened to the rest of the summer crew? I did run into Jonathan in town…but do you ever hear from the others?"

"Emily I'm not sure about. Nick gave me the slip a couple of months into our freshman year of college. He did come to visit me one time after our summer together, before college ended, and then…nothing. Never heard from him again. I hear he is engaged to a girl that runs in his family's circle. When push came to shove, he didn't want to end up with a girl from the other side of the tracks…a Rhode Island townie like me." She pauses for a moment, and a wistful smile crosses over her lips, not quite reaching her tired eyes. "I still think about him now and then, though. He was my first love."

First love. How familiar I am with those words. Fleetingly, I shudder before willing myself to concentrate once again on the conversation at hand. Kate's chestnut hair is still pulled back into a tight ponytail, causing her brown eyes to pop. So much about her has changed; at least that hadn't. Finally our visit draws to an end, and I pull her into a hug before stepping back out onto the wooden front porch. Then peeking around Kate, I blow a kiss to her mini double. Standing in the kitchen doorway, only feet away, Hannah's fingers are clasped tightly to a pink blanky, cautiously watching the stranger that is leaving her home.

Now it is midday and I am back at my rented room once again, rummaging through my cupboard in search of something to eat. Only nothing sounds good. I've extended my stay in Watch Hill, but for what good reason? Each minute that ticks by is one more minute that I realize Tristan isn't coming to find me. My heart is heavy. Why did I have to end up running into him again? Now the old wounds have been opened, and blood is pouring from them at an alarming rate. Finally I decide on an apple. I have just taken the third bite of it when I hear a hesitant knock at the door.

My heart stills.

Holding my breath I stand paralyzed. Was I just hearing things? But the knock happens again. This time louder. I startle into motion. Quietly crossing the room, I lift one of the blind louvers on the window that is situated next to the entrance and peer outside. *Oh—my—word!*

Spinning back around, I fold my arms across my chest trying to calm myself. *It's him! He came!* Tristan is standing outside my door right now, this very minute! I shut my eyes tightly and then reopen them before running my fingers through the blond locks of my hair in attempt to make myself presentable. Taking a relaxing breath, I open the door.

I am greeted with an uncertain expression filtered through sea green eyes and gloriously perfect features. It takes every bit of effort for me not to come completely undone.

"Hey—" Tristan's voice is deep and soft.

"Hey," I say back equally as soft. Our eyes are locked. I don't move. Finally he breaks the trance and motions to the doorway.

"Can I come in?"

"Um...sure." I rotate slowly, leading him through the entrance of my room. When we reach the living area, I turn back around and eye him hesitantly. He has on white shorts and a tight-fitted gray tee shirt that reads *coastal engineering* etched in small letters across the left side of his chest. And he looks so freaking hot! Suddenly I feel shy. I have to force myself to speak. "Did you...have a hard time finding me...finding this place?"

He shakes his head, and immediately I am captivated by the tousled, sunstreaked strands of his hair. "Yes...it took some asking." He pauses. "But I'm here." He watches my face and I can't help it, I know I'm blushing bright red. Giving me a chance to recover, he looks away, his gaze taking in my small rented room instead. "This isn't too bad...it has everything you need."

I nod. We are making polite small talk as though we have just met and hardly know one another at all. And yet there is this unspoken tension between us bubbling below the top layer of the conversation, just waiting to surface. But neither of us seems to know how to address it. And so both of us carry on, making niceties with each other, offering tentative glances, dancing around the topic of *us*. Finally Tristan looks me directly in the eye.

"It killed me to leave you, Bethany."

I suck in a breath, speechless.

As he continues, the expression on his face becomes serious. "I want you to know that I didn't want to leave you, and that it killed me."

I nod, listening.

"I knew if I told you that I was leaving, you would try to talk me into staying, and I couldn't. I feared for your safety. Going away was the only way to protect you. I also knew that I was hurting you, and that killed me too. But I couldn't change what needed to be done…I missed you so much, Bethany. I love you."

That's it! That's all I need. I go to his arms and press myself into his strong chest. He crushes me into him, and this time I'm very aware of the tears that are pouring down my cheeks, getting his gray tee shirt wet. "I love you too," I say into the black lettering that is etched into the cotton cloth. And I know he hears me, because he squeezes me tightly in response.

I pull away in order to get a tissue, and when I return, Tristan is sitting on my bed. I settle in beside him, and he places an arm around me. "So I take it you heard about them catching the real yacht murderer then?"

"Yes," he sighs. "I heard." He doesn't sound very convinced. Does that mean he's *not* convinced? Surely he doesn't still believe the killer is Keuran!

"When I couldn't find you, when I realized you went away, I found Mr. Horton's house and he explained everything to me, so at least I knew what you were thinking, why you left…He told me about your cousin Keuran." Tristan had been rubbing my arm with his fingers, and as I say Keuran's name, he stops. I glance up at his face in time to catch a flash of anger crossing over his features. Watching the muscle in his jaw twitch, I wait for a response, but he isn't quick to offer a reply. The room is quiet.

"I don't trust him!" The emphatic tone of his voice startles me. "I knew he was coming on land watching me….me and you….and I didn't trust him and the lengths he would go to hurt anyone involved with me. The only way to keep you safe was to go away and get him off your trail." *Really? Keuran?* I narrow my eyes, deep in contemplative thought. He just doesn't seem *that* bad! Maybe a little devious, but the accusations that Tristan is throwing around are pretty stiff. I make a decision that right then might not be a good time to bring up the fact that—*by the way, I'd met Keuran and that he is actually the one who'd talked me into staying in town for a bit.*

"It tore me up how emphatically you were searching for me, though." The gentle tenor of Tristan's words breaks through my thoughts. "When I saw you on my island waiting for me, I almost lost my resolve. And then when you almost drowned on the way back, I reached a breaking point. When that happened, I didn't know if I'd be able to hold out and stay away after all."

I gasp. "You knew about the near drowning?"

He nods solemnly, his expression pained. "I was there." I narrow my eyes, confused, as he continues. "In the water. I was right there by you." *What?* I shake my head. *Of course!* Of course he was there! It finally all makes sense.

"You saved me, didn't you? It was you, there…the presence I sensed around me. You brought me safely to shore."

Tristan presses his lips together and nods. "Yes, it was me." My eyes are wide as I recollect all that I felt that night through the intense haze of my oxygen-deprived lungs and brain.

"Thank you," I mouth, still a little overwhelmed. He shifts on the mattress beside me. For the first time that day I become very aware of the intimate setting we are in. We've never been together alone on a bed. I work hard to fight off the aching sensation that surfaces as I stare at the strong muscles in his thigh that is only inches from mine. Folding my fingers tightly together, I press away the thoughts that are captivating my mind.

Tristan shakes his head. "Of course! I didn't want any harm to come to you. That is the very reason I left in the first place. I never wanted to hurt you. It killed me to see how bad you were hurting. I kept thinking, if I could just get you home safe and sound and on to Penn State, you'd be able to get over me and move on. You'd end up meeting all sorts of college boys."

"Huh," I roll my eyes. "Well, it wasn't just that easy."

"So did you?…Meet some college boys?"

I heave a resigned sigh. "It took a long time, but eventually I did try dating again. The truth is though…I never really moved on." Goose bumps cover the skin on my arms as I watch the measure of relief that is revealed in his green eyes. I take a deep breath, preparing myself for an answer to the return question I'm about to shoot his way. "What about you...and the college girls of Rhode Island?"

Tristan looks me right in the eye, and my heart begins to pound. "I told you before. It's always been you. That hasn't changed." *Oh!* I am instantly elated! But in some ways frustrated too—he didn't *exactly* answer my question. *Did he?* Before I have time to perseverate on the thought, he is jumping off the bed, offering me a hand to pull me with him. "Do you want to go for a walk down by the water?"

I smile then. "Of course." Where else on earth would I possibly want to be? He keeps his hand wrapped around mine as we make our way down by the flowing surf that is waiting only a baseball's throw away from the front of my building. My heart skips in my chest as we walk along. I can hardly believe it—it has been so long since I've felt the sand between my toes and Tristan's fingers laced with mine at the same time. I inhale the ocean air that is wafting against my face and catch a whiff of Tristan's clean scent. *Oh—my!* I glance over at his profile. He catches me looking—and smiles. Immediately every part of my body goes weak. I look away and exhale slowly. This is it! This is what I've waited four years for, and here I am. I want to pinch myself. Then I remember something I've been dying to ask him.

"Hey...what about that dream I had...the coral reef dream. I woke up wet with sand and seaweed on my feet...How could that have happened?"

"I took you there."

"I knew you had...it was all so real! But how did you do it?"

"I wanted to help you move on. I was so worried about you. I knew you weren't going around town anymore. I got wind that you weren't even getting out of bed. I had to help you get over me. So I used my music, our song, to put you in a trance. If I kept you close by me, I could help you breathe underwater for a longer time." *The electrical current I'd felt coming from him.* "I used every ounce of my power to pass on to you not only oxygen while you were in the water, but steadfastness and strength as well. The strength you needed to move on…And I also wanted to keep my promise to you…of taking you to a coral reef."

"Wow." It all seems so surreal. "Well, it worked in a lot of ways. It really did help me at the time. It never made me *all* better, but it helped. At least I was able to get out of bed." I offer him a sheepish grin, truly embarrassed that it ever got that far.

Tristan narrows his eyes and shakes his head. "I'm so sorry that I made you feel that way. I wish there was a way I could take it all back…or at least make it up to you." His gaze doesn't waver, and I begin to tremble. There *is* a way. Standing in front of him I become riveted by the look on his face. Involuntarily my mouth parts. *I'm pretty sure I can think of a way.* His hand brushes a strand of my hair that is blowing across my face. He cups my head with his fingers. Staring back, I resist the urge to run my own fingers against his perfectly chiseled cheekbones. *Oh how I've missed him!* Very slowly, he leans toward me.

His lips are soft as they move against my mouth. Instantly, I am breathless. The minute space between us vanishes quickly as we melt together. My fingers quickly find his hair and then his back, pulling him closer toward me. I can feel his strong hands all over my arms, and then my back—sliding down to my lower back. I suck in a breath. How far will he go? He pauses and then briefly I feel his fingertips as they reach for my waist, traveling up my sides. *It's okay, Tristan,* I tell him with my kiss. *I'm yours. I want to be* completely *yours.* Do I just imagine the gentle pressure of his fingertips grazing the sides of my breasts? Unabatedly I press my body into his hands, willing them to continue and expand their touch.

Instead Tristan pulls away. Holding me at arm's length, for just a moment he looks questioningly into my eyes before crushing me to his chest in a hug. *No! Not again! Another kiss cut off prematurely.* When then? It's been four years. When if not now will he be ready to take our relationship a step further? My thoughts are interrupted by a whistlelike noise that is coming from the waves, just beyond where we are standing. I peek around Tristan's chest to find the source of the sound. And there, much to my surprise, is a little, gray head bobbing just above the surface of the water. I draw away from Tristan, stepping to the side.

"Oh my goodness, Tristan, I have never seen a dolphin so close to land. Look...look."

Tristan laughs outright. "It appears we're being spied on." He takes a step toward the little nautical creature who seems to be grinning from ear to ear. "Can't a guy ever get a moment of privacy?" At this, the dolphin proceeds to dive under a wave, disappearing momentarily before shooting back up into the air for a flip.

I am dumbfounded. "What is going on? Where did he come from?"

Tristan rolls his eyes. "Meet my newest friend."

"What? Wait, is he really your...friend?"

"I'm afraid so. I can't seem to get rid of him."

Now I am laughing, breathlessly excited. "Really...what is his name?"

"I call him Drag...because he's a real drag to have around... and because it seems like I'm now destined to drag him around with me wherever I go."

I eye the friendly, marine animal that is biding his time dipping in and out of the waves. "Aw...that is not a very nice name. He obviously really likes you. You should come up with a better name than that."

Tristan shakes his head. "Nope...I'm calling him Drag."

I roll my eyes. "Well, I won't call him that...no way. He is way too cute for that."

"Suit yourself."

We spend the next while catching up with each other, walking the shoreline, periodically splashing in the waves, sitting side by side in the sand. Kissing and touching—but never taking it any further. The dolphin keeps us company, just yards from the shoreline at all times. When daylight fades to dark, Tristan tells me he needs to go. And I don't want him to. If he leaves now, will I ever see him again? My eyes watch the ground.

"Hey—" he lifts my chin. "This isn't good-bye for good...I promise." I think back to the coral reef dream and realize then that Tristan does keep his promises.

I offer a small smile. "Okay." At that, he takes his thumb and kisses it before gently pressing it to my lips. Then he turns and leaves me standing on the sandy oceanfront as he and his newest friend dive into the waves and disappear. Breathlessly, I hold my fingers to my mouth, still tasting the salt where the skin of his thumb had been.

There I remain, staring at the horizon until all that is left is me and the relentless roll of the surf. Shaking my head in wonder, I finally begin wandering back to my room. I want to pinch myself. Did I really just spend the evening with Tristan, and did I really just witness him leaving by plunging into the depths of the ocean? Most say good-bye to their dates and then watch as they slide into the front seat of their car and drive away. But not me, I think to myself, still overwhelmed with the thought as I continue my retreat from the shore, dancing on the inside and grinning from ear to ear.

Chapter Four

My newfound high is short-lived however, when Tristan does not come around to see me again for the next two days. I begin to chide myself for knowingly stepping onto the roller coaster once again. I am wallowing in my melancholy mood, preparing to go on a cathartic shoreline run, when I hear a hardy knock at the door. My heart stops and then speeds up in tempo.

"Well, hey...I see you are all ready to go." It's Keuran. He wastes no time entering the room as soon as I give him access. *What?* My head is spinning. "They are having volleyball at East Beach this afternoon." He eyes my sporty attire. "And you look like you are dressed and ready. You must have sensed I was coming to get you."

It takes me a second to gather my thoughts and wipe away my initial disappointment from the knock not belonging to Tristan. "I was about to go running."

"Running...you can do that anytime. Volleyball will be more fun." He lifts his eyebrows questioningly, and a teasing grin forms on his lips. "Come on, Bethany...what do you say?"

"Oh...all right." I chuckle out loud. Keuran can be very persuasive, and besides, he appears to *want* to spend time with me. Unlike someone else I know who seems to pop in and out of my life for brief moments—just long enough to cause my heart to perpetually ache with the thought of him.

We reach the volleyball courts and players are divvied up. Keuran and I on the same team. Flexing muscle with each hit of the ball, he steps into the game with gusto. He is an intense competitor, and there is a guy on one of the rotating opposing teams that he quickly forms a rivalry against. We have played four games already and are just vying for ownership of the fifth. The sand from the court is now sticking to my knees and thighs from the repeated digs and dives. Keuran is in the front row, his opponent just inches away on the other side of the net. Sweat drips off the bare skin of Keuran's chest with each jump and spike that he executes. The ball is in play, and volley between the two teams on the roped-in enclosure is incessant. Bump-set-spike. Bump-set-spike. It seems as though the crossfire will never end.

Then, at one point when the ball is high above Keuran's head, as if in slow motion, he leaps from the ground, abs taut, arm extended high, amber eyes focused. I watch in confusion and shock as he reaches to the other side of the net, not only slamming the ball, but the top of his contender's head as well. Immediately, the guy stumbles back, stunned, cradling the injury in his hands. *Oh…my… what?* What just happened?

The teams instantly dissolve. "Hey, grab some ice," I hear someone shout.

"Are you okay?" Keuran says to the guy, his voice laced with concern. *It was an accident then.* It had to be an accident! The victim is now sitting on the sidelines, stupefied, being tended to by his teammates and other concerned onlookers. "Man…I'm really sorry. It was an accident…I must have lost my footing," Keuran continues on with his apology. I watch the interaction from the other side of the net, preparing to head over. But then stop short as Keuran begins making his way across the sand toward me. I watch his face as he approaches. For just a split second I imagine I detect a gleam of satisfaction in the light of his amber eyes. *What?* I blink, trying to get a handle on what I'm seeing, and then that quickly the expression is gone.

I feel chilled. "That was awful! Is he going to be okay?"

"A little ice and he'll be just fine. But yeah…I feel really bad, my hand just slipped." Regret and consternation are clearly written on Keuran's features, evident in the tone of his voice. In turn, my mind is set at ease. He truly does sound sorry. *And accidents do happen.*

We are gathering our things, getting ready to call it a day and head back, when out of the corner of my eye I notice a form advancing across the sand, slow and steady, heading in our direction. I pause from packing up my duffel and look up. *Crap! Oh crap!* Its Tristan! His jaw is tight, green eyes steel. Nodding one time in acknowledgement, he looks from Keuran's face to mine as he reaches the spot where we are standing.

"I didn't realize you two knew each other," he says on approach. His voice is like polite ice. *Double crap, he is pissed!*

"Sure we know each other," Keuran announces. Me and Bethany here are volleyball buds. We just finished up a game, didn't we, Bethany?" Am I mistaken, or is it a satisfied smirk that I see splayed across Keuran's face? Suddenly I feel desperate to explain.

"I ran into him on the shore, playing a guitar. I thought I knew the song…and then I stayed and he asked me to play volleyball…" My words come out in a breathless rush, their intended meaning getting botched. Tristan looks confused. And pissed! Ignoring my explanation, he turns toward Keuran.

"Why are you on land?"

"Why am *I* on land, Tris?" Laughter rings from Keuran's throat. "Why are *you* on land, cous'?"

Tristan cuts him off. "You know why I'm here, Keuran."

"No…remind me." For a minute, Keuran's complacent attitude begins to fade, and irritation surfaces across his striking features. The intensity of Tristan and Keuran's warring gazes are mirrors of each other, and I am reminded of their relational similarities. "Oh yeah, that's right…you got the approval to go to college to get your *degree*…the degree that is going to magically help you save the ocean."

"*Our* ocean, Keuran!"

Keuran spits on the ground. "Well, if you figure out a way to save it, maybe they'll award you the Nobel Peace Prize too. That'd be nice, right, Tris?" He gives a nod in my direction. "So, I take it from what you said earlier, you know Bethany then?" Not an eye is blinked. The angst in his voice—gone. The topic—changed.

Tristan's lips twitch in irritation, and I find myself wanting to reach out and run a finger over their sun-kissed pink softness. *Just like he did to me the other night.* Making a fist at my side, I attempt to squeeze away the growing ache that is working its way through my body. "Cut the shit, Keuran, you know I met Bethany four summers ago."

Keuran sneers. "Four summers ago?" Silently, I suck in a breath. *What all does Keuran know about when we really met as small children?* If there is bait intended in the question though, Tristan ignores it.

"Yeah, we were acquaintances at the marina where we worked that summer." *Acquaintances?* Why does the sound of that word hurt so much? I watch Tristan's face for some sign of his true feelings for me, but the stoic expression I see does not waver one iota. Pressing my lips together, I make an attempt to disregard the sensation of a dagger pressing into my chest. *No—I shouldn't go there.* He told me that he loved me, that he had a hard time getting over me that summer. This current apathetical attitude is surely just for Keuran's sake. *Right?*

"Well, you just caught us leaving, Tris," Keuran's voice jumps in, interrupting my thoughts. "So I guess we'll have to have this party another time." Tristan stares Keuran down. I hold my breath in anticipation of what is sure to ensue. But before I have time to formulate an idea of what that might be, Tristan turns away, heading back the way he came—without a second glance at me. My heart sinks to the ground. It takes all of my staying power to not run after him and clear the air between us. "So... do you want to get a soda, before we head back to your place?" Keuran's voice sounds lighthearted, cheerful even.

What? "Um...sure." Ignoring the thoughts that are consuming me, I fight to draw my eyes away from Tristan's retreating form and focus on Keuran instead.

After heading over to St. Clair Annex, we settle into a booth.

"This place is great...isn't it?" Keuran's gaze sweeps through the old-fashioned ice cream parlor. He is seated across from me. I too glance around, taking in all the updates from four years ago. It still holds all the charm and nostalgia that I remembered from all the many outings with the summer gang.

"I love this place." I can't hide the wistfulness in my voice.

"Well...I'll have to remember that for future times. I'm glad I made a good choice for today."

I offer a weak smile, but it's hard to concentrate on anything Keuran is saying when my mind had exited the beach a half an hour ago. Taking a sip of my cherry soda, I work hard to engage in the conversation with the dark-haired boy sitting across the table from me. Right now Keuran is here, clearly enjoying my company. And though I wish he was, Tristan is not.

After we finish our drinks, I talk Keuran into saying good-bye and parting ways at St. Clair Annex. I am not in the mood for him to accompany me home. It's not a long walk to my rented flat, and after cutting over two streets and then up one, I am making the final approach to entrance of my room, when something causes me to stop short. I swallow down a gulp of air. Tristan is sitting on the step just outside my door. Waiting. His expression is stone, the look in his green eyes formidable.

My steps slow, but not enough. Eventually I reach him. We are only feet apart. Standing above him, I watch his face. *Say something, Tristan.* He doesn't say anything. Finally I gather my voice together. "Tristan—" His name coming from my lips sounds cracked and distant. He still looks pissed, and it is making me feel unsure about what to say next. Instead, I sit down next to him, our thighs touching.

He doesn't look at me. "Don't trust Keuran, Bethany." His deep voice so close by breaking the quiet startles me. "I think you know he is bad news."

Irritation reaches out to grab me. And I'm not sure why except that Tristan is a fine one to tell me who I can be around and who I can't. Where had he been for the past four years? I clear my throat. "Bad news? You know...I never get the feeling Keuran is trying to avoid me. He actually comes around quite a bit, so he must enjoy my company. Did you know that he texts me? *Somehow*, I was led to believe that wasn't a possibility for your kind. But it doesn't seem to be a problem for him." I can feel Tristan's eyes on my face now, but he doesn't try to stop the words I'm spewing, so I continue on. Taking a breath, I try to keep my voice calm. I don't want to get all worked up and start crying or some embarrassing thing like that. "Actually," I continue. "He really doesn't seem *that* bad...and besides, I get the feeling that it won't be Keuran that ends up hurting me anyway!"

A sigh escapes Tristan's lips, and I can feel his breath on my skin, making it difficult to stick to my point. I want to turn and find his mouth and let him kiss me and tell me he'll always stay right beside me so there won't be any room for Keuran in my life anyway. But he doesn't, so I begin playing with my fingers, trying to stay focused.

"Just...just please be careful." That's it. That's all Tristan seems to want to say on the topic, and as mad as he seemed earlier, he now seems willing to let it go and move on, and so I'm willing too. I don't want Keuran or anything else to ruin this rekindled time we have together. We sit and talk on the porch step a while longer about day-to-day things, about how his people are doing and how he came to meet his new dolphin friend, and about how my family is doing back in Philadelphia. We talk about pretty much everything *but* Keuran for the next long while, and then too soon, he tells me he has to go. And I don't want him to. "How much longer do you have this room for?" he asks. We are both standing now, facing each other.

"Until the end of the week." Just saying it sounds so discouraging. A look of surprise registers on Tristan's face.

"Oh…that soon?"

"Yes." *Yes, and unless something changes, my time here will be up and I'll be gone, and you've already missed spending two of those days with me.*

Tristan looks like he is deep in thought. Finally he looks up. "When can I see you again?" *You name the time.*

"When were you thinking?"

"Well, I have to work tomorrow, but in the afternoon?" The look in his green eyes as he watches my face makes my heart beat faster.

"Okay." My voice is soft. His eyes are still studying my face. I feel them drift to my mouth, and unwittingly I suck in a breath of air. Once again he has me in his spell. I stand motionless while he's leaning toward me, closing the inches between us. Seconds later he's pressing his lips against mine, very slowly, softly, driving me crazy. And it takes all of my reserve not to throw myself in his arms and mold myself tightly to him, deepening the kiss. Finally, when I think I can't take it anymore, he pulls back.

"Good-bye, Bethany." It's just a whisper.

I hold my fingers to my lips trying to gather my senses, watching his sexy smile and his disheveled, blond hair as he backs away from me before finally turning to leave. "Good-bye," I mouth after he is already gone.

The sound of an engine revving wakes me up the next morning. Stretching, I crawl out of bed and pad to the window to take a look. *Keuran!* What is he doing? Opening the door, I step outside. He rolls down the driver-side window of his Lexus ES. "What is going on?" I yell.

Cutting the engine, he opens his door. "I'm not sure. The engine is misfiring. I was driving by and thought I'd park it at your place to give it a rest for a while." Mentally I roll my eyes. *Well, that's the biggest line of crap I've ever heard!*

I laugh. "It doesn't sound like you were giving it too big of a rest. You just woke me and probably the rest of Watch Hill too."

"My apologies…but since you are awake now, how about going with me for a walk along the shoreline? That way my car can get the rest it needs." *Bullshit!* I cough the words, and Keuran eyes me speculatively.

"Let me grab a cup of coffee, and I'll be right out." Secretly, I'm glad he did wake me up though. I had gotten a text from my best friend Lucy the evening before. She is coming in town for a visit today. I am thrilled—so excited to be able to take her around to all the places that are jam-packed with memories from summer 2012. Maybe even introduce her to Tristan! My back is turned as I'm heading back into my room when I hear a whistle behind me.

"By the way…sexy pj's." *What?* I look down at my skimpy, striped shorts and laced camisole top and blush. I'd forgotten my attire. Shaking my head, I close the door behind me, shutting out Keuran's view.

It is a quiet morning, and the water is glass beside us as our bare feet sift through the sand. Sauntering down the winding oceanfront, I savor the crisp morning air and my first cup of coffee of the day. Beside me, Keuran chitchats incessantly. "So you met Tris four summers ago?"

My heart pauses at the mention of Tristan's name. Especially coming from Keuran. "Yeah."

"So you must have kept in contact quite a bit over the last few years then?"

I hesitate. "No…not really."

"Oh." Keuran looks momentarily perplexed. "I might have read too much into it…but I thought you two had gotten pretty close that summer…was I wrong?" *Hopefully not!* I thought we had gotten very close too! Had I read too much into it?

"Well…I thought—"

He cuts me off. "Well, at least he came to visit you a couple of times at college, right?"

I sigh, before taking a sip out of my ceramic mug. "No…no, it was too far away…He couldn't be away from the water that long." But *Keuran should know that!*

The sound of Keuran's laughter fills the air. He has a hard time curbing it. I stare up at him dumbfounded. "Is that what he told you?" he asks. "Oh…okay." Narrowing my eyes, I try to ignore the uneasy feeling that is forming in the pit of my stomach. A spray of liquid lands on the skin of my arms and legs, pulling me from my thoughts. It's from Keuran. "Hey…cheer up!" Lost in the space inside my head, I hadn't noticed him reaching for tide. "No moping on this walk…it's too nice of a morning for that, all right?"

I decide he's right. It's a beautiful day! The sun is still low in the eastern horizon, glistening on the water, bringing it to life. Beside me I can hear birds embracing the awakening hours with a song. The brisk ocean air feels refreshing on my face. Reaching down with my free arm, I scoop liquid into the palm of my hand, sending it Keuran's way.

Keuran winks. Clearly, he doesn't mind getting splashed. One bit. "That's better…much better." He stops. Looks hard at me. "Hey…do I? I do! I think I detect a smile." I can't help it—my lips curve the rest of the way upward, releasing a bout of laughter in the process.

The rest of the walk is pleasant, and we are almost back to where we started before Keuran's line of questioning has me on edge once again. "So…tell me…did you have many boyfriends in college?"

"I did date some."

"Well, that's good…it would have been a waste otherwise."

"A waste?"

Keuran runs a hand through his dark hair. "Let's just say no one else was sitting around *wasting,* if you know what I mean." *Is he referring to Tristan again? Like with other girls?* My heart constricts. I have to fight back the emotions that want to surface on my face.

"I take it you mean Tristan didn't *waste* his time during his college years."

I feel amber eyes studying my profile as we continue walking, but I can't meet their gaze. I don't want him to see the pain I'm suppressing in anticipation of an answer I won't like. "Girls like Tris, Bethany…or haven't you noticed?" *Oh, I've noticed!* I am now officially sick to my stomach. What will Keuran do if I puke into the ocean at this very minute, right in front of him? "But enough about him, right?" Keuran brushes my arm with his fingertips until I look at him. He smiles, and for a brief moment I imagine I detect a sneer in the midst of the grin. But then he blinks, and his striking countenance is charmingly boyish instead. "Did anyone ever tell you… you are one hot chick and deserve only the best?"

I laugh self-consciously and roll my eyes. When we get back, Keuran's car starts, no trouble, and he is on his way. I shut the door to my room behind me, shutting my eyes in contemplative thought at the same time. Keuran is so nice to me and seems to only want the best for me. So why is it that when I'm with him I feel assaulted with all these nagging doubts and suspicions about what I know to be true? Shrugging my shoulders, I push away these negative thoughts. The past is the past. I'm back in Watch Hill now, and Tristan is happy to see me. *He loves me!*

And Lucy is going to be here in two hours!

Lucy gets lost a few times, but finally makes it into town. When she pulls into my drive, I run out to greet her and wrap my arms around her in a hug. We both squeeze tight. She'd put up with my melancholy mood for the past four years at college like only a true best friend would do. And the last time she had come to Watch Hill four years ago, she had found me in bed, deep in depression. I never showed her around town, took her to the beaches, introduced her to anyone. *I am so excited!* This time is going to be *way* different! An ear-to-ear grin is plastered on my face; I know my blue eyes are dancing. "I'm so glad you are here!" I tell her.

She pushes a wisp of her blond, wavy hair behind her ear. "I'm so happy I'm here too! Look at you…you look so happy! I haven't seen you like this in forever. What is going on?" Her brown, doelike eyes are smiling, and I am once again struck by her beauty. I lace my arm through hers and begin guiding her toward my rented room. I can't hide my obvious enthusiasm, but I keep my lips pressed tightly together like I'm not going to say a word. "Stop…and quit acting like you are going to keep a secret from me. What is it, Bethany?"

I blow out a slow breath, trying to act calm and cool. But I am like a kid on Christmas morning, bursting with so much zeal that it is pathetic. "Oh all right, I'll tell you. I ran into Tristan!"

Lucy's eyes are wide. "Really…and—?"

"*And* I love him and he still loves me…and I am so happy!"

"Well, the happy part is obvious." She watches my face, and her voice becomes softer. "And the love part is too."

"Did I mention that he is *so* hot?" At that we both laugh. We take a few minutes to catch up on hometown news and gossipy stuff before beginning the Watch Hill tour. Filled with passion about the summer town that I am so fond of, I am the best tour guide around. Of course the first thing I am quick to point out is the all-encompassing view of the ocean. From there I take her to Watch Hill Light, the Flying Horse Carousel, the shops downtown, and finally Hill Cove Marina. I haven't stopped by the marina to say hi yet, and David Chambers, the owner, is happy to see me. Thrilled about my marine biology degree, he begins to discuss it with me at length. I could easily stay there all day delving into the particulars, but the bored expression on Lucy's face reminds me that now is not the right time. Easing myself out of the conversation, I ask about Ethan Vaughn and find out that he is still managing the marina.

"Stop in again," David Chambers tells me. "I'd like to talk to you some more, and Ethan will be sorry he missed you." I assure him I will, and we begin heading back to my room. Tristan would be there soon. He and I had made plans to get together this afternoon before I'd gotten the text from Lucy. Now as it stands I will get to hang out with *both* of my favorite people! I am so excited for them to meet!

"Just look at all that water…don't you just love it?" Once more I point out the ever-present view of the ocean as we continue the route back to my place. Lucy laughs at my exuberant tone.

"How many times are you going to ask me that—" she begins. Stopping midsentence, she grabs my arm. We are a baseball's throw from my front door.

"*Who*…is that on your steps?"

My heart quickens. I have so little control. "That's him." I smile. "That's Tristan."

I feel a squeeze on my bicep. "You weren't kidding, were you!"

I am so proud and undone by him at the same time. Even at this distance I am captivated by his gaze. Lucy's voice is now just a whisper beside me as we make our approach. "He is freakin' hot, Bethany!"

Introductions are made, and Tristan adapts easily to the idea that we now have a third party joining us for the evening. From all our long, shoreline discussions that summer four years ago, he knows how much Lucy means to me. After hanging out for a while, giving a chance for Tristan and Lucy to warm up to each other, he tells us about a party that's going on near Misquamicut Beach, and we head in that direction.

The sun has set, the horizon's warm glow vanishing into a graying night sky, when I finally get the chance to be alone with Tristan. We are standing yards away from one of several blazing bonfires when two girls walk by, barefoot in the sand, offering flirtatious smiles. "Hi, Tristan," they call out. Their voices are playful, sugary. Involuntarily, I feel myself flinch. Unwelcomed thoughts from my last conversation with Keuran come wafting back into my mind. What *had* Tristan been up to these last four years? Was I just another conquest? Did he throw around the word love to a variety of wanting ears? Could he really have come to visit me at college if he had wanted to? I am struggling with these circulating questions when I feel the warmth from his arm as he places it around my shoulder, almost protectively.

"Do you want to get another drink?" His fingers brush up and down the skin of my bicep.

"Sure," I tell him. He leads me to another part of the beach where beverages are flowing freely, never once taking his arm away. And I can't help but warm to his touch, leaving the negativity of my contemplations buried like a forgotten seashell in the sand.

"Hey, guys—" Lucy had been out mingling in the crowd for the last long while, and now she has found us once again. And when she returns, she is not alone. *Oh my word!*

"Hello there, stranger!" The gravelly voice that reaches my ears causes a shocked smile to spread across my face. Leave it to Lucy to find Ethan Vaughn in a crowd this large. I'd forgotten how beguiling his perpetually smiling eyes could be, or how the warmth of his persona could be so unsettling. I am still recovering from the shock of seeing my manager from four summers ago, when my gaze flickers to Lucy's face. Just in time, I catch the flash of admiration that is crossing over her features. *Uh-oh!* I bite my lip. And send her a look like *what is going on?* But she is too busy hanging on to Ethan's every word to catch my inquiring expression. *Oh, Lucy,* I mutter softly in my head. *What have you gone and done?*

It is very late before we leave the beach party that night, but I am so enjoying Tristan's company that I really don't mind the fact that it's going to be very difficult to pry Lucy away from Ethan's side.

Chapter Five

My good habit of running had worn off on Lucy during our college years, and now she joins me for an early morning shoreline jog. Having run nearly five miles, we are sweaty and spent, faces red, kicking back grabbing a cup of coffee when Tristan shows up at the door.

"Um…hi." All of a sudden I am very aware of my unkempt appearance. For a brief moment he eyes me up and down and then smiles, not seeming at all deterred by my grunge. He is wearing tan shorts that are resting low on his hips and a snug, black tee shirt that defines every contour of his chest. *Oh wow!* "Come on in." Lucy doesn't move from her lounging position on couch, but lifts her mug of coffee in greeting.

"Good morning, Tristan…up and at 'em bright and early after our late night last night." Lucy's doelike eyes are playful.

"Talk about up and at 'em, I'm not the one who looks like they just ran five miles." Tristan's retort is lighthearted. *Yeah, but I bet you just swam five miles.* I glance at his blond, tousled tendrils, inspecting them for any evidence of water. I can tell the ends are still slightly moist, and I have to resist the urge to reach over and run my fingers through them. He catches me staring, and I look away trying not to blush. I feel his gaze lingering on my face. "Are you all booked up for the day…or will you have a few free minutes for a walk?" *For you…are you kidding me?* I look over at Lucy.

"Why don't you go now? I need to pack up my things, and then I have some errands to run in town before I head back to Philadelphia." Lucy is insistent. Too insistent. I'm suspicious of the *errands* she is running in town, wondering if they have anything to do with copper highlights and a gravelly voice. I give her the eye.

"Okay, I'll just take a quick shower first."

After I get cleaned up, Tristan and I head for Napatree Point. We are walking through town, stopped at a crosswalk waiting for a car to pass, when Tristan reaches over to clasp a string of my damp hair left over from my shower. Taking it in between his thumb and forefinger, he lets it slide through their tips until it falls away from his grasp. "This is a good look on you." His voice is breathy and soft, and it catches me off guard. I look up into his face, and our eyes lock momentarily. Then the car passes and we both look forward again, realizing it's time to cross the street. Now my heart is beating fast.

When we finally reach Napatree Point water surrounds us on three sides, causing a maritime breeze to stir, falling across our skin. The air smells of salt and sea. I inhale deeply, catching a drift of Tristan's clean scent in the mix. It is intoxicating! The ocean that surrounds us is glistening blue, mixed-up and choppy, causing anchored watercrafts to rock and sway this way and that. Pale grains of sand shift below our feet with each step we take. It's a long walk to the tip of the point, and when we eventually reach the end, Tristan finds a piece of driftwood and pats it, inviting me to sit.

"I'm not going to be ready for you to go at the end of the week." *Oh my word!* His words are like music to my ears. Now my heart is beating triple-time.

I shake my head. "Yeah, me either."

"Really?" He stops. "Would you stay...in town then...if you could?" *With you, of course, forever!*

"I'd like that."

"Then apply for a job...There is a position posted at the Center for Marine Studies here in Rhode Island for an Environmental Educator." *What?* My head is spinning. Is he serious? His green eyes are dancing. I furrow my brow, studying his face. He looks animated, but I don't think he is teasing.

"Wow...I—" I pause, overwhelmed. "Wow...um yeah, I could look into it—"

"Great...I'll give you the information about the website where you can apply."

My head is spinning. I want to know more about his thoughts on the matter. Where this newest idea originated from. More about the job. But right then a splash in the water interrupts our conversation. Simultaneously we turn toward the noise. The sweet, smiling face of a dolphin is bobbing just above the oscillating motion of the waves. Immediately our conversation is abandoned. "Aw...Drake...how are you?" Getting up, I walk to the edge of the shore. Tristan moves to stand beside me.

"Wait—what did you just call him?"

I smile, keeping my sight focused on the friendly creature that is dancing only yards away from us. "Drake."

Tristan shakes his head, laughing. "Oh no...you must have misunderstood me when I told you his name is Drag. Not Drake."

I shake my head back. "No, I didn't misunderstand you at all, but I'm calling him Drake...Hi Drake." As I holler out to the ocean, the dolphin does a playful flip in the air. "See, he likes my name better."

"Figures—" Tristan mutters under his breath.

"What?"

"He's getting sucked in by your charms already." At that I shoot Tristan a quick glance. I can tell he's teasing. Taking my hand, he leads me into the water. "Want to get a little closer?"

I grin enthusiastically. "Sure!" We wade in. Soon we are only feet from his friend, who repeatedly swims toward us and then at the last minute, changes his mind and darts away. It turns into a game, and just when we are getting ready to call it quits and head back for the shore, Drake performs an acrobatic stunt and lands within my reach. I glance up at Tristan questionably.

"Go ahead," he says. Cautiously, I reach my hand out. Drake bobs his gray head, smiling, but this time he doesn't turn away.

My fingers make contact with his smooth skin. I want to shout for joy. But I stand there calmly, moving my arm in a slow, repetitive motion instead. At last he seems to have enough and offers one more grin before disappearing below the surrounding waves, darting beyond my grasp once more.

By the time Tristan and I turn around and reach the shore again, I realize that we are both dripping wet. I had been so absorbed in interacting with the dolphin that I hadn't even paid attention to how far out we were going into the water. Laughing on the inside, I sigh. Somehow I get the feeling if I'm to keep hanging out with Tristan and company, I might as well get used to soaked clothing. I wring out my shirt.

Feeling Tristan's eyes on me, I stop midsqueeze and look up. *Oh my!* I am frozen in place. My mouth goes dry. I lick my lips. His green eyes do not waver. There is something about his look, like he is hungry or something—hungry for me, that makes me tremble all over. We are standing facing each other, and he takes two steps forward, then another, until he is directly in front of me. The wind is whistling softly, causing my hair to blow. He tucks a wisp behind my ear, his fingers lingering on my earlobe, before gently grazing down the side of my neck. My body comes alive. "Dang, Bethany, it's so good seeing you again." His voice is raspy, his eyes intense. The words from his mouth are so sweet to my ears, making every part of me turn to liquid.

"Tristan I—" But he doesn't give me a chance to finish before his lips are pressed against mine. Wrapping our arms around each other, we cling tightly, consuming each other with our kiss. Behind us the waves continue, restless, and a dolphin scoots in and around them, waiting for its owner. An easterly breeze pushes sand against our legs as they become intertwined. The kiss continues, stealing the breath from my lungs. This is living. It feels so right and good. *He* feels so good! Before him I wasn't actually living. I know that now.

My hands press against the strong shoulders of his back, my fingers finding the place where the collar of his shirt ends and neck begins. *Oh…wow!* His skin is like fire beneath my fingertips. A powerful yearning overtakes me, and I can no longer think straight. All I know is I want to feel more of him—want more of him. Suddenly, kissing and embracing does not seem like enough. Does he feel the same way too? I've been waiting for him to make the first move. And he does.

Pushing with a gentle force against my shoulders, he separates us. *What? No!* Now I am standing a foot away from him visibly shaking, bereft without his touch. Hugging bare arms to my chest, I search his green eyes, then look away. What is he thinking? But his face reveals nothing of his thoughts. Am I the only one that's been affected this way then?

"We'd better head back." How can his voice be so controlled after what we just did?

I nod in acknowledgment, not trusting my own words.

On our walk back I am reminded of something I hadn't shared with him yet about our past. About what I'd discovered in-regards-to our history together. In some ways it seems almost embarrassing to admit that I had been so affected by him even at such a young age. But still there is a part of me that wants to let him know. For him I know it will be like putting together another piece of the puzzle. And besides I *do* really want to tell him. I clear my throat.

"So remember how you told me about how we met as small children, and I didn't remember?"

Tristan's head snaps around to face me as we are strolling, a questioning look in his eyes. "Yeah?"

"Well, that summer in 2012 when I was having such a hard time, couldn't get out of bed and all that?"

"Yeah?" The word is drawn out slowly.

"Well, one day as I was lying in bed, out of nowhere, I remembered. Plain as day, I could picture it all. You…me on the beach as little children." Tristan's silence encourages me to elaborate. "Before that though, I had spoken with my parents about it, and they confirmed that we had in fact visited the area before, but it wasn't until that day that I actually *remembered* it."

"But why—"

"But why what…did I remember it then? I don't know. Why did I not remember it for all those years? I'm not completely positive about that either, but after doing some research on childhood memory loss, I came to the conclusion that it must have been the easiest way for me to live without you…to repress you from my memory altogether."

Out of the corner of my eye I detect Tristan's jaw twitch ever so slightly. He takes a deep breath and reaches for my hand, giving it a little squeeze. "I'm sorry for that…but I am glad you can finally remember. Sometimes it made me crazy wondering why you couldn't. Because I was so *sure* it was you."

The rest of the walk back is quiet, both of us lost in our own thoughts as we consider all of the obstacles we've been through over the years, seemingly fighting a force that is trying to keep us apart.

Before he drops me back off at my room, he gives me the name of the website for the job application, and I write it down. *He was serious about me staying then!* We hadn't really gotten back to the subject of it since being interrupted by Drake, so I secretly hoped he would remember. Inside, though still slightly disappointed about the abrupt ending to our kiss, I am overjoyed that he did!

When I step inside my entryway door, Lucy is there zipping up her suitcase. Her brown eyes widen when she looks up. "What did you just do?" she exclaims. "You are all wet!" I glance down at my still-damp attire. I'd forgotten all about it. *Oh my goodness,* this whole wet clothes thing is starting to become very second nature to me. Briefly, I experience a bout of unease. I don't want to give away Tristan's secret.

"I guess we got a little too playful and ended up in the water."

Lucy's eyes go wide again. "Oh! Should I even ask?"

I shake my head, laughing. "Don't worry, it's nothing too much…stayed fully clothed. Hence the *wet* clothes."

"Aahhh…okay…hey, you don't have to explain." She is all secret smiles, and I throw a dishrag at her. She catches it mid-throw. All of a sudden I think of something.

"Hey, guess what? I'm applying for a job here, and if I get it, I'm staying."

"Really? What job?"

"An environmental educator. Tristan told me about the job. I'm going to apply online this afternoon."

Lucy runs her fingers through her wavy, blond hair, eventually forming it into a ponytail. Her brown eyes gleam proudly. "Aw, Bethany…perfect job for you, perfect town for you. I hope you get it. And if you do…it will give me an excuse to come back and visit."

I narrow my eyes, thinking back to the night before. "Ethan?"

"I never was very good at keeping secrets." She presses her lips together and nods her head. "Yes, definitely Ethan."

Oh Lucy, be careful! "Ethan's sexy-hot for sure, but he's a little older. Just be—"

Lucy reaches over and pinches my cheek. "Look at you, so cute, worrying about me. I'll be fine. On second thought, he does seem a little unsafe. Oh geez…well, too late…I like him."

We hug good-bye, and I don't waste any time getting on the Center for Marine Studies, Rhode Island's website, and filling out the online application. It tells me I need a letter of recommendation, and I remember David Chambers' words from four summers ago. So I go down to Hill Cove Marina and pay him a visit. We talk at length about the position I'm applying for and how he thinks I'll be perfect for the job, and then he tells me in more detail how things are going at the marina and finally that he'd be honored to write me a letter of recommendation.

And now all that is left for me to do is sit back and impatiently wait. And wait. Although it feels like forever, it isn't actually very long until I receive the text that tells me they want to set up an interview. Even though it's the message I've been anxiously waiting for, I am stunned when the words scroll across the screen of my mobile device. But soon shock turns to excitement, and I'm dancing around my rented room like a crazy fool.

I reply to confirm the appointment time with shaky hands before eventually putting on my sophisticated-intelligent face in preparation for the interview. *Whoa, this is such a big deal!* First real interview for my career job, after four years of college! The opportunity of living close to Tristan is hanging in the balance with this very meeting. *No pressure!*

I run into the town of Westerly to purchase something studious to wear, pull my hair into a sleek ponytail, and leave in plenty of time to find the facility. The Center for Marine Studies is a large, whitewashed brick building, located as expected, next to the ocean. I park my black jeep, take a deep breath, and proceed through the glass double doors. The receptionist greets me with a formal but warm smile and shows me where I am to sit and wait.

Before I know it, I'm whisked into a conference room, sitting at a gleaming, mahogany table, talking with a panel of human resource personnel, and trying very hard to hide the anxiety that is pulsating through my veins. It's only when I detect two of the interviewers exchange a knowing smile that I realize I've lost myself in the current question and am rambling on passionately about my love for the ocean and the dire need for humans to protect its marine environment. *Oh geez! I've probably just blown it!* Forgetting about being all mature and professional, I'd been carrying on like an enthusiastic kid.

In the end, they tell me they'll be in touch, letting me know their decision. And even though they shake my hand cordially before I exit the room, I have a bad feeling in the pit of my stomach as I slide into the front seat of my car. When I arrive back to my room, I am exhausted and yet in desperate need of a run.

By the time I reach Watch Hill Light, I am in an all-out sprint. Reaching the crest of the uphill jaunt, I pause to catch my breath, staring up at the tall, white brick tower that sends a flashing safety signal to all those that pass through Block Island Sound and Fisher's Island Sound. The waves are hurling themselves onto the jagged rocks below with a deafening force. The wind is a powerful cogency whooshing against my skin, whipping my hair, plastering my shirt and shorts against my body. Watching the frothing whitecaps, in the far distance I detect movement amongst the waves. Drawing close to the cliff's edge, I squint my eyes trying to get a better view. Is it what I think? I continue staring, concentrating, focusing my gaze. *It is!*

Drake!

I know what this means! Immediately I begin glancing in all directions, but all I find are a variety of tourists visiting the lighthouse and scattered fishermen who have come to try their luck in spite of the ferocious waves. My vision finds the water once again. Does that mean Tristan is close by then, possibly out there watching? It takes all of my willpower not to call out or wave. My eyes dart around self-consciously, taking in my fellow human companions who have gathered to enjoy the grounds of Watch Hill Light for one reason or another. Again I contemplate waving. But that would just look strange. Still I *could* yell hi to Drake—but I don't want to give away that he is there, in case some overzealous tourist decides to cause trouble for him. So I stand there quietly watching as the ardent breeze from the ocean does its best to loosen my ponytail. Finally, Drake disappears. For some time I keep my eyes peeled to the water, but nothing else materializes.

After a few minutes of leisurely stretching, I begin a slow jog back. I am circling down the path that leads to the lighthouse's summit when, for some unexplainable reason, my heart starts pounding uncontrollably. *What is it?* Just an intuition, but it feels as though something is not right. My eyes look to the sky. It's getting prematurely dark, foretelling an impending storm. Unwittingly goose bumps cover the skin on my arms, and I don't know why. Seconds later I hear movement in the bushes beside me. Glancing in the direction of the noise, I detect a faint shadow emanating from behind the leaves, in spite of the graying sky.

There is a part of me that wants to yell "who is it?" or "what do you want?" Or on second thought just outright scream, drawing attention to the problem. *My problem*, I realize as I take in my current remote surroundings, because no one else is close by. Instead, I pick up my tempo and soon I'm running at an all-out sprint once again, this time fueled by unadulterated fear.

Eventually I reach my room. Panting and nervous, I peer over my shoulder to see if I've been followed. But all that is behind me are newly formed raindrops which are beginning to spatter onto the blacktop. Closing the door behind me, I fasten the locks, all the while trying to take calming breaths. *What was that all about anyway?*

Finally marginally relaxed—though still slightly on edge—I am sitting on my couch, listening to the rain that is now coming in torrents on the roof, when I get the much-anticipated text. I got the job.

I've got the job!

Oh my word, I got the job!

Thank God! I am jumping for joy, my bizarre situation from earlier completely forgotten. I am going to get to do what I went to school for—what I love to do! Not to mention I get to stay in town by Tristan. Things are good! *Things are finally so good!*

The following day, I go back to the Center for Marine Studies and go over the particulars with the department head. Lucky for me, they were almost finished with the interviewing process when they got my resume—which they happened to like—so they were at a point where they could put me through the system rather quickly. Had I applied earlier, it would have taken a much longer time, even months. And—much to my surprise—they drop a little tidbit of information my way to let me know that while I was horrified at the enthusiastic way I was rambling on during my interview questions, it was that very zeal that sold them into giving me the position. I am to start the following Monday.

I can hardly wait to tell Tristan! In fact, I decide *not* to wait to tell Tristan. After some research, I find out where his place of employment, NEC Systems Group, is located, and drive over to give him the news. I am somewhat intimidated as I enter the front lobby and make my way over to the customer service counter. The place is huge, unlike what I'd expected. How will I ever find Tristan? I clear my throat.

"I'm looking for Tristan Alexander."

"Let me just check my computer." The dark-haired attendant is businesslike, but cordial. "Take the elevator to the sixth floor and ask for him at the reception desk. They will be able to direct you up there."

On the sixth floor the receptionist is blond. She eyes me warily, clearly more familiar with who I'm asking about. But I won't let myself be intimidated, not with the good news I have bursting inside of me. Like the lady on the ground floor, she too looks on a computer. But instead of pointing me in his direction, she tells me she's sorry, *although I can tell she is really not all that sorry*, he is currently out on a consultant run. I step back onto the elevator feeling somewhat deflated. My news would clearly have to wait. Hopefully, he will come to visit me soon so I can relay my newfound information.

Walking with a disheartened gait, I am almost to my jeep when I hear my name being called from across the parking lot. I turn to the sound of the familiar voice, and my breath catches in my throat. *Holy cow!* It is Tristan after all, dressed in business attire—dark gray dress slacks, a white button-down shirt with pale pinstripes, and a tie. He looks sophisticated and ultra-sexy. I swallow back my breathlessness, remembering why I'm here. Suddenly, I'm grinning like a Cheshire cat.

"Hey baby…what's up?" *Baby? My word!* Will I ever get tired of hearing that from him?

"Well—" I pause, trying to hold out for a few seconds, making him wait with anticipation to hear my news. But I'm not able to keep my silence for very long. "I got the job!"

For a few seconds he goes very still, his expression stoic, as he tries to register the news, and for one terrifying moment I wonder whether he wants me to stay in town after all. But then his face lights up into a grin, and I am instantly relieved. "Bethany…that is great!" He wraps his arms around me in a hug, and I am drawn into his fresh, clean scent. "First chance I get I will come over and we'll celebrate, okay?"

The sooner the better, I think to myself as I make my retreat across the Systems Group parking lot, a smile plastered all over my face. I can't believe this terrific turn of events!

Chapter Six

I keep getting the sensation that I'm being followed. I can't really explain it, because when I turn around no one is there. I am walking adjacent to the downtown docks, my mind filled with all the possibilities of what it will be like at my new job. And what experience and enthusiasm I might bring to the table— *or rather the water.* Previous to this I had stopped down at Hill Cove Marina to visit David Chambers; he had some websites he wanted to show me that I might find to be a useful resource as a marine educator. Now I am making a leisurely retreat along the lapping waves of the downtown bay. It's a perfect environment for brainstorming new ideas to implement at the Center for Marine Studies when I start on Monday. Only I can't concentrate, unable to shake the feeling that someone is there—somewhere close by. Brushing off a momentary bout of chills, I contemplate whether what I am experiencing is related to my run coming back from the lighthouse the other night. That time there really *had been* someone there—I had witnessed the looming shadow behind the bush. *Hadn't I?*

Unobtrusively, I sneak one more peek over my shoulder.

Still nothing.

And no one.

Except a young lady appearing to be in her late teens or early twenties, who might have been easy to overlook, were her features not so pixylike and striking. She is yards behind me on the boardwalk, dressed in a floral sundress and sandals. Her fine-boned characteristics, slight form, and pale skin manifests a type of frailty. I pause for a second as my eyes sweep over this stranger, recognizing in my mind that she couldn't possibly be the unexplainable phenomenon I am searching for. As I stop, she stops too. Taking a moment to peruse the screen of her mobile device, she walks over to the nearest city-provided trash container and tosses something inside. Never once does she look in my direction. I turn around and keep walking.

Several yards into my route, I spy an empty bench. Walking over, I take a seat and begin watching a barge that is chugging across the inlet looking for a place to dock and unload. After several minutes of watching its crew attempt to land the cumbersome watercraft, I abandon the performance, deciding on an ice cream cone instead. Still through all of this, I can't free myself of the feeling of being watched. Then an idea occurs to me—and my eyes shoot toward the waves. Narrowing my brow, I scan the horizon. One-two-three-four times. But there is nothing, so I continue on into the ice cream parlor.

The flavor I decide on is strawberry. Cone in hand, I opt for a quick shoreline jaunt toward Napatree Point as I work through my ice cream. A northeasterly wind has blown into town, and the surf beside me is now a deafening roar. Sand is being lifted from the ground, stinging the skin of my bare legs as it whooshes through the air. Strands of my hair have loosened from my ponytail holder and are flying across my face, obstructing my vision, making it difficult to keep my ice cream intact. Using my free hand, I pull them out of my eyes.

"Excuse me," a voice beside me seems to say. But the words lifting into the air are so mousy that at first I almost don't detect them against the backdrop of the waves. Still, the nearness of the sound startles me. Interrupting my steady pace, I turn in search of what I'm hearing. And come face-to-face with the most haunting gray eyes I've ever seen. *It's the pixy girl from earlier in the hour.* She is looking at me, seemingly taking in every detail of my countenance. Suddenly, I feel exposed. *What is this? Who is this?* Then as if remembering her manners, she stops staring and clears her throat. "Excuse me...I'm sorry," she says. "Can you tell me which highway to take to get to Newport?"

I narrow my eyes. I feel a little off kilter. Somewhat taken aback. *Was there no one closer to the city boardwalk to ask this question of that this person had to follow me all the way out to the point?* I wipe away the hair that is whipping against my lips. "Newport?" I say. "Uh…highway one. You take highway one north."

"Okay, thanks. I appreciate it. That helps." The eyes that look at me are round, watchful, swallowing up the pixy face.

Nodding, I take one last bite of cone, turn around, heading back the way I came. Now the wind is at my rear, the sand hitting my spine and calves. Unexpectedly, the waiflike girl falls in step beside me. And for a second time in a few minutes, I get the sensation of feeling thrown off my game. The silence between us feels awkward. I glance in her direction, trying to think of something to say in order ease the next few minutes as we continue our excursion back into town. In the same token, trying to decide whether it was my obligation to say anything at all. Out of my peripheral vision I see brown, shagged hair being ruffled by the wind. The resemblance of a young schoolboy. The faint line of a shadow hovers below sad, gray eyes. Clearing *my* throat, I begin speaking into the wind. "So you are going to Newport you say?"

At the sound of my voice, the face beside me lights up in surprise. It's as if she hadn't expected me to speak. And yet here we are together—walking together. A slight grin forms on her lips and I do a double take. The upturn of her mouth, the lack of foreboding being reflected in her eyes, it was giving her a different appearance. More pleasing, attractive. This too catches me by surprise. "I am," she answers. "Have you ever been?" Her voice is so soft that I have to strain my ear to listen.

"No…never. But I'd like to sometime. I've heard it's really nice."

Her countenance continues to brighten, her words becoming noticeably louder. "You should go too then!" *What?* "I mean sometime…You should visit Newport sometime too." *Oh, okay.*

I smile over at her. "Yeah…sometime." Maybe with Tristan. I'd have to make that suggestion to him. Now that I'd be staying in town for an indefinite amount of time, the types of dates we can go on are endless to think about. I'd have to add Newport to the list.

"I'm Rye, by the way."

Hesitating to answer, I look straight ahead. Was it really appropriate to share my name with a stranger who's only interaction with me was to ask for directions? The wind howls into the air, drowning out all other sound. It offers me a reprieve. When it settles, I wipe at my mouth, getting rid of yet another loose strand. "I'm Bethany," I finally say. A weak smile finds my lips. I'm not sure of where this is going. Nodding her head, Rye grins.

"Do you live here in town?"

I smile unrestrainedly at that question, the luck of my latest disposition surfacing everywhere in my thoughts. "No, not originally," I say. But I will be now."

At that, Rye's eyes widen, and her lips part as if in shock. "What—what do you mean?"

"I mean, I just got a job here, so I guess I'll be settling in the area soon." Just saying the words out loud seems surreal. *But why am I even telling this stranger private information about myself?* I know why, because I can't keep my mouth shut. I'm so excited about my new job—I want to shout the news from the top of the rooftops!

For just a moment Rye's countenance falls. I snap out of my enthusiastic reverie and do a double take in her direction. But once again her face is placid. There is no sign of anything else. "Congratulations," she finally says.

"Well, nice to meet you, Rye. Enjoy your visit to Newport." We've reached the boardwalk once again and I decide it's time to part ways. But as I walk away, heading down Bay Street in the direction of my rented room, I can't seem to shake the weightiness of the eyes I feel inscribing themselves into my back.

The next time I run into Rye, I am at McQuades Marketplace in downtown Westerly, picking up some groceries for the next few days. I have just placed a carton of strawberries into my cart. When I look up, she is only feet away from me, standing in front of a vegetable display. In both of her hands she holds a bell pepper. Turning them from side to side, she studies their size and shape, apparently deciding between the two. I pause in place, watching her.

Then much to my surprise, the next thing you know I hear myself calling her name in greeting.

Lifting her face from the peppers, she lights up. And yet there seems to be a token of wistfulness hidden just beyond her smile. "Hi…Bethany…right?"

I nod. "How was Newport?"

Her lips form into a frown. "I didn't end up going. My car broke down, and so I couldn't make the trip." In that moment she looks so despondent—so utterly frail—I can't seem to help myself—I can't seem to stop the next words that leave my mouth.

"Do you still want to go? Because if you have some free time, I do too…I could drive you." *What am I doing?*

Immediately her gray eyes fill with light. "Yes…sure! I mean are you sure?"

Am I sure? Heck no! What has just possessed me? But somehow I *do* know—the sadness in the gray eyes in front of me—the overall persona of helplessness—has just sucked me in.

The following morning, we make the drive over to Newport. The minute we begin crossing Pell Bridge, the gateway to town, I am immediately captivated by the charm and history of the place. Rye eagerly shares my enthusiasm. Small talk had been exchanged during the hour-long car ride, making the excursion a little less awkward. Now as we drive on the red brick downtown streets, we are taking the exchanges between us to the next level, reveling in the quaint tourist shops and the picturesque backdrop of Newport Harbor. Sailboats with crisp, white sails and high-end yachts fill the slips at the marina. Large, leafy trees provide a shaded canopy for the streets of the historic district. Rye exclaims over them with such enthusiasm that it's hard for me to believe that she is just one year my junior and not still an adolescent.

The days passes with us in town, and I am relaxing on a park bench at Easton's Beach, a little breathless after having completed the Cliff Walk with Rye—the three-mile scenic trail that overlooks the Atlantic Ocean. Earlier we had decided to take a tour through The Breakers—a restored historical mansion—which makes even the largest home in Watch Hill look like a bungalow. Sitting on the bench, I am watching the many beachgoers who are cavorting in the waves while I wait for Rye to return. *What is taking her so long anyway?* She had told me she wanted to run to a store that she had noticed farther back along the beach. And I could *just wait right here and relax* she'd be right back. But that was some time ago. Surely nigh onto an hour. Pulling my mobile phone from my pocket, I check the time. But I'm not even sure on the exact time it was when she left. So now I don't really know how long she's actually been gone. *It feels long though, no matter the minutes.* I am just beginning to get worried when she shows back up, fresh and smiling. Of course I am relieved. No details or apology is given. And while I don't ask the reason for her lengthy disappearance, the idea that I don't require some sort of explanation lets me know that our relationship is mildly strange at best.

After grabbing a burger and a Coke at a drive-in, we decide to find a spot at a remote picnic table in a tranquil bend in the shoreline. As we eat, everything is quiet between us. Staring at the rolling surf, I am lost in thought, thinking about all that is below the surface, when I feel Rye's eyes on me. Tearing myself from the daydream, I turn in her direction. The gray eyes that watch me are melancholy and inquisitive. "What are you thinking about?"

Her voice is just a whisper, and it takes me a moment to translate her words in my mind.

"Oh…nothing." I shrug my shoulders and offer a smile.

Her eyes, so haunting, pierce my own. When she doesn't smile back, for just a moment I begin to feel uncomfortable. She swallows, and I detect the movement of her Adam's apple in her pale throat. "A boy?" she asks.

When I laugh, for some reason it sounds nervouslike. I bite my lip. "Well, sort of…I don't know…it's complicated." *Why am I feeling like this? Like it would be awkward to broach the subject of boys.* Rye nods and looks away. Doesn't ask any more questions. Unexplainably, I feel relieved. After our burgers are finished, we cross Pell Bridge once again, calling it a day. When we reach Watch Hill, Rye asks me to drop her off at the municipal docks. We part ways and as unusual as our relationship may be, I drive away feeling like I've made a new friend.

Once back in my room, exhausted from the excursion, I plop on my bed. Scrolling through the screen of my mobile device, I notice I have several missed texts from Keuran. I sigh, wishing they could be from Tristan instead. Setting my phone on my nightstand, I decide on getting back with Keuran the following day. But before I get a chance to even glance at my phone the next morning, Keuran is at my door, asking me to try out his new paddleboard he just purchased. Intrigued by the novelty of his new toy, I easily acquiesce.

Minutes into the venture, I discover it's really a lot of fun. And more work than it appears. After an hour of fighting waves, I am finally able to balance in a standing position for a few short moments. "Whoo—hoo," I laughingly call out my success to anyone within hearing distance. My triumph is short-lived however as I plunge into the water. Dripping wet, I decide to head to shore for a break. Keuran follows me in. His amber eyes are bright as we lounge, feet apart from each other, using the paddleboard as a seat.

"You did pretty good."

"Yeah? I feel good about it...but man, that's a lot of work!" We are relaxing, taking a reprieve, chitchatting, when Keuran somehow changes the topic to Tristan like it seems he often finds a way to do. Now I am on edge.

"Man...Tris got lucky finding you that summer. Out of all the other guys who wish they could have you how did he manage to get to you first?" It's a rhetorical question, and I roll my eyes at his obvious teasing. "Seriously though," he continues. "Out of curiosity, besides Tris, how many other guys have been lucky enough to have you?" *Have you? What is he referring to?* Suddenly, I feel uncomfortable, teasing or not.

"Have me?" The minute I say the words, I wish I could take them back. I think I know where he is going with this, and it is none of his business.

He laughs a deep, dark laugh. "Oh come on, Bethany, don't play dumb. I think you know what I mean. I know you've had sex with Tris, but have there been others?" *What? I am not having this conversation with him right now—or ever!* My face heats up.

"Look at you blush! What...have there been several?" I can feel myself stirring inside, getting irritated. I have an uncontrollable need to clear the air.

"I haven't had sex with Tristan or anyone else." *Crap! Why can't I just keep my mouth shut?*

Keuran's eyes go wide. "No...really!"

I won't look at him. "Really." Why am I so embarrassed to admit this to Keuran? Probably because he seems so *worldly* in spite of his other-worldliness. Running my fingers through the sand, I refuse to meet his gaze. Keuran shakes his head as if to clear his mind.

"Whoa...I'm shocked...are you sure?" *What do you mean, am I sure? Of course I'm sure!*

"Pretty positive." My voice is dripping with sarcasm.

Keuran furrows his brow, looks away from me. Then looks back. "So I take it you and Tris are just kind of buddies then… like friends?" *Why do I feel so stupid now, suddenly distressed?*

"No, we are more than that!" *At least I think!* "Not *just* friends…why?"

Keuran widens his eyes as if something has just dawned on him. "Oh…oh, nothing."

My heart is pounding. "No…no what, Keuran? What is it?" I feel desperate to know, and yet at the same time, I wonder if I really *do* want to know.

"Oh all right, I'm only going to tell you this because I like you and don't want to see you get hurt. I've known Tris his whole life…obviously.   And I have to say, when he really likes a girl, he's not *holding out,* if you know what I mean." My face feels like seeping hot coals, heating up from embarrassment and anger. "I just assumed he liked you for more than friends, but—"

My mind is spinning. On the inside I am shaking my head, furious. I feel like such an idiot. All those times—every time— he broke off our kiss, it was probably because he wasn't even that attracted to me. I had always wondered why when it was so hard for me to stop—it seemed so easy for him. I rub my arms in effort to subdue the shaking that has begun to surface on my limbs. I want to get more information from Keuran, but I don't know if I can handle the truth.   Finally, I look into his amber eyes. His expression is nonchalant.   He can't know how deeply this information is affecting me, tearing me apart. "Did he…I mean does he…when Tristan is with other girls—" I pause to take a deep breath, these next few words hurt to say. "Do you think he has sex with *them?*"

For just a brief moment Keuran gives me a look like *Hello— yeah, that's exactly what I'm saying, you moron.* But then he looks away, and when his eyes return to my face, they are laced with empathy. "I'm sorry, Bethany, I wish I could tell you the answer was no—"

I swallow hard. I can't talk anymore. I just need to leave. I get up, not caring that my skin is pasted with sand, and hasten my departure. "I gotta go." My voice is edged in anguish.

"Wait...Bethany—"

Holding up a hand to silence Keuran, I shake my head, and keep walking. And keep walking. I intend on going back to my room but find myself going in search of Tristan instead. When I arrive at his secluded beach, I am trembling with hurt and anger. Tristan is there, and he looks surprised to see me. His green eyes reach my face. "Bethany...what is it?" But I am not fooled. I don't let the empathy that is written across his features or the beauty of his physique sidetrack me from the flood of sentiments that are bursting from my heart. Taking a deep breath, I try to slow my racing pulse. Forgoing any type of greeting, I begin spewing all the unwelcome thoughts that have been pummeling through my head.

"Well, Tristan, it's so nice to find out that we've just been *friends* all along. Do you tell all of your *friends* that you love them and then write them a song?" Tristan looks dumbfounded. He shakes his head as if to clear it.

"Bethany, whoa, stop...what is going on? Where is this coming from?"

But I don't stop, and it takes all my willpower not to cry as I continue on. "All those times you kissed me...you kissed me and that was it! But not other girls! Now I know...other girls, that you *really* like—you don't just kiss *them*, you have sex with them as well!" The angst in my voice covers the wavering threat of tears that is welling up in my throat. "Not me though...you're probably not even attracted to me. I'm just a good friend...like Drake. I'm so glad I finally found out. Thanks for playing me!" I stand, feet wedged into the sand, shaking, finally finished with my rampage. Tristan, who is standing only meters away, takes a deep breath. Eyes narrowed, he closes the gap between us. The muscles in his locked jaw are twitching as his lips press firmly together. Grabbing me by the arms, he squeezes them, the look of fire in his eyes.

"What?" he shakes his head. "You don't think I want you?" I start to look away. But he doesn't let me. Taking my chin firmly in his grasp, he forces me to look him in the eye for several seconds before covering my lips with his mouth. The kiss is unrestrained and rough, taking me by surprise. Unwittingly my body begins to react in spite of the fury that is coursing through my veins. But the ruthlessness of the act is making me perplexed as well. I am not used to this show of force from Tristan. Before I have a chance to process it all, he pulls away, breathless. "Is this what you want—for me not to respect you? You want more from me, to prove that we are more than just friends?"

I stare at him in shock, it is all happening so fast. My mind can't register a response to give back. His green eyes are smoldering, burning in a way that I've never seen before. *What is going on?* Quickly he reaches an arm behind me, pulling me to his chest before laying me down in the sand all in one swift move. Eyes wide, my breath comes in short gasps. And I am so confused. This is what I've wanted from him, isn't it? Tristan looks intensely in my eyes for one quick second before kissing me hard once again. I can't think straight. Somewhere in my mind I realize that his hand is reaching under my shirt, covering my bra. Now I am squirming, but with what sensation I am not sure. I want Tristan more than anything. *But what is this? Not like this!* This is not what I'd dreamed of!

Now I feel his hands—the hands that I love more than anything—as they travel up the skin of my bare legs. Reaching my stomach, he begins fumbling with the snap on my shorts, pulling them open. There is a small part of me that is reacting involuntarily to his physical touch, but there is a much bigger part of me that is quickly becoming terrified. *Who is this person on top of me?*

Then suddenly—he stops.

Closing his eyes, he jumps up and faces away from me. Lacing his hands on the back of his head, he exhales slowly—a long, hard, slow breath while he focuses his eyes out to sea. I am lying in the ground where he left me, sand mixing into my messed-up hair, trembling. How much time passes, I'm not sure. Everything seems surreal and out of place: the wind whistling through the trees, the sound of a boat motor humming from far across the bay, the rhythmic pattern of the water as it laps up against the rocks. Finally he turns to meet my uncertain gaze, his green eyes dark. He looks pissed.

"I've got to go." His voice reverberates as if through a hollow tunnel. Dazed, I watch as he turns and dives into the whitecaps that are pounding onto shore. And just like that, he is swallowed up and gone.

Pulling myself into an upright position, I stare at the sea for many minutes, unable to wrap my mind around all that has just happened. Covered in silt, sand, and other debris from the beach, I sit hugging my legs, crying softly. Exhausted, I watch as over and over again the ominous breakers from the sea push toward Tristan's secluded beach, taking with them a large volume of sand and tiny, shattered pieces of my heart with each retreat.

Chapter Seven

A misty shade of gray filters through my window the following morning, matching my mood. I am lying in bed, subdued, trying to sort out my thoughts on all that I'd found out about Tristan the day before—and how he reacted once I'd confronted him with it. It seems as though there are always these unanswered questions I have about him in the back of my mind. And yet uncannily, when I'm with Keuran my quandaries appear to get solved— but the elucidation is never anything I want to hear. My mind is wavering in confusion between the idea that Tristan doesn't really want me and the recollection of the forceful way he had come at me in the sand. My brain had been wrestling between the two throughout the night, and now I am fatigued with the unresolved conflict.

Snuggled into my covers, I am nursing swollen eyes, warring with myself about the need to crawl out of bed and face the day, when I hear a soft knock at the door. Startled, my heart leaps in my chest and I freeze in place, listening. The rap becomes louder, and I stir into motion. Padding to the window, I peer through the blinds, my breath catching in my throat. It's Tristan—his hair more unkempt than usual, his beautiful face haggard. Pausing, I try to collect my thoughts, then head to the sink for a cold splash of water to the face. Finally I retrace my steps to the door. Reaching for the handle, I open it slowly.

And as I knew it would be, it's Tristan—but he's standing there so unexpectedly close, looking sexy and sad and unsettling all at the same time.

Unwittingly, all the events of the night before wash over me like a tidal wave, and I jump back, startled. Upon my reaction, a look of anguish crosses over his features, and he stares hard at my face. "I am sorry." His words are tentative and soft. "I am so sorry for the way I acted last night, Bethany." I stand frozen in place, eyes round and watchful. I nod my head faintly. He points to the door slowly as if any sudden movement might frighten me. "Can I…is it okay if I come in?" His green eyes are imploring, piercing through my own, and in that moment I am reassured once again that this is the Tristan I love, and I can trust him not to hurt me—physically at least—and that *yes, it would be okay to let him in.* I clear my throat.

"Okay." My voice sounds cracked and uncertain.

Once inside, I sit down on the sofa. He hesitates before taking a seat on the other end. Everything is quiet except the continuous trickling from the sink faucet. It occurs to me then that in my daze I must not have turned it off all the way. Across the way, I hear the uncertainty of Tristan's sigh as though he is struggling with something. I stare at the floor. I can tell by his restlessness that there is something he wants to say but is not sure how to begin. This scares me! What if there is a whole big something he feels he needs to tell me, and he knows it's going to be difficult for me to hear?

"Bethany?" *Yeah?* I continue staring at the carpet—*gray carpet,* I realize as for the first time. Silence surrounds us. Drip. Drip. Drip. "Bethany—?" Drip. Drip. I inhale deeply before finally turning in his direction. "I love you…so much." *Oh my!* My heart begins beating triple-time. This is so unexpected. His stare does not waver, and I feel my lower lip begin to quiver. "And—" he continues while locking my eyes with his, "I want to make love to you more than anything." *Oh my word!* Now I am blushing—bright red, I'm sure. His voice doesn't flinch, nor does his gaze. "Know this…I am 100 percent sure about that. Please be 100 percent sure about that too." I am paralyzed by the intensity of his green eyes. My mouth is dry—I try to swallow and attempt a nod, but I'm not sure my head moves at all. "My reaction was so ugly last night. I couldn't believe that you thought the opposite was true, that I actually *didn't* want you, when I've been working so hard to control myself around you all this time. The thought seemed so preposterous! I was so mad at you for believing anything else about me, and then I almost lost that control...and I am so sorry."

"Why—do you? Why do you work so hard *not* to make love to me?" Embarrassed, I look away while I continue speaking, focusing my gaze on a piece of lint that rests on the carpet. "I *want* you to." *Did I just say that out loud?* I feel the weight on the sofa shift, and then he is beside me, closer, only inches away. His voice is gentle.

"Because I don't want to hurt you. I just want to make sure we can be together, forever, before we give ourselves to each other in that type of way...completely." I look over at him now and find his face inches from mine, his lips inches from mine. I swallow hard before I speak.

"I know it's always been complicated for us...but do you think we *will* ever get to be together...forever?" *Forever.* This last word gives me goose bumps. In some ways it seems impossible, and yet I'm desperately hopeful. *Forever with Tristan*, now that he's said it, that's all I'll ever want. Without that there will be nothing.

"Yeah, it *is* complicated. I hope so." His voice fades as if his thoughts are drifting to a faraway place. "I really hope so." He reaches for me then and pulls me gently to his chest. I can feel every chiseled muscle below the thin material of his tee shirt. His arms curve around my shoulders cautiously as if I'm a fragile piece of glass, and he's afraid that with just the wrong move he will shatter me. I wonder if his hesitancy is because of the whole episode from the night before. I want to tell him that it's okay, that he doesn't have to be so careful with me, but I just lay there instead, relishing the caressing motion of his hand against my arm.

We sit there together for a good length of time with my head against his chest before he speaks again. His voice startles me out of the lulled peacefulness. "So, I have to know, who's feeding you all this crap about me anyway—Keuran?" *Oh no!* I don't want to get on the Keuran subject right now. I am sure Keuran thinks he is just looking out for me as a friend. *Isn't he?* He must have just gotten his facts confused. I snuggle in more closely to Tristan and tighten my hold.

"It doesn't matter. I'm here with you now, and I believe you." Thankfully that puts an end to the Keuran topic, and we move on to other things like my new job starting soon, how Drake always waits patiently by wherever he's left him, and eventually about his old pal, Mr. Horton. Cautiously I think of a way to broach the subject of his noticeable decline over the past four years. I don't want to alarm Tristan—surely he's detected the change as well. "Do you still spend a lot of time with Mr. Horton?"

Tristan's eyes take on a glow that bespeaks his fondness for his friend. "Yeah, I still talk to him quite a bit."

"How is he doing? I ran into him once since I've been back to visit and he seems…I don't know, thinner, somehow."

Tristan pauses to contemplate what I've just said. "Yeah, his appetite isn't what it once was. I tell him he needs to eat more, but you know how he is—he does what he wants. I'd say he's pretty unconventional or else he wouldn't have spent all these years entertaining me, a person from the sea. But I'll keep on him. Maybe his cooking skills have gone downhill…we should bring him dinner sometime. I'll bet he'd like that."

"We should do that." Inside, I wonder whether there is more to Mr. Horton's situation that Tristan isn't ready to face but decide to let the topic rest for now.

"Speaking of Mr. Horton, now that you have a job in town, you'll need a place to stay. Mr. Horton said he'd be happy to let you stay at the cabin…if you want."

I think back to the old clapboard cabin that Tristan had fixed up for me to see four summers ago, and my heart is immediately warmed. I hadn't thought much about a permanent place to stay in the area. Luckily I'd been able to extend my stay on the room rental for a longer period in spite of the business manager's cross—"I just knew something like this would happen. Now you are really inconveniencing me, having to juggle my rooms around in order to let you keep your spot"—disposition, and so I was all set for the time being. But soon enough I would need a new place to lodge. I couldn't think of anywhere in the area I'd rather reside. "That would be great, but what about you, though? Where will you stay?"

Tristan laughs at that. "Bethany...I don't really *stay* at the cabin."

I shake my head in realization. Will I ever get used to the idea that he lives and eats and sleeps in the sea? "Right!"

Later that day Tristan takes me to the cabin so that I can look things over—decide for sure. *Like I was even going to give it a second thought.* Unlocking the weather-beaten front door, we step inside. Pausing, I suck in a breath. Immediately I am struck by the fact that everything is just as I'd viewed it in the summer of 2012. No dust anywhere, not a thing out of place. Obviously it has been kept up, but for what reason? Bemused, I glance in Tristan's direction. "Wow...it's spotless in here—so well-kept."

Tristan looks away uncomfortably. "Yeah...I stop by once in a while to take care of things and stuff."

Slowly, I begin perusing the room, running my hand over the charming antique furniture, the mutiflecked countertops, and the fireplace mantel. "I'm going to love it here."

Tristan's eyes light up. "Really?" He looks over at me. "If you ever need anything...I mean you *will* need things. I already know of things that need fixing. I can take care of that for you. Like the window casings, they should really be reinforced, and I know the roof needs some work."

I smile without restraint. I can't imagine anything I'd like more than having Tristan around the place working on this and that. *Well, maybe one thing, actually.* I glance away to hide my blush. "I'd really like that!"

The kitchen and living area are combined into one space. On one side of the room is an entry to a tiny bathroom, and beside that a bedroom big enough to house a double bed and a dresser and not much else. Tristan rests his hand at the small of my back as he leads me through the doorway. I've never been in this room before, and my eyes dart around the crowded space, trying to imagine where I'll put all of my things. "It's pretty small. Do you think you'll get all your stuff in here?" It's like he is reading my mind.

"I'll make it work. It's cozy. I can't wait to move in!"

"You like it then?" The enthusiastic schoolboy voice is back.

"Love it!"

"Well, if the bed didn't take up most of the room, I guess there would be a whole lot more space in here." At the mention of the word bed, both of our eyes drift to the mattress-box springs combo in front of us, ensconced in an outdated floral coverlet. Without warning the intimacy of the setting catches up with me, causing a hitch in my breathing. Biting my lip, I try to hide my feelings from Tristan. But one glance in his direction lets me know he is having the same train of thought. For a few seconds there is a moment of silence between us. Finally Tristan clears his throat. "Well, when do you want to move in?"

The next day I inform the business manager that I will not be in need of my room any longer after all, and he mutters a few things under his breath before informing me that there will be *no* refunds. As far as I'm concerned though, he can keep his money. I've got my dream job, and I'm staying in Watch Hill, maybe for good, and I'm moving into the cabin that Tristan worked so hard to fix up—just to impress me.

I'm on top of the world.

I buy a few needed miscellaneous household items at the store, gather what little other belongings I have with me in town, and Tristan spends the day helping me get settled in. I've called my parents to let them know the news about the job. And although they are pleased about the beginning of my career, they seem a little hesitant about me moving away, especially so quickly after graduation. But I reassure them that I'll see them soon—I'll be coming back to Philadelphia to pick up the rest of my things.

After Tristan leaves, I make a quick jaunt to the local market. Now back at the cabin, I am gathering bags of groceries out of the rear of my jeep when I detect a shadow behind me. Half expecting to find Tristan, I turn in the direction of the silhouette. *Maybe Tristan's returned.* Maybe he's thought of something else he could lend a hand with. Or something else he needed to tell me.

But it's not Tristan.

Stunned, I find Rye's petite shape instead. A bag of groceries begins to slip from my hands. Reflexively I grab onto it to keep it from falling further. "Oh...Rye...you startled me." Two days prior, I had run into her down by the docks and had given her the news that I'd be moving—soon. But I am surprised that she has found my place of residence—the cabin. And in such a remote setting.

Her gray eyes look sad as if my surprised reaction is somehow a rejection. So I muster up a smile instead, doing my best to try and make her feel welcomed. She returns the smile, but there is something about her expression that seems almost dull in appearance. I speculate about the change. "I knew you were excited about moving in," she says. "I wanted to bring you a housewarming gift." Her words when they come out are softly slurred, and I have to strain my ears to resister them in my mind. In her hands she holds a pot of red geraniums. The largeness of the plant swallows her slight frame. Eyeing my grocery bags, I contemplate whether I should continue carrying them to the house, or return them to the trunk and take care of the gift of flowers first. Rye's eyes are round, watching my face, seeking my approval. *The flowers—of course.* I start to set my packages back down.

"No…don't." Rye's voice is louder this time. "I'll just set this over here." I stop in midmotion, watching as she begins walking to the rickety steps of the cottage. After setting the pot down, she helps me unload the rest of the items from my trunk. By the time the last bag reaches the house, I become mindful of the perspiration pooling on my cheeks. It's a rather hot day, making it easy to work up a sweat. My ponytail is grimy and unkempt from the heat. Pausing, I comb fingers through my hair in attempt to push a few strands back into place. My shorts and tee shirt are plastered in dirt from the last few hours of moving. Grabbing my water bottle, I chug it down.

"Aagh! I feel like a mess!"

It's a matter-of-fact statement, requiring no reply, so I am surprised to hear Rye's mousy voice coming from behind me. "But you still look beautiful even at your worst." *Huh?* I turn around. And Rye's there, observing me, eying me pensively. Something about her expression looks dazed. Feeling on edge, I shift from leg to leg. *What is going on with her anyway?* Nervously, I laugh.

"Oh…well, thanks."

Rye watches me for an uncomfortable moment longer. "No problem," Her voice is a soft, almost a murmur.

Shaking my head, I try to clear the awkwardness in the air. "Well, I'm just going to finish unpacking all this stuff. Thank you for the flowers; would you like some water for the road?" *Speaking of the road.* Come to think of it, I hadn't noticed her vehicle—was it in the drive? Unwittingly a chill crawls over my skin. *Strange that I didn't see it!* "By the way, where is your car? I didn't notice—"

"Oh…my car?" Rye's expression clears a little. "I left it on the side of the road. The driveway didn't look very drivable, and I wasn't sure whether I'd get my car back out if I drove in." Well, she was right about that. Tristan may have kept the cabin itself in working order, but he had no need for the driveway. So at this point, at best, it is barely passable. He had already reassured me it's the first thing he'll be working on.

"Oh, okay," I say. "Well, thanks again." I can only hope the intended dismissal is clear. But Rye doesn't look in any hurry to leave. Instead, she walks over to the table.

"I can help you put your groceries away if you want." Once again, the look on her face is imploring. Too imploring. I have a hard time saying no. A short time later, we have most of the grocery items tucked neatly in the fridge and cupboards. Afterward, I excuse myself to use the restroom. I'm gone only a few minutes. Towel-drying my hands, I reopen the door. And freeze in place. Across the room, Rye is kneeling on the floor. In front of Tristan's guitar. Eyes closed, she is running her fingers over the strings in a stroking fashion. The awkwardness in the air reaches out to grab me. I feel like I've just invaded a private moment. Like I'm an intruder in my own home. I contemplate retreating back into the bath. Instead, I clear my throat.

Unhurriedly Rye opens her lids and looks up at me, offering a weak smile. Her eyes are unmistakably glassy, pupils dilated. *Truly—what is going on with her?* "Do you play?" she asks.

Shaking my head, I study her glazed eyes, my thoughts now far from the guitar propped against the wall "Oh…no. That…no. It's a friend's. He helped me move in. He'll be back for it later, I'm sure"

"Well, it's such a nice guitar. I really like it." *Ah yeah, I can tell.* I watch the dazed expression on her face with a degree of apprehension.

"Rye, are *you* okay?"

"Who…me?" Her voice resonates with surprise, contradicting her lazy smile. "I feel nice… great even." *Okay—strange answer.* I continue to study her leisurely movements.

"No...no, you're not okay. What is going on?"

Unexpectedly she giggles. "Oh okay, super sleuth, you got me. It's just a little something I like to take once in a while. It might make me a little chill. But no worries, it's very harmless. Not many know about it. It's a plant that grows in the ocean."

"A drug? So you take drugs?"

Now her gray, glazed eyes look wounded. "I wouldn't call it a drug. I told you it's just a plant from the ocean. It's harmless."

"Rye, most drugs *do* come from plants. How did you find out about it? Never mind, I don't want to know. You shouldn't take it...it can't be harmless." At my harsh words, her eyes glisten with unshed tears.

"Please don't be mad at me. I wasn't trying to upset you." Her lower lip begins to quiver, and suddenly I feel guilty for causing her any type of distress. Closing the space between us, I crouch down beside her small frame and place my arm around her shoulder.

"I'm not mad. Just...just think about what I've said...okay?"

Nodding her head in acknowledgment, she wipes away an escaped tear with a fist. A stab of protectiveness shoots through the pit of my stomach.

After three days of work, I'd make an impulsive decision on a road trip back to Philadelphia. I load my jeep with as many items as I can fit into its nooks and crannies. More than ready to start keeping house in my quaint, old cabin, I envision the belongings from my childhood home and all the places they will fit into my new place. It is time—I want all my stuff here with me at my *new* residence, in my new life in Rhode Island.

Highway I-95 North is jam-packed with vehicles, making my drive back from Philadelphia a challenge. I'd crammed a lot of activity into the past couple of days at home, and now an interstate filled with crawling traffic is the last thing I want to deal with. Living on adrenaline and little sleep for the past seventy-two hours, I am exhausted to the bone. First day of work—

Monday morning—had been so exciting, stepping through the front doors of the Center for Marine Studies and into the cubicle that I would now be calling my own. Then meeting the other staff members, organizing my space, taking care of mundane human resource details, and finally getting to the nitty-gritty—receiving an overview of the types of projects I'd be working on for the next long while. *Helping to protect the ocean!*

Then back to Philadelphia.

Mom and Dad had hugged me tightly as I stood on the front doorstep of the two-story brick home that I'd grown up in ready to depart back to my new residence in Rhode Island. They are happy for me, yet sad to lose me at the same time. And surprised that I have chosen Watch Hill as my first place to settle in after the rough summer I spent there four years ago. I decide to forgo telling them about running into Tristan quite yet. I don't' want them to think he is the reason I took the job.

Now as I grip the steering wheel in front of me, exhausted, I have to strain my eyes to keep them from closing. Glancing in my rearview mirror, I eye the driving lane behind me that is barely visible among the myriads of boxes that are stuffed into my jeep. Deciding that the coast is clear, I find an open spot and shift into the flow of traffic. The dashboard light illuminates the digital clock to my right. Two more hours. Two more hours and I'll be home. I open my driver-side window and a strong breeze pelts across my face, helping me to stay awake for the remainder of the ride. Two more hours and I'll be at my new home, in my new town, with my new job, with the love of my life.

The rest of the week passes quickly, and my body eventually catches up on the sleep it needs. When the weekend arrives, Rye asks me to meet her in town for some girl time—shopping and stuff. Now, standing on the downtown boardwalk, I am a little pensive as I watch her small frame approach. Will she be strung out on drugs once again? Will her demeanor be as strange as it had been the last time we were together? I study her gray eyes as she draws near, looking for signs of the dull glassiness that had been evident at the cabin. Timidly she catches my gaze, and our eyes lock for a few brief moments. Sadness and yearning reflect back at me, but none of the glassiness from earlier in the week. I breathe a sigh of relief. *Hopefully there won't be any mind-altering substances today!*

We fall into a rhythm of shopping, and I soon discover that the type of merchandise Rye is drawn to is both artsy and mystic: dream catchers, good luck charms, dark, melancholy items of clothing. And really I'm not surprised, considering the unspoken despondency that seems to lurk beneath the surface of her pale skin. If only I knew what the sadness is all about. I watch her small hands as she reaches into her change purse, gathering the bills needed to pay for a pair of sunglasses she's found at the front display. Sometime, when the time is right, I'd ask. Gathering up her purchase, she exits the shop with me at her side. Watching her brush a strand of brown hair away from her forehead, I offer her a smile. Now just doesn't feel like that time.

Shopping complete, we are walking up the hill on Larkin Road past Flying Horse Carousel, heading toward Bluff Avenue, when I detect a familiar form in the distance. The sun is at the figure's back, darkening the silhouette, shining around the form like an alien encounter. But I don't have to visualize each detail of the person's countenance for me to know exactly who it is that is coming our way. All at once, my heart leaps in my chest. Biting my lip, I lose all track of the person next to me. Fleetingly, I imagine I hear a sigh coming from Rye as she walks at my side, but I'm so ensconced in the person that is approaching that I am not sure. When a large shade tree blocks the sun, I am able to see the person more clearly. Tristan. *Tristan indeed!* Now only yards apart, all movement decelerates into slow motion. A stretch of time lapses, the gap between us closing, and the next thing you know we are all standing face-to-face. Noticeably, an uncomfortable quiet surrounds us. I am the first to speak.

"Tristan...hi," I say. But he is looking at Rye and doesn't answer right away. For some unknown reason, my heartbeat quickens. At last though, his head snaps in my direction, and a smile spreads across his lips.

"Hey there," he says. His green eyes are filled with warmth as they peruse my face. Inwardly I sigh in relief. *Why do I feel like there is a dark cloud surrounding this encounter?* Pausing, Tristan looks back in the direction of Rye, his smile fading slightly. "I didn't realize you two knew each other." *You two—me and Rye? What about you two? Obviously, you know each other also.*

I glance at my shopping companion and then back at Tristan. Standing next to Rye, his athletic frame swallows up her size, accentuating her frailty. Under Tristan's scrutiny, an anxious expression replaces the melancholy look I'd gotten used to seeing in her eyes. She begins fidgeting and playing with her hands. When she speaks, her voice is barely audible. "Yeah, I know her; we met awhile back. I needed directions and she helped me out."

Tristan shoves his hands in the front pocket of his jeans, nods, and looks away. I wait for him to make eye contact with me once again, but he remains turned toward the sea. My eyes follow his gaze, and it's then that I notice the repetitive motion of the waves as they collapse onto the coastline. Somehow the ocean had snuck up on us during our walk. I hadn't even paid attention to it until now. Now the roar of the whitecaps seems loud, interrupting our conversation, making its presence unmistakably known. Suddenly the silence between the three of us becomes deafening, matching the sound of the waves. I feel an abrupt need to add to the discussion. "Rye and I were out doing some shopping today, and she helped me with my groceries the other day too. So yeah, we've gotten to know each other some."

Tristan peels his gaze away from the sea and looks back at me. I watch his face closely, trying to decipher the reason for the discomfiture in the air, but his expression is completely stoic. "That's nice," he says with a shift in his countenance. His eyebrows lift. "Well, hey, I have to get going. There is something I need to do for work, and I was just on my way there before I ran into you. I'll catch up with you another time?" His words sound nonchalant, as if he is distracted and just verbalizing them as an afterthought.

"Okay," Rye and I reply in unison, and I glance over at her in surprise. I assumed his last statement was meant for just me, but had it been? *Had Rye gotten confused, thinking he was talking to her too? Or was she just trying to be polite in answering?*

"Good-bye, Tris," she calls after him. But her voice is so soft that I'm sure he is out of hearing range. Either way, he doesn't turn back or respond.

I blink, trying to make sense of the whole situation. "Yeah… good-bye," I add silently while watching the strength of his frame as he walks away. Out of the corner of my eye, I feel the weight of Rye's gaze as she looks at my face. When I turn toward her, once again I am met with a type of yearning emanating from gray eyes. *Why does she keep looking at me that way?* Without warning, a chill covers the skin on my arms, and I shiver, trying to make it go away. But somehow I just can't shake the awkwardness of the whole encounter between Rye, Tristan, and me.

Chapter Eight

The smell of bread toasting is filling the cabin. Most of the windows are opened. A cool, morning breeze fills the room. The sound of the waves is a muted hum behind the framework of trees that surrounds the weathered structure of my bungalow. I am sitting at the butcher-board table in the kitchen sipping piping hot coffee, trying to wake up. In less than an hour, I'll be leaving for work. A noise at the window above the sink draws my attention, and I look up in time to see a small, yellow bird fluttering at the screen. Unexpectedly it lands and proceeds to bob its head, peering in through the wire mesh as if it wants to join me for breakfast. I smile and offer a soft whistle in greeting while the bird cocks its head. Before long my toast pops from the toaster with a bang, and my feathered visitor takes flight. Now it's just me in the kitchen once again, alone with my thoughts.

The unwanted thoughts that keep straying back to the day before and the puzzling encounter I'd had with Tristan on my shopping excursion with Rye. The tension in the air during our unplanned meeting on Larkin Road had been thick. In the end Tristan had tried his best to act casual, but there were several moments when he seemed ill at ease, very unlike his usual confident self. What was that all about? And Rye's reaction to him—how could I interpret Rye's reaction to him when everything Rye does is a little strange? And actually, odder yet is the way I often find Rye reacting to me. Fleetingly I experience a bout of goose bumps. Downing the last swig of coffee from my cup, I decide to make it a point to stay away from her for a while.

After sliding into a pair of black dress slacks and a coral blouse, I head into the town of Westerly, driving to my new job. Locating the Center for Marine Studies' growingly familiar brick building, I pull my back jeep into the lot labeled employee parking. Smoothing my ponytail into place, I walk through the double doors and find my cubicle. A type of excitement takes over as I begin working on my first big project—pulling together a curriculum that encompasses local environmental marine issues. This assignment will need to be organized by fall and ready to implement in the classroom. Several possible topics to include are spiraling through my mind, and I find it difficult to narrow them down: the importance of the ecosystem, animal behavior in relation to humans, and of course the devastating effect pollution has on the ocean. The last one goes to the top of my list. Even before my relationship had blossomed with Tristan, I had felt a need to help protect the ocean—now that desire is tenfold.

After putting in a full day at work, I stop at Sam's Surf Shop on my way home to look at a paddleboard. I had a lot of fun trying out Keuran's. And it seems like a good way to spend some free time, connecting with the water and challenging my skill and balance at the same time. Besides, checking out paddleboards isn't the only appeal Sam's Surf Shop holds for me today. I am in need of some lighthearted conversation. And there is one person that comes to mind where that is concerned. The door chimes are set off as I step foot inside. Taking in my surroundings, I scan the interior of the small shop in search of who I've come to see.

"Girl, is that you?"

At the sound of a male soprano voice, every weight that I've been carrying with me for the past twenty-four hours is immediately lifted. I can almost visualize the funnel of heaviness as it spirals away, dissipating like fog into the atmosphere, exiting the entrance of the old, renovated house that doubles as a store. "Hey, Jonathan!" I am all smiles.

"To what do I owe this surprise? Am I being blessed by a visit, or have you taken up surfing lately?"

"Yes, and kind of."

Jonathan shakes his black hair, raising one eyebrow in jest. "Okay, now you got my head spinning. Clarify, please."

His reaction makes me laugh. "Yes, I came by to see you and the *kind of* is not really surfing...paddleboarding."

"Paddleboarding...I can see that." He gives me a once-over and nods his head. "Yeah...I can definitely see you doing that. Well, don't just stand there. Come give me a hug, and I'll show you a couple of boards you might like." After a brief embrace, he leads me to a display in the far right corner of the shop. Side by side leaning against the knotty pine-paneled wall are a bright yellow board and one in a blue and aqua print. Running my hands over their sleek fiberglass material, I inspect them both before looking at the price tag. "Well, which one do you see yourself on?"

Turing away from the boards, I scrunch up my nose. "Well, considering the price, neither one for the time being. I guess I better spend a few more weeks at work before I come back to *this* shop."

"Hey...wait just a minute, young lady, you don't have to buy a board in order to come by and pay this boy a visit."

"All right, that's a deal I can make."

At this Jonathan's eyes go bright like an idea has just occurred to him. "Hey, I was just thinking...what are you doing right now? I have someone here who can cover for me. How would you like to go for a walk down by the water...East Beach?"

"I'm ready when you are."

Together we make our way down the winding path that leads to East Beach. A warm breeze is blowing against my skin. I've slipped out of my sandals and rolled up my dress slacks, exposing my shins. The sand is powdery soft between my toes. We walk the length of the beach, Jonathan's usual energy and antics making me laugh. It feels so good to be carefree with this spirited, upbeat boy at my side. A bright orange and purple kite zips through the air high above, adding to my happy-go-lucky feeling. The rising tide washes over our feet as we saunter along, dodging young children and sunbathers. Finally clear of the beachgoing crowds, we pause, taking a seat on a large rock. Watch Hill Light is towering in the distance. Shading his eyes, Jonathan points out toward the sea.

"See that freighter out there?"

Squinting, I detecting a fine, thin line of black against the horizon. "I think so. I see something…probably a ship, it's hard to tell for sure."

"Well, I'm quite sure that's what it is. But if it is…it may not be for long."

I scrunch up my nose in confusion. "What are you talking about?"

"Well, I don't know if I'm talking figuratively or literally. It's just a rumor, but I've been told that there have been some ships occasionally disappearing from radar just north of Block Island Sound."

"Really? How strange—like a Bermuda Triangle type of thing?"

"Not sure…like I said, it's just a rumor." Jonathan jumps up suddenly. I can tell he's had enough of sitting in one place. Scooping up a pile of stones, he springs to the water's edge and begins tossing them one by one into the flow of the current. I watch his energetic frame as he makes several attempts, earnestly intent on making one of the rocks skip. Mostly with much unsuccess. Although I'm watching him, my mind is far out to sea. *What does he mean, ships are disappearing?* The warm breeze that had been caressing my arms suddenly feels cold. Watch Hill is such a nice area, but why do so many strange things happen around here? I mean, I never heard of things like this back in Philadelphia.

"When you say disappear, what you mean? Like never to be seen again?"

Jonathan remains at the water's edge, his back toward me. For a moment I think he didn't hear my question or else just is not going to answer. He continues to toss his pile of rocks. "I don't know," he finally says. "I probably shouldn't have said anything. I don't think many people know about this. A close friend told me about it, and he is not supposed to know about it either. He overheard his dad talking top-secret type of stuff. But you know how stuff like this goes, it could just be a rumor. I haven't heard of any actual boats reported as missing, have you?"

"Well, no, but then I haven't been listening for that type of news really either."

I arrive home from work the next day, still contemplating the reports of the missing ships, when I am startled from my thoughts by the sound of a deep voice.

"Long time no see." Jumping, I nearly spill the armful of work-related items I am carrying. *Keuran!* It has been a while. I had begun to be hopeful that he might actually gracefully disappear, leaving me and Tristan to have our rekindled relationship in peace. It's not that I mind having Keuran around so much, but the obvious angst between the two cousins seems to be continually causing problems for Tristan and me in one way or the other. Now as he sits on my doorstep, watching me advance, amber eyes amused, I can tell there is no plan for conceding victory anytime soon.

"Hi, Keuran," I sigh.

He laughs. A deep, dark laugh. "I didn't mean to startle you." I roll my eyes. *I'll bet.* His brow line lifts as he clicks his tongue. "Eye rolling? Bethany…Bethany, what type of greeting is that for your good friend Keuran? By the way, what are you up to right now? Do you have a few minutes to hang out?"

"Actually, I was just getting ready to go for a run, so maybe another time."

His eyes brighten. "A run…that sounds good. I'll go with you." Angling around where he is perched on my step, I pause to juggle the items in my arms, unlock the door, and proceed inside. Keuran follows close behind.

"Keuran, you don't want to go running. Wouldn't that be too much air going into your lungs all at one time?"

"Nah…I'll be okay. My lungs are getting used to being on land. They can handle as much air as you can give them."

I shake my head. "Okay. But I'm going to warn you, I'm a fast runner."

"I'll take that as a challenge." His eyes narrow slightly, and for a moment he looks slightly irritated. "I always like a good challenge."

I change into black running shorts and a bright green tank, lace up my sneakers, and begin stretching in preparation for the excursion. Feeling Keuran's eyes on me, I look up from my flexed position. He is leaning casually against the front doorframe of my cabin watching me. "You might want to stretch too, you know."

"I'll be fine."

I raise my eyebrow. "Suit yourself."

"You know, I just got done swimming, let's see, probably ten or more miles. I think I'm all stretched out." Now his face is a smirk.

"All right, you got me."

"That I did. Are you about done? Not that I mind sitting here watching you stretch really."

I roll my eyes once again. "All right, let's go."

We begin to make our way down my winding, wooded driveway and onto Oakwood Drive at a leisurely pace. Warm-up complete, I am ready to step up the tempo. I can hear Keuran's soft inhalations and the steady beat of his running shoes on the blacktop next to me as we commence running. Occasionally I offer him a sideways glance, checking for signs of distress in his striking features, but if he is enduring any pain, he covers it well. Crossing Yosemite Valley Road, we continue onto Browning. And suddenly I get an intense feeling of de'ja' vu. Surrounded by the whispers of nature at every turn, a chill skulks up my back as I recognize the secluded spot where I had twisted my ankle four summers ago.

Vivid memories of isolation and feelings of helplessness begin coursing through my mind. Anxiously, my eyes start glancing in all directions looking for any signs of civilization, but of course, just as I remembered, there are no cottages to be found anywhere. I inhale a deep breath of air. *Why am I feeling so creeped-out anyway?* Involuntarily my sight is drawn to Keuran, who is keeping a relentless pace beside me. This time when I look at him, he meets my gaze, and my heart stills. What do I see reflected in his amber eyes that is making my fight or flight response want to kick into overdrive? I shake my head and focus on the blacktop in front of me. I'd better watch my step or I might end up in the same boat I was in four years ago. Still, unexplainably, I feel the overpowering strength of Keuran's body beside me with each step I take. *I could outrun him though. I'm sure of it!* For a moment I blink as I try to erase the uneasiness that is lurking in the forefront of my mind. *I'm being ridiculous!* But in spite of attempts to dissuade thoughts of negativity, my muscles tense as I prepare to explode into a full-scale, death-defying sprint if need be.

A gentle breeze encircles us, swaying the trees and the green foliage that lines the road. The repetitive thud of rubber meeting pavement echoes through the air. My feeling of being on edge continues. *Holy cow! What is wrong with me?* This is just Keuran beside me, who I've gotten to know relatively well over the last while. If anything, I should feel safer in this remote area with a strong guy like him by my side. *So why don't I?* I am trying to reconcile these unnerving thoughts when I feel a hand on my shoulder.

Unwittingly, a yelp escapes my lips, and I make preparations to run faster—possibly for my life.

"Bethany, wait up just a sec—" Keuran's voice is breathless behind me. "I just…I think I might need a break."

I freeze in my tracks.

Doing a one eighty, I turn to find Keuran half bent over, panting for all he's worth. I blink. *My word, Bethany, don't you feel silly now.* "Oh yeah…sure." I am surprised to find how breathless my own voice sounds. Slowly, I begin making my way back toward him, shoes crunching in the scattered gravel. As I approach, I notice that his coloring doesn't look so hot. I calculate the distance we've come from the water. He probably *did* inhale too much air all at once—he could probably use a good swim. What if I need to help him back to the ocean in a hurry—will I be able to support his weight by myself? "Crap, Keuran, you look gray."

Rising from his stooped position, he offers a sheepish grin, "How does gray look with yellow and black?" *What?* He points to his hair, his eyes. *Oh. Yellow eyes—black hair.* I get it.

"Truthfully, not well. Do you need to get back to the water?

Keuran closes his eyes briefly. "No…I'll be okay. Just give me a minute."

I watch his face speculatively. "All right, but if you need to, just say the word—" Keuran holds up one hand to cut me off. For a split second a spark of anger flashes across his chiseled features.

"I *said*…I'm okay."

I bristle from the curt retort. But then his lips form into a smile and I relax. Leaning his head toward the ground, he presses hands to thighs for a few minutes while I stand by in silence, idly waiting for him to cue me as to what should happen next. Finally he looks up. His ashen coloring is starting to recede, a healthier glow once again emerging. Laughing out loud, he breaks through the quiet.

"I probably look like winter."

"What?"

"Winter. I can only imagine I looked like a sea creature in the winter right now."

I crinkle up my nose, confused. "What do you mean?"

"Tris didn't tell you about us in the wintertime?"

"No. No, he didn't."

The sound of Keuran's laughter echoes down the length of the desolate roadway. "Oh, Tris…the things he likes to keep from you." *Why do I get a feeling this conversation is going to head south very quickly?* There is a part of me that wants to stop him from spewing words I don't want to hear, but there is an even bigger part of me that is just a little too inquisitive. I don't breathe a sound. "Let's just say if you were to come look us up in the winter, you'd find us all floating in a pool of grayish black, pale-colored and lifeless."

My heart begins pounding in my chest. The picture he is painting is rather repulsive. "What?"

"Nice thought, isn't it? Beautiful Tris looking like character from a version of *The Walking Dead*. Or should I say swimming dead? All…winter…long!" A smirk forms on Keuran's mouth, his amber eyes gleaming. Clearly he is enjoying my angst.

"I don't know what you are talking about."

"Obviously. But I'll fill you in so you can be a little more knowledgeable. The icy cold water in the winter helps to preserve us. It's a type of hibernation, really. I mean, we can swim around in the cold weather season, but it's better for us if we don't, so we all float, lifeless, suspended in depths; some with eyes open, some with eyes closed. I've been one of the later ones to arrive to the sea creature zombie ice festival, so I can tell you firsthand what it looks like. And let me just say, it isn't exactly a pretty sight. But enough about me and Tris. How do you like to spend your winters?"

I roll my eyes. Trying to shake the ugly vision he has just rendered from my mind, I take a deep breath. No matter how hard I try, I can't picture Tristan in this grotesque manner. It just doesn't seem possible. Making a decision to wipe the image from the forefront of my mind, I make a mental note to ask Tristan about it at a later date. For now I won't give Keuran the satisfaction of seeing how freaked out I am by the whole thing. My face becomes a mask. "Are you ready to head back?"

The return trip to my cabin is a light jog. When we arrive at my front doorstep, I am warring with myself over something

I want to ask Keuran, but at the same time for some reason I'm not so sure I should. Pausing, I tighten my shoelace. I can feel his presence behind me as he prepares to leave. Seconds tick by. Ultimately curiosity gets the best of me. "So, I met this girl and we've been hanging out…and I wondered if you happen to know her?"

"Well…what's her name?"

"Rye."

Keuran goes still, and for a rare moment he looks genuinely shocked. Goose bumps cover my skin. "You met Rye?"

"Yeah, I have. What do you know about her?"

Keuran studies my face for a long moment. I can tell his mind is spinning—or sorting. "How did you meet her?"

"I don't know, we just kind of ran into each other one day in town. She needed directions and I gave them to her. From there we ended up going to Newport together."

Keuran looks incredulous. "You just up and went with her to Newport?"

"Well, it wasn't quite like that. But yeah, a few days later I did go with her. She was looking forward to going, and then her car broke down. I didn't have anything better to do, so I offered to drive."

"Wait…did you just say her car?" Keuran closes his eyes and shakes his head. "Unbelievable," he mutters under his breath.

"What did you say?"

"Nothing. So what else have you done with her?"

Sighing, I debate about whether I want to continue the conversation. A bad feeling is forming in the pit of my stomach. Clearly, Keuran knows Rye. Why do I have a strong feeling that I may not like what he has to say about her. Somehow though, I just can't let it rest. After the awkward encounter between Rye and Tristan the other day, I just have to know more. Closing my eyes for a brief second, I clear my throat. *Here goes.* "Well, the other day I was with her in town and then we ran into Tristan, and I don't know, it all just seemed really weird like they knew each other, and I—I just wondered what you knew about her."

Everything goes quiet as Keuran pauses, arms folded, while he watches my face. Out of nowhere the sound of the surf becomes a backdrop for our conversation. The repetitive roar and splash of the waves swallows up the silence. Unexplainably I get a sudden impulse to run and dive into them just to avoid answers that I might not want to hear. In quick succession, Keuran's countenance transforms, closely resembling a sneer followed by a gleam of satisfaction before finally settling into a look of concern. My heart pounds in my chest. *What is he about to tell me?*

"Bethany…Rye is from the water." *Oh!* I gulp in a deep breath of air. *Oh my!* Could I have known this? How could I *not* have known? Keuran pauses, watching my reaction, waiting for me to answer. Suddenly my mouth is dry. I don't know what to say, so he continues. "Yes, you could say Tris knows her. They go back. *Way* back…like forever. Sometimes, not always, but sometimes in our culture, parents get to decide that their children would benefit from a life union, so they make an agreement for their children to marry." Now my heart is exploding, popping out of my chest. An elephant is sitting on me—I can't breathe. Where is Keuran going with this?

"Rye has been pledged to marry Tris."

What? What, no! No, I just heard wrong. But the sound of Keuran's words keep ringing over and over again in my ears. The look of fascination in his amber eyes as he watches me struggle to keep from coming undone becomes faded and distant. Everything is becoming a detached shadow. Blackness is closing in. All sounds around me are muted as I fight to take my next breath. Somewhere in the distance I hear Keuran's voice as he continues to explain— telling the tale that is making my world fall apart.

"Yeah, Tris tends to keep the company of lots of girls, obviously. But the pledge is still there. It's pretty much always been there."

A horse has just kicked me in the stomach. I want to fold in half, doubled over from the pain. *This can't be true!* After all we've been through together. Had he just been toying with me? He had always known that eventually he'd be taking Rye as a wife. I was just a summer sidekick then. *No wonder! No freakin' wonder it was so easy for him to go away that summer!* I have been so hung up on him. I am the epitome of stupid. "*Oh baby, I love you. I hurt too!*" Bullshit! Bull freakin' shit! *Oh…my God…why? God…why?* I am this close to falling on my knees begging for answers. I want to throw up. Why did he go to such efforts to string me along?

He just wants to make sure we can be together forever before we give ourselves to each other completely. *That's freakin' crap!* Isn't he just so freakin' noble! He is saving himself for Rye. Or not saving himself, who knows. He probably spends his days on land with me and his nights in the water with Rye doing who knows what!

I hate him!

I work desperately to slow my breathing so I can speak. "I gotta go."

"Wait, Bethany, this has upset you…come here." *Upset me?*

"You need to leave now, Keuran. I gotta go. I'm going inside."

Once I reach the security of my bed, a million thoughts begin exploding through my mind, none of them good, as I finally succumb to an outpouring of tears. Of course, Rye referred to Tristan as Tris, just as Keuran does. I should have realized right then that she is from the water. All of his friends from the water must call him that. *Yeah, I'll just bet the whole meeting up with me and Rye was awkward for you, Tristan; your fiancée and the ignorant girl that you've been stringing along.* How uncomfortable for poor Tristan! *Guess you've just been busted, buddy!*

"*It's always been you, Bethany.*" I close my eyes tightly in an effort to push away the sound of the lie that had come straight from Tristan's lips—to push away the agony of it all—of every single word that he had murmured into my ear before and after he had kissed me and placed his hands on me so thoroughly. I have been duped.

Completely and utterly duped!

Chapter Nine

My first instinct is to track down Tristan and confront him with the news. But this time I'm not going to. Anyway, what good would it do? It won't change anything. I could scream and kick and beg, but in the end, he is still going to marry Rye. Instead, I crawl into a pair of pajama pants and a tank top and cry my eyes out in the confines of my own home. I have just weaned myself down to an occasional sob when I receive a text from Lucy. She is coming into town for a visit. Sighing, I hug a pillow to my chest before bursting into tears once again. Perfect timing—she couldn't possibly have known how bad I need her right then. But I do. I can almost feel the warmth of her shoulder as I move my fingers over the keys to text her back.

It is hard to concentrate at work with the haze of misery that surrounds me. I keep thinking back to all the things that Tristan and I had done together, said to each other, trying to analyze every move. There were little clues that something was up—it certainly explained Rye's strange behavior. But as far as Tristan was concerned, he could categorically be called a professional, because he had hidden it well. It hurts so bad! My second instinct is to bury myself under my covers for days, maybe weeks, until the pain of it has eased up considerably. But I'm a responsible adult who has a career now and a paddleboard she wants to buy and a best friend who is coming into town in a few days. So I pull myself together, drink lots of coffee to compensate for my sleepless nights, and try hard to focus.

But it hurts so bad.

Lucy's doelike, brown eyes and contagious smile are a sight for sore eyes. I run to her the minute she pulls into my drive. And

I can't help it; as much as I tell myself I'm not going to burden her with crying, the tears start up again the minute I feel her arms encircle me. "Whoa…Bethany, what is going on?" She pulls back to look at my makeup-smeared face. I can't answer. By now the tears are coming full force. Her eyes go wide and she draws me into her chest, all the while soothing my hair with her free hand. "Aw, honey, what is it?" She pauses, waiting for the answer that doesn't come. "Is it Tristan?" I nod into her shoulder, still plagued by an occasional sob. She sighs with exaggeration as we separate. "That guy is such a creep, Bethany! I am going to tell him a thing or two about what he has coming to him for continually hurting my best friend."

I shake my head. "I doubt if that will help, but thanks." Offering a small grin in response to her loyalty, I help her bring her things into the house. Once her luggage is tucked into a closet, we settle onto my brown tweed couch, and I begin sharing with her as much as I can about my situation—how Tristan has a serious old girlfriend hanging around, and how I think I might have just been played all along. In the end he is going to be with her, not me. The more I talk, the more mad Lucy gets.

And it's just what I need.

I can tell it's hard for Lucy to bring up the subject of Ethan when I'm experiencing the pain of love, but I reassure her, it's okay, I'm no dummy—I realize he is the big draw for her visit to town. Soon enough he arrives at the cabin, and we are making plans for the night. The minute Ethan sets foot on the premises, his gravelly voice and sexy demeanor have self-assured Lucy all tongue-tied and dewy-eyed. I shake my head, smiling—*I get it;* Ethan definitely has that effect on pretty much everyone. I only hope she knows what she is doing.

The evening air is chilly for this time of year. So we all dress in jeans and jackets headed to the oceanside party that Ethan is taking us to. The festivity is being held at a friend of a friend of Ethan's. And in spite of the simplicity of the small cottage where it's being hosted, the water frontage goes on forever, offering the perfect setup for a beach blowout. It's hard for me to put on a party face and act like I'm having a fabulous time when I'm feeling so down, but I don't want to ruin Lucy's visit by sulking at home all the while she is in town. Instead, I put on my shield of bravery and attend the festivity, allowing her and Ethan their space to mingle among the crowd while I spend most of my time, subdued, warming myself by the oversized bonfire.

I am staring into the inferno, entranced by the pattern of the flames, when I sense someone approaching. Tearing my eyes away from the fire, I do a double take as my gaze lands on a pair of smiling, green eyes.

"Hey, baby."

Involuntarily, my heart begins pounding in my chest. *Geez, he looks so good.* Jeans are resting low on his hips, and a black warm-up jacket is fitted snugly across his chest. I turn back to the fire. *Hey baby? Is that how you talk to Rye too?* I think I'm going to be sick. "Hey." My reply is curt as I offer a smile that I know doesn't begin to reach my eyes. In an instant the warmth on Tristan's face fades, replaced instead with something akin to confusion or maybe worry. *Yeah, I'll bet you are worried, because you have just been busted, you two-timing bastard!*

He hesitates before speaking again, all the while studying my face in the dancing light of the flames. "I'm glad I was able to find you in this large crowd. I haven't seen you in so long. I was hoping you'd be here tonight. I've missed you." I am dumbfounded. Every word that leaves his lips now holds a completely new meaning. *Oh my word, really? REALLY?* He is so good. *So* freakin' good at this! I take a deep breath, trying not to lose my cool. There is something about the perplexed look in his green eyes that makes me want to succumb to his feigned innocence. His lips are perfect, so soft, less than a foot away. I groan inwardly. Squeezing my hands tightly together at my side, I resist the urge to trace his beautiful mouth with my index finger. Or else punch him in the face with my fist, I'm not sure which.

"Yeah? I need to find a restroom, so I'll see you in a bit, okay?" *Holy cow, was that my voice that sounded so self-assured just then?* I leave the fire without once looking back, not giving myself a chance to change my mind.

The rest of the evening is spent in solitude as I carefully lose myself in the crowd, avoiding any possible encounter with the love of my life that I now know is just an imposter. I am completely strung out by the end of the evening from all the effort of hiding and from my stomach doing continual flip-flops at the thought of Tristan being so close by, somewhere in the near vicinity.

It's getting late and I keep glancing at my watch, exhausted, wondering when Lucy and Ethan will be ready to go. *Probably never!* The crowd has dwindled just enough. I finally have nowhere else to hide. In spite of the lack of sanctuary, I am caught by surprise when I see Tristan's athletic frame approaching from across the landscape of the yard. My eyes begin darting in all directions looking for an escape. But that would be too obvious, and the last thing I want to do is cause a scene tonight. I am too worn out for that. By the time he closes the distance between us, consternation is evident in his eyes, replacing the former look of bewilderment. His voice is firm. "Can we talk?"

I open my mouth to answer but am at a loss for words. Tristan's gaze is intense as he waits for my reply. Even in the darkness of the night, I can detect the muscle in his jaw twitching. I am licking my lips, getting ready to speak, when Lucy breezes in next to me, wrapping her arm around my shoulder. Her voice is light and cheery. "Hey, girl…I've been looking for you. It's getting late and I'm ready to go. Ethan is at the car, waiting. Oh, hi, Tristan… ready, Bethany?"

I nod my head, thankful for the reprieve. Tristan looks frustrated, and for a moment I think he is not going to let me leave gracefully, but then he presses his lips together and nods his head once, accepting his defeat. Without hesitation Lucy leads me away, and it takes all of my resolve not to turn around and run back to his strong arms, throwing myself at him, begging him to tell me that it's all a lie—that he loves only me. And not Rye.

But I keep walking, realizing this is just a stupid fantasy. A similar fantasy to the ones I've had about Tristan all along. Just like that summer four years ago when I thought for sure he'd be coming back to me any minute, taking me in his arms and telling me he couldn't possibly live another moment without me by his side. After all, he had come on so strong during our time together, telling me he loved me and writing a song for me and all that crap.

Only he never *did* come back. And now, I won't turn back around. With Lucy's arm laced protectively through mine as we retreat to the car where is Ethan is waiting, I bite my lip hard— so hard I taste blood. But I am determined not to turn back around.

I don't sleep a wink that night. Or maybe I do, because when I crawl out of bed in the morning I find a note from Lucy saying I was sleeping so soundly she didn't want to wake me, and that she had a wonderful time and hopes that I'll feel better soon. As a way of ending the note, she leaves me with one last word of exhortation. *Remember, you deserve the best!* I had known she was leaving to go back home today, but just didn't think it would be so early. Gingerly I place the folded piece of paper back down on my nightstand. I had probably been sleeping soundly toward the time of sunrise in order to make up for the lack of sleep during the majority of the night. Downtrodden, my mind had been filled with racing, depressive thoughts which had led to nonstop tossing and turning. The moon had shone a pale, silvery light through the windowpane, filling my room with unwanted brightness, adding to the already poor sleeping conditions. Now my bed looks like a war zone, and my hair is a rat's nest. One glance in the mirror reveals puffy eyes laced with dark shadows.

I pad to the kitchen for a cup of coffee and settle back down on my couch where I spend most of the day staring at a television screen that fills the cabin with noise. The hours tick by with show after show flooding the room with bright color, and I have no idea what a single one is about. It is late afternoon before it occurs to me that I should probably check the front door to make sure that Lucy shut and locked it properly while leaving earlier that morning.

I am so lost in my numbed state, that when I open the screen entrance the shadow that falls across my porch step almost goes undetected. But then a slight movement catches my eye and I glance up, startled. "Rye." I take a step back. "What are you doing here?" *Really, seriously, what* is *she doing here?* On first instinct, my thoughts are for her to go away. *Go away and go find your fiancé, Tristan, and leave me the hell alone.* But as I watch the eyes that are wistful pools of gray staring up into my face, I imagine for a moment that she might not know about the whole messy triangle that exists between her and Tristan and me after all. Still, either way, I really don't want to visit with her right now. Before she has a chance to answer my question, I rush to interrupt. "Anyway…I'm busy right now so—"

Rye shakes her head. Now it is she who is interrupting. "You don't look so good. Actually, you look like a mess." Her quiet tone confronting me with words of truthful reality catches me off guard. Self-consciously, I run a hand through my hair, trying to tame its rebellious strands. Her eyes follow the movement. Pausing for a moment, she stares right at me. Her voice turns to a whisper. "You know, I have something that will make you feel better," she says. "It works; trust me." *What? Of course not! NO! I would never do drugs! Besides, what do you know about what I'm feeling? Nothing! Not one freakin' thing!*

I shake my head, taking a step backward. "No, thanks. I think you better go now. I'm not in the mood for company, and like I just told you, I'm busy."

"I know that...you're not in a good mood. I can see that. But I told you I have something that will change that for you. It really is not a big deal, Bethany. It's not an actual drug; it's all natural... from the sea. Practically health food."

No!

I close my eyes tightly, exhausted from lack of sleep. One thing Rye is right about though, I *am* a mess. Here I am, having moved far away from home to be close by a boy—a boy who I've entered a relationship with that I find out is really just a sham. Now I have the job that I love, but it is going to be so hard to stay around this town with Tristan on every corner—just beyond the next rolling wave. How can I just sit by surrounded with all the sand and surf, watching him slip through my fingers into the depths of the sea?

"I can see you're hurting. Just take it—you'll feel so much better." Rye's diffused voice interrupts my thoughts. My mind is whirling with a thousand considerations, mostly of Tristan and me not being together. *Crap!* I really *am* hurting! So bad! Overcome with misery and lack of sleep, I make a decision. I'm going to do it. What do I care anyway? At this moment I really don't care about much of anything at all! Trembling, I hug goosebump-filled arms to my chest. My answer is communicated without saying a word. Rye's haunting, gray eyes fill with compassion as she takes my hand and silently leads me away.

How far down the shoreline we travel or in which direction, I'm really not sure. My mind is numb. Eventually it occurs to me that we are no longer moving, and I glance around, taking in my surroundings. Ensconced in a protective alcove, large boulders rise from the sand while frothy waves explode around them. Rye is beside me, preparing something in the palm of her hand. I stand by idly watching as she bends her head to cupped fingers, inhaling the substance she's concocted. For a moment she stands very still, staring just beyond the rocks out to the ocean. Then slowly she turns toward me, offering me her outstretched, upturned hand. I blink, barely detecting the green, flakey matter that fills her palm. She nods once, and shakily I repeat what I'd just witnessed her do only minutes before. Afterward, I too stare out to sea, waiting for some type of mystical reaction to course through my body.

But nothing happens!

Squinting my eyes in concentration, I decide that the components from this drug may only work on people from the sea, because I am not feeling a thing. "What is this stuff exactly?" My voice sounds distant, lost somewhere in the wind, but somehow Rye hears me anyway because she answers, giving a long, Wikipedia-type dissertation about Thong Weed.

"It's a green plant often found on shorelines. It grows up out of mushroom-shaped knobs, living two to three years before it dies and falls to the bottom of the ocean. I catch it right after it dies, before it falls too deep."

Yes, Rye, before it falls too deep. Waaay downn deeep where you always swim. Because you're from the ocean, right, Rye?

The biggg deeeep ocean.

I smile at her, but I'm not sure why. I'm not feeling particularly amiable toward her at the moment. She smiles back and continues her educational piece on marine plant life. *Hey, maybe I'll be able to use this information at work in some way. Good idea, Rye!*

"Sometimes I search the shorelines for the plant, looking for clusters that are on their last legs getting ready to expire. That way I'll know which areas to dive in to get them."

"You are so intelligent, Rye. You had to do a lot of research to perfect your quest for this Thong Wheel, didn't you?"

At that Rye laughs, a rich, boisterous laugh, so unlike her usual mousey self that it catches me off guard. "Weed. It's Thong *Weed*, not wheel."

Oh my goodness, she's right! Weed. She is so funny. Come to think of it—so am I. We're both funny. *And I feel so good right now.* Idly I begin playing with my hands, wondering if this wheel stuff is ever going to start working. On second thought, I don't really think I need it to—because I'm *already* feeling great. Just being here watching the ocean trying to swallow up the rocks is a great feeling. *I wonder if it ever actually does—swallow them up, I mean.*

Rye crawls up on one of the large, protruding rocks that I'm so intent on studying, rambling on and on about various subjects that aren't quite making sense to me, while I lean against a boulder that is near where I am already standing. I don't have the energy it takes for climbing, so I don't follow suit. I know she is still close by though, because I can see her through the shimmering haze that's been created by the wafts of wind that are stirring up the ocean. In spite of her proximity though, it's as if her voice is fading farther and farther away. *Rye. Rye, are you still there? Why is everything becoming so far removed?* Suddenly even the ocean seems like it is receding into itself. The transformation leaves me slightly confused. A bout of dizziness spirals through my body, making it difficult to focus for a second or two. *Do I feel okay?* I shake my head. *Yeah, yeah, I'm okay.*

Once again Rye's voice is clear. But it has become deep, so deep that it is practically astounding. How can this be? After another moment I realize that it's not Rye's voice I'm hearing at all. Someone else has joined our group. *Well, welcome. Sign your name in the sand as a way of registering.* I start to laugh, but the abrupt movement makes me feel slightly queasy. *Am I okay?* I take a deep breath. *Yeah, yeah, I'm okay, but I better not laugh.* That's hard to do though, because I'm *soooo* funny! *Kate always said I was funny, and she was right!* She was right all along.

The other voice keeps talking in low, intense tones, and I strain my ears trying to figure why it sounds vaguely familiar. Concentrating with every ounce of my being, I focus on the deep, sexy voice, trying to place where I know it from. *Sexy!* I gulp in a waft of swirling air. *Oh my word! It's Tristan!*

Tristan! Holy crap, I wonder if he's found out that he is going out with Rye and not me? I wonder if I should tell him, or should she? Looking around, I search for the owner of the voice who I'm quite sure is Tristan, but it's hard to find him, because I'm getting dizzier and dizzier with every minute that passes. Finally I spot him though, yards away, talking to someone hiding behind the rock, or maybe just talking to Rye. Either way, he sounds pissed.

"What did you do to her?" *To who?*

"Nothing. She was a perfectly willing participant. When I talked to her earlier this afternoon, she looked like a mess. I thought she could use a little help. Funny how that happens." It *is* Rye. *Funny how what happens?* Now her voice becomes a mixture of ocean waves and soft whispers, and I have to strain my ear to catch the rest of what she is saying. "Funny how the more people care about you, the more they fall apart. Why is that, Tris?" *Why does Rye's voice sound so desperate?*

But *Tris* doesn't answer, and I half wonder where he went. For a moment I contemplate whether he was just a figment of my imagination after all. Minutes before, unable to support my weight, I'd slid to a sitting position in the sand, my back still supported by the rock. Now I feel a looming presence above me, and I look up. Into narrowed, green eyes. *Tristan!* He's back. But why does he look so unhappy? Pissed actually! Through slightly blurred vision I study his strong physique and perfectly formed facial features. Pissed or not, he is still drop-dead gorgeous.

"Get up, Bethany. You're leaving." The adamancy of his voice startles me, but my reflexes are not working well at the moment, so I don't react. As he extends a hand in my direction, I watch the motion of his arm, trying to register in my mind what it is exactly that he wants me to do. Before I can mull it over, his fingers are gripping my arm, and I'm being lifted to a standing position. But my legs are weak and tingly. They begin to buckle. Before I can slump to the ground though, Tristan's arm tightens around me, and I am pulled to his chest. *Holy cow, I don't feel so good!* I cling to his body, thankful for a place to rest. Easing me away, he wraps his arm around my shoulder instead. "Come on, keep walking. I'm taking you home."

Everything is spinning. Round and round the sand and the waves and the large rocks swirl and sway around me. I take a staggered step. *Oh crap, I feel sick!* I press my eyes tightly together. *So sick!* I can barely walk. Tristan keeps pushing me forward, offering the strength of his body to support my weight. I feel the rigidity of his muscles as we walk along in silence on the shoreline route that will lead us back to my cabin. I can tell he is really mad. *And I am so sick!* What have I done to myself? Waves of nausea plummet through my head, threatening to overpower me. But somehow although I am unable to fathom how, I continue to press on, putting one foot in front of the other.

We are at the beach directly in front of my cabin when the churning in my stomach becomes an uncontrollable force. Breaking away from Tristan's grasp, I plunge to the ground, and begin puking over and over again. *Oh God, I am so sorry!* This is nightmare! I knew better. Why did I take it? The drug—why did I take it? Humiliation courses through me as I kneel, knees dug into the sand, head bent, my body lurching as I vomit repeatedly. Somewhere in the back of my mind I realize that Tristan is behind me, holding my hair away from my face as two thoughts bounce between neuro receptors; *Tristan can't be here right now seeing me like this* and *Dear Lord, I feel so ill I want to die!*

After I am finished ridding myself from all the contents of my stomach, Tristan guides me up the path that leads to the cabin. Shakily, I climb the two steps that precede the front door. Pausing for a second I try to contemplate how I'm going to get inside. I try to recall if I have a set of keys and where they might be at this moment. The more I attempt to concentrate on the thought, the dizzier I become. Swaying on my feet, I feel Tristan's arms reach out to steady me before his hand slides into the front pocket of my shorts. Pulling out my key chain, he unlocks the door. Soon I am lying on my bed. As I begin slipping into a fitful slumber, I sense Tristan's presence as he sits next to me on the mattress. While I lie there weak and unmoving, he eases me out of my sweatshirt and removes my sandals.

With parched lips and words that are nothing but an unintelligible murmur, I tell him how sorry I am that he has to see me this way. He answers by saying nothing. Tucking the sheet around my shoulders, he wipes a cool cloth across my forehead and cheeks.

Eventually I drift away into a welcomed oblivion.

The next time I wake, my body is on fire. I want to scream. Restlessness consumes me. I want to crawl out of my skin. Shadows around my room are distorted, moving shapes. Everything is closing in around me. I have a desperate need to escape from the horror and the heat. Thrashing in bed, I begin peeling off my covers and then my clothes, frantic to find some kind of relief. My cabin has become an inferno and sweat is pouring from my pores soaking my hair and bed coverings. One repeated thought plunges through my mind—*I have to find a way to leave!*

But something is holding me back. It's as if I've been placed in a torture chamber, chained and held in place. Inadvertently I begin to wonder if I've been captured by a terrorist group and this is how I'll live out the rest of my time on earth—in complete agony. There is a shushing sound above me, and I imagine that it is coming from some type of hypnotic devise that is being used to surrender my brain to unwanted antipatriotic conditioning. I continue to writhe. *I won't let it happen! I refuse to capitulate.*

"Shhhh…" The sound continues.

Finally something cool! Something chilled and soothing is being brushed across my skin; first my face, then onto my arms, down my stomach and eventually my legs. I arch my scorching body, trying to press into the coolness, hoping to find relief.

"Shhhh…" The sound continues, but this time there are words accompanying the hum of the shushing mechanism. "Aw baby…why did you do this to yourself…I love you…I can't stand to see you this way." *What on earth? What kind of terrorist talks this way?* Now I am confused, but I continue to writhe, fighting. I can't let myself be confused. I need to be lucid, waiting for the time when I can make my get away.

Still the placating motion of the caress remains until finally it begins to calm my frenzied nerves. Eventually I am lulled back into a restful sleep.

The next time I wake, the light of the sun is pouring through my window. I cover my eyes to shield them from the brightness. My head is pounding and the mouth feels like the Sahara Desert. *Oh my…what? What happened?* Detecting movement beside my bed, I turn in the direction of the motion, squinting. *Tristan!* Sitting in a chair, feet away from my bed is Tristan. A cool breeze glides across the surface of my skin and suddenly I feel naked. Reaching down to pat my torso, I discover that I have on only underwear. *Oh my word, where are my clothes?* Self-consciously I begin searching for a covering, eventually finding a sheet to conceal myself.

Then with the force of a tidal wave all of the events from the night before come flooding back. My head jerks in the direction of Tristan once again. *The drugs! He stayed with me for the puking and the craziness and who-knows-what-else all night long!* My eyes go wide. Why would he do that? I watch his face. And he looks pissed. And gorgeous. And I feel like crap in every way imaginable. He runs a hand through his tousled blond hair before finally speaking. His voice is a stern whisper.

"So tell me…what was that all about?"

All at once I become overwhelmed. With everything; the idea that I took drugs, the bad effect of the drugs, the idea that I disappointed Tristan, the realization that he took care of me all night long anyway, and finally the assaulting memory of him being pledged to marry Rye.

Without warning an unstoppable fountain of tears is unleashed from somewhere deep inside. With a concerned look on his face, Tristan crosses the room. Hesitantly, he takes me in his arms, cradling me against his chest until the crying subsides. I am lying completely spent, face against his chest, when I am finally capable of talking. "I'm sorry," I say. "I don't know...for taking that stuff. I knew better. I just...I'm sorry."

There is a long moment of silence before Tristan eventually speaks. "I'm confused," he says. "That's not like you, Bethany. Why did you do it?"

I try to shift my position in order to have the conversation that I know needs to be aired and immediately the room begins to spin. *Oh crap!* Closing my eyes and then reopening them, I try again. "I'm not trying to justify what I did. Trust me, when I say I won't ever do *that* again. I still feel like crap—shit actually. But..." I look away.

"But what?"

I raise my eyes to his and stare unwaveringly. "But I want you to know...that I know the truth."

Tristan goes very still. "What truth?"

Unwittingly, my voice goes small and I have to fight the tears that want to start up once again. "The truth about you and Rye."

Chapter Ten

Tristan's face is unreadable, but for a microsecond I detect a flicker of worry crossing over his perfect features. My stomach is in my throat. It's so hard to confront him about marrying someone else—and not me. In my fairytale dreams I imagined it would be me walking toward him, down the carpeted aisle in a little white church. I brace myself, hugging the oversized nightshirt that I'd discreetly slipped on, preparing to hear him admit something I know is going to tear me apart. "I found out about you and Rye…and how you are going to get married someday."

Now that I've said it, I want to look away. I want to crumble to the ground, folding myself into a tiny, little ball, never speaking to anyone again for the rest of my life. Instead I stand there unmoved, continuing to watch his face. He closes his eyes as if in agony. *Or in response to straight-up getting caught!* My heart is pounding. Seconds feel like minutes as I wait for him to say something. It becomes increasingly difficult to breathe.

"It's not true," he finally says. *What? Will he continue to lie?*

"What?" My eyes flash anger. I will not be played any longer!

His shoulders slump in defeat, making tears rush to the surface of my eyes. I shake my head. *No, no, I don't want to hear it!* As much as I know I need to hear the truth from his mouth, there is a big part of me that isn't ready to face what I can tell he is about to say.

"Well, it is true that I was originally *supposed* to marry Rye. At a very young age, my parents and her parents made an agreement." He looks me straight in the eye. "But since I laid eyes on you, all bets were off."

I suck in a breath of air. This is not what I expected. Narrowing my eyes, I cock my head in confusion. "But…what about the agreement…and Rye…and your parents—"

"Both sets of parents know where I stand. They aren't thrilled about it. I know they hope I'll change my mind about it. But I won't."

"And Rye?" My voice is a cautious whisper.

"Rye knows that I have no feelings for her. She has known this for years. At times she's had a hard time accepting it, but she *knows*. I've always made it clear." He pauses, running his fingers through his rumpled, sunstreaked hair, and in spite of our serious conversation, I am reminded once again of just how sexy he is. "Bethany…is this what all of this has been about? The way you so obviously avoided me at the party the other night? And now this mess?" He sighs—an exasperated expulsion of air. "Girl, I am going to tell you one more time…it's you, it's always been you for me and no one else. Please…*please* come to me when you hear something you have questions about. Instead of torturing your body like you just did last night."

I am overjoyed by his revelation. It feels like a heavy weight is released from my chest. But there is still something bothering me. "But how come you didn't tell me…about Rye and all that?"

"I didn't know it would turn into an issue. I didn't want to worry you over nothing. As far as I am concerned, it is a done deal. I'm not marrying Rye, and that's it. It's in the past. I've always told Rye to stay off land, or it could get her into trouble. So I was surprised to see her walking around with you the other day. I am going to have to give her a little reminder about that."

Relief courses through my veins. Tristan's green eyes become soft, and he takes a hesitant step toward me. "I'm sorry you had to worry like you did. I love you." My heart melts. When he opens his arms, I attempt to take a step in his direction. But the room tilts. For a brief moment I close my eyes. When I open them again, Tristan is directly in front of me. Taking me gingerly in his arms, he pulls me to his chest, soothing my unkempt hair with his hand. I sigh softly.

"I love you too," I whisper. For a while we stay that way, holding each other in silence, relishing the feel of our bodies pressed together. Eventually the muffled sound of Tristan's deep voice begins speaking into my hair.

"By the way, you were not the only one who was tortured last night. It was pretty much torture for me to have to sit here and watch you lie there all night long after you ripped off your clothes. I want you to know, you look pretty damn sexy in your underwear." *Oh my word!* A blush spreads across my cheekbones, covering my face from ear to ear. I turn my head into his chest, grateful that he cannot see the bright red coloring that is displayed on the surface of my skin.

It is so nice to finally lay all of the questions and issues to rest and spend uncomplicated time with Tristan day after day. We do all sorts of real-life boyfriend and girlfriend types of things together without any drama surrounding our relationship. No Rye. Even Keuran seems to have disappeared, leaving me and Tristan to enjoy each other in peace. Then the day I get a call from my mom telling me my twin brothers want to come to Watch Hill for a visit, the peace ends. But the chaos that accompanies their visit is a different kind of anarchy.

"Hey, sis, whassup?" Having just arrived in town, Josh walks, or rather struts, through the front door of my cabin and lifts his hand for a high five. Jake follows close behind.

"Yo, sista."

Ignoring both of their upraised palms, I grab them, gathering them in my arms for a hug. There is no attempt on their parts to hide the simultaneous eye rolling over the apparent uncool gesture from their sister. Furrowing my brow, I eye them up and down. Why does it seem like the last time I saw them, less than a month ago, they were two snot-nosed, cootie-obsessed kids playing in the dirt? Now standing on the wood planks of my kitchen floor dressed in low-slung jeans and fitted tee shirts with their hats turned backwards, they look like two thirteen-year-olds who are going on eighteen. A type of self-imposed swagger resonates from every ounce of their youthful bodies. *Oh good grief, how long did I say they could stay?* The minute my parents leave my driveway to head back to Philadelphia after dropping them off, I want to run out to the road and yell after them, "Hey, you forgot something! Two boys!" Instead I sigh, leaning against my kitchen cabinets, watching the duo as they saunter around my cabin running their hands over things, checking out *my crib*. Josh's hair is more sunstreaked than I remember, heightening his resemblance to Mom and me as well. Jake's hair, on the other hand, is the darkest it's ever been—now he is a spitting image of Dad.

"When can we go to the beach?" Jake asks.

"Yeah, the beach, man," Josh echoes.

The first mistake I make during my brothers' visit is taking them to Misquamicut Beach. The minute we step out of my black jeep and onto the wooden boardwalk that leads to the main thoroughfare of the beach, loud, pulsating music fills the air. In response the twins' eyes begin to glimmer with energy. I shake my head. Why did I think that a spring break atmosphere would be a good place to take two young, adolescent boys that are entrusted to my care? One glance at the pair and it becomes obvious that hormones are beginning to rage through their youthful frames. The sand has barely hit the soles of our feet before two young girls pass our way, making eye contact with my brothers. Without hesitation, Josh and Jake nod their heads with cocky confidence, smiling in the girls' direction. From my peripheral vision I watch as the girls nudge each other, breaking into giggles. Josh and Jake silently high-five each other with their eyes. *Oh no, this might be a long week!*

I herd the boys through the partylike atmosphere of the boardwalk, planning on taking them to a more secluded spot farther down shore. But it's difficult to keep the progression in motion when their eyes are darting in all directions taking in the many concession huts, Jamaican-styled cabanas filled with a variety of seating, and the dance floors that will come alive later in the evening. All of it, plus a sea of people are creating a small city of fun. They linger as they walk, the expressions on their faces filled with amazement. I can tell we will not be getting to the place I intended anytime soon.

"Hey, that sign says *teen dance party tonight.*" Jake's voice echoes with excitement across the beach.

"Awesome! We're going." Josh matches his enthusiasm.

Say what? "Um, if you look more closely, I believe the small print reads *ages fifteen and up.* I don't believe that includes you boys. Last time I checked you were still thirteen." *Thirteen and how!* In tandem they crinkle their noses.

"Aw...we could pass for fifteen," Josh says.

"Um, no, you couldn't. Let's keep going. We're heading over there...to the far end of the beach."

"What? No, that looks boring over there." Jake folds his arms together defiantly. "We want to be where the action is. We want to stay close to the lifeguards."

Josh nods his head in agreement with his brother before nudging him in the arm. "Yeah, definitely by the lifeguards." My humdrum ideas clearly forgotten, they give each other the thumbs-up sign, all-the-while smiling. Conceding the battle, I shake my head, deciding it's not worth the fight. Setting our paraphernalia on a small, uncluttered area in the sand, I find a spot to call home for the next few hours midst the myriads of people that have already laid claim to the waterfront. As I settle into my beach chair, Josh and Jake begin tossing a football back and forth to each other. Before long one of them conveniently fails to make the catch, and the ball lands on a blanket filled with young girls. After an apology and a dazzling smile from the boys, three of the girls join them, and it becomes a five-way game of catch. Again, I shake my head. Closing my eyes, I relax into my chair, allowing the sun to warm my cheekbones and lashes. Before long, I begin to doze.

"Hey, baby." A deep, familiar voice startles me awake.

My heart picks up in tempo. Shielding my eyes from the sun, I look to meet piercing, green eyes and a breathtaking smile. "Hey."

Kneeling beside me, Tristan takes one finger and runs it fleetingly across my lips. Instantly my body reacts. "I see your company has arrived."

My brow lifts in mock exasperation. "You can say that again." Simultaneously we look in the twins' direction. The girl companions are in the midst leaving the game, heading back to their blanket. Tristan squeezes my shoulder and hops up.

"I'm going to go say hi." Arm extended, he starts a light jog through the sand. "Hey, throw me a pass," he calls. Pausing, my brothers look in Tristan's direction. They appear confused. *Who is this guy, and why does he want us to throw a football to him*—is clearly written all over their faces. But after a brief inspection, Josh sends the football spiraling through the air, and Tristan effortlessly makes the catch. The return throw is made to Jake. After a few tosses, Tristan makes his way over to where they are standing. They watch him approach, mesmerization flashing in their eyes.. "Josh and Jake, right?" He extends a hand. "I'm Tristan. Your sister's boyfriend." Tristan proceeds to shake their hands, and I can't help but be impressed with his ability to get both of their names correct. *Wow, he has a good memory!* A little subdued, the boys return the shake, looking up into his face in awe. Now they are on their best behavior. *Hey, how does he do that?*

No matter. Right then I make a decision. I would be keeping Tristan close by for the rest of the twins' visit.

Not long after the beach episode, Josh and Jake talk us into taking them to the movies, the arcade, the go-cart track—and pretty much anywhere else they can find girls. And somehow, amazingly enough, the girls they meet quickly become attached and find a way to track my brothers back down in return. One morning as I'm preparing chocolate chip pancakes and the boys are lounging on the couch playing a computer game, my cooking is interrupted by a knock at the door. When I answer, I discover two doe-eyed girls looking sheepishly at me. "Umm, are Josh and Jake here?" *What?* I peer around their young, slender frames, looking for their means of transportation out to the cabin and find two shiny bikes perched against an oak tree in the side yard. Before I can help it, I'm blurting in exclamation.

"You girls seriously rode your bikes all the way out here?"

They glance at each other uneasily. "Yeah?" The twins hear the sound of female voices and soon arrive at the door. The group of four talk for a few minutes, and I tell the boys—and girls— *sorry about the long ride on the bikes,* but their newfound friends will have to exit the premises before I go to work. The visit short-lived, I get into my black, four-door jeep, and leave Josh and Jake to consume the stack of pancakes I've made for them as I make my way into town.

The morning passes, and I work it out with my boss to leave at noon so I can head home for the rest of the day. Knowing that a week in Watch Hill will pass by quickly, I want to spend some extra time with the twins before they head back to Philadelphia. But when I arrive back at the cabin, the boys are nowhere to be found. Frustrated, I spend the afternoon in an unsuccessful search. At wit's end, I finally head over to Tristan's work and ask for his aid in finding them. I'm starting to get worried. I imagine the uncomfortable call I'd have to make to my parents, telling them I managed to lose their bratty—*I mean*—sons. Once Tristan joins the search team, however, it isn't long before he spots Josh and Jake coming out of St. Clair Annex, ice cream in hand, the two doe-eyed girls from earlier that morning at their side. Taking a deep breath, I try to calm myself before heading in their direction. I am this close to wringing their overconfident, squirrely necks right out in public. *But only after sending their sidekicks to an early demise.*

"You're in a whole lot of trouble," is all I say. Maybe it's the insufferable look on my face or maybe it's the dead-serious tone in my voice—but either way it seems to be effective, because the girls instantly scatter, and the boys don't take the time to finish their ice cream cones, pitching them into a nearby trash container instead. Once back at the cabin, we leave Josh and Jake inside while Tristan and I take a shoreline walk, giving me time to cool off. By Tristan's relaxed manner on our stroll, it's evident to me that he is not as distraught as I am over the whole thing. This becomes even more apparent when he leaves and goes back inside the cabin to check on twins. Returning with the boys at his side, he announces that he is taking them fishing. I begin to choke.

"Fishing?" Two things instantly come to mind. First of all, Tristan does *not* fish! He had made it clear to me in the past that fishing is not a hobby that he will ever partake in. In some ways it would feel like he was trying to catch a distant relative or something like that. So the idea that he is willing to take the twins fishing is a really big deal! Second—go figure—the boys are being punished, and yet he is taking them fishing? Oh, and yes, there is a third thing too.

I realize right then and there that he is one heck of a guy!

As the rest of the week passes without event, it becomes clear that Tristan is the boys' idol. Whenever he is at the cabin or hanging out with us in town, they follow him around showing lots of interest in whatever he is doing, even if it is the most menial task. Unknowingly, *or maybe knowingly*, they start talking like him and mimicking his pet phrases. Even their walk changes—they throw back their shoulders and stick out their youthful chests as if this alone will make them look bigger and stronger.

"If they only knew you lived in the sea, they would probably pick up some scuba gear at a local store and dive into the ocean to see if they could live there too." At that, Tristan shakes his head and laughs and laughs. Although he never verbalizes it, I'm sure he notices that he's turned into a celebrity in the boys' eyes too.

The day before Jake and Josh have to go back to Philadelphia, they ask if they can go to a party being held in the Watch Hill area that evening. It takes some prying, but finally I get out of them that the party is at the house of one of the infamous girls that they had been running around with in town that day. One of the same girls that had ridden all the way out here on her bike that morning—*most likely without her parents' knowledge.* My first instinct is to say *no way!* But the imploring look on the boys' faces, accompanied by their rather pristine behavior since the original day of the incident, leads me to give them the answer they want to hear.

The catch is, it is a private party—no jeans allowed, and all male shirts must have a collar—and in order for the boys to attend, they will need a chaperone. I let out a slow breath of air, knowing where I'll be spending my evening. After I get ahold of Tristan, he is soon roped into the situation too, and we are on our way, driving through a shaded boulevard winding up a hilly terrain that overlooks the ocean. Ancient, leafy trees and giant, historic mansions line the paved streets. After our vehicle is valet parked, we follow a red brick sidewalk that leads to a spacious backyard where table after table sits laden with drinks and hors d'oeuvres. Fountains splash playfully into marble receptacles, while elevator music plays over strategically placed speakers that blend in well with the landscape.

Glancing at the boys' polo shirts that have recently come untucked, I hope we are dressed appropriately for the occasion. Behind me, Tristan is sporting white pants and a baby blue, pinstriped button-down shirt. I'd already given him the once over—several times. So I don't have to recheck his attire to know he looks better than good for the party. But I do anyway. And once again I'm not disappointed. Offering him a smile, I hold his gaze for a second or two, and by the look in his green eyes, I can tell he thinks my pale, yellow sundress looks okay too. Taking a calming breath, I try to relax in the stuffy, rather formal setting that I'm going to be immersed in for the rest of the evening.

And I don't do half bad: mingling with the wealthy, eating fancy snacks, making small talk—learning about others and telling a little bit about me. But when I hear irate expletives flying out of the hostess's mouth as she rushes across the lawn, displaying a punch-soaked dress, yelling, "Those kids just knocked the punch fountain over on me!" I begin to glance around nervously, looking for the twins. A half an hour later I spy Josh walking beside girl number one, his polo shirt suspiciously wet across the front. I motion him over and ask if he knows anything about a knocked over fountain. But before he can answer, the girl at his side is quick to reassure me, "Absolutely not!" Exasperated, I roll my eyes as they quickly turn to leave, wondering if it was little spots of red that I detected smeared throughout Josh's water-soaked shirt.

Soon after the fountain incident, I begin searching the crowd for Tristan, realizing that I haven't seen him in some time. After a few sweeps through the partygoers, I am convinced he is nowhere in the vicinity. Instinctively, my eyes are drawn to the water. I begin to make my way slowly down to the beach. After a few twists in the shoreline I spy him standing, facing the sea, lost in thought. Pausing, I stop in my tracks watching what I can only describe as a troubled expression evident on his features. Of its own accord, my heart begins beating forcefully against my chest wall, and I swallow down the bad feeling that wants to rise into my throat. I'd seen that far-off look before. *What is it, Tristan?* He appears oblivious to my presence, so I begin cautiously walking toward him. Padding across the sand, I approach him from behind. Wrapping my arms around his mid-secttion, I rest my face against his back. For a minute he does nothing while I hold him. All around us the whitecaps repeatedly rush to shore. For a moment or two I wonder whether I should have come at all or left him to welter in his solitude. It's not until I feel him reach for my hand that I realize I've been holding my breath.

"What are you thinking about, Tristan?"

He sighs and for a moment says nothing. I wonder if he can feel my heartbeat accelerate nervously as I lean against his back. "Nothing," he says. I close my eyes together tightly. *No! Not that answer—clearly it's something.* I am fighting back the emotions that are playing havoc in my mind when he finally speaks again. "Nothing I want to burden you with at least."

"If something bothers you, it bothers me too," I say back, recalling the times in the past that he'd kept things from me *for my own good.* I hate it. I'm not a frail person that can't handle all the secrecies that seem to be associated with his world. How will we ever have a real relationship together if he is continually keeping things from me? "I wish you would tell me."

Gradually he breaks free from my hold and takes a step away while running a hand through his hair. It's then that I detect the dampness in his strands. So he'd been in the water very recently— probably moments before I'd arrived. "Pollution." His one-word answer interrupts my musing over his latest swim. Silently I wait for him to expound. "Pollution in the ocean is increasing around this area. Especially at the bottom of the ocean. Right now it is at an all-time high."

I furrow my brow. "Are the shipping companies increasing their dumping? Isn't there something that can be done to stop them?"

He shakes his head as he presses his lips together. "I'm just not sure who or what is doing it. But somehow the lower levels in the sea, my world, are taking a direct hit." His shoulders tense. From past experience, I know how badly this is affecting him. The look that is etched into his features is a combination of hurt and anger. "But eventually if this new onslaught of polluting keeps up, your world will be affected too."

"Tristan, you *are* my world. Your world is now my world too. I can no longer differentiate the two." At this he turns and offers me a small smile, but it doesn't quite reach his eyes. Ignoring the implications, I continue my line of questioning. "Why is there such an increase anyway?"

Shrugging his shoulders, he walks downs to the water's edge. Scooping up a handful of water, he peers into his cupped palm, examining the contents that are helplessly slipping through his fingers. Finally he turns back to face me. "I'm not sure." The look in his green eyes is distant, not focusing on my face at all. It's as if he is lost in thought, somewhere else far from the sandy shores of the beach. "But I'm doing my best to find out."

Okay. I nod my head in acquiescence. There is something about the look on his face that tells me that this is the end of this conversation.

And there is something about his contemplative stare as he turns and gazes back out to sea that tells me there is much more to the story than he is telling me.

Chapter Eleven

When it comes time for Josh and Jake to return to Philadelphia, they are not ready to go.

"Can we come back in a couple of weeks?" Jake asks.

"Or sooner?" Josh interjects.

"We'll see." *Probably not!* I offer them a hopeful smile.

The cabin is profoundly quiet after they drive away with Mom and Dad, and I plop on my couch, relishing my newfound peace. But after one afternoon of solitude, I begin to feel like something is missing: loud rap music, balls being insubordinately tossed around indoors, trails of sand on the floor, leftover piles of dishes in the kitchen sink. I glance around the interior walls of my cabin, taking in my neat and tidy surroundings, and unexpectedly I experience a little pang in my chest. Contemplatively I reach for my phone. *No, I won't do it!* I set it back down. Maybe next summer. Next summer I'd have them back again. But not before. I think back to the recent party we had taken the twins to and how it was such an effort to find them at the end of the evening when it was time to leave. Somehow, in spite of the boys' feigned innocence, I had a suspicious feeling that in protest to leaving, they were conveniently avoiding us. Then when we did eventually make our exit from the venue, the hostess gave Josh and Jake a dirty look. In response, my thank-you-for-everything smile turned into more of a cringe.

Even Tristan had sensed the angst between the owner and our ensemble and had hurried the boys along as we exited through the side-yard gate. After finding Tristan earlier in the evening, sequestered on the beach, he had walked back with me to the party, and I had taken the opportunity to ask him about something I had been wondering about for the last while—Keuran's description of their winter hibernation. After Keuran had described the scenario, I hadn't been able to quite shake the unpleasant image from my mind. As I bring the subject up, there is a part of me that hopes Tristan will refute the story. But when his head shoots quickly in my direction, eyebrows furrowed, carefully watching my face, I know that Keuran was indeed telling the truth. I shake my head and look away.

"This bothers you, doesn't it?"

"No, I—"

"I know it not a very picturesque thought, but this is actually how it does happen for us. It helps us to conserve energy so that we can stay healthy the rest of the year and live out a normal life span."

"So I guess that means I won't see you as much during the winter?"

"No, not as much, but I can try to minimize my hibernation and come see you as often as I can."

"No!" My tone is adamant. "I don't want you to jeopardize your health for my sake, and besides, I want you to live a really long time. Hibernate all you want; I'll be okay." As I contemplate the speculative expression on Tristan's face, I think of how appropriate it is that he resides so close to a summertime community. Essentially his people are summertime folks themselves.

"I can come out of hibernation safely every couple of days for a short period of time, so I won't be completely gone all winter." He offers me a tentative smile. I smile back, a little breathless, once again coming slightly undone by his beauty. Then I'd learn to live with those small moments of having him around me in the winter. I'd have to—by now I have no other choice. I love him so much.

For the next couple of weeks, work at the Center for Marine Studies keeps me busy as I'm wrapping up my environmental classroom project for the fall. After the last few items needed for the assignment cascade into place, I begin working on the next thing on my agenda: biweekly classes that will be offered to the community year-round, held at Community College of Rhode Island. The focus of the curriculum will be Endangered Marine Animals of the Atlantic. Very quickly my research starts to concentrate on the rising levels of CO_2 and the havoc it plays on the ocean environment—and in turn, how it affects the aquatic creatures dependent on the underwater milieu. Increased levels of CO_2 are being absorbed by the ocean, which leads to increased marine temperatures and increased acidification and decreased oxygenation of seawater. All of this leads to destruction of kelp forests and coral reefs, which are home to many aquatic creatures.

Taking a break from the coalition of work on my desk, I leave my cubicle behind for a few minutes as I head east toward a grassy park that offers a distant view of the ocean. Cup of coffee in hand, I situate myself on a wooden bench and gaze beyond the tree line, past a fisherman's wharf, out to the still waters of the sea. With no breeze in sight, in spite of my shaded seating arrangement, the heat of the day begins to warm my skin, causing my white blouse to stick to my back. Taking my hand, I wipe the sweat that threatens to pool across my forehead, all the while focusing on the body of liquid that is peeking through the leafy foliage in front of me.

Right now the color of the water that stares back at me is a vibrant blue, glistening with the promise of vitality. But what will a future without the right compilation of ingredients necessary to maintain the vibrancy of life in the ocean look like? Dull? Lackluster? Ominous? Diseased? My heart rises to my throat as I contemplate the worst. Squeezing my eyes tightly together, I try to erase the image from my mind. Realizing that it's time for my break to be over, I unglue myself from the strips of wood that are sticking to my thighs and head back to my desk. With one more glance over my shoulder at the ocean, I enter the building.

There is still so much work that needs to be done.

It's two o'clock in the afternoon, the sun is beaming in the sky, and a soft wind is blowing the borderline-hot temperatures across the parking lot of the Center for Marine Studies. As I cross the pavement to my jeep, hurrying to avoid the heat that is radiating off the blacktop, I make a decision to spend the rest of the afternoon at the beach. As of late, I had been putting in long hours at work, and today my boss, Jada, suggested I go home early to avoid burnout. After tying up a few loose ends on the project I am currently working on, I close down my cubicle and head for the cabin.

Soon my work clothes are exchanged for a turquoise bikini and a floral sundress. Traipsing through fine granules of sand, I make my way toward Napatree Point. The farther I walk toward the southeastern end of the narrow peninsula, the sparser the beachgoers become. And that is perfectly fine with me. I've chosen Napatree Point over some of the more congested beaches in the area in order to avoid the crowds, trading them in for solitude and the soothing sounds of nature, instead.

I've just settled my chair next to the shoreline and pulled my favorite classic novel from my tote, *Jane Eyre*, when I detect a slender shadow teetering close by in the sand. *Apparently, I wouldn't be as alone as I'd hoped.* Shading my eyes from the sun, I look up in search of a face. Unexpectedly, my heart picks up in tempo—for what reason I'm not exactly sure. Except that it quickly becomes evident in my mind that Rye is the last person I was expecting to see at the beach today. As Rye steps directly into my view, the sun becomes completely blocked. Now I am able to make out her hauntingly ashen eyes and the gentle lines of her face more clearly. She stands above me, two pools of gray, gazing not only at me, but through me—as if staring deep down into the depths of my soul.

I shift awkwardly in my chair. "Rye!"

"Bethany." Her voice is soft as she answers my greeting. "May I?" She points to the ground beside my chair. I nod my head, and before I get the chance to offer her a towel to sit on, she positions herself on the powdery sand. A million different thoughts begin coursing through my mind as I eye her pixielike features and her pale skin—like: *Oh my!* The last time I was with her I took drugs. *Does she think I'll be willing to do that again?* Or—Does she know that I know the whole story about her being from the sea and that she was promised to marry Tristan and that he has rejected her? *I mean, obviously Tristan came and took me away that night, so she must know that I'm connected to him somehow!* Does she know how much? Does she know that he loves me—instead of her? Or—*What was it* that Rye said to Tristan that night while I was stoned and sick, about hurting girls?

"Is that your dress?" Rye's question startles me from my reverie. Confused, I begin glancing around. "Over there. Is that your floral dress?" Looking to my left, I see my discarded coverup lying next to my tote.

"Oh…yeah."

"'Cause it matches mine."

Taking in the dainty pattern of orange and pink flowers that make up her flowing garment, I widen my eyes. "Yeah…I guess it does."

Rye studies my face for a moment or two, not saying a word, and I begin to feel uncomfortable. I know I could say something else in regards to the dress or initiate some other type of conversation, but I don't have much else I really want to say. Eventually she clears her throat. "I hope you were okay that night, the last time we were together. I was worried about you after you left."

The drugs! Here goes. "I was fine!" *That's a lie!* "Well, actually not really, that stuff made me feel like crap. I won't do that again!"

"I'm sorry." Her voice is laced with concern as her delicate, pale hand reaches for my arm. I freeze in place, not expecting this type of familiarity. "I really *am* sorry, you know." Her eyes search my face until I turn and look at her. Something washes over me. And for some unexplainable reason, I feel strange—in a creeped-out kind of way. Still, I hold her gaze as she finishes what she has to say, wishing she would remove her hand from the goose bumps that are now forming on my skin. "Maybe next time it won't be like that for you."

I jerk away. "There won't *be* a next time, Rye." She drops her gaze to the sand, and I can tell that I've hurt her feelings.

Aaagh! I sigh inwardly. Why does this have to be so complicated? Taking a deep breath, I force myself to sound lighthearted. "So anyway, I haven't seen you in a while...are *you* doing okay?" *Why am I asking her this?* I really don't even *care* about how she is doing. I only want her to go away and leave me and Tristan alone.

At this she turns to look at me once more, a smile lighting up her face. It's then that I detect the glazed look in her gray eyes. Furrowing my brow, I scrutinize the hazy lagoons of pewter that are blinking up at me. I shouldn't be surprised. She's made no secret about how the drugs are a big part of her life. But as she commences into jubilant chatter at my side, taking no concern over my nonchalant—rather detached—reaction, I begin to wonder if there is more than just a chemical substance involved here. Something more inherent going on inside of her inexplicable mind.

The sun begins to lower slightly, and the shadows made by objects scattered on the shore begin to take on an evening glow. I am getting an uneasy feeling that the solitude of my leisurely afternoon is slipping right through my fingers, when Rye begins brushing pale granules of sand from the translucent skin of her legs, preparing to leave. Inwardly, I sigh in relief. But after a measure of time she stops short, perusing my beach tote where my *Jane Eyre* book is peeking out of a side pocket. Bending down, she reaches for the book and begins thumbing through the pages. After a minute or two, she sets it back in its place once again. Slowly, she stands back up and looks me directly in the eye. Unexplainably, my pulse accelerates.

"I wonder...would Jane have allowed herself to fall in love with Mr. Rochester had she known all along he already had a wife that was hidden in the attic?"

I stare back at her, shocked. Why do I get the feeling that she is referring to far more than the paperback novel that I've brought with me to the beach? Before I have a chance to further contemplate the meaning of her words, she turns her small frame away and begins walking slowly, purposefully, as if by rote, into the distance. Step by step through the sand. Step by step out into the ocean. Step by step—until her head disappears, and she is completely immersed under the swelling waves of the sea.

My heart begins pounding against my chest and I have to remind myself to breathe. My mind dissolves into a tumultuous storm as I try to wrap my thoughts around what I've just witnessed—what I've just seen. *Rye walking into the ocean.* My eyes stay glued to the waves—the emptiness of where she's just been. *She knows!* I gasp for air. *And she knows that I know too!*

Every hair on the skin of my arms is standing on end.

The following day I get a text from Keuran wanting me to meet him by Watch Hill Light. I'm not all that sure I want to spend another afternoon with any more of Tristan's seafaring friends. But Keuran is very persuasive, as I know he can be, and besides, his plan to hang out on the rocks by the lighthouse and watch a storm roll in sounds like fun. And if I'm honest with myself, I do kind of miss his adventurist, albeit sometimes alarming, personality. So after putting on a pair of tan shorts, my green Philadelphia five-K tee shirt, and tying a gray zip-up sweatshirt around my waist in case of a temperature shift, I head into town in my black jeep.

By the time I am making my way up the winding path that leads to the lighthouse, the sky is already becoming a canvas of rapidly shifting clouds. The air that I breathe in tastes of a pending storm, causing a rush of adrenaline to shoot through my veins. When I reach the crest of the hill where Watch Hill Light stands proudly piercing the sky, preparing to do its job in the face of the storm, I notice Keuran right away.

"Hey...Bethany. Come on!" His voice is full of enthusiasm as he waves me over. His amber eyes are all lit up. "Look at that dark sky...this is going to be freakin' awesome!" His fervor is contagious, and soon I find myself getting all junked up on the rush of the approaching inclement weather. "All right, well, let's go. Down there on those rocks." *What?* I shoot him a look of concern as I eye the jagged boulders that are resting many feet below us. He nods his head. "Yes, down there. That is the perfect spot to experience the maximum effect of the storm's advance."

Before I can change my mind, he is grabbing my hand, and we are heading down a steep embankment, the wind whipping at our faces, pressing our clothing against our skin. But he is right: once we are settled onto the massive rock formations at the bottom of the cliff, it becomes obvious that we've got front-row seating for the storm. In the distance the grayish blue sky is rapidly converting to black. And in turn, a baby blue ocean is being swallowed up by a steel-colored, traveling shadow. The mounting whitecaps glow stark white in contrast.

The wind picks up in velocity, and the waves twist and writhe as they prepare to enter combat with a force of nature. Keuran and I are sitting side by side watching the world transform around us, reveling in the edgy thrill, when he unexpectedly brings up the subject of Rye. Immediately I feel my shoulder muscles tense.

"So, have you seen much of her lately? Are you two still hanging out?"

A lot had gone down since I last talked to Keuran about Rye, and I am not in the mood to discuss it with him. The exasperated sound of my heavy sigh is swallowed by the blustering wind that is increasing in tempo. I force my voice to sound nonchalant. "Yeah, I just saw her yesterday actually."

Keuren's head snaps in my direction as if he is surprised. "Oh...so you two are still hanging out then?" He appears to mull the idea over for a moment. "Well, good. Yeah...that's good. She really is an okay friend to have around...when you can get her away from lover boy that is." *Oh no, here we go again!* Keeping my eyes planted on the growingly turbulent sea, I try not to react to the words that are spewing from his mouth. *I'm not going to react!* "Geez, I swear that's how it's always been with those two. Growing up, I'd try to get Tris to go on an adventure dive, and he'd be all set to go, and then Rye would show up, and she would want to go too. But Tris knew it wouldn't be safe for her. So he would change our plans and stay back with her instead."

On the inside I am shaking. I hate to hear these endearing childhood stories about Tristan and Rye and how their relationship goes way back. Out of the corner of my eye I can see Keuran shake his head in frustration as he reminisces about his growing-up years. "It's like when push comes to shove, Tris feels some sense of duty to Rye. It can be really annoying."

It takes all my effort not to let this little snippet of information bother me, but I swallow down the angst that is rising in my throat and think of a way to change the subject. "What is adventure diving exactly?"

Keuran runs a hand through his dark, spikey hair, and his amber eyes explode with light. "It's so awesome. It's going down deep—way deep—trying to find unexplored, really dark spots in the ocean. Sometimes to places so dark that even *our* eyes can't adjust. It disorients you, and it can be hard to find your way back out. There are moments of time—thrilling but chilling moments—when you just aren't sure what the outcome is going to be. Let's just say, it's a *real* challenge."

I crinkle my nose. *More like Russian roulette!* The thought of what he's just described sounds daunting—almost creepy. It is hard for me to imagine Tristan partaking in something so dark. In my mind it's hard to put him in the setting that Keuran has just described. But I don't have much time to linger on the image as suddenly the air around us becomes colder, alerting me that the storm is just minutes away. My body shifts gears, getting ready for our last-second escape.

I am scanning the surrounding seascape eyeing the storm, rocking on my haunches—getting ready to sprint, when I spot a young boy to our left floundering on the rocks. The waves have increased in size, and their outpouring is threatening to devour the place where he is standing. The look of fear is written on his face. "Keuran…look at that boy stuck over there. We need to help him." I have to shout to be heard over the now deafening sound of the surf.

"What?"

I grab Keuran's arm and point to the exact location of the kid, watching as the water gyrates and rises at an alarming rate. "I said, we need to help that boy." My voice has escalated to an urgent level. Keuran stares in the direction of the youth and laughs.

"Looks like he should have listened to Mommy. He's on his own for this one. I'll bet you next time he won't be so careless and stupid." *What? Are you kidding me?* I become frantic.

"Keuran, there won't be a next time! If you won't help him, then I guess I'll do it on my own." *Oh, God, help me, and I don't know how to swim—not well!* I begin edging along the rocks, heading toward the boy, careful not to slip off their water-soaked surface. It's a tricky venture though. And with footing not as sure as I hoped, I stumble and almost plunge into the breakers that are increasing in force.

"I got him," I hear a voice behind me say. It's Keuran. But the wind is so strong in my ears, I can barely hear. "Just get out of here, back up to the lighthouse." Turning in Keuran's direction, I get a glimpse of irritation written across his striking features. "I *said*, I got him, go on!"

I watch as he dives into the waves, disappearing, then reappearing on the rocks next to the frightened boy. Breathing a sigh of relief, I begin to make my escape, fighting the outpouring of rain that is now pelting across my face. It is a slippery uphill slope. And there are seconds when I half wonder whether I'll actually reach the protective covering of the lighthouse information center at all.

When I am safely under the overhang of the center, I bend over, heaving, in an all-out effort to breathe. Meanwhile the rain comes in torrents. As my respirations slow, I glance in all directions, wondering what happened to Keuran and the boy. Through the wind and the deluge, I finally spot them across the parking lot. Involuntarily tears begin to well up inside of me as I watch Keuran deposit the boy into the frantic arms of his mother. *Thank goodness!* Trembling with relief, I hug dripping wet arms to my chest in a calming effort.

Lightning flashes brilliantly, illuminating the darkened sky, and large booms of thunder vibrate the ground where I am standing. The wind has increased to hurricanelike speeds and the overhang I'm under does very little to keep the rain from drenching the clothes that are now pasted against my skin. I push myself up against the brick wall behind me.

Waiting out the storm, my thoughts shift to Keruan. What *was* that, anyway—back there on the rocks? Was he going to let that poor boy drown? Could it be that Tristan is right about him after all? Shuddering, I wipe away the gruesome thoughts that are spiraling through the forefront of my mind—what if Keuran had chosen not to offer his aid? Where would the boy be right now? Where would I be right now, had I needed to follow through on the attempt to save him?

"Hey girl, we made it. We *all* made it!" Keuran's smile is warm, matching the temperateness of his amber eyes. The rain has now slowed to a light, steady flow—the rumble of thunder just a distant sound. Looking up into his face, I startle, unaware of Keuran's silent approach.

"How is he doing?" My voice comes out breathless.

Keuran laughs. "Tommy? That's his name, by the way. He's just fine. You are such a good girl you know, Bethany…wanting to save him and all. But he would have been okay either way. But hey…I got him. And I'm glad you are happy."

I furrow my brow as I stare at Keuran's relaxed smile. Was he right? Would the boy really have been okay? I think back to the viciousness of the mini-squall that has just passed through, the precarious position he was in on the uneven surface of the rocks. The water heaving all around. And I get a nauseated feeling in the pit of my stomach.

Because I'm not 100 percent sure.

Chapter Twelve

"There is a really hot guy here to see you."

My head snaps up from the project I'm working on. Anna, a college intern, is smiling down at me while I sit at my desk inside my cubicle. I'd been researching the topic of endangered species in the Atlantic all morning. Now it is almost noon. Shaking the stiffness from my arms, it occurs to me that I've been in the same position for hours. Cocking my head, I smile back at Anna. "Really?"

"Yes, really. I'd say this is definitely your lucky day."

My heart picks up in tempo as I push my chair in, smoothing my ponytail en route. Excitement pulsates through my veins. When I reach the wide-open space that serves as the foyer to our building, I freeze in place. Walls four stories high constructed of glass filter sunlight into the room, landing directly on Tristan's tousled hair. He is talking with the receptionist. With his back to me, I am able to view the strength of his shoulders and the narrowness of his hips, which accentuates the perfect formation of his backside. Now my heart is thudding. Anna is right. *So hot!*

I can tell by the way the receptionist's eyes are sparkling that she is completely undone. And I get it, because so am I. Somehow, he senses my presence, because I've only barely passed through the doorway before he turns in my direction. Dressed in black pants, a pinstriped, button-down shirt, and a gray tie, he looks like young entrepreneur—and completely sexy. His eyes fill with light the minute they rest on mine. "Hey, baby."

I suck in a breath. I will never ever get tired of hearing that from him. "Hey...Tristan. What brings you here?"

He cocks his head as he narrows his eyes, a slight grin forming on his lips. "I would think the answer to that might be evident—

you." I watch as the receptionist's eyes widen, and I have to fight back a chuckle over her reaction. *Geez, he knows how to make me feel special!* And I love it! "Are you hungry?"

"Starved!" *Oh yeah, and I guess food sounds pretty good too.*

"I'm in town for a consulting meeting and thought I'd stop by and see if you had a free moment for lunch."

"Actually, now is a great time. Just give me a minute to get ready."

When I arrive back in the lobby a short time later, Tristan holds the door for me as we walk outside. Fresh air wafts over my skin the minute we exit the building. Inhaling, I breathe in the crispness of the day. Feeling Tristan's eyes on me while walking close by his side, I look up. He is biting his lip as he watches my face. My heart rate quickens. "What?"

He reaches over and tugs on the sleeve of my dusty pink blouse before taking in my gray skirt which is resting just above my knees. The perusal continues, traveling down to my spikey, high-heeled sandals that are clicking on the cement sidewalk. "I like this. It's a good look on you. I don't think I've ever seen you dressed like this before. Business diva."

I laugh to cover my blush. "Thanks."

He suggests a café that sits next to the shoreline. We are seated diagonally from each other on the patio eating salads and deli sandwiches when I detect an obscure movement in the water, yards off the coastline. A maritime breeze is blowing off the ocean, rumpling Tristan's hair, causing an occasional strand to escape from my ponytail. I brush a wisp of blond behind my ear. Tristan notices that I am looking in the direction of the ocean and turns his head that way too. "What is it?"

"I just thought I saw something move out there." A knowing look passes through his green eyes. Now I am more certain. "It happened so quickly I didn't get a really good look, but does that happen to be Drake out there?"

Tristan laughs and then glances around discreetly, making sure no one is listening to our conversation. "I think you are probably right. Like I've said before, he's always somewhere close by, never too far away from where I am. He's pretty smart though, and I've made it clear that he can't show himself in public areas or it will draw attention to him and me. So he always waits patiently for me, trying hard not to be seen. But once in a while he gets too close to shore and can't resist popping his head above for a quick look."

"I want to say hi to him. Can I? Is there any place we could go and call him in to shore?"

Tristan contemplates my question for a moment. "I think I might know a place."

Taking our last few bites of food, we head to a secluded area just north of town. Wading through the surf with Tristan by my side, I wait for Drake to present himself. It isn't long before I am rewarded by a grandiose flip in the air. "Drake," I laugh, calling out to him. He proceeds to perform two more airborne stunts before making his approach. I have waded in as far as my skirt will allow me to go, and now he is swimming through the shallow water, full speed ahead, traveling in my direction. But just as he reaches me, he does a turnabout and swims away. This action is repeated two more times before he eventually stops an arm's length away from where I am standing. Attentively, I reach my hand out and begin petting the smooth surface of his skin.

I look over at Tristan, and he is smiling his approval at our friendship. I want to stop time. Stay on the beach forever, interacting with my aquatic buddy and the sexiest boyfriend anyone could ever have. Too soon though, it's time for me to head back to the Center for Marine Studies and go back to work. Contemplating the inevitable of spending the next few hours in a swivel chair, I wonder how much more information could be gleaned about endangered sea creatures just by talking to Tristan instead of spending hours on a computer, sitting at a desk. But then people would want to know the source of my information, and I would run into problems, so I click my high heels across the parking lot, migrating toward the tall brick building that houses my job, preparing instead to spend an afternoon of research inside the confines of four walls.

We are standing in the shadow of the four-story structure, hidden from the view of my coworkers by a shade tree, as Tristan leans in to offer me his good-bye. It's just a soft sweep of his lips across mine. Not the long, lingering kiss that I have been missing from him ever since that unsightly episode on the beach that day. Disappointment floods through me. It takes all the control I possess not to wind my fingers through his hair, pulling him close, pressing my body into him while I show him how much I love him by kissing him long and hard with my mouth.

Instead I let out a quiet sigh, holding contact with his green eyes for a prolonged moment before whispering a soft good-bye. And for a split second something passes over his features that makes me think he is going to take a step in my direction and pull me to him, kissing my lips uncontrollably. But then he shakes his head as if to clear his thoughts and the moment is gone, and I turn and walk into the building.

When I arrive back at home that afternoon, Mr. Horton is there fiddling around with a downspout on the side of the cabin. He is so engrossed in his work that he doesn't hear me approach. Clearing my throat, I give him a heads-up that I'm there, so I won't startle him when I speak. "Hello, Mr. Horton."

It takes some time for him to straighten to an upright position, and when he finally turns to face me, I am caught off guard by the pale, almost-grayish coloring of his skin. "Well hello there, Bethany. I was hoping I might run into you while I was at the cabin. Just doing a little inspection of the eaves troughs. Sometimes we've had some trouble with them in the past, getting clogged with leaves and such."

I eye the frailty of his condition and experience a sudden impulse to run in his direction, take him by the arm, and lead him to a chair where he can sit and rest. I choose my words carefully in order to conceal my thoughts. "Oh, Mr. Horton, you shouldn't have to do that. Tristan's been helping me with those types of things around here. Everything is working just fine."

"That boy is a good helper for you, huh? Well, that's good for an old man to hear. Guess I raised him right after all." *Tristan, his surrogate son.* My heart is immediately warmed.

I smile, a beaming grin, trying to hide the sadness that wants to claim me as I contemplate the reasons for his obviously poor state of health. "It's good to see you though, so I'm glad you stopped by."

In spite of the dull coloring of his countenance, his brown eyes still twinkle with life. "Well, what's a worn-out geezer like me to do, sit at home and stare at the moon? I got things that need checking on. In the morning when I wake up, I think to myself, I got things that need checking on today, so I crawl out of bed and go about my business, making sure that everything is still doing okay."

He needs a purpose for life. I eye his weakened condition and bite my tongue. It doesn't matter whether I think he would be better off relaxing in the comfort of his bed. This is what is giving him a reason to live. "Well, how do things look so far?"

"So far not bad, but the cabin is not the only thing that I came to check on today. Today I came to check on you."

"Me?"

"Yes, you. Let's see…you're back in town, reunited with your young beau, Tristan. Are you finding the happiness you always thought you'd have with him? Are your dreams finally coming true?"

Contemplating Mr. Horton's question, I become overwhelmed with a premonition—is he is trying to get his affairs in order? *No!* I take a sweep of his ailing exterior and fight back a rush of tears.

But if this *is* true, if he is feeling a need to know that the people he cares about are settled and happy, then there is only one answer I can leave him with. I swallow down the lump that is forming in my throat.

"Yes."

His eyes smile before his lips do. "Good…well, I'm glad to hear that. I always knew it would happen. Always hoped it would happen. You two youngsters were meant to be together."

I nod my head, hoping that what I've just admitted is accurate—hoping that what Mr. Horton is saying is accurate. Right now, things between Tristan and I are the best they've ever been. But the details surrounding our relationship are complicated. There are so many obstacles that we still need to overcome in order for us to have a real happy ever after. *But that's not the point at the moment.* Unable to stand the tenor of this conversation any longer, I have to know the true catalyst for all the questioning.

"Mr. Horton, how are *you* feeling?"

"Me? I'm doing all right." His chuckle is nonchalant, edged with nervousness.

I narrow my eyes, wondering if I should just let it go. But I can't. Proceeding ahead, I measure my words cautiously. "Since I've come back in town, I've noticed that you've lost weight and your coloring is pale. I'm concerned for your health."

"You know, as you get older you get slower. It's part of the circle of life."

"But you're not *that* old, Mr. Horton. Have you been to a doctor?"

"Doctor? Bah! I've lived my life so far without any mad scientists poking and prodding at my body. Haven't taken any chemical substances. And I've done just fine…I'm not about to start now." I nod my head as I look away. I can tell my words are falling on deaf ears. "Besides, I sure can tell you've been hanging out with that boy Tristan a lot. You are starting to sound just like him."

I know better than to press any further. But as I'm standing in the store parking lot loading bags of groceries into my jeep later that evening, I can't seem to wipe away the image of Mr. Horton's deteriorating stature from my mind. Feeling melancholy, I decide to take a drive to Tristan's beach—just the thought of his arms around me begins to soothe my temperament. Applying a little more force to the gas pedal, the motor accelerates as I head toward the shoreline.

Parking my jeep in a little side gravel drive, I begin walking down the winding path that leads to his beach. My heart quickens in expectancy of seeing him—I really hope that he is there. I think back to lunchtime earlier that day, and how I wasn't ready for our date to end, and about our kiss good-bye and how I wanted it to linger. My face heats up as I imagine picking up where we left off. And then I think about Mr. Horton once again, picturing his waning essence of life, and suddenly I am desperate to feel Tristan's body pressed up against mine in validation that he is real and not fading too. The sand shifts below the soles of my feet as I near the bend in the coastline that leads to his protected alcove. Pausing for a brief second, I suck in a long, anticipatory breath of ocean air as I prepare to round the corner, hoping.

And he is there!

But my heart plummets, because he is not alone.

Kneeling side by side only inches from the rising tide, lost in a recognizably intimate conversation, are Tristan and Rye. I stop dead in my tracks. Then take a step back. My heart hammers against my chest wall. Nausea begins welling up from the pit of my stomach, and I have to resist the urge to puke all over the dune grass, drawing unwanted attention to myself. Sliding behind a clump of foliage so that I am sheltered from their sight, I watch as they speak to each other in serious, hushed tones, occasionally glancing up at one another, holding prolonged gazes.

Closing my eyes tightly together, I breathe a desperate prayer that the whole scene will just disappear. But when I reopen my lids, Rye is still there staring longingly into Tristan's face, looking hauntingly beautiful. The way Tristan leans toward her, compassion written so overtly across his features, makes me want to sob uncontrollably. *Oh God, no! He has to think she is so appealing!* The vulnerability of her body language, the imploring look in her round, gray eyes, the frailty of her petite frame— it's all there slapping me across the face with each breath of air that reaches my lungs—her need for him is so explicit. My body begins to tremble as I experience an overwhelming sensation that I'm intruding on an engaged couple's private moment. Bile burns my throat and tears sting my eyes as I edge myself quietly away from the scene, suddenly frantic to get away.

Retreating from view, my attention is drawn to the ocean by a splash in the water. Freezing in place, I watch as Drake bobs his little gray head above the waves, feet from where Tristan and Rye sit, knees nestled into the sand. They notice him too. Easing out of their sedentary positions, they begin heading in his direction. Now Rye's countenance is alight with fresh laughter as she reaches out to pet Drake's head. Tristan stands close by, smiling, as he observes their interaction. My heart constricts with the realization that Drake, who I'd just started winning over, is obviously taken with Rye too.

I can't watch anymore!

Without making a sound, I edge the rest of the way down the sandy, winding path the way I came, until I'm completely sure that I am out of Rye and Tristan and Drake's sight. From there, I run with reckless abandon the rest of the way to my black jeep, throwing myself into the front seat and resting my forehead against the steering column while I cry like a baby.

Chapter Thirteen

When my tears have dried to an occasional, hiccupping sob, I sit staring out the front windshield of my car into green, leafy trees, scattered clumps of wildflowers, and undomesticated shrubbery. But I see nothing. The place where I'd parked my jeep on my way to find Tristan is shrouded in wildlife, so I am well hidden for the time being, allowing myself the interval I need to grieve over what I've just seen.

But what *have* I just seen?

Nothing really! *Right?* I mean there had been no intimate contact. *Right?* And besides, it was only very recently Tristan had held me in his arms, *and not Rye*, as he nursed me back to good health while my body, in a state of a feverish sweat, rid itself of the toxins from the drugs I had taken. He was with *me* that night telling *me* he loved me, *not Rye*. He had taken me home and left Rye abandoned on the beach to spend her sleeping hours in forlorn seclusion. Obviously, he loves me and not her!

So then why do I feel so bad?

Why had the air between them looked like it was filled with intimacy? Why do I feel like I've just encountered a pair of star-crossed lovers spending the evening lounging on the beach? I close my eyes tightly trying to erase the image of what I'd just seen. Nausea tries to claim me once more, and I take a deep breath to stave it away. Not ready to go back to the cabin, I drive into town. Maneuvering my car into a two-hour parking space, I perch on a bench that overlooks the municipal boat docks. I am sitting, idly watching various shapes and sizes of boats as they sit rocking back and forth in the gentle sway of the waves, when I feel a burst of air beside me from someone plopping down on the seat inches from where I am.

"What is so interesting out there?" The voice is gravelly. And I smile in spite of my dismal mood.

"Nothing really, I—"

"Well, there must be *something*. You've been staring at the same spot for a quite some time now. I've been watching you on my way over from the marina. I figured I better come over and find out what it is. If it is that interesting, I want to see it too."

A light chuckle escapes my throat. "I guess I was lost in thought."

"Well, don't hold out on me…was it a good thought or a bad one?" Ethan's eyes are crinkled at the edges, playful.

I crinkle my nose. "You don't want to know."

"Awww…no! Are you having trouble with our ex-employee again?"

"Kind of." There is a sheepish edge to my voice. Ethan is watching my face trying to see into my thoughts, sitting so close by. My heart gives a momentary flutter, and I look away.

"Do you like baseball?" *What?*

"I don't exactly dislike it. I wouldn't really call myself a big fan either."

"I was on my way to Waves to watch the Red Sox play. Why don't you come too? I think you could use a distraction tonight."

Waves is a pub down the coast from Watch Hill that caters to surfers and other summertime sport enthusiasts. Ornamented in vibrant colors and coastline paraphernalia, it offers an outdoor, beachy feel, making it a second home to many of the locals. And even though it isn't an intentional part of the décor, sand somehow always seems to find its way onto the rustic wooden flooring, making the ambience complete. We enter the building and take a corner seat with a perfect view of a large screen TV. Ethan does his best to draw me into the game, and after a couple of drinks, I am right there with him, cheering on the Red Sox, vocalizing my disenchantments with unfair calls made by the umpires and occasional bonehead mistakes made by the players. A commercial comes on, and he looks at me from across the table. He exudes sensuality and worldliness and self-assuredness all in one. I can feel the movement of my Adam's apple as I swallow, my gaze riveted by his lazy smile. *How does Lucy handle someone like him?*

"So, do you want to tell me about it?"

I shake my head and roll my eyes. "It's the same old song and dance, really. I'm sure everyone is getting sick of hearing about it. Probably as sick as I am of dealing with it." Ethan keeps watching me, letting me talk. Finally I pause. "Listen to me. Shouldn't it be obvious that I need to quit this? It's just a repeat of more of the same."

At this, Ethan grins at me while his eyes shimmer and turn up in the corners in that way that they do. "Sounds like you are quite capable of giving yourself the advice that you need. I don't really think that you need to hear what I have to say. But I'm glad you came with me tonight to watch the game."

I can't help it, I smile back. I'm glad I came too. He is definitely the distraction I needed. "How's my good friend Lucy doing? Have you heard from her lately?"

He contemplates my words for a moment. "Lucy...yeah Lucy, she's good. I like that girl. I talk to her a lot. She needs to come for a visit soon!"

"I'd like that too. Invite her, maybe she'll come."

"I'm going to take your advice on that...soon. So you think she'd come to town if I'd ask her, huh? What makes you think that? I'm just not sure about her. There is something about her that I can't read." *Aha, that's how Lucy is dealing with someone so unnerving like Ethan. He can't read her. She keeps him guessing.* I eye Ethan's sexy, confident grin and decide I better go along with Lucy's plan.

"Actually I'm not 100 percent sure at all, but it's worth a try, right? And besides, I'd like to see her too." The flicker of disappointment in Ethan's brown eyes is almost undetectable. He'd been hoping for more, and I hadn't delivered. *Lucy could thank me later.*

By the time our conversation about our dating life fades, the game is back on in full swing. Bottom of the fifth. Red Sox, four. The Tigers, six. The Red Sox are up to bat. Two outs. Two strikes. One man on base. Ball three. Will there be a walk with no scoring? Hopefully not an out, sending the Tigers to the dugout once again. Ethan glances over at me, and I wave crossed fingers at him. He nods his head, offering an anticipatory grin. The bat is swung.

And the ball flies. Far into the outfield, over extended mitts, right into the grandstands. The crowd erupts into roaring applause, two players round the bases, and the score is tied. Now I'm into the game. Jumping out of my seat, cheering, I reach my hand up to give Ethan a high five, but he grabs me instead, pulling me into his arms for a congratulatory hug.

I am laughing as he releases me, and he laughs too. Pretty much everyone at Waves is talking animatedly around me, smiling, enjoying the transient victory for the Red Sox. Ethan reaches for his beverage and holds it up for a *cheers* moment. I reach for my own drink and clink it against his glass before taking a sip. He takes a drink too, keeping his eyes peeled to my face.

"You like baseball now, don't you, Bethany?" His gravelly voice is shouting over the din in the room.

I am all smiles. "You are right, I do!"

"Another drink for both of us." He scans the perimeter of the room looking for someone to serve us. I echo his motion in effort to assist in finding our waiter, but I don't look for very long. The minute I turn my head, I freeze in place, eyes riveted to the front entrance of the building. Suddenly I can't breathe. I want to look away, but I can't. The eyes that flash green at me are filled with confusion, possessiveness, and anger all at one time. And he looks so gorgeous.

Tristan! And he is so gorgeous! My heart beats double-time in my chest.

Oh God, I love him!

Closing my eyes to rid the sight of his beauty, I conjure the image of him and Rye on the beach instead.

Oh God, I hate him!

Seconds tick away, but they feel like minutes as we remain frozen with our eyes locked onto one other. Finally I look away. But I don't need a clear line of vision to feel him advancing toward me as if in slow motion from across the room. My hands reach for my drink, and I begin nervously playing with the wet accumulation on the outside of the glass, while staring at the liquid on the inside. Ethan notices him too, but when he speaks, his voice does not hold any of the warmth that I've come to know.

"Tristan…what brings you here tonight?"

"Possibly the same thing that has brought you here."

"The game then?" I look up from my glass in time to see Tristan's jaw harden. "Sit down and join us." Ethan's gravelly voice has warmed a touch, but it's difficult to tell if he's being genuine.

Tristan ignores him. "Are you ready to leave?" His words sound forced as if they are coming through gritted teeth. *Who, me?* I look up from my drink. *So I take it you're done with Rye for the evening? Time for Bethany, now?* He looks pissed, but there is something else glinting in his eye that makes my heart pound. *God help me, because I just want to stand up and shout yes…yes, I'll go with you right now.*

I set my jaw and look away. That one gesture is all the encouragement Ethan needs. "Looks like she is enjoying the game. Bethany, *are* you enjoying the game?"

I swallow and nod. My voice comes out cracked on my first attempt, so I try again. "I am."

"Like I said before, join us."

Tristan hesitates before eventually taking a seat kitty-corner from me. Close enough that his knee presses into my leg, burning into my thigh. I let go of my glass and press my hands tightly together. *Oh no, he will not distract me with that! User!* Ethan immediately relaxes as if there is no tension circling around our table. "Exciting game, huh? Let's see if the old Red Sox can pull ahead here."

Tristan glances up at the screen briefly before resting his eyes on me. "Sure." I force my gaze on the game.

"Let's see if he will get a hit here." Ethan's fervor helps me to stay focused, ignoring the unsettling pull I am feeling beside me. It would be so easy to give in, allowing myself to be swallowed up by Tristan's stare, falling into his arms, begging him to tell me everything is going to be okay. *But everything is not okay!* What I saw earlier on the beach tonight tells me that everything is definitely *not* okay! I'd be stupid to sweep it all under the rug and pretend that Tristan and I are exclusive.

Forcing a smile, I lift crossed fingers into the air. Ethan looks over and smiles a wickedly sexy smile. Tristan glares. One ball. One strike. And then finally—a hit. The ball soars above the infielders, just above the head of an outfielder, grazing his overextended mitt before landing in the stands. Once again the crowd on the T.V. erupts. Almost immediately, the assembly inside of Waves echoes their sentiments. Without a second thought, I am right in with the group. "Yes!"

Ethan lifts his drink into the air, and I reach for my own to clink it against his. Ethan looks over at Tristan. "Hey, you need a drink. What are you having?"

"I'm not. We're leaving."

"It looks like she is staying, dude." Ethan flags down a waiter. "He'll have what I'm having." Tristan's eyes are like steel as he looks over at me. Ignoring him, I motion toward the screen.

"Too bad the bases weren't loaded for that hit."

"For sure." Someone from a table away agrees with my comment. I turn, half surprised, not realizing my voice had carried. Soon the waiter brings Tristan's beverage. He doesn't touch it. I continue to watch the game with coerced enthusiasm, careful to avoid eye contact. After having a couple of drinks and many *cheers,* I feel the need to use the restroom.

Taking my time, I use purposefully unhurried movements, eyeing myself in the mirror afterward, fixing my hair, making small talk with others at the sink. Butterflies swarm my stomach. Somehow I have an uncanny feeling that when I leave the safety of the Ladies' room, I am no longer going to be *safe.* Taking a deep breath, I open the door slowly and step into the corridor.

And I am not wrong.

Standing in the dimly lit hallway, adjacent from the restroom entrance, arms crossed, leaning against the wall, is Tristan. I freeze in place, my heart pounding. Our eyes lock. Even in the darkness of the space, I can feel the intensity of his gaze as if it is piercing straight through my soul. Licking my lips, I make an effort to rid my mouth of the sudden dryness that finds it. I am overcome with a sense of helplessness. "Are you ready to go *now?*" His voice is so deep, calculated. It's hardly a question.

No! No, I am not going with you. I'm going to stay here and finish watching the game with Ethan. I swallow. "Okay."

His expression softens minutely as he watches my face. A flash of confusion crosses over his features, and he shakes his head as if to clear it. "I'll meet you back at the cabin."

And just like that he is gone, and I skulk back into the neon-lit room to tell Ethan good-bye. "You sure you know what you are doing? You don't have to go," he tells me. But I shake my head because I know that deep down inside this is something I need to do. I need to air my feelings about what I'd seen on the beach earlier in the evening. Let Tristan say what he has to say and then make a decision.

When I arrive at the cabin, Tristan is not there. I pause for a minute to think. I know I heard him right; he was pretty adamant about us leaving. And I know it was the cabin he told me to meet him at. He wasn't just trying to get me away from Ethan, was he? My eyes stray toward the water, and I begin heading in that direction. Soon I reach the beachfront. The moon shines down brightly, glistening over tranquil waves as they roll to shore. My heart stutters in my chest. Because he's there. Standing at the ocean's edge, turned partially away from me, hands shoved in the front pockets of his jeans, staring at a pale light that is reflected over the night tide. From the corner of his eye he sees my approach. When he turns I am able to see every perfect angle and line of his face. I suck in a breath. He looks pissed.

Bringing my steps to a halt, I fold my arms across my chest. *I'm pissed too!* Silence surrounds us. He stares hard at me, apparently waiting for me to talk. Well, I can wait too! *Longer!*

"Looks like you were having fun with Ethan tonight," he finally says.

"Yeah, I guess it wasn't such a bad time, actually, considering the way I started out the beginning of the evening."

He narrows his eyes as he watches my face. "Really? And how was that?"

"Having to witness you and Rye together, having a nice, cozy time on your beach." I pause, my voice becoming a painful whisper. "On *our* beach." In some ways that is what was hurting the most, the idea that he was having an intimate time with Rye at a place that I had assumed was ours exclusively. A place where we had shared many special moments.

Tristan's eyes widen ever so slightly. "You saw us then?"

Pressing my lips tightly together, I look away. "Yep."

Tristan sighs, and then there is only the sound of the rolling ride. Over and over again it pushes onto the sandy shoreline in a peaceful, lulling motion. But my body is fighting against it, refusing to be pacified. How can I be drawn into the ocean's serenity when my heart is hammering in my chest along with every nerve ending that is screaming out, waiting for Tristan to give me an explanation that I don't want to hear?

"I have to tread very softly when it comes to Rye, Bethany." When he first starts talking, his voice is quiet, and I have to strain my ear to catch everything. Then he clears his throat, and it becomes a little easier. "Every conversation I have with her, I am telling her that there is no me and her. But she is very sensitive, and I know she is hurting, so I have to be careful to get it across to her in just the right way. I want to play my cards just right so I can be with you. Everything I do is about playing my cards just right so I can be with you." He stops talking, and I look up from where my eyes had been focused in the sand. His gaze meets mine. "I only want to be with you." My mind is still processing everything, and so I don't say a word. Eventually, Tristan begins talking again. "*And...* in case anyone hasn't figured it out yet, you are mine so Ethan Vaughn can—"

"Can what? Ethan is completely taken with Lucy. He was just being a friend. And I was hurting so I needed a friend right then after what I'd seen. You know, Tristan, Rye might be fragile, but I have feelings too!"

Tristan groans and closes his eyes for a moment. "I'm sorry, Bethany. Everything I do, I always have you in mind. My whole goal is never to hurt you, and yet somehow it keeps happening. I just...I don't want to hurt you. I never want to hurt you." His eyes become soft as he watches my face, waiting for something from me—some type of reaction. I stand shivering, rubbing crossed arms with my hands. I want everything that he is saying to be true—want it so desperately I can taste it. But it is hard for me to erase the hurt so quickly. Slowly, very slowly, he begins edging toward me, taking steps through the sand, closing the space between us. His green eyes stay carefully glued to my face as he advances. It is as if he is approaching a frightened puppy and knows that if he makes the wrong move, the creature will bolt.

When he reaches where I am standing, he stops and stares right at me, narrowing his eyes in question. *Are we okay? Does he have permission to touch me?* I swallow hard. *I'm just...I'm just not sure.* He reaches his hand out tentatively, eventually finding a stray strand of my hair. Very gently he tucks it behind my ear. Everything his fingers touch leaves a trail of fire behind. It takes every ounce of my being to control my breathing, not giving my vulnerability away. *I'm just not...just not...* With a slow, deliberate motion his hands reach for both sides of my head, cupping my face. His lips are only inches away. He licks them and I begin to tremble, betraying everything I've been working so hard to hide. Now he is leaning in and I hold my breath, waiting. Involuntarily I feel my mouth part. But instead of pressing his lips full on mine, he catches only the very corner of them. Next he lightly grazes my cheekbones and then the tip of my nose. Shuddering, I close my eyes, and then his mouth is on my eyelids.

When I open them again, he has taken a step back from me and is looking intently at my face. "I love you," he mouths to me. Taking me in his arms, he pulls me to his chest and begins stroking my hair over and over again reverently, kissing the top of my head.

Sighing, I whisper into his chest. "I love you too." *God help me, but I love you too. So much!*

We stay locked in each other's arms for a very long time, and eventually I shift my position, leaning my head back, looking up to the sky. The heavens are filled with shimmering lights, shining their approval on the love that we share. Tristan tightens his arm around me. "It's a beautiful night...do you want to spend it with me? I mean the whole thing...sleep out here under the stars. We could get a blanket."

I freeze in place. My heart thuds in my chest. "Do you mean—?"

His voice is gentle. "No, I don't mean that...not yet. But someday...we *will*."

I exhale. *Spend the whole night with him!* We've never done that before. Well, there was that one night when he stayed with me while I came down from the drugs that I took, but this is different. This is a real step for us. I can't think of anywhere else I'd rather be.

We get linen from the cabin and steal back onto the beach, situating ourselves in a bed of sand. Wrapped tightly in each other's arms, we lay together, allowing a maritime breeze to float across our skin. And I want to pinch myself. Am I really lying here with Tristan getting ready to spend the entirety of the night with my body pressed up against his? The earlier images of him and Rye have now faded from my mind. I have decided to give him the benefit of the doubt where she is concerned. I have to trust that he will know how to handle her. I only hope that he now understands that I have feelings and needs too.

The waves of the ocean gently graze the sandy shore that we occupy, singing us a bedtime lullaby. I am torn between the comfort of sleep and the continual reminder that the guy that I am so attracted to is lying close to me and with just the right touch, just the right kiss, things could happen between us—intimate things that make my mind go crazy with just the thought. I let out a long, slow breath.

And he squeezes my shoulder to let me know *what?* *Is he having the same thoughts as me?* "*Someday* seems like a long time away." His words fade into the rolling surf, and I have to strain my ear to listen to their echo as I replay them over and over again in my mind. *He is!*—having the same thoughts as me!

Eventually I allow myself to relax enough to drift into sleep. Upon waking the next morning, I squint my eyes, sheltering them with an upraised hand against the glare of the rising sun. Disorientation overwhelms me, and it takes me a moment to focus on where I am. Then realization hits me full force, and my heart accelerates into overdrive. Startled, I glance at the pillow beside me. And he's still there! *Oh my word!* *It's morning on the beach, and I just spent the entire night with Tristan, and he's right here beside me looking all sleepy and so freakin' hot!*

He looks over at me and offers a lazy grin. "Hey, baby."

"Hey," I whisper back, my voiced cracked, a blush spreading across my cheekbones.

On the inside I am screaming with delight because I am the happiest girl in the world!

Chapter Fourteen

The following Saturday a knock at my cabin door rouses me from my lounging position on the couch. It had been a long, hard week at work. Besides the current project I am working on, my boss, Jada, had thrown some emergency ventures on my desk, requiring me to burn the candle at both ends. The local library in Westerly is having a weekly themed summer, the topic on two of those weeks being ocean friendliness. At the last minute they requested that we come up with some workshops that would not only reach out to the children attending, but the accompanying parents as well. It was hard interrupting my thoughts on my current endeavor, putting it on the back burner, but after transitioning my focus and putting in lots of extra hours, the assignment was finally completed in the time allotted. And after thumbing through the finished product, I am actually quite surprised and pleased to say I work well under the gun.

But now I am exhausted, and I don't feel like moving a muscle. Getting up anyway, I pad slowly across the worn, creaking planks of wood that make up the cabin floor. Turning the lock, I open the door. And am well-rewarded for my effort. Standing on my steps, the sun providing a golden halo for the disheveled tendrils of his hair, is Tristan, smiling like a schoolboy. His green eyes dance mischievously, drawing me in, snapping me from my somnolent state. Biting his lip, he studies my face carefully, as if I should be able to guess what his animation is all about. I cock my head in question. It is obvious something is up.

"Good morning, sexy. I didn't wake you, did I?"

"Not really, I'm just kind of slow moving today." His eyes give me a once-over, and suddenly I am mindful of my appearance.

Running my fingers through my hair, I attempt to tame it into place uselessly. His lips form into a lighthearted smirk as he watches my unsuccessful endeavor.

"Just-waking-up hair suits you, Bethany. Don't try to fix it on my account." *Oh my word!* I blush and look away. "I heard you had a rough week at work. I'll bet you are tired."

My head snaps up. "How do you know about that?"

"I have my ways. Trust me when I say, when it has anything to do with the ocean, I know all about it. I am continually finding out what is going on to either help or hinder marine life in the area."

"Really! Does that mean you spy on me at work?" I feign indignation.

"Well, not on you directly, so you can rest easy." His charming grin makes my heart increase in tempo. "But I do make a point of finding out what your company is up to and what more could be done. I *am* a consultant after all."

"And a darn good representative for your people!"

His face become contemplative, his voice soft with a serious edge. "I hope so." For a moment or two everything is quiet, and then his eyes light up again. "Come outside. I want to show you something!"

"Okay. I just need a minute." Retreating back into my cabin, I head to my bathroom for a hair tie, pulling my unkempt strands into a ponytail. When I walk back out into the main room, Tristan is there leaning against the kitchen counter, waiting. For just a second a look passes through his eyes that makes me freeze and catch my breath, but then he blinks, and the moment is gone. He holds out a hand and smiles.

"Ready?"

I put my hand in his. *What is going on?* He leads me down to the shore in front of my house. The sun is making its ascent, filling the blue sky with radiance. The water is sparkling crystal, lapping playfully toward the shore. We've just set foot in the sand when I stop in my tracks.

There wedged onto the beach, gleaming in the light of day, is *Blue*. I look from the shiny wooden boat to Tristan's face. He is beaming. "What? How? I thought you sold her."

His lips form into a momentary pout. "I did…and was sorry the very minute she left my sight." I swallow as his eyes lock onto mine. Why do I get the feeling that he is referring to something more than just the boat? His gaze leaves mine and rests on *Blue*. "I've been watching the boating circulars and websites ever since, hoping it would go back up for sale. Finally, after all these years, I found it again. I bought it and here it is. I think it was meant to be…don't you?"

By now I'm sure there is double meaning to his words, but either way the answer is *yes*. I smile. "Definitely!"

"I'm glad you agree. Sooo…now that I have it back in my possession, there is something else I want to do with it. There is someone I want to give it to." *Huh?* My mind begins spinning with all the possibilities of who he could be referring to. No one seems worthy. *Why would he do this? Could it be Mr. Horton? Of course!* Of course, it is Mr. Horton.

His deep voice interrupts my deliberations. "Will you accept *Blue* as a gift from me, Bethany?" *What?* I furrow my brow contemplating his words.

"Me? What—I—" My syllables are a mixed-up jumble, mirroring my thoughts.

"I've spent four years wishing I could do this very thing. Please accept this gift from me. You would make me very happy if you did." A slight grin is captured on his face, but his eyes are dead serious.

"Okay…wow! I mean, are you sure? You love that boat." I let out a slow expulsion of air.

"Very sure. And I *do* love the boat!" Once again I get the impression that he is not just referring to *Blue*. My heart pulsates in my chest. Slowly I begin walking toward the boat as it sits on the shorefront gleaming proudly, looking just as it had four years ago. Running my hand over the glossy mahogany wood of its bow, I realize that it hasn't changed a bit. It is as if the temporary owner had kept the boat locked in a glass showcase for every second of the time lapse, taking it out only to tune and polish it. I eye the pristine crème leather interior.

"When can we go for a ride?"

"Today of course, now if you want to."

"I want to. Just let me change." My countenance is alight like a kid on Christmas morning. Tristan points to the far section of the beach, and for the first time my attention is drawn to a pile of lumber neatly arranged and stacked high.

"I took the liberty of getting material to build you a dock. You are going to need somewhere to keep her properly housed. So after the boat ride I can work on it."

I shake my head. *Wow!* "Yeah…sure. That will be great… thank you." At a fast pace I begin counting in my mind just how many hours will it take for a dock to be built? Surely many! *Tristan spending the whole day at my house working on this construction project*—this day just keeps looking better and better.

We are just pulling *Blue* away from the shore when I notice we have a visitor—a little, shiny gray head dipping in and out of the wake of the boat. "Hello, Drake," I call out. The greeting is returned by a generous flip into the air.

"I think he's missed you. Look at him showing off."

I smile at Tristan and then glance back to the water, watching our dolphin friend's repertoire of antics. For a brief moment my mind flashes to another shoreline, where I'd last seen Drake interacting with Rye. He seemed to enjoy her company too. A stab of jealousy pierces through my veins. Like an eight-year-old child, I want him to like me more. Unwittingly my gaze travels to Tristan's perfectly chiseled profile as he sits inches away from me driving the boat; an even greater stab of jealousy pierces through me as I recall him interacting with Rye on that same beach. And like a twenty-one-year-old that is rekindling romance with the love of her life, I want him to love me more. Blinking hard, I clear my mind of these unwanted thoughts.

It is a beautiful day, and I am riding in a gorgeous boat with a heartthrob at my side, and as a bonus, a nifty little sea creature is keeping tempo with the waves fashioned from our increasing speed. A spray of liquid reaches into the air as the bow of the boat plunges through the exterior shell of the deep, blue depths, parting the water neatly as it goes. The wind whips through our hair as we glide across the surface of the ocean, soaring full speed ahead.

Suddenly the boat slows. Tristan looks over at me. "Your turn to drive." *Drive the boat?* Visions of a reckless storm filled with biting raindrops and damaging waves with me at the wheel permeate my mind. *Four years ago—on my unsuccessful search for Tristan.* Lacing my fingers tightly together, I try to stop them from trembling. Tristan looks carefully at my face seeming to get it. My angst. Reaching out a hand, he covers mine with his. "Not ready?" I shake my head.

"Not yet."

A pained look passes through his eyes as he watches my face, and I can tell he is blaming himself for my hesitancy. Reaching out cautiously, he gently runs a thumb along my cheekbone. "No rush." I nod in answer, then he pulls me to his side while proceeding to drive the boat with a protective arm around my shoulder.

After the ride, I busy myself in the cabin cleaning, doing laundry, and baking zucchini bread while Tristan works on the dock he is building for *Blue*. Now and then I wind my way down to the shore, sneaking a peek at Tristan while he is working, never disappointed by what I see. And he always catches me watching, giving me a look that makes my heart race before setting his tools down and coming over to talk for a few minutes. Twice I bring him a tall, cold drink and once a warm piece of zucchini bread taken fresh from the oven. This results in several *looks*. "I could get used to this," he tells me, swallowing down the last bite.

So could I! I think to myself. *I could get used to all of this!* I smile in response to his comment. "I'm glad you like it."

Kate texts me midmorning; she wants to come over for a visit along with Hannah. When her car pulls into my drive, I go outside to greet her. "Could you be any farther out in the sticks?" she calls out while stepping from her vehicle.

I laugh. "This is pretty remote out here, isn't it?" *But it is Tristan's cabin, and I love it!* We hug and she reaches into the backseat to pull out the miniature version of herself. Large, guarded, eyes look up at me as I watch her undo the straps. A head full of wispy, brown curls, staring, ready at any moment to bury into her mom's shoulder. But in spite of the bashfulness evident in her demeanor, she surveys my face, intrigued for the moment by what she sees. "Hello, sweet Hannah," I coo.

At my words, the wispy curls quickly turn away. "Aw, don't be so shy, Hannah. This is Miss Bethany," Kate chastises her lightly. "You remember her? She came to visit us before." Two brown eyes pop out at me once again, and I reward her with a playful smile.

After showing Kate around the perimeter of the cabin, pointing out the handful of flowering pots that I'd been nurturing, I lead her and Hannah inside. Kate's eyes peruse the interior. "Not bad. It has a kind of storybook charm."

I nod my head and smile like a proud mom. "I think so too." We settle down in the living area, sitting feet away from each other on the sofa, while Hannah hangs onto her mom's legs, eyes round, examining the new surroundings. As we sit talking, reminiscing about old times, unveiling the new, Kate begins to slowly transform into the girl that I used to know. The bottled-up energy that was once her signature trademark emerges, and soon she is tapping her foot with nervous energy, bouncing in place as we lounge on the couch. Hannah breaks free from her self-imposed tether and proceeds to cautiously explore all that is around her. Now Kate jumps up from her seated position, continually redirecting Hannah from potential mishaps. On one near miss, an idea comes to me. "Let's take Hannah down by the water. Tristan is here putting in a dock."

Kate's eyes go wide. "Tristan, eh?" she says. "Are you still hanging out with that guy?"

My voice is soft. "Yeah...yep."

"Ouch...well, clearly you enjoy pain. Wasn't one summer's worth of misery enough for you? Geez, Bethany, we couldn't even get you out of bed."

Reactively, I flinch. "Oh my word, that *was* awful. What am I even thinking?" *That I am completely and utterly in love with him, and I am not able to break free. Crap!* "I do believe I need an intervention."

"Oh, I can definitely arrange that. Where is he?"

"No...no, don't do that." I chuckle. "I'll figure it out. I'm older now, wiser. I won't let it get that bad." *Right?* "Anyway, let's go down there, let Hannah play in the water, and say hi." Pausing, I narrow my eyes at Kate. "But be nice...promise?"

Kate lets out an exaggerated sigh. "Oh, all right, I promise. Let's go see him. Is he still Mr. Hottie Pants?"

"Unfortunately, yes." *Fortunately and unfortunately!*

When our trio of girls reaches the water's edge, Tristan is hard at work. Shirtless, sweat pours off his skin while the muscles of his back and arms stretch and flex with each movement. Kate looks over at me and rolls her eyes. *Yeah, still hot! Way too hot!* I swallow, trying to stifle a grin. "Hey, Tristan, we have company."

Tristan stops his hammering, turns, and looks up at us while running a hand through his tousled hair. It takes him a second to register who it is that I've brought with me down to the shore. His eyes shift to take in the baby in Kate's arms. "You remember Kate Owen, don't you?"

"Bethany, have you ever met Tristan Alexander?"

In an instant I am transported back to a beach from the past where Kate is the one doing the introductions. My heart twists in my chest with the memory. So much has happened since that moment in time. I shake my head to clear my thoughts.

Tristan wipes a hand on his shorts and reaches out for Kate's. "Hi, Kate." His voice is deep and strong. "And this is?"

Kate's face lights up. "This is Hannah. She's mine."

Tristan chuckles. "Well, I couldn't tell by looking at her. Hi, Hannah." Hannah immediately buries her face. Kate glances over at me, and I can read her thoughts. *Smart girl, Hannah, hide from boys like him!* Suddenly I feel the need to say something before Kate does.

"So your dock…it is looking great! You've really come a long way."

Tristan steps back to eye his work proudly. "Yeah, I think I'm getting somewhere." Hannah wiggles in Kate's arms, eyeing the ocean's rippling surf. Removing Hannah's sandals, Kate sets her on the ground. For a moment Hannah stands mesmerized by the feel of the sand between her toes. Then she begins padding her chubby little legs towards the water. Kate stays right at her side with me following close behind. Tristan folds his arms across his chest, watching with a hint of interest flashing in his green eyes. For many minutes Hannah plays tag with the rhythmic pattern of the waves that dart across the shoreline, disturbing the formation of the sand with each sweep. Eventually she tires of this game and turns back in the direction of Tristan, somehow realizing that he is the stranger in our group of girls. Her eyes, large pools of brown, watch him cautiously as he sits resting on the partially constructed dock.

He smiles at her. "What is it, Hannah? I think she likes me."

"Oh, I wouldn't be so sure," Kate mumbles.

"What?" Tristan jerks his head up.

"No," I am quick to interject. "I think you are right, Tristan. She does." As if to confirm my words, Hannah begins toddling in Tristan's direction, stopping just short of his strong legs. Now Tristan looks slightly uncomfortable. Hannah glances back at her mom before taking one more hesitant step toward Tristan. Then, reaching a tiny finger in his direction, she gently touches his knee.

Kate laughs and I join in. Tristan shifts awkwardly in place. "She is rarely around guys. You must be a real novelty to her. I'm surprised you don't scare her." Seconds later Hannah puts both of her small, dimpled hands up in the air, surprising us all. Reflexively, Tristan leans backward. "On second thought, I think it's you who is scared, Tristan," Kate says. "Well, what are you waiting for? Pick her up!"

Tristan hesitates, then gingerly reaches for the small child in front of him. Picking her up, he dwarfs her in his muscular arms. At first he holds her awkwardly, like she is a diseased specimen that he is afraid to touch. But before long he succumbs to her baby charms and is talking sweetly to her while she babbles, trying to impress him with her limited vocabulary. And as I stand by spectating, I can't help but wonder why I am so mesmerized by the picture that is being created by the two of them, thinking that somehow, if possible, Tristan has just become ten times more sexy in my eyes.

Later, after Kate and Hannah leave and Tristan has completed his work on the dock for the day, he joins me up in the cabin for dinner: fettuccine Alfredo and garden salad. Afterward we take a walk beside the water, watching as the sun makes its descent into a shimmering pool of liquid. It doesn't take me too long to realize where he is leading me. *His beach!* I cross my arms over my chest, trying to forget about the last time I set foot on this piece of property, not sure how I feel about being here now. I feel Tristan's gaze on me. When I turn toward him. His brow creases. "You okay?"

Shrugging my shoulders, I glance around, trying to envision only him and me standing on the sand, waves from the sea skimming over the tops of our feet. Closing my eyes, I will Rye's soft, pouty lips and the vulnerable expression on her face as she stared up into Tristan's smile to disappear from my sight. "I think so," I say with shaky resolve.

"I brought something…something I think you might like." He points to a piece of driftwood where his guitar is resting.

I suck in a breath. "Oh."

"Can I play for you?"

I nod my head slowly as he grabs my hand, leading me to a comfortable spot in the sand. Situating himself across from me, he begins to strum the guitar. Moments into the song, I recognize the tune. Without warning, I am overcome with the chords and the melody and his beautiful voice as he sings. My heart begins beating to the rhythm of the music, tears forming in my eyes. Breathlessly, I am transported back to this very spot on the beach—four years ago.

And out of nowhere I am overcome with a strong sensation that everything is okay. *Everything is going to be okay.*

Chapter Fifteen

I am screwing the gas cap into place on the side of my black, four-door jeep when I first hear the news. David Chambers' face is solemnly lit as he crosses the gas station parking lot toward me, and so right away I recognize that something is going on. But when he says, "I'm sorry to hear about Tristan's friend, Mr. Horton, passing away," I am caught off guard.

What? No! Well, of course—this should really not come as a surprise. But here I stand visibly shaken, throat swollen, lost for words right out in public. "I'm sorry, you hadn't heard?" David Chambers continues. I shake my head in response. "Well, it only happened very recently, so that's understandable. But please give Tristan my condolences when you see him. I know he and Mr. Horton were close. And if you need anything—"

Once again I nod my head, astounded. When I speak, my voice sounds as though it belongs to someone else. "Thanks... thank you...sure." Once David Chambers leaves, I fall into the front seat of my jeep, forgetting to grab my gas receipt from the kiosk. Resting my hands on the steering wheel, I stare immobilized into unoccupied space, as one continual thought sweeps through my mind. *Tristan! What must Tristan be going through right now?* He knew Mr. Horton was sick; we both knew he was sick. But certainly this wasn't anticipated—not so soon. I know I find the news to be shocking, so God only knows what hurt Tristan is enduring at this very moment.

Without giving it a second thought, I turn my black jeep in the opposite direction and begin heading toward Tristan's beach. Once parked in the now familiar side gravel drive that sits a baseball throw away from the alcove, I pause for a moment or two before opening the car door and stepping out into the salty ocean air. Closing my eyes, I take a few seconds to embrace the ache in my heart that is slowly seeping through the rest of my body—the ache that belongs to Tristan. The walk to the beach is slow and painful. Upon reaching it, I take a deep breath. As expected, he's there, standing inches from the creeping tide, deep in thought, looking forlorn, staring out to the waves that are a roof to his home in the sea. At the sight of him, the ache in my chest increases tenfold.

Soundlessly, I approach him.

His stare remains focused on the sea.

"I heard…about Mr. Horton." I have a hard time saying his name now that I know that he is gone. Now that I know there is no more Mr. Horton living across town in his dilapidated bachelor pad with a house full of intricately constructed model ships. Tristan offers a barely perceptible nod but doesn't speak. Little droplets of water fall from his hair. As I eye the wet strands that are resting on the back of his neck, it occurs to me that my timing has been just right. Had I arrived at his beach only a short time before, I may not have discovered him on land, and it would have pained me to not know how he was doing. I would have kept searching though. Until I found him—even if it took me all night long.

Uncertainty pokes at me as I begin walking toward him, stopping when I'm an arm's length away. I want to reach out and touch him: run my fingertips across his hurting shoulders, wrap my arms around him from behind—resting my cheek on his back, absorbing his hurt into my skin. Instead I stand frozen by the force field of unapproachability that he has shrouded himself with, not knowing what to do next.

"I'm sorry," I whisper.

Jaw set, eyes glued to the water, Tristan offers no reply.

"Well, I—I guess I'll just go then. You want—I know you must want to be alone—" Backing away, I turn to leave. It's the unmistakable sound of hurt in his voice that stops me dead in my tracks.

"I'll be busy the next few days...making arrangements."

My feet pivot in the sand until I am facing Tristan's frame, but there is no eye contact between us. "You are the one to make the arrangements?"

"There was no one else. Besides, I would want to." *Oh, of course.*

"Do you need...do you want help?"

"No, I'll be okay." Now his voice is stoic, masking the pain that had been evident only seconds before. I wait, wondering if there will be more from him—anything else he wants to say. But all is quiet around us except the recurrent surge of the waves.

"Okay...well, good-bye." Closing my eyes, I fight back the tears that are trying to surface. "Please know that I'm really sorry, Tristan."

He answers with a nod of his head. And I turn to leave.

On the day of Mr. Horton's funeral, the skies are oppressively dark, and I can't help but think how fitting it is that the atmosphere, too, should be filled with grief. I haven't seen Tristan since that day I went to him on his beach. Every minute since I've wondered how he is holding up. When I park my jeep at the edge of the cemetery, I can't help but also think how appropriate it is that Mr. Horton's service and burial site should be located so close to the sea. But of course with Tristan making the arrangements, he would have thought through the importance of the location, so it makes perfect sense.

The pounding breakers beside me are a steel gray reflection of the sky as I make my way into the graveyard. The crowd in attendance is sparse. Inconspicuously as possible, I situate myself in the midst of the few that have gathered, waiting for the service to begin. The wind whistles and scourges through the air, plastering my floor-length, black skirt against my legs. An occasional wisp of hair escapes the bun that is tightly pulled, resting at the nape of my neck.

Within moments my eyes find the casket that is positioned on a platform, held in place by a contraption that will soon lower Mr. Horton's body to the ground, forever. Close by stands Tristan dressed in a dark suit, eyes shaded by sunglasses in stark contradiction to the lack of sunlight in the dull sky. My breath catches in my chest. Damp, blond hair curls recklessly on his neck as if in rebellion to the situation. Jaw set, expression resolute, he stares straight ahead, revealing none of the grief that I know beyond a shadow of a doubt is racking his body at this very moment. My heart leaps in my chest, overwhelmed both by his beauty and with his hidden sorrow at the same time. It takes all my willpower not to run to him and take him in my arms in a comforting gesture. Clenching my fists into tight balls at my side, I take a relaxing breath in order to prevent myself from making a scene. Today isn't about me or what I want to do.

As the minister clears his throat, I focus my attention back on the closed, ornamented casket.

"The Lord is my shepherd, I shall not want.

He makes me lie down in green pastures—*or green waves of the sea,*

He leads me beside quiet waters—*or the reckless waves of the sea,*

He restores my soul.

He guides me in the paths of righteousness for his name's sake.

Even though I walk through the valley of the shadow of death,

I will fear no evil, for you are with me—"

As the stranger in the black robe continues to site Psalm twenty-three, my gaze drifts back to Tristan. Still not a hint of his true feelings are revealed behind the darkness of his glasses.

But in spite of his resigned expression, I know he will be hurting over the loss of his elderly, male companion for a long time to come. Eventually the sound of the minister's declarations fade, being replaced instead by a melodic voice, ringing out the lyrics of "Amazing Grace."

As the prose of the song pierces my heart, it takes all my resolve not to break down into a fit of sobbing. Carried away by the moment, for a brief interval I imagine it is Tristan's breathy voice that I hear singing the words of the chorus instead of the hired vocalist. Now my heart beats wildly in my chest as I swallow down the lump that is engulfing my throat.

Finally all the conventionalism subsides, and it is time to say our conclusive good-byes. One by one, the small, gathered crowd marches by the rectangular wooden box that houses Mr. Horton's body in order to pay their respects. I take my place in line. A single red rose flutters from my fingertips, floating downward, until it takes its resting place on top of the casket. *Good-bye Mr. Horton.* Tears begin to plaster my cheeks. *Good-bye, and thank you. Thank you for always being in our corner. Thank you for being such a good friend and confidant for Tristan all of these years. I hope you knew—I hope you could feel it—how much he loved you too!* For many moments I stand staring at the collection of flowers that lays scattered like a fallen bridal bouquet on top of Mr. Horton's oak enclosure. Finally I move away. Lifting my eyes from the ground, my gaze travels until it finds Tristan. Just feet away from the casket he stands in his dark suit, talking in hushed tones to the minister and the funeral director. For an instant I hesitate, allowing my vision to take him in, wishing I could go to him, but it just doesn't seem like the right time. *When will be the right time?*

Reluctantly I turn to leave, heading back to the cabin instead. But I don't go inside. For some reason I can't bring myself to leave the shoreline—as if just being close to the ocean will bring me closer to Mr. Horton somehow. As my bare feet sift through the rising tide, there is something that occurs to me. There are two things that connected Mr. Horton and me—two things we had in common: we both shared a love for the sea, and we both shared a love for Tristan. For the next hour I wander the beach, my mind filled with thoughts of the deceased and what a great, though understated, person he was—and how much I will miss him. And more importantly, how much Tristan will miss him.

Eventually the gray light of day begins to fade, but I am not ready to call it a day. There is something inside of me that just can't let go of Tristan's hurt. How long will he need to mourn? How long will he shut me out and grieve alone? I can't stand it. The not knowing. The wondering. So once again I go in search of him. And find him as before, on his secluded beach. Similar to the other day he is staring out to sea, this time dressed in his black suit from the funeral, tie loosened, shirt opened at the throat. A dark pillar of strength. But I know the vitality of his body is masking the burden of pain that he carries inside. The breath inside of my lungs exits at the sight of him. For many reasons. He senses my presence and turns partially in my direction as steel-colored waves push to shore.

"I wanted to see how you were doing."

The nod that comes from underneath the tousled strands of his blond hair is barely perceptible before he turns to face the water once again. Undaunted, I proceed ahead bravely.

"The service was beautiful. You...did a really nice job. He would have been proud of you...he *was* proud of you."

Raindrops begin to spatter periodically, falling from a darkening, cloud-filled sky. Tristan's silent retort is deafening in my ears. I long for him to say something, anything, to let me know how he is doing with this whole thing. Once again I experience an overwhelming need to touch him, comfort him. But I can't bring myself to cross the invisible line in the sand that separates us. I suck in a breath and hold it. Somehow, shrouded in his suit, he seems even more unapproachable and intimidating than earlier in the week when I'd found him here at this same place.

"Well, if you need me…you know where—" My voice fades into the reverberation of the surf. I am almost to the bend in the shoreline where I'll soon disappear from Tristan's sight when I turn back. The words that leave my mouth are shouted, fighting to be heard above the relentless noise in the background.

"I love you!"

All that answers is the ocean and the increasing precipitation that is now dripping at a steady rhythm from the sky.

By the time I get back to the cabin, the temperature outside has dropped several degrees, making the evening air downright nippy. Slamming my door shut behind me, I rush inside, trying to avoid getting soaked. Taking a towel off the hook in my bathroom, I begin drying my damp hair before changing into plaid pajama pants and a white, thermal, long-sleeved shirt. Unable to shake the chill from my bones, I start a fire in my fireplace. After heating up a bowl of chicken noodle soup, I grab a thick slice of whole wheat bread that I'd purchased at a local bakery and hunker down in front of the hearth, trying to gather warmth from the lambent flames of the fire.

The rain that had started as a smattering of droplets earlier in the evening is now coming full force, pelting against the roof and the windows of my cabin. The wind is howling, banging the loosened shutters on the exterior walls, jolting me alert with each loud crash. I make a mental note to nail them back into place the next chance I get—or ask Tristan to. *That is, after he is speaking again.* I sigh, snuggling into a fleece throw that I'd grabbed off the couch. *Just how long would that be exactly?*

My thoughts on the matter are interrupted as amidst the noise of the inclement weather, I hear another sound that makes me take pause. Stiffening my shoulders, I sit listening for the hammering thud that I'd heard only seconds before, as it filtered through the commotion of the pounding rain and the swirling wind.

After a short reprieve, the sound emerges once again. Thwack. Thwack. Bang. Bang.

My heart stops and then begins hammering with the realization that the racket is coming from my front door. I don't give it a second thought. Dropping the blanket from around my shoulders, I dash through the kitchen and into my entryway. With fingers fumbling, I undo each of the locks.

Finally after what seems like an eternity, I turn the knob and throw open the door.

And standing before me on my front doorstep, face wet from a mixture of rain and tears, is Tristan. *Oh my word!* My heart leaps in my chest, and an incredible ache rushes unexpectedly through my body. For a moment I stand frozen, mesmerized by his tormented beauty, until I realize that my immobilized state is causing him to get even further soaked.

The minute he walks into the warmth of my cabin, I throw my arms around him and pull him tightly to my body, not caring that I too am getting completely drenched. Since first hearing the news about Mr. Horton I'd wanted to do this. I'd wanted to show Tristan how much I love him—how much I wanted to grieve with him. But he had shut me out. Not only had I hurt for the loss of his good friend, Mr. Horton, but also for the way he was keeping me at a distance—not wanting to share this intimate part of himself with me. Now he is finally here.

"Geez, Bethany, I miss him so much already," he whispers into the skin of my neck. His voice is tearful. My heart constricts painfully.

"I know you do, Tristan, I know you do—" My answer is just a murmur. We stay that way, clinging to each other for a long time. Occasionally I feel something hot and wet trickle onto the exposed area just above the collar of my shirt, and I shudder in response. The thought of steadfast Tristan crying is almost too much. I shut my eyes tightly, trying to fight back my own tears in response. Eventually we ease apart and he turns away from me, wiping his eyes with his fists. I look away too giving him the space he needs. I can tell it's difficult for him to show this type of vulnerability in front of me.

After a moment or two I reach for his hand. "Come sit by the warm fire. You are soaking wet. And cold." He hesitates and I read his mind. *Oh yeah, that's right, you spend most of your time immersed in liquid. Wet does not bother you. Well, come sit by the fire anyway.* As if reading *my* mind, he crosses the floor as I walk at his side. Before settling onto the rug in front of the mantel, he shrugs out of his drenched suit coat, laying it on the cement inlay that extends from the masonry of the fireplace. Now all that is left covering his chest is a sopping-wet, white button-down shirt plastered against his skin.

I swallow and look away. My vision finds a place to focus, landing on the throw that is strewn across the couch. Reaching for it, I hold it up. "Would you like a blanket?"

"Ah…sure."

I hand it to him, and he wraps it around his shoulders. Pulling my fleece coverlet across his chest, he inhales into it. "It smells like you." He offers a tentative smile. "I like it."

I bite my lip and give a shy grin back. Sitting side by side, inches apart, we stare into the dancing flames in front of us. Outside, the wind pushes rain hard against the windows. Inside, the fire crackles and pops, lulling us into a quiet abstraction. After many blurred moments of time, I am startled into reality by Tristan's voice speaking into the subdued air.

"He was like a dad to me."

Sucking in a quiet breath, I wait, hoping he'll keep talking. But for a long while he says nothing else. Gently I reach for his hand and offer it a squeeze. Finally he continues. "All those years I came on land, he put up with me…little shit that I was. I would spend hours every day, every summer at his house, and he never acted like he was tired of having me around." Tristan pauses for a moment and chuckles pensively. Shakes his head. "Looking back on it now, I'm sure I was nothing but a nuisance…but he put up with me anyway…always without complaint."

There is a part of me that wonders whether I should let him carry on with his reflection without any interruption. But there is a bigger part of me that feels the need to share what I know to be true. I clear my throat. "I have to tell you. That day that I talked to Mr. Horton in detail about you four summers ago, when he spoke of you, his face lit up. He enjoyed every moment he spent with you. He told me so himself. He loved you so much…you *were* his son. The son he never had…he told me that too."

Tristan turns to look at me. *Really?* he asks me silently with his sea green eyes. I nod once, holding his gaze. My heart picks up in tempo. Finally he faces the fire once again, and my throbbing pulse subsides.

"I'm so mad at him." *What? No, no, I get it. Keep talking.* "He wouldn't go to the doctor. Several times I asked him to go to the doctor, but he just wouldn't go. He was so stubborn about it. Why did he have to be that way? He might still be here now if he had gotten treated for whatever it was that killed him." Shifting my position, I look over at Tristan's grief-stricken profile and have to resist the urge to run my fingertips along his beautifully chiseled cheekbones, across his perfectly formed lips. Tristan adjusting the throw around his shoulders snaps me out of my line of thinking. "Maybe he just didn't care."

"Once, I talked to him about going to the doctor too. Maybe he just wasn't ready to face that something was wrong." My voice is soft, reassuring.

Tristan runs his fingers through the damp, disheveled strands of his hair and exhales deeply. "I wish he would have cared! I just wish…I'm going to miss him…so much."

I shut my eyes tightly together, willing myself to take on his pain. Then turning toward him once again, this time I do what I imagined doing only moments before. Lightly I run the tips of my fingers along his cheekbones before tracing his jawline. Finally I pause. "I'm so sorry...so, so sorry—"

Tristan's gaze leaves the fire. And I come face-to-face with hurting, green eyes. Intensity is written in them. My heart begins pounding in my chest, and I lose track of my word. I am paralyzed by his stare.

Before I can blink, he moves lithe as a cat, bringing my body to his, pressing hard against me as his lips find mine. Immediately, I match his stride. It had been so long since he'd kissed me without restraint. In an instant I am right there with him making up for lost time, not able to get enough—never enough of *him*. His heart beats fast as it pushes into my breasts. My breathing comes in short gasps. As my hands press into his back, I feel the moisture that is still dripping from the cotton material. "Your wet shirt—" I say into his mouth. Without hesitating he pulls away from me and rips it off before finding my lips once again. Now all the smooth contours of his chest and back are exposed. I shudder as my fingertips touch bare shoulders.

Seconds later his strong hands are reaching for my own thermal shirt, loosening it from its fitted position, lifting and pulling until I raise my arms, allowing him to tug it over my head. All the while his lips leave mine only for a split second. Now my head is swimming with new pleasure. I can't think straight anymore. He eases me unto my back and lies directly on top of me until all that is separating our bodies from the waist up is my sports bra. His skin feels like fire pressed up against mine. Every nerve ending that makes up my anatomy is melting into liquid. Over and over again his hands run up and down the length of my spine as I lift myself off the rug, flattening myself against him.

And then in one swift move he rolls off of me, and we are lying shoulder to shoulder while he cradles his head with his fingers, and the kiss is over as quickly as it began. Staring up at the ceiling, he exhales a long, hard breath. My body, in a state of shock, tries to slow its own breathing. Gradually I turn my head until my eyes rest on the rapid rise and fall of the chest. "I better go, Bethany." I lift my gaze to his face. He is speaking with closed eyes, a painful expression etched across his brow. Sitting up, I find my shirt that is lying discarded on the floor. Without saying a word I pull it over my head, all the while sensing his eyes on my back. Glancing over my shoulder, I nod to acknowledge his statement. But on the inside I'm wishing he wouldn't go at all.

Tristan dresses back into his wet clothes, and I walk him to the door. The wind has died down, and the precipitation has all but stopped, but somehow I just can't imagine sending him out into a night full of cold, drizzling rain, as scant as it may be. I tell him this much. Standing less than a foot away from me, he rests his hand on the doorframe, green eyes staring down into mine. I swallow hard. He is breathtakingly good-looking. "I know this is hard for you to believe, but I am used to living in these conditions. *All the time.* Besides, if I stay, I'm going to do something I'll end up regretting."

"I won't—" My lips form into a pout. My gaze doesn't waver.

Tristan laughs. "Trust me when I say if I do it, you are going to be doing it too."

"Regret it…that is." I hadn't finished.

The laughter stops and his grin fades. Groaning, he runs a hand through his hair before looking right at me. "Someday when it's finally our time, you're not *going* to regret it…I promise you."

Now I am blushing. He pulls me in for a hug. "Oh, sweet Bethany…you are my too-good-to-be-true." Gently, reverently, he kisses the top of my head. "Good-night…okay?"

I sigh into his chest and pull back so I can see his face. "Okay, and if you need anything, a hug, to talk, anything, I'll be here, all right?"

"All right." He nods one time, then runs a finger gently down the length of my nose, giving me one more prolonged look before exiting out into the cold, spitting moisture of the night.

The following morning I startle from sleep.

My heart is pounding, and it is as though I can't quite catch my breath. Deftly, my eyes scan the bedroom in search of the cause for what I am experiencing. Nothing is out of place and no one is there. Yet an overwhelming feeling hovers over me like I am bereft—unexplainably violated. Once more my vision travels to the bedroom window, but the glass is just as I'd left it the night before, the fitted screen still in place. Nevertheless, I can't shake the panic that has a grip on me. Out of habit I reach across my chest to find comfort in the leather rope that rests perpetually around my neck. And all at once I know what is wrong.

My seashell necklace is gone.

Chapter Sixteen

My mind begins to whirl with every possible option. I don't *remember* losing it. *Could I have lost my necklace?* My dearest necklace that I never, ever take off—not even to shower. How many times a day do I reach for that thing without thinking—just out of an ingrained habit? When do I remember feeling it last? Yesterday? Could I have lost it yesterday then? Maybe while I was with Tristan in front of the fireplace. Certainly I was distracted enough—it was possible that it could have pulled free during the midst of—um, everything. But no, I remember lying down to go to sleep, snuggling into my covers and reaching for the contours of the shell just before my eyes closed. My little piece of Tristan, my way of saying good-night to him, hoping that somehow he was feeling all the love I was sending to him in the process. No, it was definitely around my neck before I went to sleep.

A chill runs up and down the length of my spine, and I have to fight the anxiety that wants to possess me. Hastily I jump out of bed and throw back my covers, beginning a search that I have an eerie feeling isn't going to turn up anything. The exploration expands onto my bedroom floor and then eventually into the rest of my cabin. But nothing turns up. Over and over my eyes return to the window that is situated only feet from where I just spent the night in slumber—completely unaware. *Completely unaware of what—an intruder?* Closing my eyes, I try to shake the feeling of violation that is quaking through my body.

Last night I was not alone in my room!

And now my necklace is gone.

And then my second thought is—I can't tell Tristan. He will worry. He will worry about me and think the only way to protect me is to leave. Past experience had proven this to be all too true. *Oh no, please, Tristan can't leave again!* Grabbing a steaming hot cup of coffee, I try to pull myself together. Tristan will be coming over later today to take me out on *Blue* for an afternoon ride. My mind conducts a quick inventory of my wardrobe. Certainly I have some shirts with high enough necklines to conceal the shell. At least I think I do. Maybe he won't even know the difference.

For now.

When Tristan arrives at my cabin, it's hard for me not to throw myself into his arms and cling to him for dear life. *Oh my word, Tristan, I am so scared and creeped-out that someone was in my room with me while I slept and took my seashell. They had to be standing right, right over me—practically touching me. Maybe even touching me!*

Instead I take a calming breath and smile pleasantly. "Hey."

"Hey, baby." He pulls me into his arms for a hug. In return I give him a little squeeze followed by a chaste pat on the back. Avoiding eye contact, I chat animatedly about the ensuing boat ride all the while he prepares the watercraft for departure. We are skimming the misty, blue plains of open water with Drake leaping and diving at our side when Tristan glances over at me. "What are you doing so far away? Get over here!" Resting his arm on the back of the crème-colored, leather seat, his fingers beckon me to him. I slide over, my heart beating wildly for several different reasons. His arm reaches protectively around my shoulder, and we keep driving that way, hydroplaning across the waves. All too soon his hand moves toward my ear, tucking a windblown strand behind it before grazing the length of my neck. Unwittingly I freeze in place. As his fingers caress my exposed skin, his thumb lingers at the nape of my neck. For a split second, I feel his hand pause and explore where the back of the necklace should be resting. I hold my breath, waiting for the anticipated question. But then the stroking continues, and I have to wonder whether it was just my guilty imagination spiraling out of control, and there was really no hesitation or inspecting on Tristan's part at all.

After that the day proceeds like any other between the two of us; together we enjoy the fresh, open air of the ocean, playfully interacting with each other, occasionally calling out friendly words of endearment to Drake. So later when the boat is anchored, still miles from shore, swaying lazily amongst the waves, and I catch Tristan studying me from behind the steering column, it throws me off guard. Unexpectedly my heart rate skyrockets. Uneasily, I look away, focusing my efforts on talking to Drake instead. Thankfully the moment passes, and I breathe a sigh of relief.

The bow of the boat has just barely entered the quiet waters of the bay on the return trip as we head into town, the engine now only a soft hum, when Tristan's deep voice startles me, causing me to practically jump in my seat.

"So…where is your seashell?" *Oh crap!*

"I, ah—" *What? My seashell?* "Um…you know I'm not sure. It seems I might have…I must have misplaced it."

All is quiet but the whirr of the boat motor and the splashing sound of Drake swimming away from us, knowing that he can't be seen too close to town. *Double crap!* When I can't take it another second, I turn to look at Tristan. He bites his lip, steadily watching my face. His tone is edged with a trace of skepticism. "Really?"

I swallow hard. "I know… I can't believe it! I am going to keep looking for it every chance I get. I feel so awful. It means so much to me. I *love* that thing." My words are dripping with double meaning. Nothing else is said about the matter, and afterward I have to wonder how we stand on the subject.

As *Blue* continues to slow down on our approach to the Watch Hill municipal docks, my attention is drawn to two figures standing on one of the wooden structures, lost in a seemingly serious conversation. Immediately every muscle in my body tenses. Stealing a sideways glance at Tristan, I secretly hope he will decide to steer the boat in a different direction in order to avoid confrontation. But much to my dismay, we stay right on course. The moment Keuran sees us, he sends a friendly wave in our direction. Tristan stiffens in response. I lift a hand in polite greeting. Tension fills the air as Tristan brings the boat in closer, getting ready for a landing.

"Hey, Tris. Whatcha doing out with my main girl?" Keuran winks at me. *Oh no! What type of game is Keuran going to play today?*

We slide into a dock and Tristan jumps out to tie the boat up without looking at Keuran. After a few moments of silence, he begins speaking, all the while wrapping the rope, looping and twisting, still not once glancing in Keuran's direction. "I'm not going to take the time to answer that, Keuran." After the rigging is secured, Tristan finally looks at his cousin while sending a nod toward his cohort. "What brings you and your friend to the docks today?"

"Business." *Business? What type of business does Keuran have on land?* I narrow my eyes contemplatively. Outside of drop-in visits to the shore, I assumed he mostly stayed out to sea. Is this guy that he seemed so earnestly engaged with also from the sea? I eye his companion questionably. For some reason the outdated comb-over on his head along with his weasely appearance don't seem to ring true to the ocean. Moments later introductions are made, and I discover the guy's name is Wes Bent. After a brief conversation takes place amongst the group, I decide that, rest assuredly, Wes Bent is not a sea creature and indeed is from on land. Keuran asks us to join them for dinner. And although I can tell Tristan doesn't want to, after checking in with me about my time frame for the rest of the day, he acquiesces to the plan.

At the restaurant, Tristan seems only half engaged in the conversation. In contrast, Wes Bent eyes Tristan speculatively, sometimes almost eagerly—like paparazzi with a rock star or a UFO hunter with an alien. Come to find out Wes Bent is conducting some independent studies on marine activity—life spans and cycles of the underwater world. He'd come to know Keuran and through him had heard of Tristan and his job as a marine systems consultant. He hoped Tristan might be willing to give some added insight on the topic. Throughout the meal Wes Bent talks on and on, questioning Tristan about nautical statistics and information concerning the sea. And although at times he answers his inquiries, mostly Tristan just looks bored. Once our check is paid, Tristan captures my attention from across the table, giving me the eye like *are you ready to leave?* But before I can nod yes, Wes Bent interrupts.

"So listen, I have some free time right now. Why don't we meet up at your house, Tristan, and continue this conversation? What do you say? Just give me your address, and I'll plug it into my GPS." Wes' beady eyes gleam openly at Tristan as he waits for a response.

A muscle in Tristan's jaw twitches. "I'm going to have to pass. Now isn't a good time."

Wes Bent looks overtly disappointed. He glances over at Keuran and in response, Keuran seems all too happy to take the ball and run with it. "When *would* be a good time, Tris?" he asks, a type of eagerness evident in his voice. Tristan's head snaps in Keuran's direction.

"Why the rush, Keuran? What information are you looking for anyway? Is it the yacht harbor residents you are curious about—someone need the axe lately? Or are there bigger plans in the works these days?" Keuran,s nostrils flare. I gasp for air. What is Tristan openly insinuating? Anxiously I wait for Keuran to refute his obvious claim. *Keuran—the yacht murderer!* Instead his lips curl into a sneer as he holds Tristan's gaze unwaveringly. Pressing my fingers tightly together, I tuck them on my lap beneath the table to hide their visible shaking as I try to sort out the situation. Taking a slow breath, I remind myself that the yacht murderer is currently in custody with a documented confession. Surely it is time for Tristan to let it go. Justice has been served.

An amused smile permeates Wes Bent's face as he observes Keuran and Tristan's blatant sparring. Finally he interrupts coming to some sort of rescue. "Well, maybe another time then, Tristan? You look eager to take your girl and get back to the sea. You seem to really enjoy the water. I wouldn't want to keep you from it."

A spark of irritation flashes in Tristan's eyes, but his voice remains well controlled. "Those that live in Rhode Island usually do enjoy the water. It would be silly to live in a state that is surrounded by the ocean otherwise."

"Of course, you are right. But it would seem some enjoy it more than others."

Ignoring this last statement, Tristan lifts his eyebrows and looks at me. "Ready?"

On our way back to the boat, we stop at Sherling's Hardware to pick up a part for the newly installed dock at my cabin. Tristan holds my hand tightly as we walk in silence through town and onto the municipal boat docks where *Blue* is parked. The ride back through the bay as we head toward the open ocean is deafeningly quiet. Eventually I can't take Tristan's taciturnity any longer. Glancing over at his strained profile, taking in the forceful grip of his hands on the steering column, I clear my throat. "Don't let him get to you."

Tristan looks over at me, staring hard into my eyes, and I continue my plea to him in silence. *Talk to me. Tell me all that you are feeling right now about that whole uncomfortable encounter we just had back there. I want to know what you are thinking.* In response, he nods and looks back to the wide expanse of sea that we are approaching. Once out of the no-wake zone he accelerates full throttle, and the engine roars loudly in our ears, eliminating any chance for conversation. Frustrated, I look away. Focusing my thwarted stare at the choppy waves, I keep an eye out for

Drake, waiting for him to join us once again. After many minutes it occurs to me that he hasn't resumed his normal place beside the boat. *That's funny: where could he be?* I begin glancing in all directions thinking maybe I'll spot him behind us or at an angle that I have not yet explored. But after looking all around, I discover he is nowhere to be found.

"Hey, where is Drake?" I shout loudly over the din of the motor.

"Huh?" Tristan peers over at me, his blond hair whipping through the air.

"I said, where is Drake?"

Tristan takes a sweeping gaze of the water around us. "Not sure."

I don't let it go. "Shouldn't he have joined you by now?" I can't hide the concern in my voice. Tristan shakes his head nonchalantly, but for a split second I detect a flash of worry in his eyes, and my heart plummets. My throat is getting dry and cracked from having to yell. "You don't think something happened to him, do you?"

Tristan closes his eyes briefly, and I have to wonder if he is getting irritated from the tenacity of my questioning. Eventually he shouts back. "I'm sure he'll show back up."

But he never does show back up on the drive back to the cabin, and the unspoken reality of it hangs heavy between us as we tie the boat up at my dock. Instinctively I reach for my seashell as way of comforting myself over the situation. But of course it's not there either. A jolt of uneasiness shoots through my body. Now my necklace is gone, and maybe Drake is gone too—all in the matter of twenty-four hours. Compulsorily my eyes shoot up to Tristan's face. He looks away. *Oh God, no!* What is he thinking? *Everything is okay. Everything is going to be okay!*

I force a smile. "Do you want to come in for a while?"

He hesitates before smiling back. "Sure." I lead him inside and offer him a piece of blueberry cheesecake that I'd made earlier in the day. Sitting on my tweed couch we eat mostly in silence, afterward chatting about mundane things: what a beautiful boat *Blue* turned out to be, how the kitchen in the cabin could use some new cabinets, and how the tourist season is doing in Watch Hill. Polite, meaningless chatter, considering all that has gone on that day. At one point I remember Keuran's reference to adventure diving and think to ask about it. Tristan goes still and eyes me questioningly, obviously knowing who'd enlightened me on the topic. "Yeah…I've tried that once. That was enough. If you are sane at all, you know never to try it twice." His correlated inference to insanity and his diving companion—Keuran—is rather blatant. I don't press him for more details about what the adventure entails, and he doesn't offer anything else on the matter. All too soon he announces that he needs to go, and so I walk with him away from the cabin back down to the shore.

Before he leaves, he pulls me into his arms for a hug, and I have to restrain myself from clinging to his body for dear life. He strokes the back of my hair for a long while, then gives one hard squeeze and presses his lips to the top of my head before finally easing me away. I study his face looking for a sign, anything that will give away what he is about to do. But he masks his thoughts very well. He tells me good-bye and begins walking away toward the water. I leave too and take a few steps onto the path that will lead me back to the cabin. I just about have myself talked into the idea that I'd been wrong about Tristan leaving me again, when I turn back around. Shrouded behind wild brush I watch as he pauses, waist deep in the water, getting ready to make the dive in—back to a world that is hidden below the sea. Long seconds tick by as I wonder what he is thinking, why he has stopped, what he plans on doing next. Is he contemplating coming back to me? My heart thuds in my chest. For one moment he looks back in the direction of the cabin without noticing where I am, just yards away, concealed by the untamed foliage that separates my housing from the beach. And in that moment what I see revealed on his beautiful features is unadulterated pain.

I've seen that look before. Four years ago. This time heightened by the illusion that no one is watching. *No!* I close my eyes tightly together until the sound of splashing water fills my ears. When I open them again, my focus is pulled to the repetitive motion of waves as they spill onto shore. A weighty feeling settles onto my chest. Will it be the same as before? Will Tristan leave without saying good-bye just as he had four years ago? The sun begins to lower in the sky, disintegrating into a rainbow of orange, fuchsia, and purple. The atmosphere surrounding me is heavy just like my heart. In spite of the beautiful sunset, the humidity in the air feels like a precursor to a storm. After the final tip of the sun disappears into the horizon, I turn and head back to the cabin. Maybe I am making too much out of Tristan's apparent angst. After all, he is never thrilled to be in Keuran's company, and after the tension-filled night with Keuran's new friend Wes Bent, it would be understandable for Tristan to be on edge. With that thought in mind, I settle in for a night of sleep, making sure my windows and door are tightly secured.

Sometime during the middle of the night, I wake to the rumble of thunder, brilliant flashes of lightning, and the swirl of wind and rain against my bedroom window. The storm that I had sensed earlier has arrived full force. Now I am wide awake, tossing and turning in bed, listening to the unbridled sounds of nature. Amidst the bursts of light and the resounding booms that are shaking the walls around me, my mind begins sorting through the events of the previous day. Out of nowhere, Rye's image comes floating into my thoughts. I haven't heard from her or seen her in some time now. Why was that? Had Tristan's last conversation with her on the beach finally gotten through? The possibility of that idea pacifies me enough to relax and ease back into slumber, my thoughts waning along with the now fading storm.

One, two, three days, a whole week passes, and I hear nothing from Tristan. Each sun that sets and rises has me more and more convinced that my original intuition about him was correct. Each moment of the day I feel sick with the thought. One thing I really don't understand, though: if he were going to leave me, why couldn't he have at least said good-bye? Finally I cannot stand it any longer, and knowing that he does not carry a phone, I call his place of work instead. A female receptionist answers using the phrase "Hello, N.E.C. Systems may I help you?" After trying to connect me to his office, she eventually returns on the line to tell me he is not answering, and asks would I like his voicemail? I swallow down a wave of disappointment, say no thank you, and hang up.

After a week and a half goes by, I decide to take a trip back to Philadelphia, wanting to get away from the emptiness of the ocean water for a few days. Everywhere I look it is right there drawing my attention to it, causing me to search through the pattern of its waves, always looking and hoping. I have just crammed the last few items of clothing into my suitcase when I hear a car pull into my drive. A quick glance out my window reveals a red Lexus ES. Keuran. For a moment I debate whether or not to go to the door at all. But then decide that I'd hate to miss out on information that might lead me to Tristan's whereabouts should he be privy to it. Unfastening the locks, I step outside, sparing him the need to knock.

"Hi, gorgeous, what are your plans for the day? We haven't hung out for a while...and you've missed me, haven't you?" Keuran radiates energy as I step out onto my front doorstep, his countenance bright, dark hair wet from either the ocean, a recent shampoo, or maybe a styling product.

I roll my eyes. "Hi, Keuran...I don't really remember missing you, but if you say so."

Keuran grabs his chest. "Ouch, that hurts. Seriously, though, let's hang out."

I chuckle, knowing I've just beat him at his own game. "Sure, that will be fine…as long as you don't mind spending the day in Philadelphia, because that's where I am heading."

"Are you trying to ditch me? Because that is just not going to work." I can tell his mind is racing as he tries to come up with a solution for the problem I've just presented. It's hard for me not to grin from ear to ear as I watch him flounder. "All right, I'm in," he says. His answer surprises me.

"I thought you couldn't be away from the ocean that long."

"Is that what someone told you? Sounds like *someone* was trying to blow you off, if you ask me."

I take in a deep breath, trying to erase the pain of that statement. Sighing, I resign myself to the situation. It doesn't sound like I'm going to be able to thwart Keuran from joining in on my plans. He is leaning against my front doorstep railing, arms folded, watching me, a hopeful expression on his face. His striking looks reach out to me, waiting for me say the right word.

"All right, if you think it'll be okay, then let's go. I'm almost finished packing."

He jumps out of his casual position. "Great, you grab your stuff and I'll be right back." I watch his retreating form, realizing that he is probably headed to the ocean for one more swim before hitting the road for the long trip—his long day away from the water. I shake my head, hoping he'll really be okay. Does he know what he is doing? For him it's just another game of Russian roulette. But for me it's probably a good added distraction —the perfect interruption of all my pessimistic thoughts.

While I am loading the last of my things into the back of my black jeep, closing the hatch, Keuran is jogging up the path that leads to the shoreline, tugging a tee shirt over wet skin. Droplets of water are running off his spikey hair, spilling onto his face. His voice is slightly winded. "Ready! Got a towel?" *Huh?* I cock my head in question. I didn't think these boys from the sea bothered with towels. He reads into my questioning look. "For your front seat. I don't think you want me to get it all wet."

"Right." I reach into my back seat, grab one of my beach towels, and toss it to him. He catches it no problem. Soon we are on I-95 South, heading toward Philadelphia, listening to music on the radio, talking and laughing about any ridiculous topic that Keuran brings up. Several times he tells me that I'm going way too slow and points out that I'm being continually passed up by grandmas and great-grandmas. But each time he accuses me, I set my jaw stubbornly, refusing to accelerate any faster.

"Come on, Bethany, don't do boring. Live life on the wild side just a little bit."

I flash him a dirty look. "I'm about to drop you off on the side of the road and let you walk. Is that wild enough for you?"

At that he sends me a wicked grin. "Actually, no. Sometime though, I'll get a chance to show you just how wild I like to get… but that will come later."

Without wanting to, I feel my cheeks heat up, and I focus a steady gaze on the road, trying to ignore the goose bumps that are covering the skin. Keuran snickers, enjoying my unease, but says nothing else. We ride in silence for a while after that. The stop and go traffic in Philadelphia is difficult to maneuver around. But after many curse words and several near fender benders, I get my jeep safely parked into a lot off Market Street. Intrigued by the novelty of city life, Keuran hits the sidewalks with me, looking all around, taking it all in. We walk through Independence Mall, and I show him the Liberty Bell. He notices the variety of tourists gathering at our side, some taking pictures of the symbol of freedom. Sidling up next to me, he whispers into my ear.

"You human folk really get into this stuff, don't you?"

I cock my head in question. "Meaning?"

"Meaning…loyalty, freedom, democracy, and all that crap."

Perusing the people that could be within hearing distance, I search for a reaction in their faces, but no one seems to be paying any attention. Furrowing my brow, I turn toward Keuran to see if he's just kidding. But the dead-serious, slightly annoyed expression that is written on his features tells me he is not. "Yes, we do care—at least in this country. Many soldiers have given their lives for the freedom we enjoy every day. Freedom isn't free, it—"

"Okay, got it." Keuran cuts me off, seemingly incensed by my speech. Clearly he doesn't want to hear the rest of my dissertation. I bite down the anger that wants to well up inside of me, and we continue walking the streets, looking at other landmarks and shops. We are ambling down Broad Street, pausing to watch a group of high schoolers file out of Kimmel Center for the Performing Arts, when I do a double take in Keuran's direction. His face is looking noticeably pale. Reactively, I reach for his arm.

"Hey…Keuran, are you okay?"

"What? Yeah, I'm fine." He shakes his head. And his natural coloring returns.

I study his face. "All right, 'cause we can go. Maybe we should go now. It's a long drive to the ocean—"

He takes a deep breath. "I said I'm fine." We continue walking, circling back to where the jeep is parked, taking a slight detour on the way. I want to show him one more place before we leave the city, Reading Terminal Market—an indoor market with an outdoor atmosphere. We step through the double doors by way of the Twelfth Street entrance. Filled with restaurant booths and vendors selling meats, fresh produce, books, and all sort of other eye-catching trinkets, the lively venue ensnares us. Scooting past the myriads of other shoppers, we begin eyeing the variety of merchandise displayed at the array of jam-packed stands. As we come upon Golden Fish Market, I glance uncertainly in Keuran's direction. The smell of fresh, raw seafood is overpowering. But he doesn't flinch. Instead, he inhales deeply, his nostrils flaring.

What? Sensing my surprise, he looks hard at me until I turn away, confused and somewhat disturbed.

After grabbing a Philly cheesesteak sandwich for lunch, we weave in and out of the long rows of retailors and delis in search of an exit. As we pass by Market Blooms, a florist shop, Keuran reaches into a wooden bucket in their front display and pulls out a single pink carnation. Handing the guy at the counter a dollar, he walks back over to where I am standing. Stopping a foot away, he goes very still, his amber eyes looking into my face, almost through me.

"For a beautiful girl who deserves to be happy…who deserves a guy's undivided attention." He offers me the flower. Cautiously I reach out and take it in my hand. "*Are* you…happy, Bethany?" I suck in a tiny breath. *He knows!* I'd never said a word about my troubles with Tristan, and yet he seems to sense my underlying melancholy mood. My mouth goes dry.

"I'm okay."

"Really?" He steps closer. His voice is just a whisper, matching the soft touch of his fingers as he reaches out and runs a thumb over my cheekbone. All around us the crowds in the market are coming and going. *What is he doing?* Caught off guard, I stand frozen in place. The look in his eyes is dark, revealing desire. But there is something else there too, something that I can't quite put my finger on—something so unsettling that it makes me want to shudder. Unknowingly I take a step backward. A split second later Keuran begins gasping for breath. Out of nowhere a wave of gray coloring washes over his face. *What?* Such a quick turn of events. I can hardly keep up.

"Keuran, you don't look so good!"

Sweat begins to pool on his forehead, and he wipes at it with his hand. I glance at my watch. It has been over six hours since we left Watch Hill—the amount of time Tristan had told me they can be safely out of the water. I swallow down the feeling of panic that is rising in my throat. *Great, what now?* I had tried to tell him that this trip wasn't a good idea. Something resembling irritation crosses over his features.

"I'll be all right; let's just get back to the car."

Without hesitation, I start into action, practically jogging down Market Street with Keuran keeping a fast pace at my side. We are halfway back to the parking lot when he suddenly stops. Half bent over he gasps for air—*or more likely water*. "Go on." He motions me away from him. My eyes go wide.

"What? No! I can't just leave you like this!"

The look of fire is in his eyes as he speaks through choppy breaths. In spite of the lack of life-sustaining substance in his lungs, his voice is surprisingly adamant. "I *said*...get *out* of here!" *No!* I place both hands over my mouth, forehead furrowed, immobilized with indecision. In desperation I stare at him, pleading through frenzied eyes. But before I can make a move, Keuran bolts away from me, running in the opposite direction from the car lot. *Oh my word! What is he doing?*

"Keuran!" I call after him. Over and over I yell out his name, drawing several inquisitive looks from passersby. But he is already gone, darting in and out of cars, crossing busy streets, scuttling behind tall buildings. Too soon I lose sight of his spikey, dark hair and well-built frame. Spending the next few hours in search of where he may have gone, I come up empty-handed. Finally I head to my family's house for the visit that I'd originally intended for the day. The next morning, I make the drive back to Watch Hill, my heart heavy not only with thoughts of Tristan leaving me, but now with Keuran's whereabouts and the state of his condition as well.

Chapter Seventeen

In a tired haze, I step out of the shower onto the tiled floor in my bathroom. For a minute I stand there doing nothing, letting the water drip off my naked body, collecting in a small puddle all around me. In the past thirty-six hours I've done nothing but worry. About Keuran and whether he is lying in some forsaken alley curled up in a shriveled ball, dehydrating—essentially dying. And about whether Tristan is about to repeat history and give me the slip—or rather already has given me the slip. I haven't heard from him in close to two weeks now. Grabbing a towel from the rack, I begin drying off the skin on my arms, legs, neck, stomach. Taking a comb from the shelf, I run it through the long, dripping-wet strands of my hair repeatedly, trying to free it from the mess of tangles that it has become. After slipping into a pair of black running shorts and a light blue tank top, I fill up a water bottle and head to the shoreline in front of my cabin to watch the morning sun make its ascent into the daytime sky.

When I reach the beach, almost like a reflex, my vision is drawn to *Blue*. Sitting so serenely next to the fresh wood of my dock, it rocks gently back and forth in the waves. Like an old friend it calls to me. Quietly but without hesitation, I make my way over to where it is resting. Stepping into the crème-colored interior, I position myself on the front seat, legs tucked under my bottom, head leaning on the backrest behind me. Within seconds, my hair, still damp from my shower, begins sticking to the leather material. I run my fingers through it to loosen the strands and then close my eyes in attempt to shut out the barrage of overwhelming thoughts that are running through my mind.

Why did I have to fall for someone as complex as Tristan anyway—someone who can't fully commit to me? Frustratingly, he always talks a good game, telling me he loves me, that he wants me. Always making me come so undone in his arms but then always holding back, never quite finishing the job. And why am I always second-guessing how he really feels? Maybe because every time he leaves, just disappears into thin air, I don't feel like I'm number one to him anymore. If he really loved me, wouldn't he find a way to stay? The dissertation of thoughts are agonizing as they repeatedly stab at my mind, causing my eyes to squeeze more tightly together. I can feel my face twisting into a tortured expression. Why couldn't I have fallen for a boy in high school or the Marine Biology Department at Penn State? Instead my heart belongs to a boy from the sea, who brings with him so many complications. Will I ever be over him—be free of his grip on me? The answer to that question leaves me exhausted.

After several minutes I open my eyes again. Blinking to filter out the brightness of the sunlight, it takes a second for my vision to focus. When it does, my heart jump-starts in my chest, causing every nerve ending to stand on end. On the shoreline, only yards away, stands a figure silently watching, an intense gaze radiating from his eyes.

Tristan!

How long has he been there observing me? Green eyes lock onto my own blue. And in that moment volumes are spoken between us. Instantly my heart begins taking a slow dive in my chest. *He knows that I know!* He knows that I know something is going on with him.

And that I'm about to get hurt again.

Slowly he makes his way to the boat. I begin trembling. Climbing over the varnished, wooden side with ease, he situates himself on the seat beside me, every gorgeous inch of him. I want to look away from him, but I can't.

"I need to talk to you, Bethany."

That's it! That's all I need to snap out of my daze. I am shocked to hear the bitter sarcasm lacing the words as they leave my mouth. "Really? You mean you are not going to just leave me high and dry without an explanation?"

Tristan looks away guiltily. "Something like that." *Oh no! Please, no! I don't want you to go!*

"Don't tell me…I don't want to hear it!"

Tristan sighs, an exasperated breath. "See, this is why I didn't tell you last time. I knew you wouldn't hear any of it."

Without warning a feeling of panic takes over my body, and although it's never happened to me before, I have an overwhelming sensation that I'm going to start hyperventilating. In attempt to gain control of myself, I inhale unhurriedly through my nostrils. Instead of hyperventilating, my body begins shaking from limb to limb. Instinctively I hug shaky arms around my chest. Tristan reaches a hand toward me but stops short as he watches me recoil away from him. He looks like a wounded puppy. "Will you please just listen to what I have to say?"

What could he say? What could he say that would make any difference to me now? He is going away. I focus my eyes on the sunlit, sparkling water that is gently gyrating and lapping up onto the side of the boat where I am sitting.

"I want to tell you what is going on. So just *please* hear what I'm saying, okay?" I don't tell him okay. But I don't say no either. I just sit rigidly in place staring at the water. He takes my silence as a go-ahead. "Wes Bent saw me come out of the water."

I snap my head around. "So what? That doesn't mean anything, lots of people go swimming."

"Maybe, but lots of people don't just emerge from out the water out of nowhere like I do. He was in my spot, the place where I always exit the water to go to work. It's in a very remote area. It's almost like someone had to tip him off about me. When I came out of the ocean, he looked away like he hadn't just seen me and then kept walking as if he was out for a morning stroll on the beach. But I saw the look on his face. He seemed very suspicious. Then later that evening I thought the coast was clear when I dove back in, but at the last minute I heard movement behind me, and I have a strong feeling it was him again."

For a moment Tristan pauses, and I don't say a word. By now I am staring at the folded hands that are resting on my lap. I know that I need to hear what all he has to say about the situation that has led to his decision to leave, so I force myself into silence. Finally he continues. "I'm also quite sure that Wes Bent is connected to all of the pollution that is skyrocketing in the deepest parts of the ocean lately."

"Really? What makes you think that?"

"I've been doing some investigating for a while, and his name keeps coming up, linking him to the whole thing. And then when we all went out to dinner the other night, my suspicions were all but confirmed. He was clearly baiting me over and over again. All that I'm trying to do on land to help my people, instead is only putting them at risk." Once again Tristan pauses, and my heart rate accelerates as I wait for him to continue. "I spoke with my work."

"And?"

"And they gave me permission to consult in a different area for a while. I need...I just need to go away for the time being... and protect my people." From out of the corner of my eye I can tell that he is having a difficult time looking at me. When he speaks again, his voice sounds defeated. "I just...I just wanted to tell you this time."

"I don't see how your going away is going to help anything."

"Well, for one, if Wes Bent suspects what I really am and pursues the issue, I could expose my whole family. I don't want to do that. And then—"

"And then what?"

Tristan closes his eyes for a few seconds before revealing a serious face. "And then there is you."

"Don't!"

"Don't what? Tell you that I'm worried about you? That I know that you didn't just *lose* your seashell? Every time I think about the fact that someone came right up to you and ripped it off your neck it makes me crazy. Don't tell you that you were right about Drake the other day? He's gone now. And I didn't just *lose* him either. The more I'm around you, the more you are at risk. The only reason you are a target is because of me. It's only to make me suffer."

I shake my head. Surely he is not still referring to Keuran. I'd gotten to know Keuran quite well over the summer and although at times he seemed odd, I could never accuse him of the things Tristan does. *Could I?* Tapping my fingers together nervously, I bite my lip, thinking of how Keuran may not even *be* at this moment. I so badly want to ask Tristan if he's seen him in the past couple of days. *Like since that day I spent with him in Philadelphia.* But I know he'll get upset if I tell him about *that* whole story. I swallow. "You don't think Keuran—"

"I think anything is possible when it comes to Keuran. I don't trust him, and I wish you wouldn't trust him either. And…I believe he is also connected to the rise in pollution."

"What? Why would he try to destroy his own environment?"

"I know it might sound far-fetched to you, but Keuran *is* far-fetched. I have never been able to follow his line of thinking. I do know he'd do just about anything to make me pay for simply existing. After all, he *is* older than me…he came first. For some reason he has it in his head that I interrupted his life." Tristan shakes his head. "I don't think many people *could* really understand Keuran— he is not right."

I eye Tristan suspiciously. He is not saying all of this just to keep me away from Keuran while he is gone, is he? Maybe he is thinking if he can't enjoy my company, then Keuran shouldn't either. I lower my eyelashes. If Tristan is leaving, then nothing else really matters. I could care less about Keuran. When I speak again, my voice is just a whisper as I work hard to fight back tears. "For how long? How long will you be gone?"

"I'm not sure how long it's going to take. There is so much going on with the pollution problem and all. It is quite an operation actually." Tristan takes in a deep breath and sets his jaw. The little muscle below his cheekbone begins twitching like it does when he is really pissed or upset. I can tell there is more he wants to say, but now it appears he is having a difficult time speaking. Eventually he swallows hard and looks away from me. But in spite of him facing in a different direction, and even though his voice sounds like a choked whisper, I hear him as clearly and loudly as if he is shouting through a megaphone on top of the tallest mountain. "So don't wait…don't wait around for me, Bethany."

What? Maybe I didn't *hear him right!* "What…do you mean? What are you saying?" My voice sounds as if it belongs to someone else. Like it is coming from a long, hollow tunnel.

"It may take a long time, but I need to do this. I need to make everything all right…for *everyone*." He closes his eyes in anguish. "It might take years and that is not fair to you, so please…please don't wait for me."

The tears that I was trying to hold back are now rolling freely down my cheeks. Groaning, Tristan leaves his spot on the opposite side of *Blue's* front seat and reaches for me, wrapping his arms around my back. "Shit…shit, Bethany, I hate this. Hate this so bad. In a perfect world, the world I dream about, I wanted to marry you. Marry you and live with you on the edge of the ocean. Make love to you. Have babies with you…like baby Hannah…only even better because they would be yours and mine."

His words make me want to sob into his arms. This is all such a revelation—all I've ever wanted with him, all I've ever dreamed of. And now he's finally telling me that he feels the exact same way. But all the joy I should be experiencing from hearing his words is being helplessly sucked out of me like tiny beads of moisture at a carwash during the drying cycle.

Because now he is leaving.

He is leaving and telling me not to wait. I am devastated! Completely and utterly devastated! For a long time he holds me against him while I cry painful tears of good-bye into his chest. After the weeping has subsided, he squeezes me tightly, murmuring into my hair, "Know this...I love you, Bethany. More than anything."

I don't answer. By now I am all cried out and numb—too numb to speak. But as anesthetized as I am, there is one tiny thought that wants to answer his last phrase as it rings out in my mind. *More than anything? Then don't leave!* Instead I look away as he eases out of our embrace, not giving any verbalization to my feelings. I've said all I am going to say. Resignedly I realize there is no use, anyway. He has already made up his mind. As he gets out of the boat, I can feel his eyes on me, willing me to look at him once last time. But I won't. I can't bring myself to look at his beautiful face or the tortured expression that I know is radiating from his green eyes.

He continues backing away as if he can't stand to take me out of his line of vision, leaving me with one more exhortation before he turns. "Please, Bethany, I can tell you don't quite believe me about everything, but just please listen to me and have faith in what I am saying. Don't trust Keuran."

Emotionlessly I nod, giving him what he wants—some type of good feeling in his chest as he leaves me high and dry. The closure he is seeking. *Why not!* Maybe with that single nod he will now have a clear conscience in abandoning me, enabling himself to rest easy and get some good sleep at night.

And I guess that's a good thing—because one of the two of us might as well.

Chapter Eighteen

The rest of the day unfolds in a state of disorientation. My mind seems as though it has depleted itself from any type of emotion, so when the tears start again mid-afternoon I am almost surprised. I didn't think I had one drop of moisture left inside me. But here I am lying on my couch, hugging a throw pillow to my chest, crying like a baby with only the walls of my cabin to comfort me. And some comfort that is—Mr. Horton had left all of his property and belongings in the care of Tristan. Intermittently another question filters through my distraught mind—where does that leave me now? Will Tristan make me find another place to live? If I do stay here, where will he be when I need help with repairs on the aging structure like he originally promised? Void of appetite, not a bite of food touches my mouth the rest of the day—I don't even attempt to walk into the kitchen. By the time I go to bed that night, I am lying prostrate on my mattress not able to move a muscle—succumbing to sheer exhaustion.

Sometime during the middle of the night, I awaken. Still in a semi-state of sleep, I become aware that a type of physical numbness is overtaking my body. My heart begins pounding in my chest. I contemplate whether or not I have fallen into a state of shock. Can I even move? Should I be calling an ambulance? As I'm playing around with these thoughts, the paralysis that seems to be holding me hostage shifts into a feeling of weightlessness. A strong sensation overcomes me. It's like I'm being suspended in midair. All at once what I'm experiencing seems rather pleasant—soothing and caressing. Helplessly and yet willingly I relax into it, allowing every muscle and nerve ending in my body to be stroked into placidity. Suspended in a quiet abyss, it feels almost as if I am floating.

Floating?

What? No!

My eyes flash open, and I take in my surroundings. Nothing but deepened shades of misty blue. *Another dream! No!* How could this have happened? Eyes wide, I glance around in desperation, looking for clues of where I am. Immediately I tense up. I want no part of this fantasy dream. Tristan had shrouded me with type of thing four years ago. Back then it was just a ploy to keep me pacified, and now it is only more of the same. The perfect way to keep me appeased while he goes off to gallivant on his own. How many years of mollification will a dream like this be worth this time—another four years? *Oh no, that's right; this time it will have to be longer—because he told me not to wait!* Well, this dream must have a lot riding on it then. *Forever!*

Well, forget it! I am smarter and wiser this time. "You won't fool me twice, Tristan. Take me back! I want to go back to land!" My voice comes out as a gurgled sound or no sound at all, I'm really not sure. What I am sure of, however, is that I want out of this thing! Desperately and frantically out of this dream! Not able to stay in one place and just *take it* anymore, I begin soaring through the muted depths of the ocean. Clouds of water surround me as I dive up and down trying to find clues that will lead to the end of this underwater realm. Feet turn into yards and then yards into miles. On and on I swim with no end in sight. How long will it take to find an escape from all this fanciful nonsense? On and on I continue to swim. Uselessly.

As I'm gliding along in and out of marine plant life, up and around underwater creatures who seem oblivious to my existence, I cock my head trying to strain my ear. And there it is, just as I'd expected. Barely audible, but still there, nonetheless. The song. Being played over and over again on some underwater stereo system in complete surround sound, drawing me into this enigmatic, shadowy realm. Just like Tristan had explained to me before, the power of his music could do miraculous things to humans—for good or for bad. In the past I'd let his music take complete possession of me, pulling me into a trance. He had control over me each time played. And I had let him, willingly.

But not this time.

Soft, whimsical chords continue to play, as Tristan's voice croons softly into my ears. Diligently, I search for a way to escape it. And after many minutes of struggling, I begin to hear another voice joining in, singing along with the song. A voice that sounds so familiar. It's only after several repetitions of the chorus that I realize that it belongs to me. In urgent, I shake myself. I don't *want* to do this—I don't *want* to sing along.

But the song is so beautiful—the words so personal, written just for me, tugging right at the edges of my soul. Could anything else, anywhere, have so much depth and meaning? Without intending to I begin to relax, not quite remembering what it is that I was trying so hard to fight against anyway. With this loosening of my mind comes an overwhelming feeling of peacefulness. Now gliding through the warm, salty liquid that envelopes me, I relish each touch as it reaches out to my skin. The tranquility that is claiming my body is sensational. I can't help myself—I surrender to it completely.

Somewhere though, in the back of my muddled mind there is a little voice calling to me, telling me not to do this. *Fight this! You need to find your way out of this oblivion and get back to reality!* I shake my head in desperation, trying to free myself from the array of conflicting thoughts. I *shouldn't* be pacified into complacency like this. Deep down inside I know I don't really want this. But it wants me! Every ripple of water that caresses my legs, arms, and stomach feels so good. It's so hard to fight! Maybe I *do* want this. On and on I dip and plunge into a mystical world of blue. Would it be so bad? To just give in and enjoy?

No!

I begin using every ounce of strength I have to pull myself out of the dream state that I am in. And for a few moments, it almost feels like I'm making progress. But then my mind gets distracted for only a split second, and I begin to ease back into it again. Exhausted from the difficult struggle, I am lying in limbo, mind wrestling with all the reasons I am fighting so hard in the first place, when in an instant it all becomes crystal clear. I want no more fantasy life with Tristan. I had deluded myself over him for far too long already. I only want reality: a real, live existence with him and I together.

Or nothing at all.

The last thought cuts deep—so deep down inside that I can practically feel the scars that are beginning to form on my heart. I heave an immense sigh, and a mass of tiny bubbles fills the water around me. The pain inside me is immeasurable. Maybe I *would* be better off drifting in this underwater oblivion, letting my mind take a vacation from all the hurt.

Once more innate feelings rush to the surface of my thoughts. *No! I won't succumb to this!* I can't! My body begins flailing through the current that is continuing to caress my skin. Focusing all my energy, I begin the fight that will take me back to real life.

But how will I get there?

My mind runs down a list of possible how-tos. Could I just swim back? Can I use all my brain power and wake myself up? So far that had not been working so well. Frustrated, I shut my eyes, squeezing them tightly together, ready to give up hope. And then something occurs to me. The music. If I stop the music from playing, then I can go back!

Turning myself around, I begin to swim up-current. Somehow I need to get away from the music that is keeping me in this trance—holding me hostage in this underwater state. Fighting against the strong flow of the water, I begin searching everywhere for the source of the song. But the more I swim, the more tired I become. And still the melody that is reaching out to fill my mind continues.

Then a light switch gets turned on as another thought occurs to me. *Plug my ears.* In order to get rid of the song, I just need to plug my ears. Eyes darting through midnight blue liquid, I begin searching for something I can use to help me drown out the sound. It isn't long before I spy a patch of seaweed swaying like dancing ladies in perfect rhythm to the music. Reaching down to the plants, I pluck some and place it in my ears. Now I wait. Will it work? My heart rate pounds out the seconds as they slowly turn into minutes.

And all at once I know that my plan is succeeding. Full force! Because I am losing my ability to breathe. A surge of panic courses through my veins. Tristan had explained to me that not only did the music put me in a trance; by putting my body in that state, it aided in allowing me to breathe underwater as well. The only other thing that could help me with that was Tristan himself. He had explained that even though I could breathe for a while in a hypnotic condition, as long as he was at my side sending me the needed electrical current, I could breathe underwater for a much longer time. Once again, my eyes begin flitting around as I realize Tristan is nowhere to be found and without the music helping me to sustain, how will oxygen be exchanged? My heart hammers in my chest. *What will happen now?* Will I end up drowning in this water—in this water that is really just a dream? Could that actually happen? Should I just unplug my ears? Over and over I gulp salty liquid, each swallow burning my lungs. I am losing a grip on my surroundings. The murky existence that I am immersed in is now fading in and out of focus. One moment I am still floating in the misty streams of the sea, and the next I am thrown into limbo, unable to appreciate what is going on around me. But in those alternating seconds when I am able to think and feel and exist, I realize one thing to be true—the water from the ocean is suffocating me.

Just when I've reached the moment of desperation, thinking that I am going to have to succumb to the music after all in order to keep from dying, I find myself surrounded by air. Glorious, unadulterated, breathable air. Over and over again I gulp it down, trying to fill up my water-drenched lungs. Something bumpy and hard is pushing into my face. With much effort I move my head a fraction of an inch to figure out what is going on—where am I? It takes a minute for me to have enough air and presence of mind to realize that I am lying facedown in the dark on some rocky beach. Completely drained. It takes all my effort to roll onto my side. Dripping wet and cold, I continue gasping for air. Wrapping myself in a hug, I try to stave away the shivering that is now racking my body. Many minutes go by as I hold myself that way, cradling my limbs with some sort of comfort.

Then without warning, a surge of fury passes through me in spite of my sheer exhaustion, and I lift my head off of the pebbly sand. "It's not going to work this time!" I yell into the night sky. "You can't just play that song and take me swimming and think that it's all going to be okay this time." A lump forms in the back of my throat as I lay my head back down, face resting against the jagged stones and grit. "This time it's not okay," I whisper into the ground. Tears along with water left over from my nightmarish swim are now dropping from my eyes and lashes, running down my cheeks onto the surrounding, pasty ground.

This time nothing is okay anymore!

Chapter Nineteen

For what seems like hours I lie there, face to the ground, but in real life it is probably only minutes. But what is real life anymore anyway? Although my head feels like a brick and my lungs are still on fire, my breathing has calmed considerably. Pulling myself from the gravel and grit, I stand slowly. My feet are shaky. Glancing in every direction, I try to decipher my surroundings. *Where am I?* It's a rocky beach that does not look at all familiar. Using sheer intuition and the glow of the moonlit sky, I attempt to gather my bearings. I figure that I must have landed somewhere south of the cabin. After a few staggered steps, I run my hands up and down the wet, shivering skin on my arms and begin heading north in hopes of reaching home.

Disoriented and cold, I have no idea how long it is taking me to travel along the darkened, seemingly forsaken shoreline. It is as if I am in a time warp or still partaking in some lurid dream. I pinch my forearm hard. *No, really, I am awake now.* Trudging along while attempting to untangle my reality, I am soon startled by a sound. My heart begins to palpitate. In deft motion, my eyes dart left where the landscape consists of mostly trees and bushes. Surely the noise came from that direction. Or was it the water? My head swings toward the sea—so calm and soothing in appearance even after its attempt on my life. There is not one tiny ripple in its smooth surface. *Not from the ocean then.* I keep walking in a forward direction, my steps now a little more hurried, my vision making continual sweeps of the dim topography around me. It occurs to me then how alone and vulnerable I am out in the middle of who knows where, in what I am to assume is the middle of the night. *What time is it anyway?*

Making a quick glance at my wrist to eye my watch, I realize it's not on.

On one scan of the shrubbery that is growing adjacent to the ocean, I detect a looming shadow, long and teetering in appearance. Without warning my heart rate skyrockets, and an intense fear grips me as I realize the sound I'd heard moments before was not a creation of my imagination after all. Now I stand frozen in place not knowing whether to hide or break into an all-out sprint in effort to get away. Before I have time to decide, the shadow fills with a person stepping into the glimmer of the night sky. On instinct I scream.

"Whoa…such lungs!" The voice drips sarcasm. Incredibly deep, dark, and so familiar.

Keuran!

Keuran is still alive then!

For a split second the light from the moon reflects off his amber eyes, and they flash an unearthly brilliance, mimicking that of a cat in the dark. I gasp and step backward, recalling the night that I witnessed the same thing from him as we twisted and turned on the dance floor at an outdoor party. Back then I had assumed it was just trickery from the flickering lights. Was it the same illusion tonight, this time brought on by the rapid movement of clouds passing over the moon?

Irises normal once again, Keuran reaches a hand slowly in my direction. His voice has completed a one eighty and is now filled with concern. "Bethany…what are you doing out here?"

Don't trust Keuran! Don't trust Keuran! Tristan's words keep playing over and over like a broken record through my mind. His figure, distorted by the murkiness of the night, hovers over me only feet from where I am standing. Little by little it inches closer. Little by little I back away. A shudder quakes through my body. Why do I feel so uneasy? Finally in spite of my reflexive retreat, Keuran reaches me. Now we are standing face to face in the light of the moon. My eyes don't leave his as I search his expression for some type of warning—some type of impending danger that might be radiating from him. But his countenance is nonthreatening, altruistic even, laced with worry. I've just run into Keuran on the beach at night and nothing else. I shake my head in relief. It is no wonder my imagination has gone wild, considering all that I'd endured already tonight.

Don't trust Keuran! Screw it, what say does Tristan have on the matter anyway? Tristan is gone now!

Probably forever!

This thought once again brings with it fresh pain! It hurts so bad! Suddenly I have an uncontrollable urge to double over, hugging my arms around my stomach in effort to keep the discomfort at bay. Quickly though, the pain turns to anger. *Screw it! Screw Tristan!* His name alone brings thoughts of hate to my mind as I think of how he has left me once again. "I–I think I was just sleepwalking." My words come out raspy.

"What?" Keuran's eyes narrow, all the while watching my face. "I'd say that's a little unusual considering you are so far from home."

"I know. I…think I've done it before too. It must be something I'm prone to."

His look is still skeptical. "Well, I'd say sleepwalking doesn't suit you. You look awful!" Reactively, I reach a hand to the wet strands of my ratted hair, not at all caring about my appearance after everything I'd just gone through. The gesture does not go unnoticed by Keuran, and his expression softens. "Let me at least walk with you and make sure you get home safely."

I hesitate. *Safe* and *Keuran*—are those two words that should be used together in the same sentence? According to Tristan— *no*. Again though—what do I care what Tristan had to say on the matter? I exhale a long, slow breath. "Okay." My one-word answer does not sound at all convincing, and Keuran looks at me uncertainly before taking his place at my side. Lightly he presses his fingers into the small of my back as if to guide me, and we begin walking. It isn't far into our travels before his hand abandons position wandering up to encircle my shoulder. I feel my body tense. His touch feels so strange. But comforting as well. Allowing myself to relax, I lean into the strength of his physique and let him escort me back to the cabin. I am overcome with exhaustion, and so the trek back along the winding shoreline is made mostly in silence. Keuran seems to sense that I need this quiet interlude and easily acquiesces.

Once through my cabin door, I take in my appearance in the light of the room. I am covered in grit and seaweed. I glance up at Keuran. What I've just now realized about my condition I see reflected in his eyes—I am a complete mess! Excusing myself, I head to the bathroom to clean off my dirty skin and change my clothes. When I reemerge a short time later, Keuran offers to tuck me into bed, but I tell him I'd like to rest on my couch for the remainder of the night. What I don't tell him is that there is a tiny part of me that fears if I go to my bed, I'll get sucked back into that same dream once again. And I don't have the strength to wage that fight for a second time in eight hours.

"Why don't you let me fix you something hot to drink?"

I nod my head. Keuran has just wrapped a blanket around my shoulders and is now watching me while I lay shivering, trying to gain some type of warmth from the fleece material. He begins rummaging through my cupboards and eventually finds some tea. Bringing back a steaming ceramic mug, he hands it to me. In the process a splash of liquid spills over the rim, burning my skin. It takes all my effort not to jump, risking dumping the whole thing on my lap. I am almost positive Keuran notices the spill but makes no attempt to apologize; instead, he stares hard into my eyes as if daring me to flinch. I bite my lip to hide the two-second interval of pain and look away. *Strange.*

Afterward, he settles into a relaxed position on the opposite end of the sofa, playing with his hands as I sip on my tea. Now and then he looks up at me with an unreadable expression in his amber eyes. Each time, unexplainably, a chill shoots down my spine. Intermittently we talk about this and that: whether the tea is doing its job warming me up, how often I sleepwalk, and how I like living out here in this remote setting. As is a usual habit, while conversing, I reach toward my neck to clasp my seashell—only this time to find an empty space. Once again, I am assaulted with the realization that it is gone. Taking a deep breath, I contemplate asking Keuran what he might know about its disappearance. Apprehensively I eye his strikingly dark features, wondering whether I even want to broach this topic with him at all. Maybe due to my fatigue from nearly drowning and lack of sleep or maybe just out of pure curiosity, I throw caution to the wind.

"So…I don't know if you've ever noticed that I usually wear a seashell around my neck, but I haven't been able to find it recently, and I just wondered…you haven't seen it around anywhere, have you?"

Keuran lifts his head to eye me lazily, confusion clearly written on his features. "No, I haven't seen any necklace lying around. But to be honest, I haven't really been looking either. Let me guess, a present from Tris?" I flinch. A teasing grin spreads across his lips. "You didn't lose it, did you? Aw, Bethany, I'll bet you're all worried about that. My cousin is not upset at you… about that…is he? 'Cause he just needs to chill."

I shake my head, no longer wanting to continue the conversation. Plainly Keuran had no part in the disappearance of my necklace. I breathe a small sigh of relief. "I don't think he is too bothered by it," I say dismissively. *I really don't think Tristan is too bothered by anything that concerns me actually, considering that he is long gone!* With that thought on my mind, my attitude shifts. I can feel the anger over everything that has happened lately with Tristan as it seeps into my skin. My change in disposition does not go undetected by Keuran as he studies my face.

"All right—what is it?"

I shift uncomfortably in my spot on the couch. "Nothing, I—"

"Yes, something. Just say it." Keuran looks slightly irritated, but I'm irritated too. But for a different reason. He doesn't have to push me any further. I speak willingly.

"I don't know, I'm just sick of Watch Hill...sick of the ocean!"

Keuran doesn't move an inch, but for a split second something flickers in his eyes that causes me to believe he is having *some* type of thoughts on the matter, but of what I'm not sure. "Well, that is some type of statement, *sick of the ocean*, considering you have a Marine Biology degree."

I close my eyes. He is right. Why do I have a Marine Biology degree? Subconsciously was it all for Tristan? A sick feeling settles into the pit of my stomach. Every move I'd ever made in life since meeting Tristan on that beach as a small child—was it all for him? I thought I'd just had a strong conviction for saving the environment. But was it really that—or was it all just for him? *Oh my word!* There is so little left of myself! He has taken everything: my heart, my thoughts, my subconscious intentions. Well, *almost* everything. He had never wanted to take me completely. He had taken me—mind and soul—but never body. Not mind, body, and soul, making the trio complete. *Well, how gallant of him!* I shake my head in disgust, but mostly in disgust at myself for falling for him and his convincing charms once again.

Now my thoughts shift to the future. Keuran is right; what will I do if my career doesn't involve the ocean? Why hadn't I picked something like teaching, or healthcare, or even the field of law like my father? Opening my eyes again, I speak into the near distance without once seeing a thing. My voice is a dull murmur. "I'm thinking of moving back to Philadelphia."

"Really? Something must have happened to you to make you so desperate to get away. What is it?" Keuran's tone is incredulous, jarring me out of my daze. The sigh that leaves my mouth is deep and heavy. *Crap!* I might as well tell him. I'm sure it's no big secret to him that I'm in love with Tristan. He might as well know the whole story.

"Well, if you have to know, Tristan is gone."

Keuran's jaw tightens. "Gone? How do you mean?"

"I mean gone!" It's not hard to detect the bitterness that is dripping from my tongue as I spew the story to Keuran. "Perfect, gallant Tristan is off to save the world! Or at least *his* world... the sea. Always at my expense, of course! In order to do this, apparently he had to go away...again. Leave me...again. This time probably forever." I lower my head in defeat. "I am so over it! Just so over it!" The words as they are leaving my mouth are like raw flesh being ripped from my chest.

I am so involved in my own distress that I haven't taken the time to see Keuran's angle on the matter. Haven't noticed his trembling hands—until now. Taking a reprieve from my own misery, I look up into his face. For a quick moment his eyes flash anger before he returns my gaze. Lacing his fingers together, he swallows three times as if to gain control of himself. I begin to feel uneasy. Why does he look so bothered by what I have told him? *Is he okay?*

"Keuran?"

He blinks before offering me an unsettled grin. "I'm just... just so sorry for all of your hurt, Bethany." His words come out stilted. My heart begins to pound in my chest. *What is going on with him? Why the sudden change?*

Keuran rises from his lounging position and begins pacing. For some reason I feel the need to make myself as small as I can, curling into a ball on the couch. Stopping midstride, he turns to face me. "I think you should go to bed now, Bethany. Try to get some sleep. It might help."

"You are right," I say with unhidden relief in my voice. Under the current circumstances I'd feel a lot better if he were to leave. Whatever is going on with him seems very strange, and even though I'd gotten to know him quite well over the summer, the person I see in front of me is making me feel on edge. "Well, thanks for everything. For getting me home safely and for listening and stuff." In my mind I can't get him to the door quickly enough.

He turns to look at me once last time before leaving, and this time his countenance seems almost like the Keuran I've hung out with for a good portion of the summer. His voice is pretty much back to normal. "Well, try not to sleepwalk anymore tonight."

I nod vehemently in agreement and then shut the door behind his exiting frame. Fastening all the locks into place, I lean my back against the wooden, interior structure of the entrance and heave a loud breath. What *was* all that anyway? Maybe Keuran was hurt by his cousin leaving and not telling him about it. In spite of their differences and disagreements over the years, maybe there is a real attachment between them. Maybe Keuran is upset right now too. Maybe he is more emotionally involved with Tristan than I realized. *It makes sense.* As much sense as this night can possibly make.

Letting my thoughts rest with that, I crawl back onto the couch, cover myself with my throw blanket, and fall into a deep, dreamless slumber, sleeping into the late hours of the morning the following day.

When I awaken, it's groggily. Out of sorts.

It's hard to think straight. It's hard to think at all. Soon enough though—it all comes back. The whole sorry mess. All the hurt. All the disappointment.

I just want it all to go away. Erase everything completely.

But I'm a big girl now, and even though my first instinct is to stay under my covers and sleep and sleep and never eat again, I pull myself off of the couch, shower, and decide I had better head into town to pick up a few groceries. After searching my kitchen for some much-needed sustenance, all that I discover in my refrigerator is a stick of butter and a rotten apple. When I peruse my cupboards, all I can scrape together is an inch worth of cornflake crumbs in the bottom of the bag. Dumping the box upside down, I empty the contents into my upturned palm and proceed to shove the morsels into my mouth, gulping a glass of water to help wash them down.

Now after picking up some needed items at the store, I am in a daze, carrying bags of groceries to my black, four-door jeep, getting ready to head back to my cabin to do who knows what for the rest of the day.

"Need some help with that?" a familiar, high-pitched voice calls out to me. Before I have a chance to turn in the direction of the vocalization, Jonathan's energetic form pops out in front of me, grinning from ear to ear. "Here, let someone strong like me help you out with that." He grabs the bags from my hands and motions his head toward his upper arms. "Muscles right here."

And I can't help it, now I am grinning. *Jonathan, my personal little angel.* Whenever I am feeling sad, he somehow magically appears. I unlock my back hatch, and he sets the grocery sacks inside. "Thanks," I tell him, my voice sounding like a distant echo. It's as if from all appearances I'm participating in the daily activities of living, but on the inside I am detached, viewing life from the end of a dark tunnel. Jonathan starts thumbing through my items. "Hey, whatcha got in here anyway, anything good? I'm hungry." Half wondering if he's kidding, I watch as he pulls out a bunch of bananas and removes one. *Apparently not.* He passes one over to me. "Here…you have one too. You look like you could use it." Then as if just noticing me for the first time since running into me at the grocery store parking lot, he does a double take in my direction studying my face intently. "Hey… you feeling okay?"

I force a smile. "I'm fine."

He doesn't dwell on it. "Good…you got a few minutes to go for a walk then? What do you say? I'm free if you are." *Yes, I'm free. Too free, actually.*

"Sure."

We head through the streets of Westerly until we reach the waterfront park and Jonathan cocks his head. "This way?"

"Okay." My answers are mostly one-worded, but much to my relief, Jonathan's enthusiasm carries the conversation well all on its own. Before you know it, we are heading off the beaten path onto a more remote setting along the winding shoreline.

"You never came into the shop to get your paddleboard." Jonathan looks over at me. "I know you must have saved up some bucks by now. You didn't go all traitor on me and buy it from that evil shop the next town over, did you?"

I chuckle. "I wouldn't do that. No, I just haven't bought one yet."

Jonathan facial expression comes alight with mock exasperation. "Well, you better get on it. The summer's not going to last forever." *He is certainly right about that. It seems for me that once again mine has already come to a premature closure.*

Shaking my head to rid myself of these types of pessimistic thoughts, I focus my vision on the whitecaps as they arc and roll onto shore. In the wide expanse of the sea, I detect the long, thin lines of a cargo ship as it plods along miles away from land. I glance over at the dark hair on Jonathan's head as he darts in and out of the waves while they stretch onto the sand. In an instant I am taken back to another conversation when he had divulged secrets about mysterious, disappearing ships. Suddenly I am desperate to know more. *Is it possible that these vanishings could be related to Tristan's talk of the growing pollution in the depths of the ocean?* "So what have you heard lately about those disappearing ships you told me about before? Do you know anything else? Any new news?"

Jonathan stops what he is doing midjump through a sweep of tide. Turning in my direction, he regards me with an impish grin. "I *know* that I wasn't supposed to mention anything about it at all. I swore secrecy to my friend. His dad could lose his job if he gets caught leaking information. And I'd really hate to lose that friend in the process."

I crinkle my nose. "All right, I won't press you for more information. But I'd be lying if I told you I wasn't really curious."

Jonathan rolls his eyes and sighs. "Oh, okay, but you didn't hear this from me. And actually it's not really any type of substantial news...but I do know when any investigative crafts have tried to get close to the area, their search always turns up empty. One thing they do report though is some type of strange humming sound in that area, almost like chords on a guitar. But again, they can't find the source of that either. I don't know, it's weird." He grabs my arm lightly so that I'm looking right into his face. With exaggerated slowness he speaks the next words. "And also...*very...top...secret!*"

I smile warmly and run my fingers over my lips as if I am zipping them up. "Got it!"

As we begin heading back toward town, Jonathan's voice reaches out to me once again, capturing my attention over the receding sound of the waves. "Oh yeah, and one more thing, the ships that are disappearing...it's just a temporary thing. In the end all the vessels have been accounted for. And none of them have any recollection of anything out of the ordinary happening to them either."

I stare into Jonathan's face, right through his spirited eyes into my own world of thoughts, trying to put all the pieces of what he's just told me together. But nothing he has told me has any real rhyme or reason to it—nothing that would connect it to Tristan's pollution crisis in the ocean.

But for some reason, deep down inside I can't shake the sensation that it's all somehow related.

Susan K. Flach

Chapter Twenty

I can't tell if the pounding that is echoing through my skull is from the headache that had been threatening to overtake me throughout the night or whether it is coming from somewhere else in the near vicinity. Disoriented, I sit up in bed. A patchy fog is hovering over my sleepy mind, and it takes a moment or two before I realize that someone is urgently knocking at the door. I glance at the clock on my bedside table. Ten o'clock in the morning. *Oh my, I really overslept.* Instinctively I reach for my seashell, and like the rush of a tidal wave, everything comes back to me afresh. Immediately a pang of hurt courses through my chest. *Tristan is gone again, so what do I care about oversleeping?* Now the knocking is louder.

Startling into motion, I jump out of bed and pad through the kitchen into my small front entryway. Undoing the locks, I throw open the door hurriedly, hoping to put an end to the persistent hammering.

"About time." Keuran marches right into the cabin, practically pushing me out of the way. I take a step back to clear his path, hitting my back on the doorknob in the process. A stinging sensation shoots down my spine. Keuran turns to face me, his spikey, dark hair unkempt, his eyes bright with high-wired energy.

I run a hand through my sleep-tangled hair, swallowing twice to get rid of the pasty feeling in my mouth. "I ah...I must have overslept."

"Obviously." Keuran does a quick sweep of my appearance, and as if sensing my startled, hesitant demeanor, he smiles unrestrainedly at me. I feel myself relax just a little. "Sorry to barge in like this. I didn't mean to alarm you." He chuckles and then reaches for my face, stopping just short of touching it as if rethinking the gesture. "Look at you, you almost look scared or something." Pausing for a brief moment, he watches my face. "You're not scared...of me...are you?"

I shake my head and laugh softly, an angst-filled chuckle. "No, of course not."

His lips form into a grin that closely resembles a sneer. "Good. Anyway, what are you doing right now?" With a quick motion he leaves my side and begins wandering around the cabin, talking in rushed sentences about someone lending him a charter fishing boat to take out onto the big waters. If I hurry I can go out on a boat ride with him. I watch him, dumbfounded, as he paces through my kitchen into the living room, picking up magazines, thumbing through them fleetingly before setting them back down again. Alternately he begins straightening pillows and bending over to pick up scattered lint particles on the floor, all amidst taking a second or two to eye decorative pictures on my walls. He seems completely souped up on adrenaline. I observe his manic movements and scattered chatter with suspicion. *What is going on?*

"So which is it...you coming or not?" His question, coming at me so direct, interrupts my thoughts. I contemplate the invitation for as long as it takes me to decide that considering my melancholy condition over Tristan being gone, I'm really not in the mood for any type of hype today. And taking into account the current state Keuran is in, undoubtedly hype is all I'd get if I did go with him.

"No, I don't think so."

Keuran swallows hard. "Aw, come on...it's the perfect way to get your mind off of things."

This time I don't have to contemplate my answer. I shake my head. "No, I'd rather not. I have a lot of things I need to do around here today. I'll pass, but thanks anyway." For a flicker of a moment a look of anger crosses over Keuran's countenance before a wounded expression stares back at me. Then he looks away, and instantly I feel bad. Maybe his unexpected fervor is due to the anticipation of sharing his boat ride with someone else, and now I've let him down. I sigh. "How long will the ride take?"

He looks at me through narrowed eyes. "Take? How long will it take?"

Immediately I chide myself for being so rude. "That didn't come out right," I clear my throat. "Sure…I'll go." With an uncertain expression, he continues to watch my face. "I…I mean…I'd *like* to go. *Really.* When do we leave?" Keuran nods, bites his lip, and grins. "I got the boat. You go get ready."

After shoving down a poppy seed muffin and gulping some orange juice, I spend some time freshening up in the bathroom, slipping into a pair of jean cutoffs and a yellow tee shirt. Taking one last glance in the mirror, I open the bathroom door and present myself ready to go. When I enter the room, Keuran unashamedly eyes me up and down. I look away, an uncontrolled shiver climbing up my spine. Then quickly he changes gears as all the vigor from earlier returns, and he motions me to the door with grandiose gesturing. Once outside, I stare back at the now closed entryway to my cabin. For an instant, one fleeting thought repeats itself over and over in my head.

Don't trust Keuran!

Blinking, I take in a deep breath of ocean air in effort to dismiss the notion and begin following Keuran's retreating frame as he winds down toward the water. Walking while rubbing the skin of my bare arms, I contemplate his erratic, almost outlandish behavior since he showed up at my door this morning. Being honest, it isn't as if Keuran's past behavior has been completely free from strange—today's has been just a little more so, if anything. I chuckle a light, uneasy chortle. *Besides, it's just one boat ride.*

When we arrive at the beach, all that is resting on the shoreline is a rowboat with a small outboard motor. I glance around, looking for the vessel that Keuran had been speaking of earlier, but I don't see a thing. "Where is the charter fishing boat?"

Keuran walks up to the rowboat and pats it. "Too big to bring in to shore. We have to use this little thing to get out there."

We jump in the dingy and begin heading out to sea. Several minutes later, the horizon gives way to a large watercraft. With eyes as round as saucers, I gape openly at the vessel we are advancing toward as it looms like a small ship out of the water. *Whoa!* In my experience fishing boats are about half this size. "Do you even know how to drive something like this?" When Keuran doesn't answer, I glance over at him. But he appears deaf to my question, amber eyes wild, lost in some feverish thought. For one second I have an overwhelming sensation of apprehension as I study the look on his face, and I contemplate asking him to take me back to land right then and there. Then, out of nowhere a sickeningly scary thought occurs to me. *Even if I did—ask—I'm not sure that he would.*

"So little faith, Bethany." Keuran's voice startles me, and fleetingly I wonder if I've spoken my thoughts out loud. "Of course I can drive this thing. Remember I'm from the water. I *command* the sea. This thing is peanuts compared to all I can do out here." His laughter rings out loudly, echoing across the waves. Before I know it, we've reached the ship. "Go ahead, climb on up," he says while motioning to a ladder, hull side. I follow his directions, planting one foot after the other on the rungs that will take me to the ship's deck, all the while fighting down the feeling of unease that is beginning to churn in my stomach.

Once on board, Keuran takes his spot as captain at the helm. Firing up the engine, he calls out *bon voyage* as we pull away. With growing dread, I watch as the little rowboat that shuttled us here is left behind to float aimlessly all alone among the ocean waves. "Won't we need that boat to get back off this thing?" I yell over the din of the motor. *Maybe he just forgot and needs a little reminder.*

Keuran turns his head slowly in my direction and shoots me a look like I'm either crazy or stupid. And at that very moment, one thought hits me full force. *Crazy and stupid—I am crazy and stupid for being out here with Keuran alone at sea!* I swallow hard and fight down the panic that is rising like bile in my throat. Keuran smirks. "I don't believe I *do* need a little boat to get off this thing. Oh, but that's right, you do, don't you?" At this he laughs loudly, seemingly enjoying his own wit. Inadvertently I begin to tremble, and he winks at me. "Don't worry so much, Bethany. Worry does not become you. And you are far too pretty to let something like that ruin your looks."

With Keuran's words of admonition ringing in my ears, I leave his side and stare out over the deck's railing, watching as we get farther and farther away from land. The bow of the boat plows through the open water, creating a wake that reaches high into the air. The more outlying the water, the deeper blue it becomes, at times turning into a bottomless, midnight hue caused by shadowing clouds over the sun. It's while anxiously watching the last trace of civilization disappear, that I detect distant movement in the waves. I stare hard at the water—and then see what's caught my attention. A Boston Whaler—approaching at full speed. My heart leaps with joy as I observe what may be my potential for getting back to the mainland. Raising my arms high into the air, I wave them for all they're worth.

But hope quickly dissolves as a cold sweat breaks out across my forehead. Now just yards from our ship, the whaler continues its approach. As it comes into a closer viewing range, I am able to get a clear visualization of the driver. *Wes Bent!* I shoot a look at Keuran to see if he is aware of our impending company, desperately hoping that it is just some uncanny coincidence that we are running into his comrade in the middle of the ocean.

All hope is thwarted though as I watch Keuran leave his spot at the rudder and proceed to aid Wes Bent in boarding the fishing boat—as if he knew that he was coming all along. And I can't help it, all I can think of is how Tristan had repeatedly warned me about Wes Bent and Keuran and their possible ties to criminal activity and now, unbelievably, here I am stuck out on some ship with both of them. Completely vulnerable and alone.

Once again I glance in Keuran's direction, this time searching his face, hoping to find a glimpse of the boy that was my friend for most of the summer: the person that I considered my buddy, who at times was a little overbearing and even strange, but surely not capable of anything felonious. But the shadows I detect on Keuran's face as he engages in conversation with Wes Bent on the ship's deck are anything but reassuring.

What now? I feel sick. Then it occurs to me: *that's it*—I feel sick. Inching closer to Wes and Keuran, I clear my throat. "Keuran, I'm not feeling so good. Could you…ah…would you mind taking me back in?" Keuran's eyes blaze with irritation, and in that moment I know for sure I am no longer the friend that he liked to *hang out with* over the summer. Immediately my sickness turns to fear.

"What? No—no, I'm not taking you back right now, Bethany." Turning away from Wes, he shakes his head. "Sick, huh?" He pauses, eyeing me up and down. "I hope you're not getting sick of *me*, 'cause I'm not getting sick of you. Look at you, so pretty… such an attractive little thing. I rather like having you along for the ride. Nope, you're not going back now, so you might as well settle in and relax." Turning away from me, he begins to resume his conversation with Wes Bent. Then seconds later snaps his head back around in my direction again, his voice radiating overt annoyance. "Geez, Bethany, I said relax. Look at you trembling all over. Hey, Wes," he calls over his shoulder while still watching my face. "I think we have a little hitch in our plan today. Just a little something that needs to be taken care of. See that rope on the shelf…tie her up."

What? No! In an instant my mind becomes a scattered mess with all my fears coming to life. Like a speeding freight train, my fight or flight reaction kicks into high gear. Eyes darting in all directions, I desperately search for a way to escape. For one split second I consider jumping into the rocking waves of the ocean that are waiting far below the deck of the boat. Then vision flicking to the far left, I spy the Boston Whaler that is still with us, fastened to the side of the fishing vessel. Maybe if I play it smart, it could be my means of escape. Taking a deep breath, I try to reel in my runaway emotions so that I can make sensible decisions. But the panic keeps hovering just below the surface—ready to take control.

Inside I am chiding myself. Deep down I had to know that there was something wrong with Keuran—that he was disturbed and dangerous. But I had chosen to ignore all the signs. Tristan had warned me many times, but I had stubbornly blown off his admonishments. What is wrong with me, anyway—do I have some type of death wish for myself? My frantic desire to survive at the moment is telling me otherwise.

Wes Bent looks momentarily stunned and confused as Keuran issues the command of tying me up, but then a look of amusement spreads across his face. As ordered, he retrieves the rope, only to appear once more befuddled as Keuran grabs it out of his hands. "On second thought, I think I'd rather enjoy doing this myself." In slow motion, Keuran begins his approach toward me, rope in hand. Instinctively I begin backing away. Soon I am pressed into the boat railing with nowhere else to go. Keuran watches as I flounder in terror, my spine pinned to the barrier that is holding me in place. He stops in front of me.

Grabbing my face, he pinches my cheeks hard with his fingers, forcing me to look at him. With untamed, amber eyes, he stares at me while shaking his head in apparent wonder. "You are so damn naive, Bethany! Can you really be that stupid? You have to be the easiest prey anyone could ever find! Little Miss

Altruistic is too innocent and ignorant for her own good." With exaggerated movement he lets go of my face and then re-reaches for it, this time running light fingertips over my cheekbones, trailing them down to my lips. He pauses, looking deep into my eyes as if peering into the depths of my soul. A sneer curls over his lips seconds before he presses them hard against mine. I struggle to get away, but I am pinned in place, unmovable. Seconds turn to minutes as I numb my mind to the feel of his wet mouth covering mine, taking what it wants from me as I sit by helplessly.

Finally he pulls away, his breathing jagged, his eyes revealing a deep, carnal desire. *Don't trust Keuran! Don't trust Keuran! How could I have been so dumb?* My heart is slamming against my chest as I anticipate his next move. "You say Tris left, did he? Well, he's not going to one-up me this time!"

My mind is whirling, trying to figure out where Keuran is going with this anger-driven statement. The intermittent sparks of ire that I'd seen periodically emanating from him over the summer are now completely unleashed. His eyes are on fire. "All my life, ever since Tris was born, he's tried to outdo me. But not this time. He might think by going away he will put an end to my plans. As if! Like that would really stop me." Dark, echoing laughter spills from the depth of his throat. "Holy shit, he is as ignorant as you! No wonder...you two together...no wonder." Now his lips curl into a snarl, and he shakes his head as if shifting gears—changing thoughts. "He knows. Tristan knows that Wes Bent is on to him. By going away he thinks he's going to *save* his people by not exposing them. My ass! Truth is he doesn't give a crap about his people, and that's the real reason he went away. The weak sucker just abandoned them. He is just going to ignore the pollution syphon and let his family rot in it."

My ears burn with his last statement. *So Keuran really is involved in the increase of deep water pollution then.* I close my eyes. Once again Tristan was right. A thought occurs to me then and I force myself to speak out loud. "*Your* people too, Keuran. The people you are talking about are your people too. Surely you care about them. You don't want to hurt them." As the words leave my mouth, I am surprised by how mousy my voice sounds, pathetic and weak. In answer to my incitement, Keuran focuses his gaze on me for one short second and then continues speaking as if I haven't said anything at all.

"But I'm not fooled though, I know a way to bring his ass back here and carry out my plan. For once he is going to acknowledge that it *is* me that holds all the cards." Licking his lips, he turns his attention on me once again. Taking his index finger, he starts at my forehead and traces an imaginary line down the center of my nose lingering on my mouth, staring into my eyes, before continuing onto my neck. Slowly he keeps going, etching a fiery trail down the center of my chest before grazing lightly over my stomach, stopping only when he reaches the top of my pelvis. I hold my breath, waves of nausea trying to overpower me. "I'm not an idiot, Tris." He speaks into the air. "You might act all casual around Bethany in front of me, but I know how you really feel about her. And my guess is this is really going to hurt. Piss you right off. Although why *you* never wanted to have sex with her is beyond me." Once again he laughs, and it registers in my mind that the sound is very unlike Keuran's own voice, closely resembling that of a crazed killer. This only adds to the terror that is now coursing through my body. Keuran sneers as he watches me shrink away from him in revulsion. Still he continues shouting into the air as if his audience is far removed and not standing right in front of him. "Guess I'll just have to show you how it's done. Then you'll get to see what you missed. Yes, I think that's exactly what I'm going to do."

In one quick movement his hands reach to circle my neck, and for a second I believe he is going to strangle me, but instead he tears my yellow tee shirt right down the middle, yanking it wide open. Salty ocean air whooshes in to cover the bare skin on my chest and stomach, accentuating the fact that I am now exposed. Instinctively I reach to cover myself, but he deftly grabs both of my arms, pinning them behind while he presses his mouth over mine, this time devouring me with a crazed roughness. Uselessly I struggle to free myself. Sloppily he runs a hand over my chest, brutally grabbing at my breasts before he reaches for my jean shorts. I suck in a panic-ridden breath. A soft whimper escapes my lips as I wait for him to tear them away from my skin.

From across the deck the intonation of smirking laughter fills the air. *Wes Bent.* Distracted, Keuran stops and turns toward the sound. For a moment he goes very still, his eyes blank slates as if he's forgotten what he was doing, what he is thinking. A second later he gives me a hard shove, pushing away from my trembling body, while zipping up his pants at the same time. *I hadn't even realized they were undone.* The air that leaves my lungs comes in a series of heaving breaths. I try desperately to stifle the sound, not wanting to draw Keuran's attention back on me.

But it seems his urge to defile me is fleetingly forgotten as he is back speaking to Wes Bent or the winds of the sea, I'm not sure which. Leaning over the boat railing, he shouts out his plans into the salt-laden atmosphere. "Soon, very soon, I'm going to get the pure joy that has been owed to me for a lifetime. The pure joy of watching Tris' face while he watches his little sweetie die by the very thing that gives him life…the water." The second Keuran makes his announcement, my life flashes before my eyes. *He is planning on drowning me!* Overcome with desperation, I frantically try to think of a way to free myself. My eyes dart all around in search of random objects, anything I could use as a weapon. Finally my vision rests on Wes Bent. Surely he doesn't want to be an accomplice to murder. Surely he must realize by now that Keuran is nothing but a crazed lunatic! Aiding him in some pollution scheme is one thing, but all-out homicide is another.

Locking my terrified gaze onto his, I begin pleading with my eyes. But by now Wes Bent is grinning like a Cheshire cat. A sick, helpless feeling settles in the pit of my stomach. "So when you say his people…are you saying that there really are humanlike creatures that live in the ocean?" he asks. *Wes Bent does not give a crap about me!*

Keuran's eyes are all lit up and wild, as if revealing the news that will destroy his people is giving him some type of intense rush. "Oh yes, Bent, that's exactly what I'm saying. Tris is one of them. I'm one of them. And there are many, *many* more!"

Wes Bent gasps, pupils dilated as he processes this big piece of information that he's just been handed. Looking like a greasy, used car salesman that has just hit the jackpot at a casino, his countenance lights up like he is counting the dollars in his head, imagining the fortune he can make off this bit of mind-blowing material. *No, he is definitely not concerned with something as measly as my murder!* My vision drifts back to the Boston Whaler as my only hope.

Startling into motion, Keuran picks up the rope that is lying on the ship's deck next to where I am huddled, shivering, and throws it at Wes Bent. "I said, tie her up." Wes Bent looks momentarily confused, but then does as he is told. In the meantime, Keuran takes his place at the helm, turning up the speed of the boat to an unnaturally fast momentum. The waves of the sea become miniature typhoons reaching high into the air on either side of the hull. Their spray begins to saturate any reachable object that is located close to the railings, including me. Shutting my eyes to keep the liquid from blinding me, I foolishly fantasize that when I open them again, this whole nightmarish situation will be over, and Tristan will be here with me smiling into my smile, holding me forever in his arms.

The watercraft jerks to a halt, causing me to lift my drenched lashes and face what is reality. It feels like the boat is swaying. Without the use of my hands, it takes a second for the water to clear from my line of vision. Rotating my neck sideways, I focus on my surroundings. Keuran cuts the ship's engine, making the sound of his voice that much louder. Now the rocking motion seems ten-fold. "Good, a northbound vessel is due to be coming in within the next hour. Maybe Tris will get to witness his little girliefriend take her last breath and his precious water get massively polluted at the same time. You get two shows for the price of one today, Tris."

I strain my head to take a look over the boat's railing to see what Keuran is talking about—desperately hoping to find the ship that he is referring to. The ship that might be my saving grace. A strong wind whips the water-soaked strands of my hair and sweeps across my face, making it difficult to focus. Squinting my eyes in deep concentration, I am finally able to observe what is causing the unsettled currents in the ocean, creating a swirling motion in the airstream as well, rocking the boat. A giant eddy is spinning out of control, interrupting the normal flow of water in the ocean. I can't stop the gasp that escapes my mouth or hide the shocked expression that crosses over my features as I peer over the railing into a cavernous hole—deep down into the bottomless center of what appears to be a massive funnel in the middle of the water.

Keuran notices me looking. A smile lights up his face. A smile laced with deranged amusement and disgust. Inwardly I wince, still not believing that I had allowed myself to be so gullible where he is concerned—still not believing that this guy in front of me who I'd spend a good part of the summer with is now talking about ending my life like it's just another day at the beach. "It's the perfect place to syphon off the sludge and who knows what else from the ocean liners. The pollution is not easily detected on the top of the water because it's getting sucked right down to the bottom of the ocean. So you humans have several years before it will become blatantly obvious. The sea creatures, however, aren't so lucky. It's invading their environment full force right now." I furrow my brow. *Why?* Why would he want to destroy his own people, destroy himself?

As if able to read my mind, he answers my silent questioning. "They've always worshipped Tris. Always! He was always the hometown hero. Tried to make everyone think that he was better than me. Stronger than me. Faster than me. Could outdo me in anything. But not this time. This time everyone is going to know who really held the ultimate power all along. It's a sorry thing that I'm going to have to destroy their lives just to prove it. But maybe now they'll all be sorry they treated me this way. Bet you *now* I'll get the respect I deserve."

Bile rises into my throat. He really is disturbed. I cough and swallow it back down, willing my voice to come out steady when I speak. "What about you? Are you willing to destroy yourself in the process, Keuran?"

Keuran's laugh sounds deep and troubled. "Life is fleeting, Bethany. Or don't you know that yet? Oh yes, that's right, you're about to find out. Anyway…shut up, I didn't ask you to talk. I heard enough talking from you all summer long." All traces of humor, as disturbed as it was, disappear from Keuran's face as he lunges for me. Squirming in place, I try desperately to free myself from the ropes that are entrapping my legs and arms, all the while attempting to use my head, my shoulder, anything I can, as a weapon to fend him off. But I am no match for Keuran's strength as he frees my bound limbs and pulls me to his chest, dragging me with him as he dives into the waves of the ocean that are looming several feet below the ship's deck.

Down, down, down we dive into a silent world of misty gray. Instantly everything around us becomes distant and muffled. One, two, three, four seconds pass. I lose count. *I'm going to die! My life is really going to end right here and now!* Finally we resurface, with Keuran's arm encircling my neck. Both of our heads are bobbing just above the surface of the choppy surf. The deafening roar of the eddy fills the space around us as it swirls viciously, only yards away from where we are treading water. "Tris…Tristan Alexander, I know you can hear me. I know you haven't gone too far away yet. Come on back…come watch the show! This is one I know you're going to want to see," Keuran yells loudly into the salty sea air.

I gasp, trying to take advantage of the few moments I have been given to fill my lungs with oxygen. "Where are you, cous'?" Keuran continues to shout thunderously in my ear. Distracted by the idea of putting on a show for Tristan, he waits with useless endeavor for Tristan to show up and watch me drown. Taking advantage of his preoccupation, I put all of my strength into my elbow, digging it full force into his abdomen. Stunned, Keuran grunts in pain, and his grip around me loosens. Sliding beneath his bicep, I swim away, an arm's length from his reach. My freedom is transient though as he recovers quickly, easily closing the gap between us, grabbing me again. Now his hold around my neck is excruciating, and it occurs to me as I struggle to inhale that he won't need water to steal my breath away. I am being strangulated—certainly seconds away from death. Fading fast. His grip eases up just a tad, and I intake two short gulps of air. *A moment of hope.* But it is soon demolished, as he begins bringing my head under the surface of the shifting waves once again. Over and over he repeats this process, and each time we reemerge, I am given only a scant few seconds to suck in treasured air. Each time I go back under, I am less and less sure that I am going to be able to sustain life.

This time as Keuran holds me under, he presses hard against my shoulders as if he is purposely trying to finish me off. And it occurs to me right then and there that this is it! *I am really going to die!* By now I am so utterly exhausted, what can I do but surrender to it? I've had a good life really, so I actually have no reason to complain. But still, I know I will miss those I love. I will miss Tristan and the future that I secretly, still hoped we would share together when he was finally able to come back to me. My heart aches with hopelessness for those years that will be cut short. *I love you, Tristan!* I tell him telepathically. With every part of my heart and soul—with my very last breath.

A complete calm settles over me, and a moment of gratitude fills my essence as I give thanks that Tristan was not here to witness my drowning, was not here to confront Keuran and possibly lose a fight that would take his life in the process. These are the very last thoughts that ebb and flow through my mind before a powerful, explosive force disrupts the water around me, separating my body from Keuran's, lifting me higher and higher from the depths of the brackish world of muted gray. Up beyond the ocean and all that is in it. Up into a realm filled with miles and miles of open sky.

And life-sustaining oxygen.

My mind spins a million miles per minute as I contemplate how I got here, how I came from being seconds away from drowning, submerged in the far reaches of the sea, to now gulping breath after breath of air with the real possibility of continuing on with life again. Waves slosh all around me, trying to devour me, but I'm floating on top of them, never once taking in a drop of water down my airway. *How can this be?* My oxygen-deprived intellect searches for answers, and I question whether I have actually died and this is my passageway into heaven. And then in one moment of clarity, my vision becomes uncluttered from the turbulence of the surf and swirl of confusing thoughts that are plummeting through my head. And in that one moment, my vision connects with my answer.

In that one moment I come face-to-face with the piercing depths of sea green eyes.

Chapter Twenty-one

Relief and joy rush through my veins!

Tristan!

I have only a few precious moments to gaze on his intense and seemly ethereal face through the spray of seawater that is gyrating around us on the outskirts of the eddy. In one fell swoop he scoops me into his arms and lifts me onto the charter fishing boat. For one split second he stares hard into my eyes before leaving me behind to hurl waterlogged breaths on the ship's deck. Within seconds every ounce of energy departs from my body as I sink to the uneven panels of wooden flooring, limp as a dishrag. How long I lay there wavering in and around the edge of consciousness I'm not sure. But eventually my mind clears with a jolt, and I jerk into an upright position, wondering where Tristan is at—where Keuran is at. My heart is hammering double-time in my chest. Are they out there—somewhere—in the ocean right now fighting? Killing each other? *Oh God, Tristan!* Will he be okay?

Pulling to a standing position, on shaky legs, I teeter toward the railing. Leaning over it, I allow the paint-chipped iron to support my weight. All the while scanning the water for any sign of the cousins. For many heart-stopping moments, all I detect is a vortex of liquid and a bottomless, gaping hole. My heart is in my throat. Pounding. Anxiety stirring. Then out of my peripheral vision I spy lightning-quick movement. Two figures shoot from the waves. Tristan first. Followed by Keuran. The look on Tristan's face is focused and formidable as Keuran leaps toward him. In slow motion their bodies collide, causing a blast of liquid to discharge like a tidal wave high into the air. For many moments all I can see is a fountain of water—disruptions in the pattern of the sea, alerting me to the fact that they are still there, continuing the combat.

It's only when I see the emersion of Keuran's black, spikey hair with a chokehold on Tristan's neck that every fiber in my body screams out in distress. In spite of my exhaustion, I fill with the energy needed to jump overboard, ready to come to Tristan's aid. Without warning, an outpouring of guilt fills my chest as I realize that Tristan would not even be there compromising his life had I heeded his words of warning over Keuran. Not giving it another thought, I grab a nearby rope and begin my dive. But before my second leg can shimmy the barrier of the boat, with the deft move of a panther Tristan breaks free from his pinned position, finds a split second to shout "No, Bethany," in my direction, and then lunges toward Keuran, causing the duo to disappear below the surface once again.

I go still in my tracks. Every part of me is fighting the urge to proceed as intended. *To listen or to jump?* The sound of urgency in Tristan's voice keeps me momentarily suspended in limbo.

Minutes later the cousins resurface, now hovering dangerously close to the eddy. Instantly another thought assaults me—I know Tristan is a practiced swimmer, but if he were to get swallowed up by the powerful swirl of the vortex, would he be able to survive? Keuran's wild eyes are whizzing in all directions, and I know that he is contemplating his next move. More than once he looks over his shoulder checking the proximity of the churning hole behind him, and I can almost read into his thoughts—he will stop at nothing to get Tristan down into that waiting chasm. My stomach rises into my throat. I have to think of a way to alert Tristan, to tell him of Keuran's plans. Before getting a chance to voice my concerns, Keuran yells out loudly, calling Wes Bent to his aid. *Wes Bent!* I'd forgotten all about him.

Hearing movement behind me, I whirl to face Keuran's accomplice as he moves steadily across the ship's deck, waiting for instructions. Keuran points to a large piece of equipment, some type of commercial fishing apparatus, and tells him to throw it overboard. My mind begins frantically spinning. *What does he intend to do with that?* As Wes Bent bends to lift the heavy gear and Keuran dives in the direction of Tristan, in an instant I know the plan.

The sound of my scream fills the air as I watch Tristan's beautiful body getting hurled in the path of the oversized piece of equipment as it plummets toward the water. No one could survive a blow to the head with something so dense—so filled with sharp edges. If I could do anything to stop what I see happening right before my very eyes. If I could reverse time. If the power of love could traverse Newton's law, could defy and overturn gravity, then the large piece of fishing gear would not be traveling toward Tristan's head. And I would not be getting ready to jump overboard to be with him—throwing my body onto his fatally injured body, allowing myself to be swallowed up by the circulating abyss, pulled headlong into the depths of the sea, our souls together forever in death, because I no longer want to live without him.

In slow motion time stands still, and in that fraction of that moment, I watch as three things happen all at once. Tristan maneuvers his body, twisting in a southward direction away from the line of fire. Keuran frenziedly grabs for Tristan in an effort to keep him in the path of the object, putting himself in harm's way instead—taking the direct hit. And Wes Bent, caught by a piece of hook and wiring attached to the device, gets pulled into the swirling waves of the water, left to flounder frantically beside the ship.

Too late to stop my own self in motion, I continue to dive overboard, watching as a lifeless Keuran and a hysterical Wes Bent are being pulled into the eddy, followed by a spiraling trail of blood. Gone forever down into the deep, gaping hole.

Now I too am heading in that same direction, but with a still very alive Tristan left to watch me go down. A wave of irony sweeps over me as I uselessly fight the magnetic draw of the whirlpool.

But the force of the circulating water is not stronger than the arms that come to encircle me stealing me from harm's way, enfolding me in a secure hold. The fight does not come without much effort expended, but slowly, surely, I am tugged away. After swimming a safe distance from the eddy with me still wrapped tightly in his arms, Tristan treads water with my head cradled against his heart. For a long while we stay this way, both seemingly in shock, both overwhelmed by the knowledge that we are still alive and together in this moment. All around us the salty waves of the ocean toss and turn. Yards away, the force of the eddy continues to spin. Soon my body begins to tremble beneath the shifting liquid, my head swaying at the same time.

"It's okay, Bethany. Baby, it's okay…It's finally all okay." Tristan is trembling too. Soundlessly, he takes me to the Boston Whaler that is still tied in place next to the larger, fishing vessel as it shifts back and forth in the surf. Settling me in at his side, he starts the engine. Within minutes, we begin flying at breakneck speed back to the mainland. Never once does he take his arm away from my shoulder during the entirety of the ride. Not once do we say a word. Muted and motionless, we sit staring straight ahead as the wind whips across our faces while we soar through the open plains of the sea.

So much has happened today. Both of us have waded through a roller coaster of emotions; having had near-death experiences; having come this close to losing the one we love right before our very eyes. Tristan beaches the whaler on his own private shore instead of driving to the public marina in town or the dock at my house. Taking my hand, he gently pulls me to my feet and helps me onto solid ground. For a moment as my toes touch down on land, I feel my legs buckle. My head begins to spin and I think I'm going to collapse onto the sand. Apparently my body has reached its limit of shock for the day—most likely for a lifetime.

Reflexively, Tristan reaches out to steady me, pulling my body in to his chest. I hold on tight. In turn he squeezes back, holding me securely against the firmness of his frame. I want to cry. I want to weep with relief that both of us are still alive. I want to break into a sob over all the devastation and the near devastation we just witnessed today. And at the same time I want to shed tears of joy that Tristan and I can finally be together.

As Tristan is holding me and I am sorting out this multitude of feelings, I detect a slight movement coming from the shrubbery that serves as a protective barrier around his secluded beach. Lifting my eyes from Tristan's shoulder, I tense marginally and look in the direction of the sound. Tristan's breathing remains undisturbed. In the brush just yards away from where we are standing, I detect the flicker of a shadow. Holding my breath, I watch as a figure, small and timorous, steps into the light, bringing the darkened silhouette to life. *Rye!* With a haunted expression she gazes in our direction, staring openly with eyes full of longing at Tristan. And in that moment it becomes evident to me that she knows! All that's happened today, all that went down on the open waves of the ocean—she's been privy to it all! And she wants to run to Tristan and take him in her arms, offering the comfort she feels he deserves. But instead, she stares directly into my eyes for a heart-stopping moment before finally, quietly, turning to leave.

In complete obliviousness to the scene that is being played out only meters away from our embrace, Tristan continues to hold me tightly in his arms, his breaths coming in a soft, rhythmic pattern as he presses his face into my hair. And I am left with the burden of the concern of what I've just seen.

Chapter Twenty-two

It's with heart wrenching emotion I contemplate the look I have just witnessed coming from Rye before she disappears into the bushes. There is one thing I can't deny. Her concern for Tristan is very warranted. I squeeze my eyes tightly together in effort to dispel the tears that are trying to come. Guilty tears over all I've just made happen today—all that I hold responsibility for. But it's no use; faster and faster salty drops of liquid begin rolling down my cheeks. "I should have listened to you, Tristan. Oh my word…I should have listened. I didn't believe you about Keuran…didn't *want* to believe you about him. And now look what—" The words I speak are muffled by my lips being pressed against Tristan's chest. And by the sobs that are starting up. "I am so…so sorry."

"Shhhh…" Tristan pries my clinging body gently away from him. Taking his thumbs, he begins wiping the tears from my face. Ashamed, I try to turn away, but he won't let me. Cupping his fingers beneath my chin, he applies mild pressure, forcing me to look up at him. "Don't think any more about it. I'm so glad you are okay, baby. What would I have done if something had happened to you?"

Staring up into his eyes, I can tell he means business so even though I don't want to, I let it go, persuading the tears to recede. Pressing my lips together, I nod once. Tristan offers a solemn smile in response.

"That's better. Come on; let's go." Taking my hand, he begins guiding me along the shoreline pathway that will eventually take us toward the cabin. But he is so quiet en route. *Too quiet.* I stifle the urge to scream out in frustration right into the wide-open air. *Tell me what you are thinking, Tristan. Tell me it really is all-my-fault after all. But please, please just tell me something! Say something!* Instead, I too don't utter a word, and the silence between us becomes deafening. Occasionally I steal a glance over at him as we walk, trying to get a glimpse of his thoughts if perhaps they are written on his face. What an awful thing for him. To confirm the truth of what he had already suspected—that his cousin was instigating a plan to destroy his own people. And then to have to witness evil in action as his close relative attempted murder against the girl he loves—gloating over it even.

Then finally—probably the worst part—to have been the one responsible for the death of one's own flesh and blood. *Though in all actuality, it did happen in self-defense.* If Tristan hadn't been quick at maneuvering, he would have taken the blow from the large, sharp object instead of Keuran. Still, the fact remains that the boy who was like a brother to Tristan, that he grew up with his whole life, who he'd shared his first memories of existence with, is now gone forever. Sighing inwardly, I focus my gaze on the sand as we continue on the path. That's a lot to go through in one day—a lot to go through ever.

Time.

That's what Tristan will need to get over all of this—to try and heal. And that's what I'll give him. However long it takes. My heart aches for him. Also aches to be with him both physically and mentally. Like Rye, I want to take him in my arms and comfort him—but beyond that, taking it a step further, I yearn to console him in ways that I'd never been able to do before. Intimate ways. From beneath my lashes I peer up at him and instantly blush, wondering if he can sense my thoughts. But his profile continues to face straight ahead, solemn and laced with hurt. My heart constricts in my chest. Right now I'd settle for even just talking.

After long miles of quiet, we reach the cabin. Stopping just short of my dock, Tristan turns to look at me. The waves behind us splash up around *Blue* in a calming sort of way, while he studies my face. Finally he shakes his head. "It's over," he says. Turning away for a quick scan of the sea, he looks at me once again. For a second time he shakes his head, this time biting his bottom lip in contemplative thought. "I can't believe it's finally over." His voice is just a whisper. *What is over?*

The problem with Keuran and the whole pollution thing that was destroying his people? Us having to be separated? I really want to ask him if that's what he is referring to by—*it's over,* but I don't. This time when he speaks, his words come out in a breathy rush, edged in anguish. "I love you…so much!" Grabbing me, he pulls me into his arms and hugs me so tightly it's almost frightening. Once he loosens his grip, I cling to him in return. *What now?* Finally I get the nerve up to ask. Pulling away from our embrace, I look up at him questioningly.

"So will you…do you still need to leave?"

He shakes his head and lets a slow breath escape through his lips. "No."

Now it's my turn to sigh. In relief.

Tristan runs a hand through his already tousled hair and looks out to the ocean once again as if turning his thoughts toward home. "No, I won't…but there is so much I need to do now. I have to go see my family." He sighs again, continuing to stare out to sea. "Tell them—"

I watch the strong muscles in his back as they tighten with unease while he faces away from me. Every part of me is screaming to reach out and mold my fingers over the tense blades of his shoulders. From there I would work my hands downward, not stopping until I'd touched every ounce of his skin. Without warning, I begin trembling all over. Hugging myself, I attempt to relieve the growing ache in my body. Finally I look at the ground, anywhere but at him. "Okay." Even I am surprised at how raspy that one word sounds as it leaves my lips.

Tristan snaps his head around and for one moment stares hard into my face, trying to read into my thoughts. I swallow.

Tristan's green eyes turn the color of jade, and for a heart-stopping second, everything around us goes very still. Then he blinks and the electricity in the air slackens just enough for us to exchange our good-byes as he prepares to leave by diving into the sea.

Once inside my cabin I put every effort toward reveling in the joy that Tristan and I can finally be together, but instead my mind keeps flashing back to the menacing spark in Keuran's amber eyes as the weight of his body held me in place pinned beneath him—the sordid feel of his skin as it rubbed against my own naked flesh. In silence, I touch shaky fingertips to my lips, tasting over and over again the metallic flavor of Keuran's mouth as it devoured mine on the ship's deck. Without warning a wave of nausea overcomes me, and I rush to the bathroom. Sinking to my knees, I proceed to puke repeatedly into the toilet. When I am finished, I sit in stunned stillness before I finally begin peeling off what is left of my shredded clothing. Stepping into the shower, I turn the temperature control to scalding. For many minutes I stand beneath the burning stream of liquid, allowing it to turn my skin a seared color of red. It's only when the water has changed from hot to lukewarm and then eventually cold that I snap out of the guilt-ridden daze that I'd entered. Slowly I begin soaping my body from head to toe, trying to wash away the shame and stench of Keuran's touch—and the memory of all that had happened that day.

Keuran was right—I am so unbelievably dumb!

Tristan is gone for one day and then another. And I am stuck on the mainland—without him. I go into work and try focusing on the newest project that's been added to my list—*superstorms and their impact on the ecosystem*. But it's so hard to apply myself when everyone else is carrying on like nothing has happened. And yet I have just lived through a huge ordeal that was carried out unbeknownst to everyone else, right in the middle of the sea. Obviously the news of it has not reached land. There is a part of me that wonders if Tristan has gone back out to the scene and cleaned things up, causing the crime to vanish into thin air. And what of Wes Bent? Surely he had to have been missed by now. As I bring to mind his greasy persona and the sleazy smile that covered his face, a shudder is my response. *Or maybe not.*

Several more days go by. And still Tristan is gone. I begin to question all that he had communicated to me on the day he left, back before the whole thing went down with Keuran. He had told me that in a perfect world he had wanted to marry me and have babies with me and more or less live happily ever after with me at his side. Did he really mean those things, or was that just something he said to make me feel better because he was leaving? Every hour that he is gone is an hour that my mind fills with increasing doubt.

So when I receive a text from Lucy telling me that she is rolling into town for a visit, I breathe a sigh of relief, knowing that she will be the welcome distraction that I need.

"This dress would look cute on you. You should try it on. Almost as pretty as the one you have on."

I smile, eyeing the striped dress that Lucy is holding out to me. She had arrived in Watch Hill the night before only to disappear a short time later to spend most of the evening with Ethan. So it wasn't until the following morning while we were lounging around in our pajamas, cups of coffee in hand, that she had detected my subdued state. In turn, I had told her the abridged version of Tristan's current problems concerning the criminal activity involving one of his family members. Later, around noon, she had gone rummaging around in my closet and reemerged with a baby blue sundress, telling me to fix myself up really cute; we would be going out for an early dinner and some shopping in a few hours. I can't help but grin from ear to ear, as I remember how she always came to the rescue when trouble found me during our growing up years, seeming to know that some frivolous girl time is just what I needed. Having done what she had suggested, taking extra pains on my hair, it was falling in cascading waves over my shoulder, with a few strands pinned in a decorative barrette at my ear.

Now we have just finished a delicious dinner at the Olympia Tea Room and are mindlessly perusing shops, giggling and rekindling a kind of high school girl ambience, causing a few interrogative looks to be sent our way. I run a hand over the striped dress that Lucy is holding out to me and try to decide if I can see myself wearing it, and for what occasion. Lucy's doelike, brown eyes sparkle as she sends me an imploring smile. For a moment her irresistible beauty reaches out to me, and I am tempted to go to the dressing room and try on the dress just to please her, but then the inducement passes, and I crinkle my nose. "I don't think so. I just don't see myself in that one."

Feigned disappointment crosses over her features. "Oh all right, but I think it would look awesome on you. Sometimes you sell yourself short. Like today…I hope you know how gorgeous you look today. The color of that dress brings out the color of your eyes completely, making them practically pop." For a quick instant she eyes me up and down, appearing to work hard at containing a big smile. "You look so perfect."

Slightly confused at her demeanor, I cock my head in question. "Okay?"

In a flash her disposition changes as she grabs my hand. "Come on…what do you say, do you want to check out the art gallery? I heard from a reliable source that there are some cool new pieces being displayed."

"Let's do it. By the way, the reliable source doesn't happen to be someone named Ethan Vaughn, does it?"

Lucy giggles and bites her lip. "Maybe."

I let go of her hand and nudge her with my elbow instead. "How is it going with that boy anyway?"

"Well—"

"Well what?"

"Well, I really like him, Bethany. Maybe even love him. I really think he might be *the one.*" *Seriously? Flirtatious, sexy, make-everyone-come-undone Ethan Vaughn? And he might be your ONE?* Inside I am shaking my head, picturing a million ways that my lifelong friend could get hurt by someone like Ethan Vaughn. Out all of the guys that would happily volunteer to be Lucy's suitor, she picks him as the *one?*

"Just—" My voice sounds slightly cracked, and I have to clear my throat. "Just be careful, Lucy, Ethan's so—"

"So...what?" Lucy interrupts me. "Just so perfect for me, that's what he is."

We are entering the art gallery. The door closes behind us and we pause, looking at each other. Lucy's brown eyes are daring me to challenge what she's just said. I swallow down the lump that is trying to form in my throat. I just want to don a suit of armor, grab a sword, and protect my friend from all the dragons that are out there. A small sigh escapes my lips. "I just want you to be...to be happy."

For a moment longer she stares into my eyes, her voice soft. "And I am."

We both turn away—end of conversation. It isn't long before the old lightheartedness between us returns. Soon we are oohing and aahing at the beautiful scenery and landscapes captured in various paintings, exclaiming over the clarity in some of the close-up photo shots, and making silly interpretations of abstract drawings. A couple of times a patron or two dressed in crisp business attire shoots us a perturbed look, and we try to rein ourselves in, trading our exuberance for hushed, serious tones. Nodding our heads in a formal manner, we proceed to examine the displays in front of us.

It isn't until we step foot back on the pedestrian-filled sidewalk that we speak at a normal decibel again. "Well, that was fun," Lucy chuckles.

"I know. Good idea. I really love all the artwork. I just don't understand why you have to be so serious when you look at it."

This time Lucy laughs outright. "Did you see the look the guy in the red mustache gave us?"

Now I am laughing too. "Seriously! That was priceless. I wonder what he does for fun?"

We stay that way joking and kidding around for a while longer as we saunter down Bay Street in front of the boutiques, restaurants, and souvenir shops. The ocean surrounds us, splashing playfully in the background, creating a charming, touristy ambience. Eventually Lucy turns to me. "Well, listen, I have to get going, and you should be heading home, but I'll catch up with you later." Her eyes are shimmering with excitement. *Okay, she really does like Ethan.* But I am sad to end our afternoon of fun. Lucy detects the flicker of disappointment that crosses over my features, but her enthusiasm doesn't waver. She reaches out to pinch my cheek. "I promise I'll catch you later, okay? And smile, you look so pretty when you smile." Her voice almost sounds giddy. Heading in the direction of home, I leave Lucy to her carry out her own plans for the remainder of the day while I narrow my eyes in contemplation. *Okay, that was a little weird. Something is up with her.* But what?

The trip back to my cabin is an unhurried, shoreline stroll. I am in no rush to spend the evening alone. Coming down from the high created by a fun day spent with Lucy, my thoughts unwittingly turn to Tristan. I can't help but wonder if he's having a hard time dealing with all he's recently been through. Or if he's had trouble revealing the news to his parents and other family members. Or if he even remembers all that he once told me about his thoughts and feelings for our future. Or if he's ever really coming back. I am winding around the last bend in the coastline before I reach the beach in front of the place that I now call home when I pause in place. My heart goes still.

Just yards away Tristan is leaning against *Blue*, arms crossed, green eyes looking my way. My heart, remembering that it needs to beat, breaks into a runaway rhythm. How long I stand there staring at his wind-tossed hair and the perfectly chiseled features of his face, I'm not sure. Somewhere in the back of my mind it registers that he is more dressed up than normal, wearing crème-colored pants and a pale green, buttoned-down shirt. Fleetingly I contemplate the possible reason for this and wonder whether they've held the memorial service for Keuran only just today. The minute he detects my presence, his lips break into a smile, and joy floods through my veins. His gaze sweeps over me—head to toe. Immediately I am reminded of my own dressy apparel. Self-consciously I reach for the decorative barrette that holds the waves of my hair in place. He bites his lip. "Hey, beautiful."

"Hey." My voice is breathless. He holds out a hand, and slowly I begin walking across the sand toward him. Finally I reach the place where he is standing, and he curls his fingers around my palm. He is still smiling. *And I am so relieved!* He seems genuinely happy to see me. And yet I am a little confused as well—this is different from any reaction I've received from him in the past. In previous times his face has always been edged with a fraction of seriousness when he'd greeted me, like he was warring with some type of inner struggle. I want to attribute this new demeanor to the idea that he finally feels free from the burden of thinking we'll never really be together. *I can only hope.*

He looks deep into my eyes for a few heart-stopping moments. "I've missed you." His voice comes out sexy and deep, and that rush I can only accredit to him comes surging through my body, making me feel incredible all over.

"Same here."

"Are you busy? What are you doing right now?"

Not a thing. Not a darn thing but spending every second I can with you. "Nothing really, I was just walking home from town."

"Do you have time for a boat ride on *Blue*?" *Do I!*

I can't restrain the grin that forms on my lips. "Sure."

Tristan watches my reaction, winks and smiles back, then we load the boat. We are settled into the front seat when he turns to me. "I love that blue dress on you. It really brings out your eyes." Experiencing a sense of de'ja'vu, I think back to Lucy telling me that very same thing earlier in the afternoon—and actually she'd been the one who picked it out for me to wear. This along with another thought occurs to me, something else Tristan and Lucy seem to have in common today—their perpetual, extremely happy smiles. On the inside I am shrugging my shoulders. *Compliments and smiles, that is not such a bad thing.*

Many minutes into the boat ride, I begin to get a premonition of where we are going. I glance over at Tristan, but his face gives nothing away. But the second I detect the small body of land rising from the water, I know I am right. Tristan's island. This time when I look over at Tristan's profile, he returns my look with a heart-stopping grin. After beaching the boat, he grabs a duffel bag and takes my hand as we begin the same walk that we'd made only once together before. My chest pulsates with the cherished memory.

A few short minutes later, we enter the setting of a postcard-perfect beach. Tristan spreads out a blanket and motions for me to sit down. I watch as he takes a bottle and two long-stemmed glasses from his bag. He looks over at me. "Champagne?"

I nod my head slowly. *Okay, what is going on?* Deftly he pops the lid. Filling both of our glasses, he hands me mine. He begins searching my face and the smile from earlier fades. "So how have you been? You went through a really scary ordeal that day. That day out there on the water with Keuran. I'm sorry I had to leave you when you were coming off all of that." He swallows before continuing. His tone is sober as he looks me in the eye. "And I'm never going to leave you again." *Oh my!*

Now I swallow hard. "I'm okay…and you? You went through a lot too."

Slowly he nods. "I'm good. I've worked through a lot of things and I'm good. Right now, I'm really good. Right here and now, being with you, I'm really *really* good." Instantly goose bumps cover my skin. A slight grin crosses over his face. "Are you thirsty? Take a drink." As if just noticing the flute in my hand, I take a sip of the fizzy liquid that is shimmering in the glass. The bubbles slide effortlessly down my throat. Instantly I become warm all over. For a moment or two we sit in silence drinking from our long-stemmed glasses. The heady rush that I am experiencing from the champagne and from being so close to Tristan is overpowering. When Tristan begins speaking again, I pause, listening. "All my life I've waited to be right here with you." He shakes his head in disbelief. "And I can't believe it…I can't believe that I am actually here…that you are here…with me. We've had so many obstacles to overcome, I wasn't sure it could actually happen. But now it has, and I don't want another minute to go by. I don't want to waste another second." He situates himself so that he is looking directly into my face. Involuntarily my lips part slightly, an innate reaction from having him so near. "There is something I want to ask you." *What?* My eyes go wide. Without warning I begin trembling all over.

Tristan shifts his spot on the blanket until he is on one knee, positioned exactly in front of me. I press my hands together, trying to stop their uncontrollable shaking. My heart is pounding in my chest. He clears his throat, green eyes looking deep into my own blue. "Bethany, I love you so much…Will you marry me…be with me forever?" *Oh my word!*

I struggle to fight the tears of joy that want to escape from somewhere deep down inside me. Losing the fight, little droplets of liquid begin streaming down my cheeks. Inhaling the ocean air around me, I try to catch my breath. "Yes…yes…I love you, yes!" *A thousand times yes!* A relieved smile forms on Tristan's lips, and he reaches into his pocket, pulling out a sparkling diamond ring. Taking my trembling hand, he slides it onto my finger while I watch from somewhere in the nearby atmosphere high above, somewhere outside of my own body. Finally I float back down. Tenderly he pulls me into his arms, and I hold tightly to his back, my head cradled on his chest. While we are pressed into each other, for a brief moment, all of the day's unusual behavior from Lucy comes floating back to me—her picking out my dress, the continual influx of encouraging words, the giddy behavior, her shooing me toward home—cutting our time together short. And I wonder: *Was she privy to this whole thing beforehand?* A slight grin forms on my lips—because I'm pretty sure I know the answer to that question. Seconds later every other thought fades from my mind, and it's just me and Tristan again, together in an embrace. I squeeze tight.

A few moments later, I press my hands against his shoulders and begin to pull away. Now our mouths are only inches apart. A soft moan escapes from my lips as a thought comes rushing into my mind. In the past Tristan had said that we would share our love physically when he knew for sure we could be together forever.

Now is finally that time.

Unexpectedly my body goes weak with anticipation. I can barely breathe. Slowly my face moves toward his, our gazes locked. Tristan's green eyes are dark. But my lips have barely brushed against his before he turns away, leaving me to kiss his cheek instead. *What?* Tristan lets out a light, nervous laugh and nudges me gently away from him. "I better not kiss you right now, Bethany."

I am so confused. This guy completely confuses me! I narrow my eyes in question, hugging my trembling arms to my chest. "I don't understand...I thought—"

"If I kiss you now...I guarantee you I won't be able to stop."

"And? I thought that—"

"Bethany, we've waited this long...let's wait until we get married."

No! I let out a long, slow breath. "But we've already waited so long, and now we're really going to be together forever, and you said when we knew that for sure, we would give ourselves to each other completely. I don't want to wait anymore."

Tristan takes my hand and squeezes it, his voice filled with enthusiasm. "Well, let's get married soon then. Very soon!"

Now he has my attention. "Really? When?"

"As soon as we can make the arrangements…and talk to our parents about it."

I watch his face to see if he is for real. The light in his eyes does not flicker even for a second. "All right, I'm in. Let's do it." *What am I saying? Of course I'm in!* "But really…I can't kiss you?"

Now Tristan exhales long and hard. "Knowing that we are free of the obstacles that held us apart, I just don't think I could do it and still hold out for the rest until we're married." He lets out an edgy chuckle. "Or should I say *not* do it."

Resignedly, I sigh. "Okay." Tristan puts his arm around me, and we sit together watching as the sun slowly dips into the sea, leaving a trail of burnt orange and purple laced with ribbons of fading magenta. Beneath the horizon, turquoise waves explode into intervals of frothy, white seaclouds. The postcard-perfect atmosphere. And I am completely captured. With toes dug into the sand, I enjoy every second of the moment with Tristan at my side. On occasion though, he glances over at me with a look that makes it difficult to breathe. Attempting to take a calming breath, I turn away. After a few of his *looks,* I can't take it anymore. Holding his gaze, I clear my throat. "You know, if you keep looking at me like that, I am not going to be able to restrain myself from kissing you…and then I won't be held responsible for what happens after that."

Breaking into a cat-got-the-canary grin, Tristan nudges me playfully. "Duly noted," he says.

Laughter is exchanged between us. We are both on cloud nine.

Packing up our duffel bag, we begin heading back to the mainland. All the while my heart is dancing in my chest as I begin to mentally make plans for our wedding, which will be taking place in the very near future.

Chapter Twenty-three

True to his word, Tristan seems eager to carry out our plans for marriage. Now that things have settled down and the pollution syphon has been taken care of, we are able to focus on the rest of our lives together. Mostly Tristan seems reluctant to talk about the whole thing concerning Keuran and the operation he had going on in effort to destroy his own people. But he is at least willing to answer a few of my questions, explaining in more detail some of the particulars of the illegal venture. Although the sailors had been willing participants, Keuran had been using his music to put all the ship's captains and crew into a trance so that at best, after the dumping occurred, they only had a foggy recollection of the event and zero knowledge of the whereabouts. Keuran had picked a perfect spot, using the unstable sea conditions of the giant eddy to throw the detection of the ships off radar, having had very similar effects to that of the Bermuda Triangle. Now that the whole operation had been shut down, no answers would ever turn up to validate the mysterious disappearances, and it would all be considered an unexplained phenomenon.

Tristan had worked hard to eradicate any evidence of the scheme in order to avoid drawing unnecessary attention to his people. But now that we are jumping into the next phase of our life, one major thing needs to happen first: I need to meet his parents. Tristan is certain that his parents will accept his choice for a life partner if they just meet me, but the problem is they aren't willing to come on land to make this happen. So I have to go down into the depths of the sea. And even though I've done this twice before with Tristan in a dream, I am really anxious about going there knowingly again. Although Tristan has explained the way it works in detail, on the inside I am nervous that I will panic once I'm submerged in the far reaches of the ocean floor and then it will be too late—there won't be enough time for me to get back out.

But Tristan reassures me more than once that as long as he is right by my side feeding me his life force, my breathing will be perfectly okay. Although I completely trust him, I am smart enough to know that things can go wrong. Unplanned things and what then? What if for some reason he has to leave my side? Stifling a shudder, I try not to think about it.

The one thing Tristan does make crystal clear to me is that this is a one-time type of deal. The past two times he'd taken me into the depths of the ocean, it was as a desperate attempt to help me move on with my life. Each time I am submerged at those distances below sea level, it is really hard on my body. And every time I go under it takes a little more of a toll. I won't be able to sustain this type of activity too many more times before my physical makeup will no longer be able to survive against the extreme depths. And then basically I will become very sickly and die. Tristan's face becomes grave as he tells me again that this will definitely be the last time.

Now we are preparing to submerge, and Tristan keeps eyeing me apprehensively. I can't help but wonder if the cause of his angst is because he isn't sure that I should be going under even this *one* time. Does he worry that I won't be able to withstand the descent after all? Or are his features tensed in anticipation of his parent's possible reaction to him bringing home a girl from on land? Either way his trepidation is doing little to set my mind at ease. Without warning, I begin shaking all over. Tristan is situating a blanket on the sand, and he stops what he is doing.

"Are you okay?"

I chuckle nervously. "Me? Better yet, are you okay? Because you really don't seem like it, and I admit that has me a little worried."

Tristan blinks and opens his arms. "Come here." I go to him and tuck myself in his embrace. "I'd be lying if I told you I'm not a little on edge, but it's just because I need to focus and make sure everything goes perfectly, that's all. But trust me, I'm going to take very good care of you, I promise you. Everything is going to go great."

I snuggle deeper into his chest. "And your parents?"

"And my parents are going to love you. How could they not?" Even though I can't see his face, I can sense the smile that is forming on his lips. In reaction, a grin works its way onto my own, albeit an anxious one. I squeeze his chest and pull away.

"So tell me one more time how this is going to work exactly. What will actually be happening?"

Tristan tucks a loose strand of hair behind my ear. "Okay. So you're going to lay down on the blanket and just relax, and I'm going to play and sing for you until you're ready to go with me."

I interrupt. "So basically you'll put me in a trance, right?"

Tristan hesitates. "Yeah, basically. And then even though I'll actually stop singing, the music will continue for you only to hear, keeping you—"

"Keeping me in a trance."

Tristan nods his head slowly, watching my face. "Right."

I sigh, still slightly on edge. "Will I actually experience getting up from the sand and following you into the water, diving under?"

Tristan presses his lips together and shakes his head. "No... I'm going to keep you pretty sedated until I feel like you're ready to wake up. By then you'll be down in the depths quite a ways. The descent can be difficult so you shouldn't ...it's best if you are asleep for that. And then coming back will be the same way. I'll put you into a deeper state right before we ascend." He squeezes my hand. "And I'll be right there with you the entire time, giving what you need to breathe."

I close my eyes and then open them again, trying to convince myself that this whole thing is going to go off without a hitch.

In some ways it would have been easier if Tristan would have come and stolen me from my sleep, taking me there completely unaware like he had in the past. But I have to admit it feels good that he respects me enough to include me in all of the plans.

"And in a couple of weeks we are going to be married." The tenderness in Tristan's voice breaks through the silence of my deliberations. His words are like a soft caress in my ear. *That's it! That's all I need.*

I look him in the eye. "Okay. I'm ready."

Situating myself on the blanket that Tristan has laid out on the bay of sand, I close my eyes and will myself to relax. Unsure of what to wear for such an event, I've chosen a floral sundress, with a swimming suit slipped discreetly beneath, of course. Tristan begins singing, and I am instantly reminded of how beautiful his voice is. Breathy and seductive. Inadvertently I wonder what condition my apparel will be in by the time I reach Tristan's home. In all actuality did it really matter what I wore? Will my floral dress float above my head, exposing too much skin—? Maybe I should have just settled for a simple, one-piece swimming suit instead of the bikini that I'd selected. Will Tristan's parents even care? Does everyone just swim around down there naked? *Oh my word, I should have asked Tristan that question!* Blushing, I imagine Tristan—in that *condition.* For a moment, I contemplate trying to fight the relaxing feeling that is sweeping over me. Maybe I should stop this whole thing. Get a little more information before I descend. But the music is making me feel good all over, and I can't imagine in a million years allowing the sound of Tristan's voice to stop resounding in my ears. So I relax into the warmth of the soft material that is positioned below me, allowing myself to experience the feel of the musical words as they float over me.

By now little else matters but the reverberation of the music anyway. Any other thought is just a distant reflection.

My next recollection is miles and miles of an endless, misty blue void. For a split second I panic because it feels like

I am completely alone underwater. And although it seems questionable, I know this is very real and not some sort-of dream. Soon though, the vaguely familiar feel of an electrical sensation slides over me, and I begin to calm. Tristan. I turn to my left, and he is there as promised right by my side. He smiles and I smile back, relieved. *We made it here!* I allow my lungs to expand, then retract. And I seem to be breathing okay. Not saying a word, he motions for me to follow him and begins guiding me through an endless, hazy sphere. All at once it occurs to me that we aren't conversing aloud, and I have to wonder if his people only communicate silently to each other. Just one more thing I hadn't considered. How he will introduce me to his parents? Will I understand what is going on if they don't verbalize their thoughts? Suddenly I become nervous all over again. In response, the electrical buzz that is surrounding me heightens, and I know that Tristan is doing his best to slacken my angst.

And it works—immediately I relax. Now bits of color begin to fill the space around us, and I start to notice the encompassing underwater sea life as we swim. Schools of fish. A family of seahorses. Deep-sea turtles. Even the waving arms of an octopus. Opposite of what I'd expected, the greater our descent, the more vibrant life around us becomes. I shake my head in question— why is that? I turn toward Tristan and mouth *wow*. And he smiles back knowingly like *of course this is completely awesome, this is my home and I love it.*

I snicker outright, surprising myself that I can actually hear the sound of my laughter. He is so confidently sexy even down here. I guess personalities don't discriminate over land and water. An unexpected rush shoots through my veins. He winks. I blush and we keep swimming.

The more we keep going, the more the landscape changes. Soon we are surrounded by bundles of sea grass and a variety of underwater vegetation. Hollowed caverns and stone formations protrude from the ocean floor at every angle, creating a busy atmosphere, making me feel like we've just arrived somewhere—as if we're on the outskirts of town. Tristan looks over at me and smiles, and I know I'm right. We're getting close, and he's getting excited to show me his home. We continue swimming in and amongst the rocky configurations, and before I know it a metamorphosis occurs, transitioning the excavated boulders into well-sculpted castles, no longer making them seem random and organic in appearance. The realization of it hits me all at once. Stopping the fluid motion of my propelling arms and legs, I glance in all directions, taking in my surroundings. *Oh my word!*

It's a small city!

An underwater city! All around me are intricately constructed structures and dwelling places ornamented with precious metals and glistening gems. Light from the conglomeration of crystals refracting off each other causes the region to shine brightly. Taking in a sharp breath, I gasp from the unadulterated beauty. I'm not sure what I'd expected but not this—definitely not this. I can feel Tristan's eyes on me watching my reaction as I take in his world. "So beautiful," I mouth to him, and he nods his head as if to say thanks.

Then out of the corner of my eye I detect movement, interrupting my impromptu tour of his city. With a slow, sinuous motion I turn my body toward the activity that has attracted my attention, and once more I am taken by surprise. *A real, live being swimming underwater!* I stare openly in amazement. I sense Tristan's laughter beside me, and it hits me that this should not be a surprising phenomenon—after all, I am engaged to a sea person. But in spite of this and in spite of having known Rye and Keuran as well, I am not prepared for my reaction. All of a sudden everything seems very real. This whole underwater-realm-sea-creatures-actually-do-exist situation is completely absurd—and to think that I'm now a part of it seems even more preposterous! But I'd experienced this with Tristan for so long, watched him dive into the waves at the end of a date, swam side by side with him in a lucid dream—am swimming beside him even now. And yet the sighting of a real, live sea being in this organized environment has me completely dumbfounded.

As if to compound the overwhelming situation further, one, two, three, four, several more swimming people arrive on the scene, going about their business as if I'm not there invading their space. As if I'm just another person walking on a downtown sidewalk. *Swimming! Swimming on a downtown sidewalk!* I want to pinch myself. "Are you okay?" The sound of Tristan's voice startles me. *We can talk! It's actually possible to converse out loud in this place.* Suddenly I'm relieved.

"Yeah, I'm okay. It's all just so…incredible! I'm not sure what I expected." My voice sounds slightly muffled as it resonates through the water, but still I am able to vocalize my thoughts and feelings, and that causes a weight that I hadn't even realized was there to fall off of my shoulders. The humming sensation that is perpetually hovering in the background intensifies, and once again I know that this is Tristan's way of giving me a reassuring hug, all the while keeping our connection intact so that I can keep breathing.

"Well, let's keep going; we're almost to my place." We resume movement, falling into the flow of the others that are swimming around us, but now it's hard for me to stay focused on our forward motion. I am continually checking out the ethereal scenery of the carefully constructed fortresses and turrets in the underwater domain, always mindful of the beings that are subsisting only feet away from our plunging arms and legs.

"Hey, Tris…dude, Tris." Two deep voices call out in unison, and we pull to the side to greet a pair of males with light brown hair, looking to be around the same age as Tristan. Their blue eyes dance as they take in Tristan and then me swimming so closely at his side. Identical twins. For the first time since I'd arrived at the city, I am conscious of my attire. Glancing down at my floral dress, I am surprised to see that it is staying in place rather well.

Now my curiosity gets the best of me, and with one sweeping gaze I take in several of the other traveling creatures' apparel around me and notice that most of the females are clad in dresses as well. Lightweight, ribbony, fairlylike flowing concoctions, but dresses nonetheless. Thankfully the males are covered in shorts, most wearing ornamented chains or scarflike collars around their necks—some so large that they cover most of their bare chests. The twins in front of us are no exception.

"Zepther, Seth…it's all good. Brothers…what are you up to?" Tristan enters a playful repartee with the identical sea creatures, his face lighting up in a smile.

"Us—what about you? She's the one, isn't she?" The one on our left, who I find out seconds later is Zepher, focuses his gaze in my direction.

"Definitely, she's the one. This is Bethany. Bethany, these are my good friends Zepher and Seth." All three of us smile and say hi in greeting but don't shake hands, causing me to speculate that handshaking is not a custom in their culture. We carry on a lighthearted exchange before Tristan tells them it's time for us to get going, and I wonder whether we are on a time clock due to me and the whole lack of oxygen thing.

"Meeting the parents?" Seth questions. Tristan nods in answer. "It's all good, Tris. It's all going to work out." Once again Tristan nods, and for a fleeting second I detect a worried expression cross over his features. A swarm of butterflies begins fluttering in my stomach. Immediately the buzz around me intensifies, and seconds later I'm okay again. Curiously I ponder how he manages to keep doing that to me. How does he have such a keen sense of my need?

After that we say our good-byes and keep heading toward our final destination. All around us the underwater city is alive with activity, and I briefly speculate whether we will run into Rye in the midst of all the commotion. All at once my heart starts beating wildly with the thought, and I take a deep breath to calm myself before Tristan detects my newest anxiety. It seems to work, because my rapid pulse rate quickly subsides as I remind myself that Rye is not an issue anymore now that I'm engaged. Now that it's official, Tristan is finally going to be completely mine. My heart warms with the thought, and Tristan glances over at me, sensing my change in mood. For a few seconds he eyes me up and down, and now my *entire* body is warm. That heat stays with me for the remainder of our swim. Through the series of dips and turns we take amidst the labyrinth of castlelike rock formations. Through the vast array of underwater plant life and coral landscape that takes my breath away over and over again. Finally we stop.

"Well, this is it." We are paused in front of a large, arching doorway covered in a teal, nylon curtain. *Apparently not much crime at these depths.* Right away my thoughts shift to Keuran and his elaborate plans involving felonious activity—his attempt on my life and on Tristan's life—and a shudder racks my body. Apparently he hadn't followed the crime-free attitude of his fellow sea creatures. Tristan looks at me with concerned eyes, interpreting my apprehension as fear over what is about to happen. He reaches a hand toward my face. "Hey, baby, I love you—It will be okay."

I force a confident smile. "I know...I'm ready."

He pulls back the curtain, revealing a room with high, marble ceilings and opulent décor. Gold, silver, and other precious metals are etched into the walls, making me feel like I've just entered a palace. Although I am unsure of the source of the light, a serene glow is cast on the space, making it seem that much more grandiose. Elegantly carved sculptures and pillars are strategically placed around the open-concept living area. In the far reaches of the room, several smaller chambers can be seen adjoined to the large expanse that we've entered, making me wonder how far his home stretches out.

"Tristan, you're home." A warm, female voice causes me to stir from the stupor I'd entered while taking in the magnificence of the dwelling where my fiance' grew up. Reflexively I float to Tristan's side. Across the way a lady clad in an elegantly flowing dress with carefully styled silver blond hair stands ready to greet her obviously cherished son who has just arrived through the door of their family home. Instantly the affection in her green eyes fades as she detects me at his side, her previously congenial features turning to ice. Apparently she had not realized Tristan brought a visitor with him upon first entering the room. I swallow hard, trying to rid myself of the pasty feeling in my esophagus as I stand riveted by her stare. "What's this, Tristan?" The warmth in her voice is now all but gone.

"Hey, Mom." Undaunted, Tristan goes to his mom, reaching in for a hug. His voice is filled with affection, laced with undeterred enthusiasm. "Mom, this is Bethany Kuiper. Bethany, this is my mom, Charlize Alexander." The minute Tristan steps away from me, I can feel myself becoming short of breath. It is at that moment it occurs to me that his music is still playing in my ears. It had become such a staple during our excursion that I'd almost forgotten it was there at all. Tristan glances back in my direction while he attempts to carry out the introductions and notices my struggle for air. Instantly he is back at my side. It only takes me a quick second to recover, and I send him a reassuring look in effort to dispel the worried one that is now written on his face. Clearing my throat, I prepare to say hi.

"Who is she? Where is she from?" Charlize dispenses with all the niceties and skips right to the point. Tristan's jaw clenches almost unperceptively.

"She lives in Watch Hill. *And* she is the girl I'm in love with."

Charlize closes her eyes and then opens them again. "Land? She is from on land?" For several seconds she is quiet as her piercing eyes rake me up and down. Unwittingly I grab ahold of the hem of my floral dress, fidgeting with it nervously.

Had I ever encountered a woman so beautiful and regal in appearance? *And intimidating?* "Tristan, I think you better call your dad in the room." Briefly she shakes her head and then looks away.

"Call me in the room for what?" A deep, booming voice echoes from an adjacent corridor. Tristan visibly stiffens. My heart pounds in my chest. This time the electric buzz around me does not heighten, and I realize that Tristan is obviously too consumed with his own angst at the moment—he doesn't have the time nor the presence of mind to worry about pacifying me. Using all my effort, I work hard to calm the runaway pulse that is tripping through my veins. Seconds later a being who I can only assume is Tristan's dad enters the room. Instinctively I shrink toward Tristan's well-built frame.

The older version of Tristan, only with an unapproachable, aristocratic edge to him approaches our group, taking his place beside his wife, arms crossed formidably over an unbelievably broad chest. The minute his awareness expands to take in my appearance, his ocean green eyes flash anger, and his silver hair seems to stand on end, creating a frightening aura about him. For a split second I consider whether it would have been wiser just to elope. Tristan could have kept our marriage well-hidden on land, and no one would ever have been the wiser. Out of the corner of my eye I send Tristan a look of desperation, hoping he is able to read my thoughts and we can split this joint at record speed. But Tristan seems impervious to my despairing and yet astute ideas.

"Tristan?" The imposing man's one word bellows loudly, shattering the liquid around us, demanding an explanation for my existence. Tristan throws back his shoulders rebelliously, bracing for the worst.

"Dad, I want to introduce you to Bethany Kuiper. Bethany, this is my dad, Britton Alexander."

Tristan's dad, Britton, stares straight ahead, not even glancing at me. I mumble a weak hello, but I'm not sure the sound of my voice is heard above the deafening beat of my heart. Tristan continues without backing off.

"I brought home Bethany with me today to introduce you to her...and to tell you that we are going to be married. Soon."

"What?" Britton's thunderous voice resonates off the rocky walls in the room. Charlize doesn't try to hide the gasp that leaves her mouth. Tristan takes a step closer to me. My fingers pinch more tightly on the sides of my floral dress.

"I love her. All of my life this has been the girl that I've loved, and now I want to be united with her in marriage."

Britton closes his eyes. "I just knew this would happen." He opens them again and they are hard as ice. Green ice. "You knew the rules. You've been sneaking around seeing this girl for years?"

"I met her when I was young. But then didn't reacquaint myself with her until much later." Out of the corner of my eye I detect a slight blush creep onto Tristan's cheeks as he talks. Although he is doing his level best to stand his ground, he is clearly intimidated by his father. Charlize's gaze keeps straying to my form during the exchange as if to scrutinize me, deciding whether I'm a specimen worthy of her son. But not once does Britton address me or glance in my direction. *Geez, he is tough and cold as ice.*

"You know it would risk everything to have a permanent bond like marriage with a human. Our whole existence." Tristan's dad's words have an edge of finality to them. His mom sets her lips in a thin line.

My heart sinks. They are not going to budge. Tristan becomes fidgety beside me, and I can tell he is trying to hold himself in check. But his eyes become wild in spite of it. "Never once in all of these years has Bethany ever betrayed our secret. She is very loyal to me and to the sea and to all that lives in it. I trust her completely." *He trusts me completely.* A wave of warmth spreads through me. I love him so much. This just has to work. They have to give us their blessing.

A prolonged pause fills the room. Finally Britton speaks. "Tristan, step away with me into my study."

"Dad...I can't. I can't leave her side."

Britton sighs, but still he does not look my way. "Right." He turns to his wife and places a hand on her shoulder. "I want to talk with you." Quietly they both float from the room. Immediately my eyes seek Tristan's. *Oh my word, what now?* I know I am visibly shaking. Without wanting it to, a soft whimper escapes from my mouth.

"Shhhh...it's okay. It will be okay." At Tristan's whisper of comfort I bite my lip, but the worried expression on his face betrays his reassuring words, keeping me on edge. What will Tristan say, what will he do if they don't hand us an approval? Will he out and out defy his own people's wishes in order to keep us together? I fight back the tears that are trying to form in the back of my eyes, unable to consider the alternative. Do his parents know the whole story about what happened with Keuran? If so, will they in some way hold me responsible for his death? All these thoughts keep spiraling recklessly through my mind. In minutes the fate of our future is quite possibly going to be revealed.

Dreadfully long moments in time pass before Tristan's parents reenter the room. Two pairs of green eyes slice through the water, landing on my and Tristan's restless forms. As I wait for their verdict, a sidetracked notion shoots fleetingly through my head. *Their eyes.* The green piercing eyes—Tristan didn't stand a chance where they are concerned. They are the very eyes that I love—that I don't want to live for another second without. My fingers release the hem of the dress I'd been clinging to, and I stretch my hands across my chest, rubbing the skin on both arms in a comforting gesture.

"Son." The fierceness in Britton's voice causes me to jump. "You have and continue to do so much for our people. We have trusted you to go to the university. To work amongst the humans on a daily basis. And so now we trust you will do your utmost to keep our secret as you marry." A long, hard sigh escapes through his lips as he pauses, betraying the unshakeable power in his persona. From a sideways glance I detect the Adam's apple in Tristan's throat bob up and down as he swallows, listening intently to his father's words. "You deserve happiness. Although we would not have picked this decision as your best choice...we are going to give you our blessing."

Thank you! Joy unspeakable and immense relief course through my veins. The buzz that has been perpetually encompassing me noticeably slackens, allowing me to hear sounds that I hadn't been able to moments before. Funny, I hadn't realized how intense the electrical force field had become. Was that in reaction to Tristan's anxiety or for protection from my own? Now the water all around me bubbles and trickles in a spirited manner.

"Thanks. Thank you, Mom and Dad." Relief is evident in Tristan's spoken words. Charlize smiles fondly in Tristan's direction. Clearly she adores her son. And I get it, because so do I. Britton nods one time, his face serious. Tristan glances in my direction. "Well...we better...I have to get her back...you know...but we'll go over things later."

As we prepare to exit through the teal curtain once again, I realize that Britton has not so much as laid an eye on me, let alone spoken to me in any way. The comprehension of this stings just a little. But at the moment I am thankful for small favors. *Huge favors, really.* We are inches away from leaving through the entrance to the stately Alexander abode when I hear a soft good-bye coming from a feminine voice behind me. Turning back around, I return the sediment, wearing my heart openly on my sleeve. And for just a split second I detect a trace of compassion staring back at me in the light of Charlize Alexander's green eyes.

Chapter Twenty-four

When I wake up, I am in my own bed. The sun is filtering in through the window, rising into the east sky. *So it's morning then, but on what day?* I attempt to lift my head off the pillow, but it takes every ounce of strength I have. Giving up, I close my eyes, allowing my fuzzy mind to drift once again, heading back toward sleep. The last thing I remember, I was swimming deep in the sea with Tristan. We were outside of his city, and the music in my mind was turned up full volume as I prepared to climb through layers of the oceanic zones in order to reach oxygen-filled air. Now my energy is depleted, and I feel like I could sleep for days and days. The wooden floorboards outside my bedroom door make a creaking noise, and I have enough presence of mind to realize someone must be in the cabin with me, but I don't have the wherewithal to investigate the source. My lids stay securely shut.

But the squeaking continues, getting louder. Now right beside my bed. The weight of the mattress shifts next to my body, and it causes me to stir, opening sleepy eyes. And Tristan is there. Right beside me, watching me carefully, a slight frown on his face. "Hey," I murmur. "I guess this means I made it back."

"Yeah. We made it. *You* made it."

I reach a hand over to clasp his. But it takes so much effort. When our fingers are finally entwined, the grasp is weak, matching the sound of my voice. "Well...great news, right? They gave their approval."

Tristan's smile is tender. "They did. But you should sleep now, and we'll talk about all that later."

I fight to keep my eyes open. "I am *so* tired! Why is that? I know you said it would get harder each time but—"

"This will be the *last* time, I swear. Whatever else happens, happens, but I am never taking you under again. Right now though, you need to rest and recoup."

I smile faintly, too exhausted to argue. "Okay, whatever you say…but it was worth it." *Because very soon you will be my husband forever.* "Definitely worth it!" My words fade into a whisper. Tristan leans down to kiss the top of my head before getting up to leave again. He is almost to my bedroom door before I open my eyes again. "Hey," I call to him in a cracked voice. "Did you…um, sleep in here with me last night?"

He shakes his head marginally and offers a crooked grin. And even in my worn-out state I appreciate how breathtakingly good-looking he is. A tingling sensation spreads to every limb in my body. "No…I stayed out here." He points to the living area. "I didn't think it would be a good idea to for me to lay next to you. I wouldn't have quite trusted myself. It would have been too easy to…you know, start something… and then not stop. But I did look in on you a lot though."

I send him a feeble smile and allow my heavy lids to close, the image of Tristan *not stopping* filling my mind before I drift back into a deep slumber once more.

It takes a few days for me to land back on my feet. Tristan checks in on me several times during that time, making sure that I'm progressing along nicely back to good health, mentioning more than once that he will never do this to me again. "Do what?" I ask him. "You didn't *do* anything to me. I was a willing participant." *Well, at least this time.* "Besides, I'm okay now, and it was worth it." Tristan can't argue with that. But still he is adamant that this is the last time. And I don't debate that because what would be the point; I have him now, and that's all that matters.

As soon as I can, I'm on the phone to my parents, asking them to come to town for a visit. "There is something I want to tell you." The minute I say the words, I can feel the anxiety rise on the other end of the line. *What on earth could I be getting ready to reveal to them?* I run down the list of possibilities that could be traveling through their heads and chuckle briefly at all the ways their thoughts could go. Hopefully my impending marriage to Tristan will not seem all that bad in the catalogue of potential options. Picking a date on the calendar, we arrange a time and place for the big reveal.

The day has arrived, and we are meeting with my parents at the Ocean House Seasons restaurant for dinner. When they pull up to the circular drive and hand their keys to the valet, Tristan and I are already waiting on the veranda. I am nervous about their initial reaction to seeing Tristan again after all that went down the summer we vacationed in 2012. And I can tell by Tristan's intermittent fidgeting at my side that he is slightly unnerved as well. Heading in their direction, I greet them both with a hug. "Mom, Dad, you remember meeting Tristan? Tristan, my parents, Lisa and Kevin."

Formal handshakes and hellos are exchanged, and as we are making our way into the dining room, Tristan excuses himself to use the restroom. Thankful for the few moments alone with my parents, I take the time to discreetly tell them not to order the seafood—*Tristan has a strong aversion to it*. In the hullabaloo of everything, I'd forgotten all about this important detail and am relieved now to have the chance. Cringing, I think about how awful the dinner could have gone had I forgotten to instruct them on this small but important particular. My parents both eye me dubiously as they agree to the request.

"Isn't it a little odd to take us to a restaurant that serves mostly seafood if you don't want us to order any?" my dad questions, an incredulous expression crossing over his features. I search my mind for a quick answer.

"I know they have other things on the menu that come highly recommended. I understand the pheasant and lamb are big sellers actually," I say, hoping my voice sounds convincing enough. Tristan shows back up right then, and I send a smile his way, eyeing his beautiful physique at the same time. His baby blue and white-striped shirt shows off the tanned skin on his neck, face, and forearms perfectly. The beige pants that are fitted just right on his narrow hips cause me to swallow hard. Our group walks into the dining room, taking our seats at a table next to large windows that offer impressive views of the Atlantic. All around us soft jazz music is playing, silverware is clinking against fine china, and conversations are taking place in hushed, sophisticated tones.

But at our linen-covered table, awkward, strained silence surrounds us.

I don't have to read my parents' minds to know what they are thinking as they periodically glance over at Tristan, giving him the evil eye. I know they are remembering plain as day four summers ago when they couldn't get their young daughter out of bed. Or maybe the several years that followed when they helped a promising and yet floundering college student navigate through the rocky road of heartache and healing, hoping and praying she'd be able to stand on two solid feet again.

"So…I take it you all are friends." My dad's voice is deep voice—practically choking—as he lift a napkin to his mouth. I imagine I hear the words *for now* spoken into the cough. Instinctively I lean toward Tristan.

"We are. We've become quite close actually." My voice is steadfast as I speak the words that describe the latest phase of our relationship. By now we are eating our dinner, taking small bites of the mouthwatering dishes that have been set in front of us: locally raised beef, mouthwatering salads with goat cheese and walnuts, gnocchi, anything but seafood. Tristan had been doing his best to make polite, congenial small talk at the table, trying to engage my parents in conversation. But breaking through my dad's resilient exterior is like breaking through granite. I flash my dad a slightly irritated look. *Isn't it possible that for one moment you can put away the ruthless lawyer act and embrace your daughter's wishes, even if they don't match up with your own?*

In contrast, my mom's iciness is rapidly thawing, largely I imagine due to Tristan's warm and engaging personality. And quite possibly because of the irresistibility of his good looks to the female population. Sending me the cue, Tristan wraps his arm around my shoulder. I peer over at him and catch the look in his green eyes. *Now is the time.* I suck in a breath and take a drink of water.

"Well, thanks for driving all the way here today, Mom and Dad. I invited you because there is some news we want to share." Tristan begins rubbing the skin on my bicep, offering me support. I pause, trying to calm my nerves. "I love Tristan…have loved him for a very long time. We love each other and are going to get married…soon."

To my parent's credit, they don't audibly gasp or start gagging on their food or shout interrogative pronouns in our direction. But I don't miss the slight widening of their eyes or the miniscule breath of air that they draw into their lungs. Long seconds pass before either of them say anything. My dad speaks first, running a hand through his graying hair.

"Wow! Do you feel…are you ready for that?"

Not giving me a chance to answer, my mom interrupts. Reaching for my arm, she gives it a little squeeze while looking right at me. "Are you happy, Bethany?" I nod and she barely notices before continuing on. "You don't have to answer that…I can tell you are." I look over at Tristan once again. *So happy*, I tell him with my eyes. *Just counting the days*, he tells me with his. My heart rate picks up in tempo. Tristan clears his throat, preparing to speak, and I involuntarily stiffen. *Oh my word, what is he going to say?*

"I'm sure you probably have worries where your daughter is concerned. Especially about me…considering our past. But I'm here to tell you that although I can't go into the details over all the obstacles we've had…we *have* made it through them. I love Bethany more than anything, and I have for a long time now. I promise to be a good husband to her." My dad is studying Tristan's face, trying to decide if he can actually believe him or not. My mom is grinning, wiping tears from her eyes. And I am rubbing the skin on my bare arms, trying to tame the goose bumps that now have surfaced.

Finally my dad nods. "So when? You said soon." Once again I glance over at Tristan. We hadn't really set an exact time. We wanted to tell both sets of parents first.

"Very soon," we both say at once and then break into a chuckle. Secretly I'm glad we are on the same page with that.

"We'll get back with you on the particulars once we have them planned. But definitely sooner than later," I say. Tristan nods his head in agreement, reaching for my hand.

By the time our plates are cleared and we've enjoyed an after-dinner drink, I can feel the tension that had been surrounding our table of four slacken considerably. Although I'm sure my parents still have certain reservations in regards to the news we've handed them, they seem ready to go along with our plans in an amiable manner. And that's good enough for me.

Chapter Twenty-five

The weeks that follow fly by. Wedding preparations and the thought of being with Tristan forever consume my life. Deciding on a Saturday at the end of August for exchanging our vows, we have very little time to get things in order. I am now fully recovered after my trip into the depths of the ocean, and it is a good thing—I need all the strength I can get to pull off a wedding in so little time. But something curious has been perplexing me in the back of my mind: how is it that the first time Tristan had taken me into the ocean in a lucid, dreamlike state, I had come back with a resolve to move on—and yet this last time especially, I felt completely drained on my return to land? I know this is a touchy subject with Tristan, because he feels responsible for my weakened state. He had cringed visibly each time he saw me during the aftermath of the dive, knowing the toll that it had taken on my body. Eventually I get the nerve up to broach the subject.

He explains to me that the first dive was so new to my system it hardly affected me at all. And what little it did affect me, I wouldn't have known the difference between the fragile depressive state I was in and the consequence of the dream. Knowing this, he had been actually able to *give* me strength instead, through the use of his energy. But with each deep immersion, it only continues to get worse on the makeup of my human system.

After his explanation, I throw another question at him— something that has been puzzling me. How was I able to go into the second dream state through only the use of his music and not his presence as well? Answering my query, he explains that it wasn't his first choice—he knew the submerge would have been much more effective with him at my side, directly feeding me the force I needed to sustain breathing. But he didn't think I would have been very receptive to seeing him right then, knowing full well what he was up to. And he was right, I had fought that dream every step of the way.

But that is the past.

Now it's the morning of my wedding, and all those thoughts are far behind me. Thanks to Tristan, the pollution operation that Keuran had started is completely shut down, and life is loaded with a promising future for him and me.

And I couldn't be happier!

Or more nervous.

Wrapping my arms in the duvet that is used as a cover for my bed, I pad over to the opened window at the far end of my room, close my eyes, and inhale the cool, morning air. This is what I've wanted for so long—practically craved for years, and now the day is finally here. Keeping my lids shut tightly together, I stand there for many minutes, breathing softly. I fight the urge to open them again—scared to discover this whole fairytale day in my life isn't real after all. *I love Tristan so much.* The thought of waking up next to him for the rest of my life gives me butterflies. *How will it go tonight?* Every cell in my body has desired him for so long—has craved to be melted together with him for so long. And now the wait is finally over! An overwhelming thrill courses through my veins as I imagine every single inch of my skin touching every single inch of his. *Oh my…wow!* My body tingles with excitement, and my cheeks succumb to bright red blushing.

Okay, enough about that.

Time for breakfast.

My small, rustic cabin is overflowing with female chitter-chatter, all getting primped, pampered, and polished for the ceremony that will be taking place later that day. A local hairdresser and his team have agreed to come do our hair, nails, and makeup at my humble but quaint abode. Mom, Lucy, Kate, and I fill up the crowded space flitting here and there, talking excitedly, snacking on fruit trays and cream cheese-filled muffins while we wait our turn. Later we will be boarding a cabin cruiser crossing the miles of open sea to Tristan's island where the wedding is to be held. Tristan couldn't think of a place that would be more suited to our affair. And I couldn't agree more. He wanted to surprise me with the provisions of the arranged site that his fellow sea creatures were putting together for our special day, so I was informed that in no uncertain terms was I allowed to go help set up, decorate, or view the venue ahead of time.

This frustrated me in some ways, because I wanted to be included in the plans. But when I found out that his parents volunteered to have a major part in putting together the arrangements, I reluctantly acquiesced, relieved that they were taking some type of ownership in our special day. And I know this means a lot to Tristan too.

Now I am all dressed in white, my dress hugging curves in some places and flowing freely in others. Eyeing myself in the full-length mirror just outside of the boat's bathroom, I almost don't recognize the blushing beauty that stares back at me. Hair in pin curls fastened high on my head shrouded by a beaded crown and folds of snowy mesh, my face practically glows beneath. After one more spin and glance at the dewy-eyed girl in the glass, I go to be with the others—the bridesmaids and my mom that have now boarded our vessel, getting ready to help celebrate the beginning of the rest of my life.

My attendants are dressed in baby blue. Lucy, of course, is my maid of honor, and I decided to ask Kate as well. She seemed so much a part of my and Tristan's beginning that I couldn't imagine anyone else filling her spot. Except Jonathan, that is. There is a small bit of me that wishes I could have had my fun, supportive buddy stand up as a bridal attendant. But with a speculative grin

I had nixed that idea, deciding that he probably wouldn't have looked very cute in the silk dresses I'd picked out.

For a moment or two I watch the wake of our watercraft as it splashes up around the boat, spraying the cabin windows, wondering if Tristan and his groomsmen, Zepher and Seth, are already there. How easy it will be for them to step out of the water, throw on their tuxes, shake out their hair, and show up in the lineup, joining the minister up front. I think of the others from the mainland that will be coming to the wedding as well: my dad, my brothers Josh and Jake, David Chambers, Ethan Vaughn, coworkers, and other close family friends like the Callahans, wondering if they too have already boarded the provided transportation that will be whisking them away to the island.

Then for one depressive moment my thoughts drift to Keuran, and I wonder if it would have been him standing up for Tristan had he still been alive. Then I remind myself that although Tristan would never have wished for Keuran's death, there wouldn't even *be* a wedding had he still been alive. I shudder with the thought. Everything seems so crystal clear to me now. All the times that Keuran had tried to plant subtle and not so subtle ideas in my mind, attempting to make me doubt Tristan's love—all along it had been due to his consuming jealousy over his cousin. He had tried his level best to sabotage our relationship. And yet here I am today on a boat, skyrocketing across the open plains of the ocean, heading toward a landmass where I will say vows of forever with the person I love more than life.

Some things are just meant to be.

By the time we arrive at Tristan's island, my heart is beating wildly in my chest. *This is it! This is really it!* In a very short time I will be getting *married!* To Tristan! A young man who I assume is a sea person greets us on the beach and guides us on the familiar trail that I've taken before—only today the path seems a little less cluttered by untamed foliage, the ground ostensibly more level, making it easy to pass through even in a fancy wedding gown. Shaking my head in wonder, I question whether I'm just imagining the subtle change. Finally we round the corner that I know will take us to the ultimate destination—the place where I've spent special moments with Tristan in the past—and I audibly gasp for breath.

Instead of the usual secluded postcard setting, it's like I'm stepping onto the grounds of a luxury, tropical paradise getaway. It's like a miniature five-star resort has been constructed from seemingly out of nowhere. Awestruck, I stand in place staring at the variety of freestanding patios with jutting, white pillars and miniature wading pools exhibiting sprinkling fountains. Scattered, thatched-roofed, open huts lined with flowing, see-through curtains serve as shaded seating areas, while others are filled with minibars and a variety of edible refreshments. Wooden walkways lined with brightly colored flowers are strategically placed, ready to take guests from point A to point B effortlessly. Palm trees and marble statues stand in greeting at every turn. My eyesight expands, and I notice a remote venue that has several round tables covered in white linen with fine china and sparkling crystal arranged perfectly on top. A dance floor with myriads of twinkling lights awaits close by for later after the ceremony.

Stunned, I stand in place for many minutes, taking in all of the newly constructed scenery. *What is all of this? Where did it come from in such a short time?*

"Wow, Tristan's family must have a lot of money. This is fancy." From somewhere behind I hear my mom's voice. But I don't acknowledge her statement. In a daze, I turn toward our greeter who has guided us back here.

"How—what—who did all of this?"

He laughs. "It is something, isn't it? Britton and Charlize Alexander. With a lot of help, of course. But they are the ones who insisted on it, who put the whole plan into action. I guess you could say they are very happy for their son."

Suddenly overwhelmed, I'm close to tears, and I don't want to mess up my carefully applied makeup. I blink several times. *Oh my word!* Tristan's parents have ordered up all of this elaborate construction for Tristan. And for me. A wave of relief and gratitude sweeps over me. This is their blessing on our wedding. Now the day feels complete, and I can thoroughly enjoy this magical experience without worry.

Once we arrive safely into the dressing room that has been created for the girl's side of the wedding party, another person arrives and hands me an envelope. I lift my brow in confusion. This is unexpected. Tearing open the sealed cover and unfolding the paper, I recognize the writing as Tristan's. My heart squeezes in my chest. I haven't seen him in several days now—purposefully. And it has been making me miss him terribly, making this day seem all that much more special and desirable. Quickly my eyes scan the page.

I can't wait to marry you today! I love you! ~~Tristan

Holding the paper to my chest, I suck in a breath. *Oh...wow!* Suddenly I want the wedding to begin, as nervous as I am.

Before long we are gathered up by another attendant, who I assume is yet another person from the sea called upon to help with the whole shindig. He herds us to the spot allocated for the ceremony located only feet from the turquoise waves of the ocean. Now Kate and Lucy are preparing to start the processional while I wait, pacing, taking repeated deep breaths next to my dad. Soon I hear beautiful, melodic music being played while my friends are somewhere now out of my line of vision on their way to the front of the gardenlike setting where the guests are eagerly watching, where Tristan is already standing—waiting. Waiting for me. A breeze from the nearby sea arises and flutters softly across my cheekbones and lashes. For a few seconds I close my eyes, allowing it calm me like a gentle caress. Then I open them again and glance over at my dad, letting out a slow breath. *Okay, ready.*

Now it's my turn.

Taking my dad's arm, holding my bouquet of pale blue daisies, white roses, and baby's breath in my other hand, I begin my march down the aisle. On and on I glide between row after row of netting and floral-lined, white wooden chairs. Somewhere in the back of my mind it registers that I am walking toward a large, white gazebo; all the while my brain is spinning with a dizzy sensation. Music is playing, people are watching, and I keep moving forward taking step after step as I survey the movement of my feet, trying desperately not to trip or faint. Finally I lift my eyes.

And everything goes still.

In front of me standing on the meticulously constructed altar is Tristan, looking breathtakingly gorgeous dressed in a black tux, waiting for me to look up—waiting to catch my eye. Now his gaze is locked on mine, and my pulse is beating uncontrollably. His green eyes are so serious as they pierce through my own blue, down deep into my soul. For a moment I am spellbound, frozen in place, completely overwhelmed. Then he smiles and I experience a sense of relief. I keep moving forward, filled with complete elation. This is the happiest day of my life.

After a few short words from the minister, my dad hands me over to Tristan, and the ceremony begins. As Tristan tells me his vows, I have to repeatedly swallow down the lump that wants to form in my throat. His words of uncompromising love completely surround me, reaching into the deepest parts of my being, causing me to want to come undone. And then it's my turn, and I tell him mine in a slightly breathless voice, taking a second or two to pause while I regather my words, trying hard not to cry. Behind me I can hear an occasional sniffle coming from Lucy, making my resolve that much harder. Somehow though I make it through anyway, and finally the nuptial is almost complete. Tristan stares down at me with hungry eyes as we wait for the minister to give his closing statement, and a blush unwittingly covers my cheeks. *Dang, he is so sexy hot!* My thoughts fast-forward to later that night, and a tingling sensation pulsates through every part of my body. *Oh my!*

The minister clears his throat, almost chuckling, as Tristan and I send each other one more *look*. "And now unless there is any formal objection, I will now pronounce Bethany and Tristan man and wife. Tristan, you may now kiss—"

But suddenly there is a loud, rustling noise from the far corner of the beach.

At once everyone turns in the direction of the sound.

"Tris…wait, no…Tris." A soft, despairing voice pleads into the hushed, salty ocean air of the gathered crowd. The weight of a sledgehammer slams against my chest, knocking the air from my lungs. On the far edge of our perfectly fashioned storybook setting stands Rye. Through haunting, gray eyes lined with deep, dark circles beneath, she regards the altar where Tristan and I are standing. Her pale yellow, cotton sundress is hanging loosely on her slight frame, falling off her shoulder, ripped in places, covered in several days' worth of grime. The wispy strands of her hair are an unkempt mess, causing her to look almost savage. Timidly and yet desperately, she begins stepping forward, inching herself in our direction. "Please…Tris, don't do this…please." Her voice cracks as tears begin streaming down her cheeks. *Oh God, no! Why is this happening?*

"Rye…stop!" Tristan's deep voice echoes in my ears, dispelling the sensation of dizziness that is trying to overwhelm me. It's in that moment of lucidity my eyesight fine-tunes to the distraught figure that is approaching, and I detect the object that is resting against her chest. Audibly I gasp for breath. *My seashell!* The beloved seashell necklace that Tristan had given to me on our starry-eyed summer night so long ago, that I had worn for four years straight, that had gone missing—stolen off of my very body during the deepest hours of the night, is now being worn as an accessory to Rye's wild, bedraggled attire. A nauseating feeling sweeps through me. *Oh my word, I am going to be sick!* It takes every ounce of effort not to run through the crowd, closing the distance between us, and tear the rope from her neck. Instead I stand frozen in place, trembling.

"You know you belong to me...you know we belong together...we were promised. I love you. You love me too... you *have* to." With pitiful, frantic eyes Rye continues to plead. A shocked but empathetic expression covers Tristan's face as he contemplates the whole ludicrous scenario. My heart takes a fast dive in my chest. He is such a gallant person—will the distraught look on Rye's face be too much for him? Will he ultimately feel an inherent need to protect his lifelong, promised sea companion from this heartbreak? Staring at her now, I take in her frail demeanor and her complete vulnerability. Clearly she does need help. Will Tristan be the one to offer it?

No! This can't be happening! I watch in horror as Tristan leaves my side, taking step after step in Rye's direction. Finally he reaches Rye. His voice is soft but firm. "Rye, you've known for many years that there was no us. I've never led you on. I've always made this clear to you...always."

At this, Rye loses her calm and begins weeping loudly, calling out frenzied words spoken through loud, hiccupping sobs. Echoes of riotous gasps from the wedding guests begin circulating around us. Out of nowhere, two men dressed in dark colors surround Rye. Taking her by the arm, they pull her away from the stunned crowd all while she struggles uselessly in their strong grip. "You never saw me. All of these years I followed you around, tried to make you see me the way I see you...the way our parents saw you and me together...but you never saw me! You *never* saw me." The despondency in her voice reverberates into the air. Tristan looks away, jaw clenched, obviously disturbed by the whole scene.

And suddenly it is all too much. My beautiful day has just disintegrated into a pile of sludge washed up onto a lonely shoreline. Avoiding eye contact with Tristan, I leave my spot at the altar and slowly walk away while everyone watches with shocked, sad looks on their faces. Lucy hurries to my side. Taking my hand, she leads me to an enclosed shelter. For many minutes we sit in silence while she rubs my upturned palm with soothing fingers. I am too stunned to cry. I want to cry, but I am stricken by an intense daze instead. "I don't know what to do." The sound of my voice is cracked and subdued. Lucy squeezes my hand to let me know she is listening, encouraging me to continue. "Maybe Tristan needs some time…needs some time to think this all through. I saw how hurt he was by Rye's pain. Maybe there is a part of him that is confused. I want him to be sure. I need him to be sure."

"Tristan *is* sure." A deep, thundering voice answers my pondering, and I turn to see Britton Alexander standing in the doorway of our enclosure. With a purposeful stride he enters the hut and joins my and Lucy's private conversation. "Although I've never faced it, I've always known there was a human girl that held Tristan's heart. All along it's been you. I know Tristan, and I am undoubtedly sure that he loves you deeply…more than anything. He is a good guy, and you will be very happy together. Please go back to him now. He is ready and waiting for you at the altar to finish what you started."

Trying to process all he is saying, I sit frantically sorting out my thoughts, trying to make a decision. "And Rye?"

"She is going to get the help she needs to get her through this. She needs to finally get on with her life. It's time. She will be closely monitored now, so you won't have to worry about her. She won't be bothering you again."

Uncertainly I look back and forth between Tristan's dad and Lucy. "Go…this is what you've wanted. It's the right thing to do." For the first time since exiting the ceremony Lucy offers her advice.

On shaky legs I walk back to the altar. Quiet sighs of relief resonate through the crowd as they watch my return. And Tristan is there—looking beautiful, regarding me carefully with concern, a deeply tender look in his green eyes. Gently he takes both of my hands in his, for two seconds he stares hard into my unsure expression. "I love you," he mouths slowly so only I can hear. I nod in return as the cloud of doubt that is surrounding me begins to dissipate. The minister resumes his place. Eyeing us both, he clears his throat.

"Ladies and gentlemen, I now want to introduce to you Mr. and Mrs. Tristan Alexander. Tristan, you may kiss your bride."

"Before I do, there is still one more thing I want to do." I cock my head in question. *What does he have planned?* Pulling up a chair for me, Tristan helps me into a sitting position before pulling up a stool for himself. Seth hands him a guitar. My heart is pounding in my chest. *Oh my word!*

Tristan's gaze sweeps over me, regarding my face for a second or two as he sits directly across from where I am. "This is something I wrote for today…for you. It's called "I Promise You."" Without saying another word, he looks back down at the instrument cradled in his arms and begins to play.

I PROMISE YOU

````A whispered prayer, innate connection
  Your life crossed with mine
````Now we're together
  Ocean waves crashed onto shoreline
````Swept away by a light that's shining
  Door to your soul
````Our loves a refuge
  You make me whole


```With you it's like swimming on the edge of the surface
  By the glow of a moonlit sky
````I'll go with you to the edge of tomorrow

'Cuz you lift me up, you make me high
````Can't believe we're here in this moment
Such relief, salty water on skin
````Forever's our future, let's go there
Come fill me up, I'll let you in

Chorus:
````When I breathe your air
````I'm surrounded by you
````My heart's yours forever (here take it)
````I'll give it to you

````Girl, I'm going to (right now)
````I promise you

# Chapter Twenty-six

The last chord of the song is played. For a moment or two I sit, dazed from the words and music, sweeping as they had—over me, extending down deep into my soul. Afterward, Tristan reaches for my hand and pulls me to a standing position. Taking me in his arms, he kisses me chastely on the lips as an official testimony of our marriage. It takes all of my restraint not to intensify the kiss—it has been so long since I've had him this close, and his mouth feels so good on mine. But I do a good job keeping it PG rated—even so, I am still breathless when we pull apart, turning to smile at the applause of the crowd.

The reception is a joyous occasion with an array of succulent foods and champagne fountains set in a backdrop of mellow jazz music. The mood is festive, and the wedding guests all appear to be having a fun time—Lucy and Ethan being no exception. Smiling, I glance over at my best friend and the person who it has become very evident is the love of her life. By the smitten look on Ethan's face, clearly she is able to handle this unnerving guy, better than handle—it looks like they are completely in love and undoubtedly meant for each other. Secretly I hope their relationship does work out so that I will get to see a lot more of Lucy around the area.

Tristan and I dance the first dance together to a recording of "I Promise You". He is a great dancer, and the sound of his sexy voice coming at me is, of course, amazing as I'm pressed against his strong body, the soapy, salty smell of him nearly making me come undone. But all of this and all of the flashing, spiraling lights in the world can't keep me in the moment, savoring the occasion of our first dance as husband and wife—unwittingly my mind keeps fast-forwarding to later that night and what it will be like finally being with him for the first time. I can't stop my cheeks from turning bright red with the thought. I bury my face into his chest to hide the evidence. At this his arms tighten around me in a subtle squeeze. *Oh my word!* Does he know what I'm thinking? After the last note is sung we finally pull apart, and he gives me a look that I'm pretty sure I've never seen from him before, and it causes me to feel weak and tingly all over. In the moments that follow I peruse the crowd silently, wishing that they could all disappear so that it could be just me and Tristan— *right now*. But then just as quickly I change my mind, and I am a bucket of nerves, completely scared to death. *On second thought, maybe everyone should stay and keep dancing all night long.* Safety in numbers after all.

As we begin walking away from the dance floor, Tristan stops us momentarily. Quietly reaching into the pocket of his pants, he places something into the palm of my hand. *My seashell.* I suck in a small breath of air as I stare at the object in my upturned hand that had been stolen from me by Rye in the middle of the night right while I was sound asleep. I raise my face to his. He looks me right in the eye. "I believe this belongs to you. Always has… always will." For a second he pauses while my heart stutters in my chest. "Just like you, and only you belong to me…always have… always will." In return, I swallow and nod. I can tell he really means it. *Enough said on the matter.* I am determined to enjoy the rest of my night without another thought about Rye.

For the next few hours our circulating amongst the guests continues. My parents, Tristan's parents, guests from land, guests from the sea, they all intermingle without the humans having a clue that there is a whole world that exists miles below the turquoise waves that surround our festive venue. Or that the person in line beside them at a beverage station that they are so casually chatting with is really from another species entirely. Thankfully it is all working out very well. The music picks up the tempo, and I dance with Jonathan, my energetic twin brothers, Kate, and even baby Hannah. Breathlessly the time passes in a whirlwind of excitement, and finally the hullabaloo dwindles. Little by little all of the guests exit the island.

Now it is just me and Tristan.

The music and lights have faded. Everything is quiet around us except the rolling tide. My heart is pounding in my chest. *What now?* Tristan looks over at me, and by the expression on his face I know that he knows I'm nervous. He reaches over and lightly takes my hand in his. "Ready?"

Too shaken to answer, I nod in return. *Am I ready?* I let out a slow breath, and Tristan does a double take in my direction. I offer him a weak, reassuring smile. He watches my face for a second or two, trying to read into my thoughts, before eventually guiding me down a Tiki torch-lit trail that leads to a honeymoon suite from out of a movie setting. Without giving me a chance to register what is happening, he sweeps me off my feet and carries me in his arms over the threshold of the room. In awe I take in my surroundings. The space is airy and open with several large, exposed windows. A light breeze is blowing in, ruffling the gauzy, floor-length curtain panels. French doors open to a brick patio with dazzling views of the night sky and the moonlit ocean. I breathe in the salty sea air, overwhelmed with all the surrounding beauty. It is truly a tropical paradise getaway. I turn back to face the interior of the room and feel my pulse accelerate as I eye the central focus of the well-ventilated chamber: *a gigantic bed!*

I swallow down a momentary feeling of panic, and then Tristan is right there in front of me. Placing his hands on both of my arms, he looks down at me. "I have to leave for a few minutes, but I'll be right back, okay?" His voice is deep and raspy, matching the look in his smoldering, green eyes.

"Okay," I breathe back. He begins heading toward the French doors, and not knowing what else to do I start padding in the direction of the en suite bath. *How should I prepare for this?*

*What do I put on or not put on? I should have asked someone more questions.* When Tristan reaches the entrance to our suite, he opens the double doors and a strong breeze swishes across the room, ruffling the silk folds of my dress. As if sensing my quandary, he pauses and turns back to face me.

"Don't…change your clothes. Don't…ah…take off your dress."

*Oh, okay.* At his words a chill racks my body. Without wanting to, I shiver and begin rubbing the skin on my arms. "Okay," I attempt to say, but I'm not sure the word is uttered out loud. And then he is gone, disappearing into the night, and I continue on into the ginormous bathroom that is attached to our room. As I begin freshening up, getting ready for what I know is soon about to happen, I stare into the mirror, and all of a sudden a thousand insecurities come sweeping through my mind. What if he doesn't like what he gets—me *out* of this dress? What if my inexperience gets in the way, and everything goes crazy awkward awful? What if after all of that he changes his mind about me, and now we are married, and he is stuck with me?

Gazing into my reflection in the glass in front of me, I watch as all the color drains from my face. Now white as a ghost, I grip the vanity edge, holding my head down as I wait for my heart rate to slow and the blood to resume circulation in the upper half of my body. After a minute or two, I slowly look back up. Eyeing the curls that are piled on top of my head, I try to decide whether Tristan would want me to leave them in place or take them down. Deciding on down, I begin unpinning each coil and twist until my hair is a cascade of blond, sun-streaked waves flowing around my face. Then taking a big drink of water from the glass that sits next to the set of double sinks, I leave the shelter of the bathroom behind and take a seat on the edge of the massively oversized bed.

Feeling a bit lost on a framed mattress of this magnitude, I sit nervously tapping my feet and playing with my hands, waiting for Tristan's return. I don't have to wait long. Sensing a change in the landscape of the room, I look up from my fidgeting, and Tristan is at the French doors, watching me. His black tux is still on, but his tie is undone and his hair is wet. His gaze is intense, causing my insides to clench. He looks breathtakingly beautiful. I clear my throat, stating the obvious. "You went for a swim."

His eyes never leave mine. "I want to have as much uninterrupted time with you as I can tonight. I needed to get the water thing out of the way." *Oh my!*

I lower my lashes to the ground before slowly looking back up. He recaptures my gaze and begins walking slowly toward the bed—toward me. My heart pounds in loud cadence with each approaching step. Without saying a word, he sits next to me on the bed. We aren't touching, but the powerful presence of his well-built frame is burning into every fiber of my skin. I am so completely aware of him.

And what I'm about to do with him.

But still so nervous as well. I had heard a variety of stories about the first time, and now I don't know what to expect. Will it hurt? Without wanting to, I shiver. Tristan detects my worry and reaches for my face, pulling it gently in his direction. "Hey, baby…it will be okay."

I nod and swallow, looking into his green eyes, unable to speak.

He offers a little smile. "Better than okay…I *love* you."

Finally I find my voice. "I love you too." In that moment I become conscious of his soft lips that are only inches away from mine, and suddenly the unease of the situation fades far into the background. All I want is his mouth on mine. And to do everything else that I had dreamed of doing with him for so long. For far too long.

My heart beats wildly as he continues to watch my face through slightly narrowed eyes. I can feel the minute distance between us edging away as we slowly lean toward each other. The air surrounding us is thick, and it becomes difficult to breathe. Every fiber of my being is craving this gorgeous boy in front of me. To touch him, feel him, taste him. Seconds later his lips brush against mine, and I let out a soft breath. He inhales it, and I can feel the shudder that rips through his body. In response, a thrill races through my veins. This is it—finally—the kiss that doesn't have to end.

The following morning I awaken to the sun filtering through the filmy curtain panels that frame the large, open windows of the room. A cool, early morning breeze brushes lightly over my face. I go to shift my position in bed and freeze in place. My body aches all over; it's like I can hardly move. *Oh my word!* Instantly all of the memories from the activities of the previous night come flooding through my mind. Intuitively I reach for a sheet to cover my exposed skin. *Oh my! Better than okay was right!* Now all of my nerve endings are tingling, and yet muscles in other places are tender, even sore—but in a glorious way. Sensing that I am all alone, I turn to the pillow beside me to find it empty. *Where is that new husband of mine anyway?*

Biting my lip, I call to mind the memory of his beautiful face and his gorgeous body—unclothed. The sexy look in his eyes. And all of the things he did with me over the course of one night. The way he reacted to me. The way I reacted to him. Unwittingly I blush without restraint right down to the roots of my scalp. *Oh my word, I had no idea!* And now—now all I can think is, with this guy as my partner, at this point forever is looking mighty good.

Carefully I ease out of bed and place my shaky legs on the floor, testing my footing to see if I can even stand. Apparently the well-conditioned muscles I'd used on a regular basis for running were not the same ones I'd used last night. Briefly perusing the airy space around me, I detect Tristan's discarded white button-down shirt lying on the floor. Picking it up, I slide it over my head, down over my naked skin, breathing it in as I do. It smells so intoxicating, all soapy and salty—just like him. Instantly a thrill shoots through my body, and I have a sudden need to find Tristan—my new husband. And I'm pretty certain I know where I can. Padding across the room, I head toward the French doors which lead to unrestrained views of the ocean.

It doesn't take me long to find him. My feet go still in the cool morning sand as I detect his powerful frame standing on the edge of the shore, eyes focused out to sea. For many moments I am frozen in place, heart in my throat as I take in his ardent muscles while they occasionally ripple through the bare skin of his back. Or the view of the rear side of his white shorts as he stands, legs slightly spread while the reaching tide flows repetitively over his feet. A soft breeze reaches across the waves to ruffle his already tousled, damp blond hair, and I swallow hard. *He is so beautiful!*

Suddenly I feel shy as I think about approaching him, remembering all that we intimately shared over the previous night. Keenly sensing my presence, he turns away from the water, facing in my direction instead. Holding my gaze, he sends me a sexy yet adoring look that causes my breath to catch in my throat. Feeling a little lightheaded I study his face, amazed that he will really be mine for a lifetime. My heart is pounding. A rush of warmth spreads through every inch of my body. This is all so new, everything I'd experienced with him last night was so new—what did *he* think about it, about me, about how it all went? For a few breathless seconds he stands very still taking me in, me taking him in as well. His white shirt that I am wearing is blowing in the gentle breeze pressing up against my bare skin. My just-woken-up hair whisks untamed around my face. Futilely I try to push a strand behind my ear. He watches my attempt and grins a little before opening his arms.

"Good morning, Mrs. Alexander," he says. The sound of his voice is soft, laced with sexy, matching the look in his ocean green eyes as they beckon me to him. And that's all it takes.

Without hesitation I run to that sound.

~~~~~~~~~~~~~~~~~~~~~~~~~~~~~~~~~~~~~~~~~~

We are wrapped in each other's arms, holding on tightly to one another, enjoying the feel of the beginnings of forever when our attention is drawn to a noise—a loud splash disturbing the rhythmic pattern of the surf. At once we both turn toward the sea in time to see a friendly little gray head bobbing above the frolicking waves, eager and smiling. *What? How? Where? He's back and he's okay!*

"Drake!" we both exclaim in unison. In answer to our greeting, the little aquatic creature proceeds to perform an acrobatic flip in the air.

Behind him an ethereal sweep of liquid unexpectedly gathers from seemingly out of nowhere. Swirling and shimmering like a large exhibit of sparkling diamonds, it sends a spray of water high into the air, fanning all around us in the sky before finally falling like handfuls of rice thrown at a wedding reception. In the midst of the fountainlike droplets, I imagine I hear the soft roar of a stadium-filled applause. Holding my breath, I freeze in place, taking in all the surreal sights and sounds that are assaulting my senses at once. None of it makes sense. None of it seems real. Goose bumps cover my skin. There is no other explanation. It's as if—

As if the ocean itself is stirring from somewhere far beneath, exhibiting its own celebratory display, bestowing an approval on our recent union.

I turn toward Tristan in search of his reaction and find him smiling. And what else can I do but smile too? Then glancing back at the ocean, grinning, I watch as the entire spectacle dissolves back into itself, and then it's just me and Tristan and the glistening, turquoise waves once again.

The End.

*Sometimes…*fairytale endings are too good to be true!

`````BOOK III`````
~**A Searchlight and a Silence**~

Read all three books in the series: A Song and a Seashell
A Sound and a Shadow
A Searchlight and a Silence
`````

www.ingramcontent.com/pod-product-compliance
Lightning Source LLC
Chambersburg PA
CBHW061936170626
46813CB00006B/2421